Sam White Owl's
Letters from a Cryptid Hunter
Volume 1

Written by Elias Ramos

Illustrated by D. M. Caulk

Hunter's Wings Publishing

Table of Contents

INTRODUCTION

Well, it's been a long time, friends. For those of you who already know me, I really appreciate you returning to spend some time with me once again. And for those of you I've never met, welcome! My name is Sam White Owl. You'll get to know me better in just a bit, so for now, let me explain what the following book is all about.

In July of 2020, I entered into an informal partnership with Robby Antilla, better known by his YouTube name of Swamp Dweller. Swamp is a narrator who focuses primarily on all things scary. On his channel, he takes submissions from members of the public and reads them aloud. People write in to him to share their experiences with the paranormal, the supernatural, and other frightening or dangerous situations. Over time, Swamp Dweller has compiled hundreds (perhaps thousands!) of accounts detailing all sorts of strange and spooky experiences, and he's drawn a wide audience by narrating them. My nephew introduced me to Swamp Dweller's channel, and as I listened, we both concluded that Swamp might be a good avenue for me to tell some of my stories. I had often thought about sharing my experiences, and this seemed like a promising opportunity. So, on July 16, 2020, I co-opted my nephew's email account and sent out the following message:

Dear Swamp Dweller,

Hello. My name is Sam White Owl. I've been following your YouTube channel for some time now, and I've been pretty impressed with your content. I'm reaching out because I have a proposal for you. It's pretty simple, but I've never quite reached out to anyone like this before, so here goes.

I'm in a very specific line of work. You'd probably call me a "cryptid hunter". I've been doing this for essentially my entire life, and I'm 47 years old, so I have plenty of stories to tell. Because of what I do, the nature of many of my experiences is different than some of the stories you share on your channel. Most of my experiences aren't just standard "encounters".

I'm getting older now, and thinking about retiring from being a Hunter, but it's been a long road, and most people still don't recognize what my organization and I do. I've been looking for somewhere to share my experiences, some place where I can let people know what's really out there and really going on, and I wondered if you'd be interested. If you are, I'd be happy to write a few letters to you so that you can post them/read them. And if not, no problem.

I realize this may be a little strange to you, but I figured I'd try contacting someone who reads stories that are similar to some of mine. If you have any questions or comments, feel free to reply with anything you might think of. Hopefully we'll talk soon.

- Sam White Owl

3 days later, Swamp Dweller responded: he was interested in the project! And the rest is history. Over the course of 2 years, I wrote a series of 19 "Letters from a Cryptid Hunter", each of which Swamp then read aloud and uploaded on YouTube for his audience. Over time, it seemed like it might be a good idea to put my stories into a text format that people could have for themselves. To do that, I've teamed up with my nephew, Elías Ramos, who I've mentioned in these letters in the past; I taught him a lot of what he knows about being a Hunter, and we've worked together many times since. And as it turns out, we also make a pretty good team when it comes to this whole writing thing!

Together, Elías and I have cleaned and polished up my original letters, and I've added quite a bit of new content to them. To go along with the new text, we put together some brand-new material that you won't find anywhere else, including some amazing illustrations by the very talented Danielle Caulk. So that's what you'll find in this book: the edited, expanded text of my first 10 letters ("Season 1" of the original YouTube series), combined with some extra, all-new material. Whether this is your first time hearing from me, whether you're one of my original listeners, whether you're interested in learning more or just looking to be entertained, I hope that this project will have something for you.

Because we shifted most of the following text over from the letters that were read in a YouTube video format, Elías and I have done a fair bit of editing to make it a single book of text.

Here's a few things you should know before getting into the letters:

Even though the letters have been updated and expanded, I've made the decision to keep them framed as they were first read aloud by Swamp Dweller. You'll hear me speak as if I'm addressing an online audience, since that's what I was originally doing. Just know that now you too are a part of the audience!

In the original YouTube series, I began most letters with a short question and answer section, where I responded to various things people asked in the comments on the videos. You guys had some great questions, and I really enjoyed interacting more personally with you. To make things smoother for this project, Elías and I decided to relocate all the Q&A segments (except for the first one, found in Letter 2) to their own dedicated section in the back of the book, where they're laid out according to the different letters that they originally appeared in. This way, you can look through them separately, without interrupting the flow of any given letter.

My first few letters weren't very long, but as I got more familiar with the audience's wishes and the format, I included longer question and answer sections, additional information, and simply more stories with more detail. A few letters even feature more than one cryptid, and you can look at the titles and headings of each letter to see what creature(s) and location(s) they cover; after all, I know that many people like to skip around.

I often refrain from giving the exact names of places and people, in the interest of safety and privacy. When it comes to places, I give at least a vague idea of the overall area I'm talking about, and I use aliases or substitute names for people who don't want to be identified.

About the term "Indian". This has been discussed elsewhere by people who are a lot smarter and more eloquent than me, but here's how I've put it in the past. The term "American Indian" is often used to refer to most of the different peoples who are otherwise called "Native American". Contrary to popular belief, some of us do use the term "Indian" to talk about ourselves, especially elders and older folks, but it's mostly out of convenience; "Indian" is inaccurate, historically loaded, and generally just old-school. Usually, we go by our specific culture, nation, or tribe (such as Cree, Wampanoag, Tlingit, Hopi, etc.). But when talking about our various peoples as a whole, across North and South America, many of us prefer to say "Native" or "Indigenous"; in Canada, the term "First Nations" is also good. Fortunately, there has been a shift in recent years towards using these terms; language has enormous power, and we ourselves were able to choose these much more suitable names. Nonetheless, the term "Indian" does crop up occasionally in my letters, but always in a specific context. You'll also hear me speak about *actual* India, the country in Asia, but that distinction should be pretty clear!

Speaking of Native folks, it's very important to remember that we have thousands of cultures, nations, tribes, and bands, all of which are unique and often very different from each other. North America, which we call Turtle Island, and South America are huge places, and people have been here for thousands of years building all sorts of societies and ways of life. Indigenous people aren't a single monolithic group, and I don't speak for all of us. The same goes for African Americans. I'm just one guy with one perspective and one type of relationship to my cultures. For example, I don't subscribe to every aspect of traditional Cherokee beliefs, but I follow some of the teachings, and I try my best to respect them all. Other folks certainly share a lot in common, but just like every culture is distinct, so too is every individual person. I encourage you: ask around, observe, and get informed about many different people's perspectives and understandings. Nobody is obligated to answer or educate you, and some knowledge may be off-limits, but you can ask and seek to learn more when and where it's appropriate.

I touch on a ton of different topics across these letters, but I'm by no means an expert on everything I talk about! Again, do your own research and observations, and talk to others. There's always more to learn.

And finally, a disclaimer about some of the details in these stories. I'm lucky (or maybe unlucky) enough to have a pretty photographic memory, and I've made it a habit to replay events in my head to better remember and process them. I also take great care to create detailed notes and journal entries both during and after any event that has to do with my job. Even so, these experiences happened anywhere from a few years to a few decades ago, and some of them were very quick and chaotic. Many of the details in these letters are down to me recreating things to the best of my ability and giving you an idea of how events played out. I've done my best to actively point out the areas where this applies the most (for example, dialogue is almost never verbatim).

And there you have it! That's everything I think you should know before diving in. Now, on to the letters. I hope you enjoy and maybe learn something new from my stories. Thanks for coming along with me on this journey, and we'll talk more soon!

Sincerely,

Sam White Owl

LETTER 1 – SASQUATCH

U.S.A. (WASHINGTON, FLORIDA), CANADA

Written July 2020

So, where to start? I have to say, I'm not very good with most technology, but my girlfriend is helping me out, and I can write just fine, so I think this will work out alright. Maybe I should start by introducing myself. My name is Sam White Owl. That probably sounds unusual, I know, but I was given this name after a special experience in which I encountered, well, a white owl. I might tell that story in more detail sometime later. Lots of Native folks, including many other Oklahoma Cherokee, have traditionally had very negative feelings surrounding owls, because they're seen as an omen of death. At the same time, owls also serve as messengers, and not everything that they represent is dark or bad. Animals have a lot to teach us, and I have my name for a reason. I'm 47 years old, and let me tell you, I certainly feel like an old man. But many people in my line of work don't make it this far, and I'm thankful to still be around.

That "line of work" is really what I'm here to talk about, and it's difficult to explain. But I'm getting close to retirement, and I figure it's time that people should know. So, to jump right in: I'm a member of an organization known as the Hunters. Capital 'H'. If you're picturing camouflage clothing, long rifles, and deer stands, then you're not terribly far off; I sometimes do that sort of hunting too. But I'm really talking about something a little more unique. There's not an easy way to say this, but our world is home to many beings that most people don't believe in or understand. But cultures across the globe have had to deal with them for thousands of years, and for over 300 of those, it's been us capital-H Hunters who have taken on the job. These beings are what we call "cryptids", "creatures", or more simply, "monsters".

Those terms are interchangeable, and they're probably bringing up some specific ideas for you right now. Most people think of "monsters" as purely fictional, the stuff of legend. But every legend has an origin somewhere, and humankind has accepted the reality of these creatures for most of our history. They're alive and well, which is why I'm writing this, to share what I know.

"Cryptid" is a catch-all term, not a formal classification; in fact, many cryptids are more closely related to non-cryptids than to each other. It's an incredibly diverse group, including everything from arachnids like the Tsuchigumo to the human-like vila and the aquatic reptilian taniwha.

Like many animals, most cryptids don't usually care about humans very much. Many even fear us, and for good reason. On the flipside, we ourselves fear many monsters, often also for good reason. For the most part, I'll be talking about the latter, the more dangerous cryptids, both because they're the ones I normally deal with and because many can threaten you.

Hopefully these letters can help you stay just a little safer. And even if you don't believe a word I say, well, maybe you'll still find this interesting.

I've heard lots of stories both here on YouTube and elsewhere about people's encounters with cryptids, and many of them seem quite true to my own experiences and knowledge. But like any topic, especially something so...unusual, there are a ton of misconceptions out there, so right off the bat, let's get rid of what might be the biggest.

Many people think that monsters can only be found in isolated areas, far from human settlement. But this is only partially true. In reality, cryptids live just about everywhere, all over the world. Most commonly, yes, they do live off the beaten path, in wilderness areas and environments away from humans. However, humans frequently pass through many of these areas, whether driving between towns or hiking on a summer vacation. And many cryptids can and do live in and around cities, towns, and villages. Some even resemble humans very closely and live right alongside us in our societies. Throughout history, various individual people or small groups have made it their job to manage the relationship between humans and monsters. Over time, they steadily joined forces, and this is how the Hunters were born.

The Hunters are a worldwide organization dedicated to preserving coexistence with monsters. It's not our job to keep these creatures secret or to hide them from you; honestly, a whole lot of us would love it if the wider world would acknowledge the fact that cryptids do in fact exist. Unfortunately, in most societies today, people actively ignore or throw away traditional knowledge, and that makes a

Hunter's work that much harder. But that's no reason for us to give up.

Most of us live job to job, taking tasks where they come up and travelling to different locations to deal with various creatures. Sometimes Hunters are able to resolve things peacefully, since many monsters are not inherently aggressive and can be handled without bloodshed. These cases are the best, of course, since nobody gets hurt and we walk away without a new set of scars. But a lot of the time, things get messy, and we're forced to fight. And that's one of the things the Hunters do best; when push comes to shove, we shove hard.

But with all that in mind, I have to make it clear up front that the purpose of the Hunters is not strictly to kill or eliminate monsters. In fact, it's the opposite: the more lives that we can protect, the better, whether that's human, cryptid, animal, or any other being. The name "Hunters" comes from an older time and a Euro-American worldview that was mostly concerned with simply wiping monsters out, rather than learning other ways to live with them. Thankfully, things have changed, and to most Hunters nowadays, it's clear that our job is just as much about preserving life as it is about dealing death. We don't always get it right, but I think all of us should promote peace as much as we can, and Hunters just have a unique way of doing so. We're far from perfect, but we take our responsibility more seriously than you can imagine.

Anyway, I won't get too caught up in philosophy. You should know just a little bit about how the Hunters function as an organization. We're pretty loose for a formal institution: there isn't a great deal of bureaucracy or restrictions, which is nice, but can be troublesome when it comes to tasks like organizing things or getting resources. For example, there are some great custom weapon makers in the Deep South of the USA, but they're tough to reach without contacting them directly. As nice as it would be, we don't exactly have a bunch of exclusive weapons depots stocked with their stuff. However, I usually have help with obtaining my specialized gear. That's because most Hunters have a Guide (capital 'G'), a person who does all sorts of behind-the-scenes work: they liaison with important members of the public and with the Hunter organization at large, give and receive records and data, sniff out potential jobs, and a million other tasks. My Guide is an older guy named Sergio, who used to be a Hunter on the ground himself. I know that he was a Guide for at least two other Hunters before me, which goes to show how short our careers can be sometimes. Sergio is pretty hardcore, and far from the most affectionate person out there, but he's very reliable and has always looked out for me.

There's so much more background information I could give, but I think this is good enough for the moment. If you'd like to know anything more about me or about my work, feel free to ask. I'd be glad to give you more information! But right now, let's get to what I'm sure you're probably here for: the monsters.

I'm thinking that this will be part survival guide, part personal account. I'll focus on specific cryptids and try to explain what each one is, what it *isn't*, how it lives, how to deal with it, and so on, before talking about my own personal experiences with it. I've interacted with a lot of creatures in my time, including pretty much all of the common North

American cryptids and many more from other places. Again, if you have any questions about any particular creatures, be sure to let me know. If I haven't had any encounters of my own with a certain cryptid, then I'm sure I can find some testimonies from people who have; I've made a lot of friends and contacts in the Hunters over the years, and I imagine that some of them would be happy to pass along their stories.

We'll start with what is probably the most popular cryptid of all: Sasquatch, a.k.a. Bigfoot. These guys are very common, ranging all across the continental United States and Canada, from Alaska to Florida. They're also (usually) relatively peaceful as monsters come. These traits in particular make them one of the most well-studied cryptids. We humans have known about and coexisted with Sasquatches for a very, very long time. My Cherokee ancestors and people of other Native nations and tribes have stories of Sasquatches that go back thousands of years before the European colonization of North America, and for the most part, humans and Sasquatches were able to get along well. But like any interaction between species, there was certainly a lot of conflict, and so my family has a long tradition of stopping violence between our two peoples, one way or another.

Physically, most Sasquatches are very close to many of the popular depictions; you could essentially describe their appearance as "ape-men", although there is quite a bit of variation between different populations and subspecies. Adults usually stand anywhere from 6 to 10 feet tall and weigh anywhere from 300 to upwards of 1000 pounds. The body structure is very similar to that of humans, although they have proportionally longer arms and larger hands and feet.

Sasquatches are super famous for their shaggy hair, which covers them completely, except for the palms of their hands, the soles of their feet, and parts of their faces, and they have nearly as much range in their fur color as humans do with our own hair. Most have chocolate brown, reddish, or russet-colored hair, but it's also common for them to be gray or black; occasionally some have blond or sandy-colored hair, and more rarely, they can be an ashy, almost white color (truly white hair on a Sasquatch typically occurs only when they're born albino, which does happen every so often). Geography seems to have some impact on the color of the hair, but maybe not the environment or climate; it seems to be more of a genetic, population-based thing. For example, take the Sasquatches of southern and eastern Ohio, often called the "Grassmen" (different groups of Sasquatch often have really fun names): all organisms pass on their genes, and since the average Grassman has reddish-brown fur, their children will probably look the same.

Sasquatch social structure is fluid, just like with humans, and it varies with location and conditions. They tend to be pretty solitary, unless they're bachelors, a mated pair, or parents with children, usually mothers. But sometimes Sasquatches make groups of up to 20 individuals, although it's incredibly rare to see so many together. For the most part, you can expect to find Sasquatches either alone or in small groups of only a few. In a group, the physically strongest one tends to take the lead, and since these tend to be more mature individuals, they've had time to get to know the land that they live on: where to find food and water, human settlements, good travel routes, and so on. They teach these things to the younger generations and pass on their knowledge. Just like many other creatures, including humans and our fellow apes, Sasquatches are able to teach each other deep and complex information. Some even have a form of spoken sounds that is similar in many ways to human language. They're very intelligent, and just as smart as humans in many areas.

I've been told about Sasquatches ever since I can remember. And because my family has been dealing with monsters for a very long time, I learned a lot about all sorts of cryptids as I grew up. For a little background, my mother's side of the family is from the Cherokee Nation in Oklahoma. My father is black, and he's from Washington state. When my parents divorced, I was about 5 years old, and I mainly grew up in Oklahoma with my mom. We lived somewhat separate from the rest of Indian country, partly because my mom is a Hunter, and especially when training me, we had to spend a lot of time living and working on our own. My dad would come to take me to Washington about three times a year or so. Although his side of the family wasn't involved with the Hunters, they did enjoy regular old deer hunting, so they'd take me out into the woods every so often when I'd go up there, teaching me how to shoot and track and such. Both sides of my family taught me how to enjoy and respect nature, and I'll always be grateful to them for that.

I should also note that I've had a number of encounters with monsters completely unrelated to my work as a Hunter. In other words, I've had experiences with cryptids that any average person might have. It's happened several times, and I can't help but think that there's something about having one cryptid encounter that almost makes you more likely to have another. After your first experience, you might become more aware of the signs of a cryptid's presence and know what to look for, but there almost seems to be some invisible force, even fate or destiny, which makes you more likely to encounter a monster again. There's no proof of this, and I don't even know how much I really believe it myself, but it's just something strange. There's a lot of strangeness associated with monsters, and some of it can be almost supernatural, so that's something to keep in mind as we go on.

My first encounter with a Sasquatch was when I was about 9 or 10 years old, while out on a hunting trip with my dad and grandfather. We were in the eastern part of Washington, in a densely wooded area. I was trekking along with them, heading through a valley of conifers. I remember it being slightly overcast, and I was feeling pretty hungry. Just before noon, we suddenly heard a knock, and immediately stopped walking. "Knocks", or "tree knocks", are a type of sound that Sasquatches commonly use to communicate, although it's usually less of a knocking and more of a cracking or smacking, which can carry for great distances through the woods. Sasquatches produce these sounds by stripping the bark off of a branch or log and then hitting it against a tree trunk, or by whacking a pair of the stripped branches together. Typically, knocks function much like shouts, just like a human might call out "Hey!" This draws attention and advertises the presence of the Sasquatch; it's often a warning or a statement of power. This time, we heard one very distinct knock, and then silence.

I remember my dad looking at my grandfather, and then taking my hand and starting forward again, moving more slowly. After a minute or so, we heard another knock, louder and closer this time. It seemed to be coming from a ridge to our left, and we all looked in that direction. Animals often like to have the high ground in situations, and this was no different. There on the ridge above us stood a Sasquatch, mostly blocked from view behind some bushes, but still partially visible. It was a male, judging by the broad shoulders, and if I had to estimate now, he was probably about 8 feet tall. He had dark red, almost brown fur, and was still carrying the stick he'd used to knock on the tree. His posture was neutral, neither threatened nor threatening. He just stood, watching us with what seemed like a mixture of curiosity and caution. Clearly, though, he wanted us to see him and know he was there.

My dad held up his hands to indicate that he had no weapons, and then turned to me and my grandfather, indicating that we should go back the way we came. We hadn't caught any game that day, but that didn't bother me. I was thrilled! I had seen pictures and remnants of cryptids before, but that was the first time I'd seen a monster so alive and active, and I was so happy. I wasn't even scared, although I guess the Sasquatch's appearance was a bit intimidating. I don't think my father and grandfather were scared either; they just wanted to keep all of us safe, and so they decided to head back the way we came and let the Sasquatch be. From my mom's family, they knew about monsters and knew to respect their boundaries, just like with any other living creature.

Many people don't know or care about those boundaries, though, and when they cross them, things can get very ugly very fast. A few years later, when I was 13 or so, my mom had already started taking me with her on some of her less intensive cases, to start teaching me the ropes of capital-H Hunting. We went down to Florida on one of these trips, in order to investigate sightings of a Skunk Ape. Skunk Apes are not actually some sort of hybrid between skunks and apes; those would certainly be interesting and cool creatures, but the truth is a bit less exciting. Skunk Apes are just a subspecies of Sasquatch that inhabit the southeastern US, mainly Louisiana to Florida. Their name comes from their smell, because they absolutely reek. Combine the odor of rotten eggs and sulfur, then bump up the power of the stench, and you'll get an idea of what Skunk Apes smell like. They're a bit smaller and often lighter in color than other Sasquatches, with a sort of mane of longer hair on their shoulders and necks.

This particular case had been called in because a Skunk Ape had apparently mauled a pair of brothers who'd been out duck hunting. The two men had been heavily injured, with cracked ribs, fractured skulls, and internal bleeding, which had all been treated at the hospital they'd managed to get to. Both had talked about a man-sized ape coming out of the trees and beating them to within inches of their lives, but the official explanation was that a black bear had been responsible for the attack. I understand this kind of willful ignorance, but that doesn't make it any less frustrating. If there weren't even claw marks or bite marks on the victims, was it really a black bear? Their injuries were consistent with blunt force trauma, which is exactly what the fists of a Sasquatch will cause. Unfortunately, people typically don't want to admit that.

My mom and I dealt with this case pretty quickly. The Skunk Ape was a lone female, and her home range was being converted into housing developments. The injured brothers were local and had been hunting ducks practically in their own backyards when they'd gotten too close to the Skunk Ape's nest. She'd lashed out, and even though she hadn't killed the men, she'd still proven herself to be a threat. However, she was not aggressive, and Sasquatches have the intelligence to realize when they've killed someone. Most likely, this Skunk Ape had intentionally refrained from killing the two men. My mother and I made the decision together that we weren't going to kill her. Instead, we'd tranquilize her and relocate her to somewhere safer and far away from humans. Along with my mom's Guide, a lady named Hannah, we were able to pinpoint a state park in Alabama where we hoped this Sasquatch would be able to find a new life.

The next day, my mom and I were able to track down the Skunk Ape and tranq her. My mom even let me take the shot! After she dropped, we called in one of the Hunter relocation crews to pick her up and take her to her new home. It was a clean job, with no bloodshed necessary (well, besides the duck hunters, who were expected to make full recoveries). I love it when things work out that way, even though it is pretty rare that they do. If this first letter goes over well, then maybe I'll tell you guys about some of the jobs that weren't so clean, and some of the creatures involved.

Thankfully, most of the time with Sasquatches, it's pretty simple. Since they generally avoid open hostility, it's usually enough to just relocate them. There's plenty of empty space across North America where we can take them to live out their lives without being afraid of humans or hurting them. But Hunters can't deal only with the nice ones, and the more aggressive Sasquatches can be a handful. A perfect example would be one that I hunted in 1994. I had only been working on my own for a little while at that time, but I had already handled some very tough and aggressive monsters. So, when Sergio told me about a Sasquatch wreaking havoc in British Columbia, I figured I'd be more than able to handle it.

When I arrived in the province, I immediately picked up a fresh lead: three people had been killed while camping in the mountains of a certain national park. One of the main jobs of our Guides is also to interface with the government and law enforcement when needed, so Sergio had already notified the relevant authorities of my coming. Though the Hunters aren't directly part of any government agency, we still have badges and licenses for our organization, and those are usually enough to let us go where we need to. This time I showed my badge to some park rangers and policemen who were near the scene of the killings, and I was let through to examine the area. It seemed that the two women and one man had died quickly, without putting up much of a fight. The Sasquatch had broken one of the women's necks, seemingly by throwing her into a tree, and had smashed in the heads of the other two. It wasn't very messy, and I had seen much worse, but that doesn't make it any less tragic. To state the obvious, nobody, especially not Hunters, wants things like this to happen.

Luckily, the Sasquatch had left some prints nearby, and after I gathered my stuff, I headed off into the woods in search of it. The next day, I caught up to it at a small creek. This one was a huge male, definitely over 9 feet in height, with dark gray hair and a physique that would make any pro bodybuilder look twig-thin in comparison. He was squatting by the creek, using his hands to scoop water into his mouth. I was downwind of him and slightly uphill, on a slight ridge that overlooked the creek. It was a perfect position. I shot him with a tranquilizer dart in the side of the neck, then began to run some distance away along the ridgeline; it'd take a moment for the tranquilizer to work, and I didn't want him catching me in that time.

The big guy let out a roar of surprise when I shot him. Just like other great apes, Sasquatch make all sorts of noises, and when they're in pain or angry, they can give loud, earthshaking roars that you can feel in your chest. I hadn't really hurt this one, but he felt the dart enough to make an enraged bellow. I turned back to see him rise to his feet and take a step backwards, looking around himself for the source of the dart. He saw me, and instead of running away, he took a few staggering steps towards me, before collapsing onto his back with a loud thud.

You might be wondering why I tranquilized this Sasquatch instead of putting him down for good; after all, he had killed three people. Sometimes, however, the higher-ups in the Hunters have plans that might not line up with your own. On this occasion, Sergio told me that some of our organization's scientists wanted to research this Sasquatch's behavior, maybe precisely because he had been so violent. They wanted to take him to an area far away from human habitation, so before the hunt, I picked out a remote, safe location with Sergio. After tranqing the Sasquatch, I called a cleanup crew, as usual. Occasionally, active combat Hunters sometimes debrief with the cleanup crews in person, especially when we have to stay with a sedated cryptid until they arrive. So this time, when I met up with the cleanup crew, they confirmed the relocation destination with me and then began preparations for the move.

Relocating an animal is always intrusive and stressful, and I had mixed feelings about letting this particular Sasquatch go, given what he'd done, but it's still valuable to learn more about cryptids. Knowledge is a key component of Hunters' work.

Before wrapping up, I should tell you that many people often report some additional weirdness about Sasquatches. I've never personally experienced any of these things, but much like the very existence of Sasquatches and other cryptids, there are too many accounts to just completely ignore, especially when many are given by people who are very trustworthy or would have a lot to lose by revealing their experiences. Even the Hunters don't know too much about some of this stranger stuff, but I would be doing you a disservice if I didn't at least mention it. Some people, including Hunters, say that they've seen strange lights or objects in the air related to run-ins with Sasquatches. Occasionally, people have also heard voices speaking in their heads during their sightings or encounters, as if the Sasquatch is communicating telepathically. Finally, it's often said that Sasquatches move in a sort of alternate world, one that allows them to go unseen until they decide to hop back into our reality. Again, I have no personal experience with any of this stuff, but I figure it should be mentioned.

At the end of the day, hopefully you can recognize that Sasquatches are not just mindless beasts. They have thoughts and feelings just like us, and for the most part they just like to be left alone. This goes for a ton of monsters, especially ones that are not predatory. But that doesn't mean they can't be dangerous. If you come across a Sasquatch, it's usually best just to walk in the opposite direction. Don't run, point, flail around, or otherwise make yourself seem obvious or like a threat. Try not to make prolonged eye contact with the Sasquatch either. Just keep your head down and walk away, and you'll generally be just fine. Like most animals, Sasquatches typically attack if they're starving, if they feel threatened, or if you're near their nests. Most other times, they're generally peaceful and even gentle.

If a Sasquatch charges you, though, you'll almost certainly have to defend yourself. Many other animals will do mock or bluff charges to scare off potential foes, but I've never seen a Sasquatch do this; once they charge, they usually commit. You won't be able to outrun them either, so you'll probably wind up fighting. If you're expecting this kind of situation, it's usually best to bring some kind of rifle with high-caliber, penetrating rounds. Sasquatches don't have very thick skin, but they have a lot of hair, and it often acts as protection against projectiles. The hair around their faces and necks is thinner, though, and that's where you'll want to shoot. Just like with a human, headshots are most effective.

I've never had to kill a Sasquatch, but I know Hunters who have, and every one of them says that it's an awful thing. Maybe that's because Sasquatches are so similar to humans. I'm just thankful I've never had to do it, even though I have had quite a few other unpleasant experiences. I'll tell you guys about some of those later, if you're interested. But the ones I just laid out should be a good example of how we operate as Hunters.

"Mercy to the wolf is cruelty to the sheep." I don't know where this phrase originated, but it's a good way to express a key part of our outlook. At the same time, wiping out the wolves would be equally cruel. Everything and everyone has value, a place, and a purpose, and if one piece of a system goes away, it's going to impact others. Hunters aren't sworn pacifists who think we can just be friends with every dangerous monster by hugging them and talking nicely, and we also aren't indiscriminate murderers who go out guns blazing with a mission to kill everything we don't like. And we definitely aren't some mysterious, magical masters of nature who keep the universe in complete harmony. But I think we do okay overall.

Anyway, I think this has been long enough. I'll certainly answer any questions that you guys ask, and if you want to hear about something in particular, just say so, and I'll definitely see if I can fit it in. And like I said, if this letter goes well, then I'll absolutely follow up with some more. For now, though, I think I've given you guys a good bit to think about. I'll be back soon. This has been Sam White Owl, signing out.

LETTER 2 – CRAWLER

U.S.A. (OKLAHOMA), AUSTRALIA

Written July 2020

Hello, everyone, it's Sam White Owl, back again. I hope everybody is doing well and staying safe during these crazy times. I'd like to start off by saying "Wow". You guys really seemed to respond well to my first letter, and I'm honestly shocked at the positive feedback I've been getting. It's been more than I expected, really, and I'm so grateful that listeners have been open to hearing more of these little tales that I have. I've also been getting quite a lot of questions, and while I can't answer them all, I will do my best to get to some of the most important and common ones. My girlfriend says that I should create a YouTube account to answer some of your questions directly, but for now I'll just try responding to some of them through these letters. Once I get some things cleared up, we'll be free to get more into the stories. Hopefully this letter will answer a lot of important questions before we move on to more stories and information.

So, Q&A time. First, I've gotten a lot of people comparing my work to the TV show "Supernatural". I know about this show, but I've actually never seen it. A lot of other Hunters have brought it to my attention, saying that it featured a monster hunter with the same first name as me, and I've been shown clips of it, but I've never watched a full episode. Supposedly it's pretty good! But I heard that it dealt a lot with angels and demons, and, well...that's not really my thing. But if the show does deal more with monsters and cryptids, I think I probably wouldn't want to watch it. Lots of TV shows and movies often spread disinformation about creatures, whether intentionally or not. They also make cryptid hunting seem like an attractive pastime, rather than the messy and violent job that it usually is. Not to mention that I've never met any Hunter who's quite as good-looking as the characters in Supernatural. I'm certainly not some attractive young white guy!

Moving on, I heard a few comments wondering why the government wouldn't suppress me or my knowledge, or why this information being public isn't a bigger deal. There are a couple things I can say to this. The first is that the Hunters are not affiliated directly with any government, whether that of the US or any other country. Our organization is a global one that's existed in some form or another for centuries, and we've become largely independent because of that. To my knowledge, we've never operated openly in coordination with any sort of outside governmental body. Maybe this is because we don't feel that we can trust others to act with our same interests in mind. Maybe it's because we'd rather keep secret, which brings me to another point.

The Hunters officially operate undercover, and always have done so since our founding as an organization. Our existence is not publicly acknowledged or accepted. But there's no hardline Hunter rule that says we can't divulge our secrets. I am one of a small minority of Hunters who believes that we should formally reveal ourselves and release information to the world at large. Most Hunters, including our leadership, are firmly against this. Due to the nature of our work, they believe that going public could compromise our organization and the creatures that we deal with. And they have a point. At the same time, it's not the Hunters' job to keep either creatures or ourselves secret. Our job is to ensure that humanity can coexist with monsters peacefully. And I believe that in order to truly do that, we need to let people know what they're dealing with. These letters are just one avenue that I found to be helpful in doing that. I'm used to people not believing what I say. It comes with the territory. I used to make a bigger deal of it, but I'm getting a little too old to care that much anymore. I just care that you all keep safe, and that's why I'm writing these letters.

Some people also asked why I didn't take pictures. There's a couple things I could say to that too. First is that cameras have definitely gotten smaller and easier to use, so maybe on a future hunt, I can try and get some photos to you guys. However, they'd probably be from my cellphone, which doesn't have a great camera, and that brings me to the main reason I don't really take many photos. If you can believe it, there are *already* tons of pictures and videos out there. All it takes is a simple Internet search to find them. However, most are of poor quality or from far away, and so people don't believe that the pictures are genuine. If you've ever worked with or been around wild animals, however, you'll know that it's often difficult to get clear and close-up shots with just a cellphone. When blurry photos of chimpanzees or wild dogs show up online, people excuse them, and nobody doubts that they're real. When it's a picture of a Sasquatch, however, then people immediately say that it's fake. Plus, no matter how good the quality was or how close to the subject I was, I have a feeling that any sort of picture or video I could take would just be brushed off as fake or as some sort of Hollywood prop, just like what's happened with so many other photos and videos.

And briefly, as for the DNA testing route, I've seen a couple of tests that were conducted and wound up discovering unknown primate DNA from somewhere in the northern US. This was almost certainly Sasquatch-related, and it had nothing to do with the Hunters. However, it's important to remember that the DNA testing agencies may also have their own agendas in mind, and even if us Hunters did send things to them that they weren't able to identify, they might have reason to keep the results secret as well. Who knows why.

I'm also not going to roll up to some government site with a dead or captured monster in tow. Absolutely not. Both of my peoples, Native and Black, survived apocalypses caused by the government for hundreds of years, and we're still surviving and still here. But we've learned from the past and have no plans of going anywhere. There's been several hundred years of experience with that. If governments still can't treat their fellow humans, animals, or the planet at large with dignity, respect, and compassion, then I have my doubts they'll act differently for monsters.

Anyway, my goal isn't to defend myself or explain everything away, and my girlfriend says I'm getting sidetracked. Like I said, what I really care about is just that you are all safe. So on to some more straightforward questions. One person at least asked how they can join the hunt for cryptids. To that, I would say: DON'T. As an active field Hunter, almost every job, every task, and every case might literally put your life on the line. There are some people who can accept that, though. To you, I say that if the Hunters want you, we will find you. There is a special wing of our group, the Scouts (capital-S), that's dedicated to sniffing out the best trappers, trackers, and regular hunters from around the world, and if you become known to them and they decide that we could use your help, they will come to you. I wish it was as simple as applying online or something, but again, our organization officially operates off-the-grid, so it's not that easy.

Do you have to have Native blood to be a Hunter? Absolutely not. In fact, most of us don't even live in the Americas, let alone have any Native heritage. The Cherokee side of my family just happens to have been in this general profession for a very long time. This has always been common knowledge in our community, and we've been known in our community as Hunters ever since we joined the organization. But again, in an official capacity, the Hunters work undercover.

How many types of cryptids are there? A whole lot! The Hunters have catalogs of several thousand species across the world. They're more common than you might think, but again, people don't want to believe. It's interesting, because creatures like the giant squid or the okapi were once considered cryptids, until humans found them and acknowledged their existence. Many cryptids are also just variants or species of more familiar animals, such as owls, frogs, and fish, so I'm sure those will have a higher chance of getting recognized by the general public. Maybe something similar will happen with other monsters as time goes on.

How do I protect myself from cryptids? Well, whenever you're away from civilization, keep your eyes and ears open. I don't necessarily recommend being armed at all times, but having a good weapon by your side can certainly help you out. Most monsters require high-power weapons and high-caliber ammunition to bring down, so you'll need equipment designed for big game. But many creatures are also scared by loud noises, like gunshots, and by the sight of people carrying large protective objects, like guns. Bear spray actually works fairly well against a number of creatures, believe it or not. And if you're a person of faith, then protective measures like praying can work wonders for your mind and soul. I wouldn't trust entirely in a prayer to stop an attacking monster, but praying before you go out can at least give you some comfort and peace of mind, which can be half the battle. I carry several spiritually important objects on me almost every time I leave the house, and certainly on every hunt. These aren't just to stop monsters outright. They also give me mental and spiritual strength and vigor, and that can be just as important as any gun.

Of course, I do carry guns on my hunts, though. Many Hunters, especially here in the US, get their weapons personally designed and customized by the branch of our organization known as the Smiths (yes, capital-S); the name comes from their role as blacksmiths way back in the old days, and they're the weapon makers I mentioned in my last letter. Nearly every weapon of mine has been either tuned or flat-out created by the Smiths. My weapon of choice through the 90s was a custom-built elephant rifle, designed for the .416 Remington Magnum cartridge. That gun served me very well on all of my hunts, and was designed to fire both bullets and tranq darts as needed. Times have changed, though, and now I use another custom-made rifle that fires .458 Lott rounds. Rifles are always my staple weapon, although depending on the creature I'm hunting, I may bring along a shotgun instead. The Remington 870 has been a solid choice for me. Sidearms aren't really my cup of tea, but since the early 2000s, the Smiths have made some great handguns that have definitely caught my attention. My current pick is a customized version of the Taurus Raging Hunter (ironic name, I know), which fires .454 Casull rounds. Finally, I often carry an assortment of melee weapons, depending on the hunt and the monster. One that I frequently use is my combat tomahawk, which doubles as a great survival tool. And the one weapon that always sticks with me is my paternal grandfather's Bowie knife, which I carry as an absolute last resort. I've only had a few occasions to use this knife, and boy, am I grateful for that.

I also got a question asking where I operate. I'm based in the US, since I'm from here, of course, but my jobs have taken me all over the world. Typically in a foreign country, I try to link up with at least one other Hunter who's actually from that region, but there have been times when I've worked abroad by myself.

Phew. It's harder than I thought to answer so many questions! I even got a comment from Sweden, asking about some of the creatures there. There are absolutely cryptids and Hunters there, and although I've never been to that country in particular, I was in Norway this past summer. I got to deal with some interesting situations while I was there. I was mainly teamed up with a Hunter named Ingrid, and we were investigating some activity in the mountains. Troll stuff. I might tell that story later.

Anyway, I think that's enough of the big questions answered for now. So let's talk about some more specific stuff. I got several questions about a certain Southwestern shape-changer, and we'll get there eventually, but before we go to that place, I'd like to talk about at least two other creatures. I got questions about these two cryptids, and they're a bit easier to discuss with non-Native people. We'll talk about one in this letter and the other in my next one.

For this letter, let's discuss a cryptid species that I got a few questions about, and which I know is fairly commonly talked about on both Swamp Dweller's YouTube channel and some others. Like nearly all monsters, these creatures have a few different names, and the most popular seems to be "crawlers". That name seems to be fairly recent, and Hunters have been calling these monsters "Ash Men" or "Pale Men" for as long as I can remember. We may have taken the name "Pale Man" from the movie "Pan's Labyrinth", but I'm pretty sure we were saying that before that movie came out.

Crawlers are typically anywhere from 5 to 8 feet tall, and

humanoid in appearance. They have long, thin limbs, and an emaciated, almost skeletal appearance; you may see their ribs or their vertebrae sticking out underneath their skin. The sockets of their eyes are usually sunken and dark, but their eyes themselves glow when light passes over them, like two little pinpricks of white or light yellow. They have mouths filled with sharp, pointed teeth, but when closed, you may not even see these mouths. They tend not to have lips or noses. Their appearance is quite frankly terrifying, and it's no wonder that most people's first reaction upon seeing a crawler is to freeze up or run in the opposite direction. I think it's because these cryptids fall near the Uncanny Valley. They *almost* look human, but they're different enough that it's still obvious that they're something else.

Crawlers are found across the United States, southern Canada, and Australia, and honestly, I have no idea where they come from or what exactly they are. They look generally like extremely pale and thin humans, but their much greater speed and strength would suggest otherwise. Did they come into being separately from us or alongside us? I truly don't know, and the Hunters don't either. A friend of mine, an Australian Hunter named William, believes that Pale Men are closely related to us, maybe as another species of human that developed a different lifestyle than the rest of us. They certainly resemble humans, and they seem to be at least as intelligent as most other apes.

As you might expect, crawlers tend to live in caverns and cave systems. They are primarily nocturnal, but on rare occasions they can be active during the day. They usually sleep when the sun is up, before emerging from their caves at night, mainly to feed. They primarily go after small game: squirrels, small rodents, and especially rabbits. They are surprisingly strong, however, and I've seen them take fawns and small deer before. In one particularly odd case in West Virginia, I even came across evidence of one having grabbed a newborn cow.

People often see crawlers on the sides of roads or trails, and nobody (except for Hunters, of course!) sticks around to learn more about them. But as horrifying as they might look, they aren't actually very dangerous to humans. When people run away from them, they rarely give chase, and on the few occasions where Pale Men have attacked people, the wounds are almost never fatal. Still, you obviously don't want to bother them, so if you see one, just keep your distance and move away. They may screech at you, but this is almost always a warning, similar to how a human might yell "Back off!" or "Stay away!" But if a crawler actually attacks you, then I'm sure bullets are effective on them. Some Hunters have killed crawlers, and as you can imagine, headshots and chest shots work well; even just the noise of a gunshot will generally scare them away. Like many nocturnal, cave-dwelling creatures, crawlers hate bright lights and loud sounds, and like most animals, they also fear fire. In a pinch, anything flaming or burning, like some kind of torch, can help stave off a potential attack.

In the early 1900s, the Hunters made a coordinated effort to kill Ash Men. They were seen somewhat as a nuisance, but one with the potential to become a threat in certain circumstances. Their terrifying appearance also didn't help matters, nor did the fact that crawlers aren't as strong, fast, or well-armed as many other cryptids, which made them more attractive targets. Many were killed, possibly as many as 350, although the exact count is probably higher. But exterminating them proved to be difficult and expensive, and combined with pushback from a significant portion of the organization, including many of us from Aboriginal Australian and American Indigenous communities, the Hunters, thankfully, abandoned the effort. This was a critical moment in our organization's history, and one of many steps that led to a very positive shift in our approach. We'll come back to this later. For now, here's my personal experiences.

My first meeting with a crawler was sometime in my early teens, and it was incredibly standard as far as these things go, so I apologize if it's not terribly interesting. I was going through some caves with a cousin of mine who was interested in spelunking. He'd rather not identify himself, but since he told me he's always liked the name Rob, that's what we'll call him. There are a few nice caves in Oklahoma that you can explore, and Rob and I were in one of these. Like in my previous letter, I won't say the actual location. I've never liked being in confined spaces like caves, but I think Rob was trying to get me into caving. He's about 7 years older than me, and he doesn't have any younger siblings, so I've always been a bit like a little brother to him. We used to hang out a lot, and this time we were pretty deep into this cave. Rob was leading the way, and I was a short distance behind him. We were able to stand up and walk for most of the trip, but we came to a fork in the path after a little while. Rob stopped here, looking off down the tunnel to the right.

"Do you smell that?" he asked, and I sniffed. There was something else along with the usual mustiness of the caves. I recognized it as the smell of aging meat, an odor which we were both familiar with. This was obviously very strange. Why would there be some *meat* so far back in this cave? I told him it might be an animal, and he looked back at me with this mischievous grin and started walking towards the smell, saying we should go check it out. I started shaking my head; I knew very well that some cryptids live in caves, and I've always been more cautious than him.

"Rob, that's stupid, come back," I told him, but he had already started clambering over some rocks into the tunnel. I had no choice but to go after him. I only had a knife on me, so if something jumped us, we would probably be in a lot of trouble.

It wasn't long before we came upon the source of the smell. There was a little rock ledge off to the right side of the tunnel. When we shone our headlamps in that direction, we saw that, sitting on top of the ledge, was a hunk of discarded meat, still attached to the bone. There were a few other small bones scattered around nearby as well. Most looked small, like squirrels and mice, but the meat was definitely from something bigger. Maybe a pig or a goat, but I couldn't tell, and I didn't want to.

"What the hell is this?" Rob asked. I remember being so nervous that I actually grabbed his arm and yanked him backwards.

"It's a feeding area, dumbass! Something lives here."

I guess Rob had finally seen enough, because he started following me back the way we'd come. As we walked, I glimpsed something much lighter than the darkness to my left with my headlamp. Spinning to look, I saw two glowing white eyes reflecting back at me from on top of a ledge about 10 feet overhead. I saw the briefest glimpse of a skinny white body crouching there in a squatting position, and a hairless head looking right at us. Rob yelled some kind of curse word and rushed past me back in the direction of the entrance. I was frozen in fear for a second, only able to watch as the lanky humanoid body scuttled backwards into the shadows. Once it was gone, I snapped out of it and took off after Rob, with no idea what I had just seen. At this point, I hadn't been told about crawlers by my mom or any of my family, so I also had clue if this being was dangerous, and I just acted without thinking. I'm a bit ashamed of that, because I knew better than to turn my back and start running away; that can trigger a predator's chase response and make things worse. I should have backed away slowly, but between the uneven cave floor and the unknown nature of what I had just seen, my reaction was just to flee.

As we ran, I heard a screech come from behind us, echoing off of the cave walls and spurring us to go faster. At one point I lost sight of Rob around a bend in the path and tripped a couple of times, hurting my hands. and hurt my hands as I fell onto the rocks, but eventually I caught up with Rob where he'd stopped to catch his breath. We didn't say anything to each other, just standing there panting and wheezing. I kept looking behind us to see if we were being followed, but there was nothing. Eventually, we kept going, not exactly running, but still moving fast. We made it safely out of the cave and immediately started driving back to Rob's house.

"I don't know what that was," I told Rob when we were on the road, figuring he might have expected me to know. But he just shook his head and kept driving.

When we got home after that, everything was actually pretty normal. I asked my mother what we might have seen, and she told me about the Pale Men and what they were. I called Rob later on and explained the whole thing to him, and even though we both realized that we probably weren't in that much danger, we still never went caving in that place again. Maybe my mother or another Hunter did something about that particular crawler, but I'm not sure.

That encounter was pretty standard, from the stories and accounts I've heard. I've seen a crawler in Australia too, while doing some recon in the outback for another job. I was in the central area of the country with William, the Australian Hunter I mentioned before. We were walking through a dried-up creek bed after dark, headlamps on, chatting quietly when we heard a pretty loud rustling from some bushes beside us. Both of us immediately turned, guns at the ready, and we saw a large, tall shadow stand up from the shrubs. This crawler was about 7 feet tall, and our lights reflected off of its glowing eyes as it stared us down. Maybe it expected that we'd run, but William and I weren't budging. I fired off two shots into the air, and faster than I could blink, the Ash Man dropped onto all fours and started racing away from us. They have a very odd gait when they're moving at full speed like that, sort of like a bounding run. I had clearly scared this one off, and after it was gone, William and I made it back to our camp without incident.

Over the years, I've seen a couple more crawlers, always on the sides of the road or on trails, late at night. I've never actually had a job to hunt one down, though. Their glowing eyes and skeleton-like bodies are certainly horrific, but as long as you just go away from them in a timely manner, you should be alright. As I mentioned earlier, the effort to wipe out crawlers was called off partly because of this: it became clear that even though they look freaky, exterminating them wasn't only challenging and expensive, but also just unnecessary, and flat-out morally wrong. I'm really glad that the Hunters realized this, because it's something that I, my family, and many others try to live by.

There's a concept that indigenous groups around the world have understood pretty much forever. Natives in the US often express it with the Lakota phrase "Mitákuye Oyás'iŋ", which usually gets translated into English as "all my relations". There's no way I can fully explain this concept here, but at the core, it's exactly what it sounds like: the understanding that everything in existence is connected at the most fundamental, core level. You personally are a member of your family, of your community, of your people, and these are mirrors to how you're also connected with the gigantic, messy, beautiful family that is the universe. That includes animals, plants, stars, rocks, and quite literally everything else; after all, nothing exists in a complete void without an environment that surrounds it.

If you think this sounds very "woo" and silly, you can also go to mainstream Western science. Every living thing is made up of the same building blocks of DNA, and we all come from a LUCA, our "last universal common ancestor", the tiny cell from the very earliest stages of life that survived and split and over millions of years gave rise to fish and flowers and mushrooms and you and me. If you want to get into DNA, we humans share 99.9% of our genes with each other, ultimately making us borderline identical. We share 98.8% of our genes with chimpanzees, which is pretty clear to see just from looks alone. But we share about 80% with mice, 60% with fruit flies, 60% with *bananas*, and 35% with *daffodils*. We're very different than all of these beings, and yet we're directly related at the core, and to live, we all depend on each other and our other relations and our environment.

Whatever you want to trust or believe, Indigenous knowledge understands all of existence as being interconnected. And like other Indigenous teachings, this can definitely be balanced with mainstream Western science, which I try to do, because there's truth to both. We're related to everyone and everything around us, with all the complexity that entails. Families never get along perfectly, and relatives sometimes do terrible things to each other, but you literally owe each other your lives. At the end of the day, you depend on each other, and although you may hate each other with a burning passion, you shouldn't treat your relatives with cruelty or without respect. That's how I've been taught as the way to approach both life and the position of a Hunter. The vast majority of Hunters are not Indigenous, and all of us have our own philosophy and ways of handling the responsibility we have. Sometimes we kill cryptids. Sometimes we capture them. A whole lot of the time we just look at them through binoculars. But it's all within the big context of being, as I said, relations. I'm nowhere near perfect, but that's how I try to see things.

Anyway, that's about it this time around. Thanks for listening! Crawlers are scary creatures, but fortunately, not terribly dangerous. Next time I think we'll talk about a certain canine humanoid that is truly a threat. I've created a short list of monsters that I'd like to talk about, so let me know if you'd like to see that. And again, if you have any more questions, please don't hesitate to ask. But for now, just stay safe, everyone, whether it's by wearing a mask and social distancing or by being aware while you're out in the woods. We'll talk more soon. This has been Sam White Owl, signing out.

LETTER 3 – DOGMAN

U.S.A. (OKLAHOMA, UTAH)

Written July 2020

Hey, everyone, it's Sam White Owl, back again. I hope you're all staying safe and keeping sane during this weird and wild year. I'm still so happy to see that you guys are enjoying this series, and I'm likewise happy to keep providing more information and stories. For now, I want to continue talking about some of the most "popular" cryptids. We'll do it the usual way: first I'll talk about the monsters themselves, and then about my experiences with them. I've gotten lots of comments asking about one particular monster, so I figured I'd cover it sooner rather than later. Let's talk about Dogmen. The names "Wolfmen" or "Wolf People" used to be the standard, but the term "Dogman" seems to be the more popular term in recent decades, and the Hunters have adopted it as well.

Dogmen range all across North America, Europe, and parts of Asia. In appearance, they're exactly what they sound like. They are humanoids with a range of body measurements, much like Sasquatches; dogmen are usually between 6 and 10 feet tall, and weigh from 250 up to 1000 pounds. Their arms are proportionally longer than humans', but otherwise their general body structure is similar. Dogmen's heads are their most distinctive and well-known feature, because they resemble the heads of German Shepherds, huskies, or wolves, albeit with proportionally longer canine teeth. Wolfman hands have five fingers on which the nails are sharp claws, but they don't have fully opposable thumbs like humans. Their feet are canine, with footpads exactly like those of any dog or wolf. Besides these pads and the palms of their hands, dogmen are covered in a coat of fur which is usually shorter than that of a Sasquatch but still grows up to several inches long. Their fur is usually dark in color; typically it's black or dark gray, but it can sometimes be chocolate brown or russet, and there are a few recorded instances of beige and even snow-white wolfmen.

Dogmen are nocturnal, but they are sometimes active during the day. They're usually solitary, but in rare cases they can form packs. These packs are usually no more than 5 in number, but the largest that the Hunters have on record had a whopping 13 members. Because these are highly aggressive and extremely dangerous creatures, it's very difficult to study them. Wolfmen have a nasty penchant for attacking on sight, and they are predators in every sense of the word. They often run on two legs but will drop onto all four if they need extra speed; still, no matter how many feet they have on the ground, dogmen are much faster than you or I. They're also very heavily muscled, with sheer strength that rivals even Sasquatches'. And most dangerously, dogmen are quite intelligent. Like wolves or African wild dogs, they communicate with each other when hunting together, and this coordination can be deadly. Dogmen are cunning, and that may be the scariest thing about them. They can be difficult to track down and they are definitely difficult to hunt. Oddly enough, many people have been stalked or have had dogmen stare them down, but haven't been physically attacked. So these cryptids have a strange and disturbing habit of actively, intentionally terrifying people, almost as if they're enjoying the fear or even feeding off of it. But wolfmen can become directly violent, and many people, Hunters included, have fallen prey to them. Overall, they are some of the most dangerous North American monsters, and should be avoided at all costs.

If you're like me, you may be asking how in the world wolfmen could possibly have come into being. How does a canine-human hybrid even emerge? I've heard a theory for this, although it could be entirely wrong. This may sound completely fantastical or far-fetched, but it's the most formal explanation I've seen the Hunters come up with. It revolves around the disease known as lycanthropy. I've personally seen the effects of this condition while working in France and England. From all the evidence, lycanthropy seems to be (at least partially) a genetic disorder, passed on from parent to child. Some people call it a curse. Lycanthropy gives an otherwise ordinary human enhanced speed, strength, and senses, along with the ability to transform into an enormous wolf.

I realize that you may see this as some mystical nonsense, and perhaps there is some other explanation for it, but humans worldwide have always had beliefs about crossing into the bodies of the creatures around us. It's been echoed in Native traditions for thousands of years as well; our various cultures are no strangers to shapeshifters and transformations, like you'll see with a certain Navajo being that we'll discuss later. On one occasion in France, I chased a man with lycanthropy into a barn, and a gigantic wolf burst out of the building moments later, rushing off and leaving behind no trace of the human he had been just seconds earlier. This is indeed a "werewolf". On full moons, the wolf transformation is virtually uncontrollable, but otherwise, it can be activated and deactivated at will. Again, it seems like a manifestation of similar abilities that have been known to people on Turtle Island, a.k.a. North America, since long before Europeans even knew we existed. Call it magic, call it a curse, call it a disease, but it is a truly strange part of this world. Do I believe that it's entirely true? Not every part of it, but I won't deny it either.

To tie this back to the subject of this letter, if lycanthropy is truly what it would appear to be, then some Hunters believe it's possible that dogmen, a.k.a. *wolf*men, might be werewolves who have somehow lost control of their lycanthropy. Rather than simply transforming into a huge wolf on the night of a full moon or when they desire, what if a werewolf became permanently stuck in a halfway, transitional state? Neither entirely human, nor entirely wolf, but something in between. I'm sure this sounds absolutely insane, but it is one of the only firm explanations that the Hunters have for the existence of dogmen. If you don't like it, feel free to ignore it or come up with your own theories. I would be interested to see what you guys think!

Whatever you believe, wolfmen/dogmen are very real, and I have had quite a few experiences with them. These guys are some of the few monsters that I can definitely say that I truly don't like. Dogmen are so dangerous and mean-tempered that it's very difficult to respect them. Like pretty much any animal or other being, though, you *should* respect them. If you don't, you might end up in a place you'd rather not be.

The first experience that I had with a dogman was when I was quite young, maybe about 6 years old. I only remember it very, very vaguely. My mother's family and I were sitting in our dining room one night, just having dinner, when there was a loud howl from outside. Dogman howls are similar to wolf howls, but usually lower in pitch and with a lot more bass to them; they'll shake your chest and can even hurt your ears if you're too close, and the audio frequency alone can really rattle you psychologically. I remember being very scared that something was so close, and there was a lot of commotion as my family responded to the sound. And that's about all that I can really remember about that incident. I assume my mother or someone else took care of that dogman, or perhaps it simply moved on, because I never really saw any more of the species in that area until much later.

I should add that we probably weren't in any danger of the dogman actively breaking into the house. There are countless stories of monsters prowling around people's homes or standing outside them, and occasionally they can even get into outbuildings such as barns, sheds, or storehouses. But it's *extremely* rare for any cryptid to actually break into a house, especially while the residents are inside. I was once asked why this is, and why cryptids seem almost incapable of getting into houses, even though, physically, they could do so very easily. There are a bunch of different theories as to why this happens, but as usual, I tend to lean towards the simpler ones.

I think that it's mainly that many creatures, cryptids included, are pretty thrown off by manmade structures and objects. It's rare for most animals to willingly enter into buildings, especially inhabited ones, unless they're familiar with them. These are unknown spaces that are known as the den of humans, and we can be very dangerous. Besides, most cryptids don't necessarily want to kill you as much as drive you off, so if you leave the area and go inside, then they might feel that they've accomplished their goal. I can't think of any reason besides seriously wanting to kill someone that a monster would break into a building to go after them, and even then, there's very few monsters that would ever want it that badly. It just doesn't seem worth the effort or the potential danger. This is also why cryptids and larger animals hardly break right into people's houses for food or shelter unless they're really desperate. Humans are more vulnerable when we're alone and away from our "dens", but it's a very different story when we're indoors, potentially with more of our kind and/or weapons. That's one reason why I'm a big advocate of traveling in groups when going out into the wilderness. So there's my best guess, although the real reason may be something totally different. For certain cryptids like faeries, though, you can safeguard a house by ringing it with salt or iron, or by putting these materials around doorways, chimneys, windows, and other thresholds and entry points. All this information will become relevant later on.

My next experience with a wolfman was not until many years later, when I was in my early twenties and starting to work alone. My Guide, Sergio, had informed me that some bison (a.k.a. American buffalo) had been mauled on state land in Utah. He suspected that it was likely the work of a dogman. Other predators like wolves and brown bears will kill buffalo, but the victims here had apparently been mutilated to an unusual degree, and some hadn't even been eaten. Apart from humans, there were also no apex predators in this area...except for dogmen. The herd that these bison had belonged to was fairly large, but surplus killing like this can take down population numbers fast. But the main concern was that everyday hunters (yes, lowercase-H) were also allowed to go after this herd, and if there were one or more dogmen still around, things could get even bloodier. It would be best for someone from our organization to step in before there were more killings, of buffalo, humans, or any other creature.

Sergio put me in touch with a local Hunter named Louis, and I drove to Utah to meet up with him. We arranged to meet up at a spot near the last location of the bison herd, and so I took my car up into the mountains. We met each other at a stand of trees overlooking a meadow, where we could see the herd below us, grazing and sleeping. They had moved away from the area after the initial killings, but had returned a day before I got there, maybe because the grass was good, or maybe because humans or other factors had pushed them back. Buffalo have traditionally been both sacred and vital for survival to countless Plains Indian nations, including many of my neighbors in Oklahoma; they're a very meaningful animal, and I found it particularly important to protect them. I also didn't want any hunters or hikers to get into trouble. Nowadays I'm much less eager for any sort of combat, but back then I was young and more of a fighter, so I was ready to rumble.

Thankfully, Louis helped to balance me out. He was an older guy, maybe in his mid-forties, with a big beard, a big cowboy hat, and a big rifle. He shook my hand and gave me a warm smile as I approached, and he immediately took to calling me "kid", which I didn't mind (luckily, it wasn't the more historically charged term "boy"). Together, we headed down onto the prairie to look for any wolfman sign. Louis took me to where he had found the four dead bison earlier, but unfortunately, they weren't much more than bones at that point. Examining the skeletons, I saw that some of their injuries were far more traumatic than anything a regular gray wolf could inflict: one of the buffalo's hind legs had been crushed, and another had had its skull fractured, wounds which could only have been inflicted by a crazy powerful set of jaws. The true smoking gun, however, were the canine pawprints we found around the area, some that were nearly a foot long.

"How many dogmen do you think there were?" I asked Louis. I thought I could see two separate sets of prints, but I wanted to get his opinion as well.

"At least two. Maybe more. They tore through these buffalo like it was nothing," he answered.

It was a heartbreaking assessment, but I agreed, and together we started to follow the prints as best we could. They led away from the prairie and up into some clusters of trees that were slightly further up the mountainside. Unfortunately, we didn't get far before losing the trail. We decided to retrieve our supplies from our vehicles, then returned to where we'd lost the trail to camp out for the night. A few hours later, while we sat having a dinner of soup, Louis told me some of his experiences. He'd mostly dealt with Sasquatches, but on a few occasions, he had fought and killed dogmen. Evidently, they were almost impervious to bullets...almost: Louis had only ever managed to dispatch them with headshots. He'd also never encountered more than one at a time, though, so he was grateful to have me with him, and needless to say, I felt the same.

The next day we went looking for any more dogman sign, trying to find a lead. Sometime in the late afternoon, I spotted a small, low cave in the side of some rocks. I called Louis over and we readied our rifles and headed inside. The odor in that cave was strange. I had expected a thick musky smell, or maybe something pungent, like a dog or even a Sasquatch. Instead, there was a different sort of scent; it wasn't incredibly strong, but it was distinct. I can only describe it as the smell of death. You may know this smell if you've been in or around a place where things have died recently. It isn't the scent of blood or of rotting meat; it's something deeper and more unnerving than that. It made me shiver, but Louis put a hand on my shoulder.

"Steady, kid. Doesn't look like anyone's home."

We took a look around, but there wasn't much to find. There were a few scattered bones, mainly deer and rabbits, as well as a few clumps of dark hair here and there, but no wolfmen. Everything looked fresh, though, meaning that the place was probably still being used, so we decided to back out and set some traps at the cave entrance. Louis had a large metal jaw trap; this wasn't a traditional bear trap, but more of a giant, spiky mousetrap, designed to lock around targets' ankles and embed spikes into them. Vicious stuff, but effective. He placed this slightly inside the cave, covering it with dirt and some leaf litter to conceal it. In my pack, I had a few ankle snares made of thick wire. These could hold cows, and although I wasn't sure if they'd hold a dogman, I figured it was still worth a shot.

"Dunno if those are gonna work, kid," Louis said as I started setting down the snares.

"Maybe not, but they'll at least distract them from your monster over there." I pointed to his much larger trap, and he chuckled and nodded.

After setting the traps, Louis and I hurried away to make camp before the dogmen returned to their cave. They would probably pick up on our scent that we had left there, but that wouldn't necessarily stop them from stepping into any of our traps. I can't tell you why they weren't in the cave or where else they might have been, but whatever the reason, we were fortunate. Louis and I didn't light a fire or set up tents, because we wanted to be ready to move quickly if we had to. We spent the rest of the day resting up for any potential nighttime action, and alternated keeping watch whenever one of us wanted to sleep. Late that evening, I was awakened by a sustained, low-pitched rumbling sound. I sat up, realizing that it had gotten dark. The sound escalated until I realized that it was a howl, just like the one that I had heard so many years earlier at the dinner table. Louis and I had our rifles in hand almost immediately, and we both sat still for a moment, assessing the situation. The sound had come from downhill, in the direction of the prairie where the buffalo were. A moment later, it was answered by another howl from somewhere in the trees off to our left, a bit higher in pitch, with a slightly thinner tone. This confirmed it: we had a pair on our hands.

After each of the cryptids had howled once, things went silent. I looked to Louis, who whispered that we should start heading down towards the meadow. One of the wolfmen was already in that direction, and we didn't want to let them get to the bison. And yet the herd would be perfect bait; we obviously weren't going to let any of the buffalo get killed, but their presence would attract the dogmen and allow us to set up an ambush. Quietly but quickly, Louis and I began to descend from the woods back to the prairie. When we got there, the buffalo were nowhere to be found, so we started heading further into the meadow. Eventually, by the light of our headlamps and the sound of deep snorting and stomping, we located both the herd and their attackers.

The bison had formed a defensive formation, pushing the young and the elderly into the middle of a ring that they formed with their own bodies. Two enormous black dogmen were circling the herd, alternating between two and four legs while they snarled and bared their teeth at the puffing, stamping bison. I gritted my teeth as I watched the wolfmen pace back and forth in front of their prey, seemingly selecting a target; there couldn't be any more needless slaughter. They still hadn't noticed us, so I raised my rifle and aimed for the one that was closest to me; this dogman seemed like a female, since she was an adult, but about a foot shorter than the other.

"I'll get the right one, you get the left," I told Louis, who nodded and took aim as well.

I squeezed the trigger a second later, and Louis' shot followed just an instant after mine. There was a sharp yelp, and I saw the male dogman stagger off to the side, whining in pain. I thought I'd hit the female wolfman squarely in the chest, but she whirled as if my bullet had done nothing. Her two glowing eyes reflected red in the light of my headlamp. She made a noise like a snarling, extended bark and charged me. I immediately fired again. I think I shot three or four times, and I even remember seeing the fur on her body twitching where the bullets impacted. Still, she didn't stop.

"The head, aim for the head!" Louis called.

I had been so used to aiming center mass, at the torso and upper body, that by the time I heard Louis, it was too late. I managed to get off one last shot, hardly aiming, before the female dogman hit me with the force of a charging rhinoceros. She plowed right into my legs, and I fell forwards, hitting the ground hard on my stomach. All the air was knocked out of me, and my vision flashed white as I hit the grass. I laid there for a moment, stunned, reaching instinctively for my rifle. I was almost waiting for claws to come shredding through my jacket and skin, but for some reason, there was no pain. I managed to roll over onto my back, gasping for air, and soon I felt Louis grab my free hand and yank me up to my feet. I looked around. Both of the dogmen were gone, and the bison had rushed away too.

"You alright, kid?" Louis asked. I was still having trouble breathing, so I just nodded. He pointed back the way we'd come, towards the woods. "You got lucky. She knew she didn't have the time to tear you up, so she just ran for the trees. So did the other one. Looks like we've got them both on the run. Can you walk?"

"Yeah, I'm good," I panted. If I could just catch my breath, I'd be able to pursue them. Luckily, I wasn't truly hurt, just a bit stunned.

"Good. Come on then, let's see if we can catch them at the cave," Louis said, patting me on the back and starting forwards in the direction of the trees.

I followed after him, gradually regaining my breath and my composure. That had been too close. The only reason I wasn't dead is because Louis had still been shooting at the female after she'd knocked me over; maybe she could have dragged me off, but she'd probably been smart enough not to risk it. These monsters were just as dangerous as I'd been told. We arrived at the woods soon enough and started moving quickly in the direction of the cave. When we were maybe about halfway there, there was a loud metallic clang and a howl of pain. Louis and I glanced at each other, then picked up speed.

When we arrived at the cave, we found the female wolfman in front of the entrance. She was standing on two legs and whining in agony as she used her hand-like front paws to try to pry the metal jaws of Louis' trap off her leg. The metal spikes were sunk deep into her flesh, though, meaning that this was our chance. It felt almost cruel, but Louis and I took aim at her head and cut her crying short in a spray of bullets and blood. As her body dropped, I heard a snarl from behind me and to the left. I whirled, raising my rifle, but it was too late. The male wolfman slammed into me, and his fangs sunk into the very top of my right shoulder, just above the bone. The pain was unimaginable, like huge drill bits were being rammed into my skin and muscle. I collapsed backwards onto the ground, using all the strength in my upper body to shove the enormous beast off me. It was completely useless; he was hundreds of pounds heavier, and his jaws simply locked, driving his teeth deeper into my arm.

With no room to raise my rifle, I let go of it and struggled to get my knife off from my hip. The second I drew it, I started stabbing across my body at the dogman, sinking the blade into whatever exposed fur I could find; I should have tried to aim at his eye, but between the pain and the panic, I was just doing whatever I could. The dogman released his jaws from my shoulder and opened them wide again, this time coming down at my throat and my face. Just then, he gave a sudden howl and blood splashed out onto my cheeks. Louis stood practically on top of the wolfman, his rifle firing into one side of its head, and the massive animal fell to the side, mercifully freeing me from underneath it. Out of instinct, I stood up and started to say something, but the shock and the sudden blood loss suddenly took their toll, and everything went black.

The next thing I knew, I was in the hospital with Louis and my mother watching over me. We'd killed both dogmen, and both the buffalo and any humans that might go to that area were safe. My right shoulder wound up being okay, although I don't have quite as wide a range of motion in that arm as I did before. Luckily for me, though, I'm left-handed. And needless to say, I try to never let any dangerous creatures get that close to me again. Everything can teach us lessons, including animals and beings like cryptids; in this hunt, the dogmen had reminded me, more strongly than ever before, about the importance of awareness and spatial positioning, and the value of teamwork and friendship.

I've got one last experience with wolfmen that you might find particularly interesting if you like interactions between cryptids. This one occurred when I was 36, and had just moved into a house in Oklahoma, off the Cherokee Nation land. My new house was up in some low hills, on several acres of forested area. When I moved in, I decided to explore the local outdoors;

I knew all the regional animals and plants already, so I wanted to see what exactly was near me. Pretty soon, I discovered some small tree structures. Sasquatches often leave behind bent-over branches and tree limbs in unnatural positions, which is a way that they signal to each other, like making signs or markers. From this, I figured that I might have a Sasquatch or two living on the land, and from then on, I was a little bit more cautious when going out.

The area was home to more of the usual animals, too. Over the years, around my house I saw deer, foxes, bobcats, coyotes, and even, once, a mountain lion. In time, most of these creatures grew used to my presence. The Sasquatches, though, remained secretive, as they almost always do. Sometimes I could hear them whooping to each other through the trees, and a couple times I gave calls of my own which they responded to. But I almost never saw them. Sometimes I spotted trees moving or shaking, and every so often I'd catch a glimpse of their big figures, but it was never anything up close. Sasquatches are masters of stealth, and if they don't want you to see them, then you probably won't, so these ones were at least reasonably comfortable around me. Even though I never clearly saw them, I did find footprints. From these I was able to determine that there was at least one adult Sasquatch with a young one. Since we all know that mother animals of any species can get defensive, I tried to keep my distance after I figured this out. Just to make sure that I was on their good side, but without interacting too directly, I sometimes left little gifts of salmon or apples out where I thought that the Sasquatches might be able to get to them, just to show that I was friendly and meant them no harm. Whenever I came back, these gifts would be gone, and of course other animals could have gotten them, but I chose to believe that the Sasquatch had taken them. And because of what happened later on, I now believe this even more.

One day when I was out just enjoying the woods, I came across a canine print in some wet mud by a small stream. This print was huge, over a foot long and a few inches deep. I immediately thought that this was dogman sign, but that wasn't a guarantee; there are many other cryptid and just animal species out there, and a single footprint can be distorted by soil and weather. But of course, I also just didn't like the idea of a dogman being so close to my house. I decided to grab my rifle and look for more sign. It was the middle of the day, so hopefully if it was a wolfman, it wouldn't be active. Over the next 36 hours or so, I was able to locate more pawprints, but I wanted to gather more information before jumping to action. Dogmen tend to leave big, noticeable trails, so it wasn't long until I found more sign, including a big pile of scat. Scat is...well, dung. Poop. You know.

You may find this next part gross, but sometimes you just have to do what you have to do. Using a nearby stick, I examined the scat to see how moist it was; the surface was dry, but inside it was still a little wet, meaning that it was somewhat fresh. Next, I continued poking the scat to open it up and see what was inside. There were a few tufts of hair and feathers, but not much else; the hair was from a deer, which I determined by snapping a few strands, but I couldn't identify the feathers. Between the scat and the prints, I realized that, yes, I was likely dealing with a dogman, and the conclusion made my stomach drop. I didn't want to have to deal with one of those again, much less alone.

I went home, thinking about calling Sergio or another Hunter. I might have called Louis, but he had retired a few years earlier, and I wasn't going to force him into my dilemma. I decided to talk to my mother for some advice, and she advised me to stay put. Perhaps the dogman was just passing through, and it might just move on. If not, then it would obviously be smart to figure out its habits before taking further action. As any hunter knows, both capital-H and otherwise, observation can be just as important as a well-placed bullet.

The next day I woke up to find that it had snowed a little overnight. I grabbed my rifle and a few other supplies in my backpack, and headed out. Snow is excellent substrate, or ground material, for tracking; we all know what a trail of footprints looks like after even just an inch has fallen. But wind and additional snowfall can easily wipe out these tracks, and in this case, the overnight snow had covered a lot of the wolfman prints I had found over the past few days, making it tough for me to pick anything up. The day was pretty fruitless, and I returned home before dark, disheartened. I was also a bit concerned about the local woods. If large predators like dogmen remain in one area for a prolonged period, they can devastate local prey populations; this is exactly what Louis and I had feared with the bison herd. The loss of life is bad enough, but it also throws off the balance of an ecosystem; that's not just bad for survival, but also because both animals and monsters can turn to humans and our civilization for food, making things even worse. Even the Sasquatch could be in danger. Dogmen and Sasquatches are known to fight over food sources and territory. I grew up around some Choctaw and Chickasaw folks (their Nations are almost right next to the Cherokee in

Oklahoma Indian country), and they even have a story about how, a few centuries ago, some of their warriors tricked the two species into doing battle, ultimately saving the people from the hostile actions of both. These clashes were supposedly brutal, and often fatal, and that made me worried for the Sasquatch mom and child. I made it my goal to find this dogman before things escalated.

That night, I was sitting watching some TV, which is a bit unusual for me; I think I just needed something passive to do. Regardless of whatever show or movie was playing, I wasn't really paying attention; my thoughts were on the wolfman and my concern that any further snowfall might make hunting it impossible. At some point, I heard a *loud* snarl from right outside, just like the dogman vocalizations that I'd heard before. This one sounded incredibly close, so I immediately shut off the TV and leapt up. That house was pretty small, so my shotgun was in the next room over, and I grabbed it just in time to both hear and feel a tremendous weight ram into my front door, rattling practically the whole house. Like I mentioned earlier, most monsters don't just break into people's houses, but I think you'll understand that I wasn't exactly going to go back to watching TV on the couch. I rushed up and aimed my shotgun right at the front door, waiting for it to come down and for the wolfman to burst in. If I could just get a clear shot at its head, maybe I could bring it down, or at least drive it off. More likely, it would rip me to shreds, but before that, I would put up the best fight I could. Thankfully, my door and my body remained intact. Instead of another collision, there was a bellow that shook the house almost as much, a sound I recognized as a Sasquatch. The thudding of heavy feet came from outside, and I ran to the window; in the trees beyond my small front yard, a pair of enormous two-legged figures were shoving and grappling. Ordinarily, I would run in the other direction, but here, one of these monsters was clearly more dangerous than the other, and my life and many others were at stake if I let that one win.

As quickly as I could, I switched my shotgun for a rifle and a headlamp, then rushed out the front door towards the woods. The cryptids were still standing upright, wrestling to bring each other low, and when I got my light on them, I saw both clearly for the first time. The mother Sasquatch was dark brown, while the dogman was the usual dark gray, nearly black; he was a male, and a good foot or two taller than his opponent. As I raised my rifle, he heaved his body to the side, muscles rippling as he tossed the mother Sasquatch to the ground. He must have noticed me at that point, because he lifted his head to fix me with glowing scarlet eyes, making me flinch but doing nothing to stop me from pulling the trigger. I fired, and the wolfman gave a yip as the bullet hit him somewhere around the eye. He staggered backwards, and around then a hefty stick came hurtling through the air and whacked him on the side of the head. I looked to the side to see the juvenile Sasquatch, no more than 4 or 5 feet tall, hurling branches at this enormous predator, doing whatever she could to defend her mother. Touching as this was, the realization that the youngster was so directly involved made my stomach drop.

The dogman leapt to the side to avoid the Sasquatch's barrage, but I fired again, landing another headshot. This time he bared his teeth at me, blood running down the side of his face. I was expecting him to charge when the mother Sasquatch rushed in from the side, slamming both of her raised fists straight down onto the dogman's skull. He dropped like a rock, and the Sasquatch repeated her attack, bringing her fists down over and over, until finally the wolfman fell still.

There was a long silence, apart from the sound of all of our heavy breathing, before the mother Sasquatch turned to look at me. I froze for a moment as her brown eyes met mine, then knelt and put my gun onto the grass; I wasn't scared, but I didn't exactly want her to stick around for dinner either. Her facial expression was hard to read, but before I could think about it much, she simply turned around and took her little one's hand. With the other, she grabbed the dead wolfman by the arm and dragged him behind her like a sack of dirt. In seconds, they were gone, disappearing into the forest like they had never been there. Everything was suddenly silent; it was surreal, and if it wasn't for the churned-up dirt and scattered patches of blood, this might have just been any other night. As I weakly picked up my gun and walked inside, my mind was having trouble processing the situation. Cryptid clashes like this certainly happen more than we know, but usually not right next to people's houses. I don't know why the Sasquatches had been there, or why the mother had decided to intervene, but I was certainly grateful for it; even if the wolfman had just intended on frightening me, it was thanks to them that it wouldn't be coming back for an encore. The whole situation was chilling, and I would never want to repeat it, but it was also incredible. To this day, it remains one of the most powerful experiences I've ever had.

And one of the flat-out best moments of my life came the following morning, when on my porch, I found 32 smooth river pebbles of all different colors, each a little smaller than a thumbnail, arranged in a perfect circle on the doormat. This was clearly a gift, and although I unfortunately had to mess up the circle, I still have those pebbles today. They're a reminder of the natural balance of all things, and the peace and protection that I work to maintain as a Hunter.

Anyway, hopefully I've taught you some things about dogmen. If you encounter one, act calm and back away. Don't try to challenge it or even look it in the eye. Most of the time, they're content to just scare the hell out of you rather than attack. But if one really *does* come at you, well...I think the best you could do would just be to shoot it in the head and take cover. You probably won't kill it, but you may at least give yourself enough time to get away safely. Carry high-caliber, high-power weapons, and hope you can do enough damage. But realistically, you won't be able to outrun or out-fight a wolfman, so this is honestly the best advice that I can give you. As with many cryptids in these letters, I hope you'll never have to encounter one in the first place. And if it gives you any comfort, odds are that you won't.

Anyway, this has been a much longer letter than the previous two, so I'll end it here. I hope you enjoyed my accounts and maybe learned something today. Next time we'll talk about a much-requested cryptid from the southwestern United States. But for now, I hope you all stay safe, and stay home if you can. We'll talk more soon. This has been Sam White Owl, signing out.

LETTER 4 – SKINWALKER

U.S.A. (NEW MEXICO)

Written July 2020

Hi, everyone, it's Sam White Owl, back again. I've been really happy with the way these videos are turning out, and with all of your responses to them. Writing these letters has given me a chance to go back over my old journals and think about where I've been and what I've done. As I get closer to the end of my days as a Hunter, it's been good to look back on my career. I think we should all look back on our lives every so often, no matter where we are currently. So, with that, let's talk about one of the stranger experiences I've had, starting with a question I've frequently been asked.

As a viewer put it: Do I believe in witchcraft or magic? This is tough to answer, but here's my best shot. As you know just by reading these letters, I've seen a whole lot of strange stuff. And behind everything you might call a legend, folktale, or myth, there is some kind of truth. There are some things that don't seem to be possible without the existence of witchcraft or magic, and in many cases, that's been the teaching for thousands of years. The English words "witchcraft" and "magic" also have certain connotations, usually as explicitly fictional concepts, whereas in other traditions, this stuff is understood as a different side to our everyday reality. For example, I can't think of any "natural" way that a human can change their form into an animal. Nevertheless, I've seen the results of these transformations firsthand. And since I have no way of explaining this besides what would crudely be called witchcraft or magic, I try to keep an open mind on the subject.

Just like you see me balance mainstream Western science with Native science and traditional knowledge, I also keep an understanding of this more mysterious stuff along with all the other information I have. I've mentioned before that I carry several personal sacred objects on me whenever I go on a task (I won't go into them in depth here, but they include a few family heirlooms and some animal body parts), primarily for the purpose of inspiration and protection, and I've conducted many different rituals and rites for certain hunts. I try to consult experts on these sorts of things, so I've gotten help from Indigenous medicine people, Siberian shamans, East African healers, and more; I trust their knowledge, and so far, it hasn't done anything but help me. Much of this truly *does* have an effect, especially on a psychological level, as well as a spiritual one, if you're into that. Many of my fellow Hunters don't believe any of this, but they still generally treat it with respect. And you can never be too safe.

I bring this topic up in order to transition into talking about the monster for this letter. This time we'll be discussing the cryptids known as skinwalkers. Honestly, this name really shouldn't be spoken. In Southwest Indigenous tradition, saying this name or even giving these creatures any sustained attention will attract them or other types of harm. I don't know if this is true or not, and even some Native people believe that it's simply superstition or even intentionally designed to scare people. But that's one reason that many Natives are very reluctant to discuss skinwalkers and related matters, especially with outsiders and non-Natives. Regardless of whether you believe them (or me), it's important to remember that many people know of skinwalkers and their power, and if they choose not to speak about it, that's because they have very good reason not to. Nevertheless, pop culture is apparently obsessed with these beings, and that can be a very slippery slope.

Even though many people won't address the topic of skinwalkers whatsoever, others are willing to give some information. Some believe that it's acceptable to learn certain things so that you're aware of what to watch out for and protect yourself from. It's also the case that walkers feed off fear and anxiety, especially the dread of the unknown, so knowing them in turn wipes out one of their biggest advantages. Plus, you don't have to know every single aspect of a topic to understand it and act appropriately. With all this in mind, I'll be trying to balance knowledge with silence: I won't go on for dozens of pages, but I will give you some information and a story.

Much of this can come in handy regardless of your situation, even if you're only dealing with the negativity of other humans. Unlike most beings that Hunters contend with, walkers genuinely cannot be understood or confronted without becoming involved with aspects of the universe that aren't exactly visible. This isn't anything too unfamiliar for many Indigenous folks in the Americas, or elsewhere, but for most people, this might be rare stuff.

First, we have to consider language. Skinwalkers have a name in the Navajo language which I am very reluctant to repeat. To get around this as much as possible, Hunters usually call these beings either "skinnies" or "walkers", which, I promise you, we were saying long before "The Walking Dead" came out. Simply altering the name like this is not enough to fully alleviate the problem, but we have to refer to these beings somehow, so this is our attempt at finding a middle ground. Speaking any of these names or discussing the topic out loud is usually understood to be more hazardous than writing in text; words always have power, but especially when spoken.

So what exactly are skinwalkers? They are beings mainly associated with the Navajo, a.k.a. the Diné, a Native group from the Southwestern USA. Walkers are rare, and are almost exclusively found in the southwestern states, although it's hard to track their exact locations. It's become ridiculously common for people across the world to claim that they've encountered skinwalkers, but I promise you that this is almost never the case. Walkers are vastly more threatening on the Navajo Nation and their traditional lands, and although they're not a problem for every person constantly, most Navajo have had at least a passing experience with them. However, as I said before, it is possible for others to draw their attention and their associated negative energy.

There are very few beings out there that can be justifiably called pure evil, but walkers can't be described as anything else. By and large, most creatures are just out to survive, and they usually don't cause harm solely for the sake of enjoyment or pleasure. But there are exceptions to this principle, such as certain humans, some of whom become skinwalkers. All their actions and abilities are intended to cause pain, suffering, trauma, and death. I'm not going to go into any deep detail, but here are the basics.

At their core, skinwalkers come from average humans. Many were once medicine people, which in the context of the Navajo means spiritual specialists who use their special and sacred skills to uplift, protect, guide, and heal through prayers, songs, and ceremonies. However, in exchange for a quick and easy path to dark powers, some people decide to commit a terrible crime: usually, that means killing a loved one, typically a family member. This is one of the evilest deeds imaginable in any culture, but it's especially monstrous for Indigenous groups, including the Diné, who value family as sacred. This is followed by a number of other ceremonies and actions that are even more gruesome, but I'm not going to get into those. Just know that there is a process which is taught and carried out in secret by these murderers. And through these rites, they gain the dark, destructive abilities that define them as skinwalkers. I know that it probably sounds absolutely crazy. However, these accounts go back centuries, and this is just how things are.

The "dark, destructive abilities" that I'm referring to come in many varieties, but I'll touch on the most frequently used ones. The most well-known power of a skinwalker is the one that gives them their English name: the ability to transform into an animal shape. By wearing the body parts of certain animals, usually their hides/skins, walkers can physically shapeshift into those creatures. They usually take on the full body forms of animals, but they can also take on a hybrid or blended shape that combines aspects of both human and animal, which is just as disturbing as it sounds. Many walkers seem to favor canine forms: domestic dogs, foxes, and especially coyotes. They're also known to become deer, elk, birds of prey, and more; it takes immense strength, but a rare few can become wolves, cougars, and bears. I'm not sure if a walker could theoretically turn into whatever animal they want, but it would probably be possible if they had the correct skin and could do the proper ceremonies and markings on it. However, walkers have a habit of transforming specifically into predators. This could just be a practical consideration, but it also reflects the danger they present.

Often, but not always, you might be able to tell the difference between a normal animal and a walker in animal form. First is the sense that something is wrong; even if you can't actually identify anything strange about the animal physically, something about it may just feel off. Next are the eyes. Human eyes look different than those of most other animals, and yet, the animal forms of walkers frequently have oddly human-like eyes. Finally, the movements of walkers in animal form may seem jerky, stiff, or just *not right* somehow. In their human shapes, walkers are often pretty conspicuous. They tend to be unusually hairy, and like before, the eyes of walkers in human form often appear like those of their favored animal form. And of course, they almost always wear various animal hides or other body parts, allowing them to transform at a moment's notice.

However, this is a good time to remind you that skinwalkers are almost unheard of outside of the Southwest USA, especially the Navajo Nation. There are certainly different shapechanging beings in other places, but it's silly seeing just how many people cry skinwalker whenever they see a deer walking with a limp in a place like New Jersey or France. Sometimes animals and people just look or act weird, and it usually has nothing to do with monsters, much less walkers. In fact, walkers couldn't even become animals in the first place if they were in these other locations. Many beings derive their power from the land, often specific geographical regions. In this case, walkers are tied to Dinétah, the Navajo homeland; the modern Navajo Nation reservation is located within Dinétah, but the region extends beyond that, with four sacred mountains roughly marking its borders. The farther away from Dinétah a skinwalker is, the weaker their abilities become. Within the boundaries of the mountains, however, they're free to change shape and much worse.

Much of the time, walkers can be heard long before they're seen. For some reason, pop culture has associated the idea of mimicking voices exclusively with the wendigo, a completely unrelated cryptid from hundreds of miles away; I have no idea where this swap started. Then again, wendigo don't have deer skulls either, so people have many odd ideas. And don't worry; we'll talk about wendigo in another letter. For their part, walkers mimic voices all the time, as well as all sorts of animal calls. They can't replicate these sounds flawlessly, though, and especially when imitating animals, their voices tend to have a noticeably human quality. Still, that doesn't make it any less disturbing to hear owls or coyotes off in the darkness of the desert calling to each other with voices that aren't entirely animal.

Other things make walkers very tough to pin down, such as the technique that we Hunters call "persuasion" or "influence". This isn't full-on possession, but if a walker looks into someone's eyes for a short period, then they may be able to gain an invisible hold over that person. According to victims of this power, they feel compelled to do whatever they're told by the walker, and it's nearly impossible to fight back and regain control of their own bodies. I've seen this in action only a few times, and I've never fallen victim to it myself, but to have someone else control your own body is nightmarish. Walkers can also run incredibly quickly over long distances and have the stamina to match. Many accounts speak of them keeping pace with cars on the highway, and Hunters have reported them covering up to 250 miles in a single night. Likewise, in both animal and human form, walkers are unnaturally fast and agile.

One of the most dangerous, and common, ways that walkers will attack is by causing sickness. The Navajo have many taboos surrounding death, especially handling or being around dead bodies. But as you may have realized, walkers pollute almost every single Diné tradition and belief. In addition to their skins, they use many other items, including weapons made from bone (whether human or otherwise). They favor knives and needle-like throwing darts, which they coat with poison by using some combination of ceremonies, plants, and worst of all, blood, bone dust, or other material from corpses, usually fresh ones; sometimes they'll just toss out clouds of toxic powder into the air. These poisons can have many different properties: walkers love to throw bone darts that will paralyze the target, and other poisons can cause everything from nightmares, fevers, seizures, and practically any kind of ailment you can think of. Without medical treatment, both physical and spiritual, a walker's poison is almost always lethal...but before then, you're going to suffer. Instead of killing their victims quickly, walkers use poison to keep them in pain and fear, usually for several days, before the end finally comes. It's sadistic, and very intentional.

And sometimes walkers don't attack physically at all. As I mentioned before, social bonds are vital and even sacred to the Navajo, whether that means families, clans, neighbors, or simply different individuals. This is the case for many cultures and groups who need to take care of and look out for one another; that includes Indigenous communities, and especially those on reservations, who oftentimes can only count on each other. Walkers will sabotage these connections, put people at each other's throats, and tear apart families and friends and communities, destroying some of the most precious and essential lifelines of the Diné. Mental health often goes overlooked, but it's a crucial part of all our lives, and a very real challenge for marginalized groups; unfortunately, in parts of the Southwest, this plays right into the claws of walkers. Even in normal circumstances, I think we all know how hard it can be to deal with something like a breakup, the death of someone you love, or losing a friend. This inner pain can hurt more deeply than any physical injury, and walkers love to cause both.

After all that awful information, you may be wondering how to deal with it. As I said, walkers are not common, and thankfully, there are ways to protect yourself from them and drive them off. And even though it's very difficult, they can be killed. If you go after a walker with just a regular gun and bullets, however, you probably won't make it back. Physical steps alone aren't enough to successfully confront creatures like walkers; it takes spiritual measures as well. Like so many of the topics I discuss in these letters, this is stuff that can take a lifetime to learn, and I'm far from an expert, so I'm just giving you the quickest of quick overviews here for this story.

Although walkers are not associated with the Cherokee, we have our own ways of dealing with similar problems, as do other Indigenous nations. Many methods involve burning important materials such as sage or cedar. Sweeping with eagle feathers can also generally cleanse an area and provide a shield against evil and negative energy. To more specifically protect from harmful beings, my grandma and some of the other elders taught me special prayers. As I mentioned before, I also carry a medicine bag with several sacred objects that serve a similar purpose. When it comes to the Navajo, many of them are very religious and have a ton of this knowledge. Like many Indigenous groups, they have a special sort of medicine bag, the *jish*, which often holds corn pollen or other important plants, as well as soil from sacred sites like the mountains. Navajo traditions also incorporate countless prayer songs, some personal and some shared, which fulfill every purpose imaginable, including providing blessings of protection and safety. Most importantly for this letter, a tried-and-true safeguard is sprinkling juniper ash on or around the area or the thing you want to protect, including yourself or other people. There are other components to many of these practices, but I'll leave it here.

Beyond simply protecting yourself, it is possible to kill a walker, but it's rarely smart to try. The straightforward way is by using weapons that have been blessed. Properly blessing anything in any tradition requires in-depth knowledge and belief, and in the case of a Hunter's weapons, the core step is coating them with white ash. Even if you're not knowledgeable about Navajo traditions, you can conduct a version of the ash-coating ceremony yourself, which I've had to do before. But it's much better to go to the professionals; before going on any job involving a walker, one of the first things I do is take my bullets and weapons to a medicine person to have them all purified and blessed. White ash is understood to be effective because of time: a core value of Indigenous culture, just like many others, is respect for your elders, and because fire is one of the oldest natural forces or powers in existence, it is said to essentially overpower other such forces, including the ones that walkers use.

Even for the Hunters, skinwalkers are among the strangest and most inexplicable cryptids out there. Their abilities are basically impossible to explain without considering witchcraft and magic, and they pose a rare and serious challenge to us.

Because walkers are pretty rare, I've only dealt with them a few times, mostly in New Mexico and Arizona. Before any of these experiences, I had already visited the area, because my parents thought it was important to show me how other Native people lived in their own reservations and communities. So I had been out to the Navajo Nation as a young boy, even though we had no family there. Nothing unusual or dangerous ever occurred on these trips, but because we were Hunters, my mother did explain walkers to me.

As I grew up and started capital-H Hunting on my own, I occasionally heard others in the organization mention these monsters, but I didn't wind up going after one for myself until I was in my 20s. It started when Sergio told me that some sheep farmers in the western border regions of the Navajo Nation were having their animals stolen. The dead sheep weren't turning up with the distinctive blood loss caused by chupacabras, so it must have been something else. Normally, the Hunters wouldn't blink an eye at this, since coyotes and other predators take livestock all the time. But something was off here. There were reports of other strange occurrences in the area. In particular, some people said that on a few occasions they had seen a strange animal-like figure in the desert at night, often wandering close to people's homes and farms. Again, many different Native groups, especially the Navajo, don't mention walkers lightly or even speak of them at all, but that's exactly what the rumors were indicating here.

Sergio brought me the job offer, but I was a little hesitant to accept. I didn't know much about Diné culture or walkers for myself, and I would have felt better with a partner. Fortunately, there are a few Navajo Hunters, one of whom was already on the task. We'll call this woman Doli for the purposes of this letter. She agreed to work together with me, and we arranged to meet up at the eastern side of the Nation. Really, this was Doli's case, and I was just there to provide backup. The next day, I got into my car and headed out. The drive into the Nation was beautiful. If you've never been to the area, there are rock formations of earthy red and orange, alongside endless open vistas of scrubland. Like many locations I've traveled to, it can be a hostile place, but it's also very beautiful.

The Navajo are one of the biggest Native nations. Just like the rest of us, the United States government forcibly removed them from their original homeland and placed them onto reservations. Over time, however, the Navajo have been able to expand their lands, and their reservation is now the largest in the country. Like any other group of people, they don't all live in the exact same manner. Many Indigenous folks are more "traditional" and stick closely to some of the original ways and customs; oftentimes these are the older generations and/or those who live in more rural or reservation areas. Others have adopted a more Westernized, mainstream "American" way; many of these are younger people and/or those who live in more urban areas, especially off-reservation, which is most of us. So on reservations, there are many different lifestyles, but you can expect to find lots of people who live in the traditional way.

It wasn't long before I met Doli at the designated location. She isn't very big physically, but her inner strength more than makes up for that. It's the kind of strength that comes from growing up and living on a rez; it might be a little difficult to understand, but it's a sort of fortitude that Indigenous folks and many other people of color share. Doli had her hair braided, with cargo pants and a T-shirt, and a slightly concealed pistol at her hip. She smiled at me as I came up, and her handshake was firm. I think she's a few years older than me, but we get along well to this day. Like all investigations and hunts, we started by gathering information, this time by driving all the way to the western part of the Nation to talk to some of the families there.

This might be a good time to mention that the Navajo Nation has its own police force to handle all sorts of internal difficulties on the rez. As always, the Hunters only get involved when there's some cryptid-related matter, which was why Doli had picked up this task. Even though I was just helping out, she gave me the chance to give some input. Our mission was very straightforward: find the skinwalker and eliminate them. With other monsters, there are often other options, but not here.

We went to a couple houses and trailer homes on those first days, just talking to the residents about what they had seen and experienced. I noticed right away that all of them, especially the older people, were *very* hesitant to even discuss the topic, let alone give any details. Native people are usually welcoming and appreciative of visitors (respectful ones, of course), but Doli and I weren't just there to hang out. It helped enormously to have a Navajo and member of the Nation as a partner, because although many people flat-out refused to speak about our task, especially to me, some of them did briefly talk with Doli after some explanation (although they almost always tried to talk her out of the mission). She collected a few stories about a strange shadow that appeared in the night at a distance. People generally described it as resembling a very large canine, often standing on two legs, with pointed ears and eyes that glowed red even when no light was shining on them. One family even said that their youngest child, a boy who was only 6 years old, had gotten sick after the creature had appeared, although it seemed like he was going to be fine. The whole thing was definitely eerie, but apart from the sick child, the walker hadn't actively harmed anyone. But as we soon learned, it was definitely trying.

After some visits, we got word of one family who had encountered the walker multiple times. Houses on any reservation can be very far apart, and this one was a long way away from any others. When we arrived, both Doli and I stopped in our tracks almost as soon as we got out of our cars. There were large scratches around the house's front door that were almost certainly claw marks. A line of ash marked the porch, forming a barrier between the front of the building and the desert outside. The scene was equal parts haunting and angering: instead of just prowling around outside, the walker had actually hit the house itself.

We went to the front door, knocking gently. In some reservation areas it can be considered rude to just go right up and knock on somebody's door, but Doli and I weren't just making a social call or a sales visit. As you might imagine, many of the events in this letter, including just about everything that took place at this house, are very out of the ordinary for the traditional Navajo way of life. This was an emergency situation.

After we knocked, a heavyset, older man opened the door and hesitated for a second. Doli greeted him in the Navajo language and exchanged some words with him, and then he let us in. Inside the house were 8 other members of the family: an older woman, a few younger adults, and several children. They offered us a seat on a big couch in one of the front rooms, but we politely declined, saying that we would be gone shortly. At first, Doli talked to them mainly in Navajo; I don't speak it, but she seemed to be trying to reassure them. Eventually, she switched to English and told me that the family would be willing to talk to us. They provided more information than either of us had been bargaining for, but it was clear that they were terrified, and maybe seeing people who were willing to help may have convinced them to open up more. The younger members of the family were also much more sociable than the older couple; the family all lived a traditional lifestyle, but like many other cases, younger generations are often more open with strangers. I'm also pretty sure that they had at least heard of the Hunter organization. Whatever the case, Doli and I were very grateful for their cooperation, and we wouldn't have completed our mission without it.

You might know the phrase "Take it outside!"; I'm personally *very* familiar with it, because my auntie would yell it at my cousin and I whenever we would get into fights in their house. Most people associate the expression with pushing physical confrontations out of a building, but less visibly, that also includes all the associated stress, tension, or negativity. Many Diné take this principle very seriously and will go outside to handle arguments or difficult conversations, so that the home can be kept clean and healthy both emotionally and spiritually. For this reason, I was a little surprised that we kept our discussion indoors. I think this is mainly because the walls and the line of ash on the porch still acted as barriers against the walker's active attention; given that the monster was already focused on the house, I wasn't sure how much we could do, but I wasn't going to question the others' reasoning.

One of the young men did most of the talking. For obvious reasons, I won't give his real name, but let's call him Mato. According to him, they had been tormented for the past several weeks. He started with a story about how he and his younger siblings had been bringing their sheep back to their house from the pasture, when they had passed a hogan. Hogans are traditional Navajo houses, made of a dome- or cone-shaped frame of wood or stone which is then packed with earth. There are many scattered across the Navajo Nation, and although occasionally people still live in some of them, others are used for ceremonial purposes or not permanently inhabited. Empty hogans can sometimes offer shelter for passersby or people who need a place to stay, and it wasn't unusual, especially in past decades, for shepherds to occasionally stay the night in these empty houses. However, Mato explained to us that the hogan he was referring to was off-limits, because somebody had died inside of it a little while ago. As he and his siblings walked past the building, they heard a rustling sound, as if something large was moving within. Mato had taken a step closer to see if he could investigate, but suddenly, a huge coyote bolted out of the door, moving faster than was physically possible. The animal almost knocked him over before it paused, looked straight at him, and then raced off and disappeared into the desert. Mato told us that its eyes "weren't coyote eyes", and he knew from its gaze alone that it was pure evil.

Two nights later, the family had been at home asleep, when from outside they'd heard the wailing, howling cry of a coyote.

This sound can be eerie enough when it comes from a normal coyote, but in this case, the quality of the noise was distorted, and the family described it as seeming to come from a human throat, almost as if a person was imitating coyote vocalizations. This unnerved everyone, especially some of the kids, and nobody left the house that night. In the morning, however, Mato and his father went outside and found abnormally large canine footprints, which matched the size of the big coyote that had run out of the hogan. Worse, when they went to check on their sheep, two were missing, having vanished in complete silence.

Whenever Mato went out with his siblings and the flock, he always carried a walking stick, and occasionally a pistol, but now he started bringing his father's rifle with him. A few more days went by without incident, until shortly before Doli and I arrived, when the family heard that strange human-like coyote call again. This time, several of them looked outside and saw the silhouette of a man. He appeared to be wearing fur on his upper body, and he was moving with a strange swaying and sliding gait, headed directly towards the home. While climbing the stairs onto the porch, his shadowy figure almost seemed to lengthen and grow taller. Then he scratched slowly and loudly at the front door for a few moments, before turning and vanishing into the darkness. The family found the claw marks the next morning. They went straight to a medicine woman, also known as a *hataałii*, or "singer", who had performed some prayers and laid down the white ash to block off their porch and the front door. Evidently, this barrier was still holding up.

Something about this situation was more troubling than usual. As a field Hunter, I've unfortunately gotten very accustomed to seeing the fear and distress that monsters can cause. Here, however, we weren't dealing with a one-off encounter on a trail or a few sightings of something unusual at the side of a road. This was basically a haunting, where the family was being stalked in their own home. It also didn't help that a lot of the people in trouble were kids, some of whom might not even know exactly what was happening to them. It was very fortunate that Doli and I had arrived when we had; nobody in the household had fallen ill, no fights had broken out, and there had been no physical attacks by the walker. And we were going to keep it that way.

After hearing the whole story, Doli and I got together and figured that the walker was likely to come back to this house. The family was considering moving out, but because the most recent incident had only just happened, they hadn't taken any action yet; on top of that, they didn't have any solid place to go. Meanwhile, it was nearly evening, so we had to plan quickly; like the rest of their kind, this walker seemed to be most active at night.

We decided to visit the medicine woman and then return to the family's house. The older folks were very reluctant, but after Mato advocated for us, they eventually allowed us to stay at their home for the night. The plan was to confront the walker when it returned. I don't know exactly how, but Doli somehow convinced the family to also stay in the house themselves, seeing as it was protected by ash and us two Hunters. They were obviously very nervous, but Doli reassured them that we would deal with the monster, which would likely be coming back to the house anyway. Again, I can't help but think that this family already had some knowledge of the Hunters, because they put a tremendous amount of trust in us.

The medicine woman's residence wasn't too far away from the house, and to keep her privacy I won't give her name.

"Medicine man" is a very generic English term that covers all sorts of different roles in different Native cultures; for the Navajo, it usually refers to the hataałii, or "singers", such as this woman. Sadly, there are not nearly as many as there used to be, but this woman had learned many of the old ways, including songs, prayers, and ceremonies. In an Indigenous context, the word "medicine" usually involves spiritual, emotional, and mental matters just as much as physical ones.

It took some communication, but eventually the singer saw that we weren't just out looking for trouble. It also helped that we mentioned another hataałii who had helped the Hunters before. She did a suite of blessings for us, and since I've already talked an awful lot about sensitive information, I'll generally say that most of these ceremonies involved prayer songs in the Navajo language. The singer's voice was steady, and because the songs didn't have much variation in notes, it let me focus more on the words themselves and the actions that accompanied them. There's something particularly moving about language when it's sung rather than spoken, even if you can't understand its meaning. Combined with the heavy situation, these prayer songs made me emotional in a way that's tough to describe; I've felt it many times before and since, but something about this occasion was especially deep. To give the least clunky analogy I can, it was almost like watching a sunset with the knowledge that things are going to be very different in the morning, and maybe not in a good way; I've been in this position many times, and maybe you have too.

At the end of the ceremonies, Doli and I swept ourselves with the smoke from a fire. Then the singer sprinkled white ash from the coals over both of us and applied it to specific parts of our bodies, before scooping up the rest of the ash and putting it into a bucket. This isn't Harry Potter; doing these ceremonies won't give you some sort of glowy magical shield, but they will have an impact if you trust in them and do them right, so just having the ash on my body made me feel steady and firm on my feet. The singer handed the bucket to Doli, telling us to use it to coat our weapons and our bullets. We paid her in cash, and then she sent us on our way, warning us to stay careful and wishing us good luck.

We returned to the family's house a little after dusk and found most of them sitting around a large table, waiting to have dinner. Despite having 11 people crowded into the room, there were two empty chairs and two full plates waiting for me and Doli. I don't remember what we had to eat, and I didn't write that part down (whoops), but I mostly remember the conversation that night. Even though everyone was still a little tense, the kids and younger adults gradually loosened up the atmosphere. They were far more outgoing and talkative than the grandparents, and they didn't hold back from asking Doli and I about all sorts of things: where we were from, what we were going to do, and even if we were married (which was just as awkward as you might imagine!). We answered as much as we could, and I could tell that the conversation made all of us feel better about the situation. Later on, Doli told me that these positive interactions did more than just improve our moods and raise morale. As I explained before, walkers thrive off of causing negative emotions and poisoning interpersonal relationships, so anything that could counteract this was a big help.

After dinner, Doli and I grabbed our weapons from our cars and began coating our guns, bullets, and knives with the white ash from the bucket, making sure not to do anything that would jam or otherwise throw off our firearms. While doing so, we decided where to position ourselves. Since Doli was equipped with a pair of night vision goggles, she decided to take the outside, near the fence of the sheep paddock. I would be inside, waiting to see if the walker would come to the front door again. We wished each other good hunting and separated for the night. I went into the living room and sat on the couch that had the best line of sight through the house's biggest front window. From there, I had a good view of the outside, and I would be able to see anything approaching the house from the front. It was nearly a full moon, so there was plenty of light to see out across the flat, open desert. It might have been nice to have full night vision like Doli, but at least my rifle scope has NV capabilities too (I also use more extensive night vision gear sometimes; I might talk about that in later letters). Pretty soon, the family was all in bed, and so I turned off the lamp that lit the living room, sunk back behind the couch, and waited in the dark.

For better or worse, that night was totally uneventful, except for a few (normal) coyote calls and the sound of the wind rustling the patchy shrubs. And honestly, I was relieved when the sky began to grow light; as much as we needed to deal with this walker, part of me was hoping that I wouldn't have to see him. But as I said, walkers gain strength from the fear and dread of their victims, so I tried to grit my teeth and remind myself that I had faced plenty of danger before; I wasn't going to give the enemy what they wanted. When the sun was fully above the horizon, I regrouped with Doli, who hadn't seen anything on her end either. We were both exhausted from the all-nighter, but the family was very understanding and let us sleep on the living room couches. I woke up just before noon and was surprised to see that Doli and some of the kids were outside, playing soccer and seeming pretty cheerful. This worried me, but Doli knew what she was doing, and I trusted her. Still, I went straight out to talk to her. After saying hello to everyone, I stepped close to Doli, lowering my voice and trying to stay casual so I wouldn't worry the kids.

"Hey, is it okay to be playing outside like this?"

"I figured you were gonna ask that. I think it's actually a good thing. We wanna keep spirits high," Doli said, before shifting to a whisper, the same way that parents or doctors or police do when they're trying to keep children or patients from hearing. "It might also throw off our target. Or trick him into acting."

This felt risky, but, well...we're Hunters. Luckily, we were much safer while the sun was up. And it was good that the kids were lively and confident enough to be out having a good time like this; keeping the fear in check was vital. I've always been decent at sports, so I decided to join the game. Even while keeping our guard up, Doli and I still had a great afternoon playing with the kids. They were way better at soccer than I had expected; still, I gave them a few pointers here and there, mainly to keep them hyped up and engaged. Doli also wasn't too bad herself, and it was a nice surprise to be able to have some fun on the job.

After playing soccer, we all needed a break, and Doli and I had to rest before darkness fell. The kids offered to show us some of the cool places in the desert behind the house, but unfortunately we had to refuse. Out there was where the walker was roaming. We needed to keep near the shelter of the house, and it was also getting late; the last thing we wanted was to be outside when it got dark. So we headed back into the house, where Doli and I both took a quick nap. After waking up, we had dinner like the previous night, and then went out to our cars, where we sprinkled the white ash over ourselves and our weapons once again. When we came back to the house, we found the grandfather of the household standing on the porch with a slim-looking rifle. He nodded to Doli and I as we came up, and she quietly asked him something in Navajo. He started to respond, but his voice broke and he quickly fell silent. He looked exhausted, and Doli put a hand gently on his shoulder, and after a moment, he lifted his head and gave a firm nod to both of us, before leading us inside. I think he had wanted to help, but Doli had reassured him that us Hunters would be fine.

That interaction stayed in my mind as I took up my spot in the living room again. It takes tremendous courage to stand against any monster, let alone one as twisted as a skinwalker. But most of our old people had to kick some major ass back in the day, and seeing even an elder still ready to fight fired me up. Obviously, I had already committed to defeating this skinwalker, and this just made me even more determined. We were as ready as we could be, so I crouched down near the couch, looked out of the front window into the dark desert, and waited.

A few hours later, I caught a strange movement; about two hundred feet away, a patch of shadows seemed to almost be sliding or spreading towards the house. I raised my rifle and looked through the scope to see a figure creeping out of the night. Even with the night vision, this being was somehow half-faded into the shadows, which it seemed to drag behind it, a bit like a grossly extended cape. Its shape was essentially human, and although it moved for a short distance in a weird crouching walk, I watched it stand up; its upper half remained hunched over, and now it began to walk in an odd, jerking gait. As it drew closer, I could see the fur of animal pelts on its shoulders and back, making it even clearer: this was our target. I lowered my gun and crept along the floor to the rear of the house, staying out of sight as best as possible. I opened the back door quietly and snuck over a short distance to where the sheep were kept. Doli was crouched against the fence there, and she was so well-hidden that I didn't even see her until she moved forwards to meet me.

We crept back into the house and as we moved towards the front door, the walker began to let out a long, trembling whistle. Something about the sound made me feel unsteady on my feet, and chills went up my spine as I carefully peeked out of the window. The walker was nearly on the porch now, illuminated more clearly by the moonlight. It was a man with long, unkempt hair, dressed in little more than a tattered pair of pants and coyote skins that hung across his shoulders and back; it was hard to tell his age, but his face was wrinkled to the point where his skin seemed cracked, and although it was faint, his eyes were illuminated from within by a pale reddish glow. The plan was to wait until he hit the line of ash, and then burst out and take him down with a few quick shots. Doli and I watched in silence as the walker slithered up the porch, before abruptly stopping about halfway to the door. He began to sway slowly in place, then gave a long growl, more gravelly than human vocal chords could produce. I realized that he'd stopped at the wall of ash. It was go time. The walker began to howl, and the noise was exactly as the family had described it: like a human imitating a coyote's cry, but with enough of the original animal's call that the two sounds clashed and merged together. I motioned to Doli, and she yanked open the door. I flung myself out and to the side, crouching down and shooting right at the walker's head. Doli fired from the doorway, and the walker staggered backwards as the gunshots cut through the night.

The monster screamed, and the sound was a horribly strange mix of a coyote's yelp and a man crying out in agony. As strange as it seems, pitch-black smoke started jetting out from his head and chest area, evidently the result of the bullet wounds. I was positive that we hadn't missed, but as I watched, the walker leapt backwards off of the porch, impossibly fast, still screaming. He crouched low, and the smoke pouring from his wounds engulfed him. Around then, a godawful stench hit my nostrils, like a combination of rotten eggs and decaying meat, almost making me gag. But Doli and I pushed through it and kept firing into the smoke, even though we couldn't see our target clearly. A hazy puff burst out of the side of the smoke cloud, much lighter in color; later, Doli and I determined that this may have been corpse powder that the walker attempted to toss or blow on us, which, fortunately, the smoke from his wounds must have disrupted.

Suddenly, the smoke seemed to tremble and twist, and the walker burst out of it, now partially transformed. Although his body structure was still humanoid, now he resembled a much leaner version of a dogman, with pointier ears and a longer snout; other than his legs, which had clear patches of human skin, the fur that covered most of his body was probably the tannish-brown color of a coyote's, although the dark made it hard to tell. I had only a few seconds to take the sight in, because the walker lunged forwards more quickly than my eyes could register, hitting Doli at a speed that made it impossible to tell if he had struck with a hand or a foot. She fell to the floor, and for only a brief moment, the walker slowed down after the strike, giving me a clear shot for just an instant. Right as he spun to face me, I squeezed the trigger. He reeled backwards, raising a claw to his neck, before taking a flying leap to the side and off the porch again. For a moment he stayed upright on his two coyote's feet, stumbling and lurching across the ground for a short distance, before collapsing in a pile of fur and smoke.

I wanted to verify the kill, but I needed to check on Doli first. She was fully conscious and alert, although she was bleeding slightly from her head. I was concerned, but she told me not to worry about her, so I quickly but cautiously made my way to where the walker had fallen, covering my mouth and nose to keep out both the horrendous stench and any potential traces of corpse dust. By the time I got there, all that was left was the dead body of the older man who had first walked up to the house. There was no blood, only lingering wisps of that strange smoke, but there was no question: he was dead, and the family could finally rest easy.

Doli earned herself a solid concussion, but otherwise she was fine. The family called in a hataałii, who did extensive cleansing rituals for all 11 of us, the house, and the grounds; this was meant to purify all of us from the spiritual contamination of the walker, and from the death that Doli and I had caused. To follow up, we had to isolate ourselves for a while, and then Doli and I decided to get going so that we wouldn't impose on the family any more. They thanked us profusely and repeatedly offered to pay us, but we refused; we were already getting paid by our organization, and this had been a necessary service. Eventually, they settled for giving us each a beautiful silver and turquoise necklace, which the Navajo are masters at crafting; turquoise is also a sacred stone, so it has deep spiritual connection and meaning in addition to beauty. I still have mine today! And although there are still walkers that roam the Dinétah, that day there was one less to worry about.

I hope this has given you some decent information about skinwalkers. You now know that they stick very closely to Navajo country, so although the chances of you running into one anywhere else are slim to none, this story might tell you something about what to do if it does happen. Walkers are truly strange beings, and they really force us to consider the more supernatural aspects of this world, which oftentimes we would rather not recognize. But there are ways to protect yourself, even if you don't have a Hunter around. And even if you don't believe any of my stories or think any of this stuff is real, just remember that there are many people who *do* know what's truly out there. So maybe you can learn from them.

For now, though, I think this has been enough on the topic. As I've said before, many people don't like to discuss it, and honestly, neither do I. So, we'll finish this letter here and talk about something else next time. I'm thinking we'll discuss either wendigo and Deer People, thunderbirds, or some of my international experiences, but please let me know if you have any specific creatures you'd like to hear about. And as always, I'm open to questions! For now, though, stay safe and healthy, everyone, and we'll talk more soon. This has been Sam White Owl, signing out.

LETTER 5 – WENDIGO + TALL DEER

CANADA, U.S.A. (MONTANA)

Written August 2020

Hey there, everyone. It's Sam White Owl again. I hope you guys are enjoying the longer letters. I know I can get wordy sometimes, but since you guys still seem to be interested, I'll keep them coming. A quick life and family update: I have a nephew who I trained as a Hunter. I also hijacked his email to send these letters! He's been working some cases overseas, and he's coming back home soon. I'm sure I'll catch up with him sometime in the coming weeks, so if he has any interesting stories, maybe I can tell you some of those. In the meantime, let's get into the monster for this letter. Actually, *two* monsters. I've gotten a lot of comments asking for information on these creatures, and they very often get mixed up in the modern day, so I'd like to help clear some of that up. So for this letter, we'll be taking about wendigo and Deer People. Because I'll be going into detail on both of them, this is going to be a long letter, so fasten your seatbelts and maybe get a snack or a drink.

Similarly to skinwalkers, wendigo and Deer People are two creatures that might simply sound too strange to be real. But our world is weirder than you might think.

Let's start with wendigo. Although some people say

"wendigos", I and most of the Hunters prefer the plural without the "s" at the end. The original plural is actually "windigoag" or "windikouk". The name "wendigo" can also be spelled a ton of different ways, including "windigo" and "wijigo". But I'm not a linguist, so I'll stop there. Now, what exactly is a wendigo? Wendigo come from the myths and stories of various Algonquian-speaking cultures, who are Native people from eastern and central Canada, and parts of the northern United States. As you may know, these areas are prone to long, harsh winters. Before modern electricity or heating, winter was even rougher and more dangerous. In addition to heavy snowfall and intense blizzards, resources were the main problem: farming and gathering were mostly out of the question, and hunting and fishing were dicey. People had to store food to get through the cold months. Sometimes, though, this food ran out, or there was a famine, and people had nothing to eat. Some starved. Others wound up resorting to one of the most atrocious actions imaginable: cannibalism. They ate the flesh of their fellow human beings, and this transformed them into monsters. This is how human beings first became wendigo.

Wendigo are usually about 8 or 9 feet in height, although on rare occasions they can be as tall as 12, and overall, they resemble enormous, walking corpses. They're extremely thin, with an emaciated, skeletal appearance; you can see their bones sticking out from beneath their skin. The skin itself is an ashy gray color, and their eye sockets are sunken into dark pits, with the eyes themselves glowing white or yellow. They don't really have noses or lips, so their teeth are constantly visible, stretching almost from ear to ear, much as you would see on a bare human skull; wendigo teeth also tend to be unnaturally sharp, but their general structure and layout mirrors the teeth of the humans they once were. Most wendigo also have long, dark hair which often falls over their backs and shoulders like a mane, although some are bald, and all are otherwise hairless. In this regard, wendigo look a bit like enormous crawlers, even though you can certainly tell the difference; wendigo also happen to be slightly faster and, despite their lean figures, *much* stronger. As I mentioned in a previous Q&A, wendigo don't have antlers or deer skulls; that whole idea was made up in modern times. In the second portion of this letter, however, we'll be talking about Tall Deer, which often get mixed up with wendigo nowadays, because Tall Deer actually *can* have antlers and deer skulls sometimes.

As you might imagine from the origins of wendigo, these monsters are very rare, contrary to many people's supposed encounters and stories; even in the old times, cannibalism wasn't common, and it happens even less nowadays. However, humans can also become wendigo by being exposed to them or in their presence for too long; this process seems to require several days, but eventually, if a human stays in close proximity to a wendigo for that extended period, they can become one themselves. Wendigo don't breed or reproduce in the usual way, thankfully, so cannibalism and staying near a wendigo for too long are the only known ways for a new one to arise. That's why they're so rare. The concept of the wendigo is often directly linked to human greed and avarice, and although the connection is metaphorical, it's very appropriate. Importantly, cannibalism alone also doesn't transform people into wendigo, not by itself. There are other additional circumstances that are necessary, but these are still pretty uncertain. Hunter research has identified some possible factors, but they're too extensive to go into much detail for this letter. Maybe it has something to do with the cold, or the geographical area. Maybe it's magic? Who knows.

What I *do* know is that the worst thing about wendigo is the way they interact with the world. They are constantly starving; no matter how much they consume, they will always be hungry. They simultaneously represent greed and starvation, gluttony and famine. Wendigo don't have the same thought processes as the humans they once were, either. The unstoppable need to devour flesh and meat is essentially the only thing they know. Because they're never satisfied and almost never rest, wendigo can devastate ecosystems, eating through everything in an area before moving on and repeating the process. As I mentioned, in more recent times this has represented how Indigenous people have pushed back against colonialism and capitalist ideals of greed and always wanting more; this principle is just as destructive with humans as with wendigo, if not more so. Wendigo will actively target and consume just about anything that moves, but they seem to have a taste for human flesh. Usually we'll become food just like anything else, but in some disturbing cases, wendigo don't eat their human victims, but instead, capture them alive and haul them back to a lair or a den; there they either force-feed the prisoner human flesh or simply stay near to them for days, and this results in the creation of a new wendigo.

Because of the danger they present to humans, other creatures, and ecosystems as a whole, wendigo are one of the relatively few monsters that the Hunters have a kill-on-sight policy for. There is no capturing or observing these creatures. They simply need to be put down. And although I often feel bad about that, I've also realized that the life of a wendigo must be hell. Everyone has experienced just how frustrated and hungry even skipping one or two meals can make you, and you may have had to go without food for even longer. For wendigo, it's *starvation*. Worse, starving every single second of every day for years and years, with no way to relieve it. No matter how much you eat, you will never, ever be able to stop your pain and your suffering. The utter agony of living like that is just unimaginable. In a tragic way, killing a wendigo is a mercy, for both themselves and others.

Granting this mercy, however, is very difficult. As I mentioned, wendigo may be skinny, but they are freakishly strong. They usually travel in a shambling walk, a lot like the stereotypical movie zombie, but when they sense prey, they can move with unnatural speed and agility. Despite their large size, wendigo are also surprisingly stealthy, making them skilled ambush predators.

Wendigo are tough, but they can be killed. Normal bullets will hurt them, but any kind of weapon that can slash them is usually a better choice. But the best option of all is fire. Because wendigo are monsters of the cold and ice, flames are highly damaging to them, whether that's incendiary rounds, Molotov cocktails, or even simple torches or burning sticks. Wendigo bodies have a limited ability to rapidly heal wounds, so it's important to take them down quickly. Their weakest point is the chest, because destroying their ice-cold hearts will kill them instantly. After bringing one down, it's also best to burn the body, preferably after cutting it into pieces; that will ensure that they're truly eliminated and won't regenerate. Again, it all sounds unbelievable, but there is a reason why the old stories came about. In the case of the wendigo, they often tell the truth.

My first experience with a wendigo was in 2001. That year, eastern Canada had an unusually long and intense winter, with lots of snow and ice buildup; some of you might remember this! While many people used the opportunity to go skiing or snowboarding, others decided to explore the wilderness. I'm sure I don't have to tell you that this wasn't a great idea. And, unfortunately, for some people it ultimately proved fatal. You need to be careful and aware when going out into the woods at any time, but especially in the winter. These people didn't take the proper precautions, and tragically, they paid for it with their lives.

At this time, my Guide (capital-G, remember?) Sergio called me offering me a job. Capital-H Hunters in Quebec had turned up remains of several missing people in the wilderness. All that was left were skeletons and scattered bones. Some of the skeletons were only a few hours old when they'd been discovered, though, indicating that something had eaten them on the spot. Based on teeth marks on some of the bones, it looked like at least one wendigo was involved. The Quebec branch of our organization had put out a request for assistance to any available Hunters in the region. At the time, I was nearby and had just wrapped up a Sasquatch relocation, so I answered the call.

A few days later, I was in eastern Quebec with two other Hunters. One was a Canadian named Katie, and the other was a fellow American named Zack. Katie was a brown-haired and tall lady in her mid-30s; she had first discovered some of the wendigo kills. Zack was around my age, maybe a little younger; he was a bulky black-haired guy who favored a shotgun. We started our investigation by going to the spot where the most recent victim had been found. We were lucky, because it hadn't snowed since their discovery; much of the snow and dirt was actually still red, pink, or brownish from where blood had soaked into it. Of course, all that remained of the victim were bones and clothing, but those could still give us some information. Both the skeleton and the clothes were in pieces, strewn out across a small clearing. The wendigo had evidently ripped off the victim's clothes before beginning to eat. The body had been thoroughly scavenged by animals, but I doubted that much meat had remained on it even before that; from what I knew, wendigo were very thorough eaters.

"The teeth marks look almost human," I remember Zack saying as he examined a long piece of bone, part of either an arm or leg.

"That's because wendigo were human. Once," Katie said. I peered at the same bone that Zack was looking at; it was a tibia, which is one of your lower leg bones, in your calf. Zack was right. It looked like a human with sharper teeth than normal had bitten down into the bone, leaving a clear semicircle of tooth marks.

One of the victim's arms had been pulled off and flung to the side, and their jacket and shirt had been torn open, but there was no evidence of the exact blow that had killed them. The pain must have been terrible, and I felt awful for this person; we couldn't even tell their gender, although based on the clothing, they were probably male. After we had brought down the wendigo, we would call in the police and have them deal with the rest. It's not our job to clean up or notify the relatives of the deceased. Katie assured me that the Quebecois police would let us do what we had to, without asking questions. It's the same for most other law enforcement groups; I'm not sure, but I think the higher-ups of the Hunters have some kind of agreement with them, even though we don't usually work together. In any case, it makes our work as Hunters much easier.

Muddled footprints were scattered across the clearing as well; upon examination, it was clear that the victim had been running when they'd been grabbed. Wendigo footprints simply look like abnormally large human ones (barefoot, of course). Some of these led into the clearing alongside the victim's boot prints. The tracks in the clearing itself were a mess, suggesting the victim had struggled for a bit before dying. And then more wendigo tracks, along with a thin, short blood trail, exited the clearing, heading east. I pointed those footprints out, and we began to follow them. The trail was probably around two days old, but it was the best lead we had.

I always wear a scarf, goggles, and/or facemask when I'm operating in cold weather, and this time was no different.

Depending on the climate, I also favor lightweight, insulated outer jackets that are designed for mobility as well as warmth. I was glad for all of it, because it was freezing cold. Since I had more tracking experience than Zack and Katie, I wound up taking point for this part. Even without snow cover, wendigo are apparently easy to track; they're huge, but more importantly, when they're not actively hunting, they hardly care about stealth. The terrain was mostly spruce trees with bare, skeletal maples or alders here and there, and dead moss and leafless shrubs around our feet. Apart from our boots crunching through the snow, the woods were nearly silent. As we walked, I remember seeing a few trails made by our four-legged brethren, so there was still animal life around, but we ignored these and kept our eyes on the prints we came there for. Eventually it started getting dark, and so we made camp in a little hollow, aiming to pick up the trail in the morning.

The night was silent except for the wind; the forest is often like this in the winter, but this time it was eerie. I knew full well that the wendigo was out there somewhere and that it could just be biding its time, waiting for the chance to strike. The descriptions I'd heard of the wendigo's appearance also started flooding back into my mind; I did *not* want to see something like that. I was able to fall asleep that night, but I remember having a horrible nightmare. You certainly know exactly the sort of dream I'm talking about: something was chasing me through the trees, and I was running in slow motion, unable to move fast enough to escape. It was definitely the wendigo that was chasing me, but I just couldn't match its speed. I turned around and saw its dead face rushing forwards, leaping on top of me, and then I snapped awake, sweating in my sleeping bag. It took a minute, but I was eventually able to calm down, telling myself that we were going to end this creature.

The next day we headed out before dawn; wendigo move slowly when they aren't on the chase, but because they hardly ever stop to rest, we would likely have to cover a lot of ground. The trail was still very clear, and we followed it until it was nearly evening. I was starting to think that we should make camp soon when we heard a sudden crashing of branches from somewhere ahead of us. Then a cry echoed through the trees. I instantly recognized the sound as a deer crying out in pain, a blood-curdling sound that you should never have to hear. Katie, Zack, and I all readied our weapons, and after pausing to check in with each other, we began cautiously advancing towards the sound. Any sort of predator could have been responsible, but with luck, it was the wendigo.

A few minutes later we came upon a dead white-tailed doe, sprawled out in a pool of still-trickling blood. She was missing chunks of flesh from her side and flanks, and some of her internal organs were spilling out of her stomach. Distressing as this was, even worse was that there was no sign of the wendigo.

"Eyes up! It's still out here somewhere," Katie hissed to Zack and I; she had seen more combat situations than either of us, so she tended to speak and act first.

We took a moment to listen and observe, but the woods were quiet. The light was dying fast, so we decided to back out. Leaving behind the deer, we retreated a short distance away and set up a light, barebones camp, making sure to keep a good view of the trees near the deer, to our northwest; if the wendigo decided to come back and finish its meal, it might give us a good opening. We kept the fire high that night, and none of us spoke much; we were all on edge, routinely scanning the trees and the shadows with our headlamps and scopes.

It wasn't long before Katie said that she caught a sound to the northwest. Even though I had been waiting specifically to see if the wendigo would come back for the doe, I hadn't heard anything. But Katie swore that she had, so we all strained our ears to listen. Soon enough, over the crackling of the fire, I heard the snow crunching from out in the trees: the footsteps of something moving on two legs, far too heavy to be anything but what we were there for. Genuine chills went running down my spine despite the warmth of my clothing and the campfire, so I picked up my rifle and double-checked it. I had loaded it with incendiary rounds made by the Smiths, the branch of the Hunters that deals with everything related to weapons and combat gear; they're very good at creating custom types of ammunition, and these incendiary cartridges are sometimes called "flamers".

Eventually, all sound died out except for the crackling of the campfire. I saw something in the darkness move, and although it was probably just a branch, it still made me flinch. Some instinct tempted me to push up to where we had heard the wendigo walking, but Katie reminded me that it was too smart for that; it would already have moved, and we didn't want to engage it on its terms, especially not out in the dark. Instead, we waited. Minutes went by, and although I didn't let down my guard, the anxiety began to let up a bit. That is, until something heavy thudded onto the ground behind me, and something sprayed across my ankles. I instinctively jumped to the side, away from the impact, and all of us spun to face the source of the noise. The dead, half-eaten deer was laying across our campfire in a splash of blood, organs, and smoldering wood; just as I realized that it had been *thrown*, the wendigo launched its attack.

It sprinted out of the darkness while we were distracted by the deer, grabbing Zack in its long fingers. Zack cried out and fired his shotgun; it was a 12-gauge loaded with dragon's breath ammunition, so each shot sent out a roaring spray of flames. As impressive as the display was, Zack couldn't turn to get a good shot on the wendigo, and the fire from his gun mostly wound up blasting through empty air. Katie and I started shooting as well, but it was too late. The wendigo opened its jaw wide, unnaturally wide, almost like a snake, and bit through Zack's neck, nearly decapitating him. I'd never seen somebody die like that, and for a moment, I froze up from pure shock. I simply watched the wendigo drop Zack's limp body and tilt its head to look at me and Katie. I'll never forget that moment; I don't even think I can. Long black hair fell around two glowing white eyes, sunken into the dark pits of their sockets; the lower half of the monster's face was red with Zack's blood, with its lipless mouth baring rows of pointed teeth in a permanent grin. I only needed an instant to take all of this in, but in all my years of Hunting, there aren't many sights that have hit me that hard.

Maybe paradoxically, the moment shook me so badly that I unfroze, aiming for the wendigo's chest and rejoining Katie's shooting. With the supernatural speed I had heard about, the wendigo charged, and although our bullets pounded into it center mass, they weren't enough. It drew an arm back and swiped at Katie, who careened backwards into the snow as its claws made contact. With the wendigo on top of us now, I dropped my rifle and pulled out my pistol, which was loaded with tracer rounds. As the creature turned its head towards me, I somehow managed to land a shot right into the side of its face. It gave a godawful scream, high-pitched and even worse than the deer's, as the tracer round did the trick; the wendigo's head burst completely into flames, with fire glowing through its eye sockets and its mouth as it shrieked. It started to stagger back towards the trees, but I kept up the pressure, this time aiming for its chest again. Now the incendiary rounds we'd hit it with earlier also ignited, and flames erupted in its chest cavity and out from its ribs and neck. Still upright, the wendigo flailed madly, until before long, it collapsed to its knees, weakly reaching out as if to push itself back to its feet. Despite what it had just done to Zack, I felt an unsettling sort of empathy as I watched it struggle, doing the same thing a human would. It was clearly in incredible pain, which must have ended a few moments later as it dropped onto its stomach and fell still.

I just stood there for a moment, staring at the massive burning body of the cryptid that had once been human. Then the memory hit me of Katie being hit. I rushed over to where she had fallen and found her unconscious. Beneath her bloodstained jacket, her stomach and chest had been torn by the wendigo's claws; the wounds didn't seem too deep, but she needed help as soon as possible. With a medicine kit from the tent, I managed to bind her injuries and stop the bleeding. From there, though, I wasn't sure how to handle things. Moving Katie could make her injuries worse, but we couldn't just sit here forever. And yet, I wouldn't be able to get her anywhere in the dark; that would be dangerous for both of us. So I decided that if she didn't regain consciousness by the morning, I'd have to do my best to carry her back out of the woods. Not to mention that, in the meantime, I had a job to finish.

After putting Katie down in the tent, I waited until the wendigo had stopped burning, which wasn't long; fire is so damaging to these cryptids that it chews through them very quickly. Then I started to hack the corpse into pieces with my metal combat tomahawk, which doubles as a handy field tool. Wendigo don't bleed, but it was still disgusting work; I think this is the closest I've ever come to cutting up something resembling a human, and I'm not ashamed to confess that I vomited during the process. Thankfully, I was able to finish, and after slicing apart the monster's remains, I set fire to each of the pieces again to ensure that they were totally burned away. While I was doing this, I was doing my best to keep myself together. Zack was still right there, and, just like the classic car crash analogy, something was telling me to look at him, despite how awful and unnecessary it was. I only gave in once, and I almost wound up throwing up again when I did. My mind kept replaying the moment that the wendigo had bitten into his neck. It had been so sudden and unexpected, and I had been right there, but unable to stop it. I had seen people die before, and I had seen people already dead, but this had been so *quick*. But Zack knew the risks of being a Hunter as much as any of us. I had barely gotten to know him, so I can't say much about him, but he was a good guy, and I will certainly never forget him.

To my relief, Katie woke up later on that night. She said she would be okay on her own while I went back to town to get help. So I left her there and made my way out of the forest as fast as I could, not stopping until I got access to a phone; nowadays we have much better and more widely available methods of communication to contact each other without having to do stuff like this, but back then, this sort of hustle out of the wilderness was pretty normal. When I got to a phone, I called in a cleanup crew to pick up Katie and dispose of whatever was left of the wendigo. To everyone's relief, Katie made a full recovery, and from what she told me later, the wendigo had burned entirely to ash by the time she was picked up. Neither of us know exactly what happened to Zack, but it's standard procedure for dead Hunters to be retrieved, cleaned up (which can sometimes include being reassembled, as awful as that is), and then sent to any family they might have; as sad as it may seem, every member of our organization who works in the field is required to fill out forms designating who and where we want to be sent to if we fall. Again, this is a dangerous job, but we all know that. So I assume Zack was sent back to any family he might have had. I hope that he got back to them.

You guys always want to hear about my most intense hunts, and this one was definitely up there. But it was ultimately successful. If there's any takeaway for non-Hunters, it should be just to use common sense when you're thinking about heading into the woods. And definitely don't go out there in bad weather. You might not like what you find.

Now, let's wrap up by talking about Deer People. These beings are often confused with wendigo (probably because, for whatever reason, people in recent years have begun to think of wendigo as having deer skulls, which, as you now know, isn't the case). Deer People can live anywhere that deer do, but they're mostly found in southern Canada and the upper half and central portions of the USA. They're shapeshifters, and although I've personally never seen them transform, they can become both humans and deer (you never would have guessed, right?).

In human shape, Deer People very closely resemble unmixed Native folks from the regions in which they live; that usually means dark eyes, black or brown hair, and skin that's colored light tan to medium brown. The only difference is that their feet always remain deer hooves. Women are more commonly sighted than men, and these are the same as the Deer Woman or Deer Lady who is found in many Indigenous stories. In human shape, she's impossibly beautiful, representing fertility and bounty, and helps women conceive. At the same time, Deer Women are famous for luring men into the woods and seducing them; if the man falls for the trap, then the Deer Woman will trample them to death. I've never seen a Deer Lady, but Indigenous accounts and Hunter reports have spoken of them for centuries, and the occasional flattened corpses of young men in the woods definitely back this up.

To be clear, Deer Lady isn't evil. She specifically saves her wrath for men who engage in destructive behaviors like infidelity and abuse, and by literally stamping those out, she protects both victims and their communities in general. Her stories aren't about simple violence, but about meaning and lessons, about how to take care of each other. I should also mention that in more recent years, Deer Woman has become an even clearer representation of female independence, especially when it comes to the efforts to locate and achieve justice for missing and murdered Indigenous women. All women across the world have to overcome so much already, and our Indigenous women fight through the efforts to take their culture and ways of life on top of that. In that way, the story of Deer Woman stands up for independence and resistance to colonialism and control.

Interpretation aside, all the Deer People that I've encountered have taken the form of...well, a deer. Usually they appear as white-tailed, black-tailed, or mule deer, always whichever is local to the area. However, similarly to skinwalkers, something about these animals may be "off". They may move strangely; they're possibly best-known for standing upright and walking on their hind legs for significant distances. When startled or angered, they may also scream in a very human-like way. In their animal form, Deer People can be unnerving, but they're not aggressive or malevolent.

Normally, Deer People seem to just die like normal animals or cryptids, passing away of old age or other causes. But there are rare cases where, for some (so far) unknown reason, they'll live on for much longer than normal for their species, and this subversion of the natural way of things can have horrific results. As they age beyond the typical lifespan of their kind, Deer People can become bitter and dark,. Their flesh will start to decay, and their bodies will warp and twist, growing much larger as their deer and human forms merge into a single, distorted shape. Their front feet will become clawed hands, and they will begin to stand exclusively on their hind legs. The skin on their faces usually falls away entirely, leaving behind only an enormous deer skull as a head. When Deer People transform like this, Hunters simply call them "Tall Deer", since they grow to stand anywhere from 8 to 15 feet in height. Even though these creatures are evidently half-dead, they crave flesh, and will settle for any kind of it, including human. This is probably another big reason why people often mix up Tall Deer and wendigo, but again, they aren't the same. Wendigo were once fully human, whereas Deer People are their own species. If a Deer Person becomes a Tall Deer, though, they gain the same carnivorous, ravenous hunger as a wendigo.

Thankfully, Deer People don't always reach this point; in fact, it's very rare for them to become Tall Deer. But it isn't known exactly why this change occurs. Like wendigo, Tall Deer can ravage ecosystems and pose a real threat to human and animal populations, and their unstoppable appetite earns them the same kill-on-sight status from the Hunters. Tall Deer don't have the speed or regeneration abilities of a wendigo, but they do share the same supernatural strength and resilience. All of this makes them hard to fight and hard to kill, but I have done it before.

Here's the last story for this letter. This took place in 2003, so only a bit after my winter with the wendigo in Quebec. Since then, I'd become more accustomed to working alone, so when Sergio contacted me about an attack in Montana and told me that there were no other available Hunters in the area, I was okay with that. Between tasks, Hunters frequently have a lot of free time, but we can't be available 24/7. I also had my experience going for me; since the western half of the US is so broad and sparsely populated compared to the rest of the country, those of us who operate here are used to traveling all across it, and I'm generally familiar with most of its major regions.

The victim of this Montana attack was a young woman; I won't give you her name, so let's call her Rachel. She was still alive, but her injuries were severe: she had lost an eye and been gored in the back, and her left leg had been amputated at the hospital. Official reports said that it was a brown bear attack, but according to her medical notes, she had repeatedly insisted that she was injured by something with antlers. I have no idea how Sergio got those medical notes, but Guides always seem to have access to just about every kind of form and authorization and person available. The conclusion was obvious: Tall Deer.

The first step was to talk to Rachel. Driving up to Montana, I tracked her down to a local hospital where she'd been going for physical therapy. When her session was over, I asked if we could talk; she was understandably confused, but I told her about my organization and explained that I was here to deal with the being that had attacked her. At first, she was suspicious, as people almost always are, but as I assured her of my intent and that I understood what she must be feeling, she opened up. Despite coming close to tears and intermittently pausing to control her breathing, Rachel told me her story, with all the detail I could have asked for.

She had been hiking with a group when she stepped off of the trail to use the bathroom, and just after finishing up, she heard a noise from the trees nearby. Rachel described it as a low creaking or groaning sound, like nothing she'd ever heard before, and when she called out there was no response. When she turned around to head back to her group, there was a crashing in the branches behind her, and something stabbed her in the back, just below the shoulder blade. The force of the impact flung Rachel forwards onto her stomach, and when she rolled over in panic, she'd found herself face to face with an enormous, two-legged creature that had a long, bone-white face topped with two huge stag's antlers. Rachel screamed, and the creature almost casually swatted her across the face with a huge hand, smashing the left side of her skull and blinding her in that eye. It then lifted her left heel with one hand and pressed down on her shin with the other, snapping her leg backwards. Between the sight, the pain, and the head trauma, Rachel had fallen unconscious. She had woken up in the hospital without her leg, surrounded by family and the friends she'd been hiking with, who had rushed over to find her unconscious after hearing her scream. She was lucky they had been with her; otherwise, I wouldn't have been talking to her at that moment.

Apparently, Rachel was the only one who had seen the Tall Deer; it must have retreated when it heard her friends approaching. She told me where the incident had taken place, but because her group had been fairly far down the trail, it was hard for me to get an exact location. I asked if she would be willing to go back to the spot with me, but she refused, which I completely understood; even telling her story had taken an immense amount of courage. But without prompting, Rachel suggested that one of the others in the group might help. After she listed some of their contact information, I thanked her and wished her a smooth and safe recovery.

Just like a crime or a news story, people who have seen or experienced cryptid encounters, especially attacks, have very different ways of handling follow-up interactions. Many of them ask a ton of questions, like what the creature had been or who the Hunters were, and I usually try to give some short answers without stirring the pot any further. But other people don't want to know anything more, sometimes because it's too traumatizing or because it's too much information to process all at once. And then there's a lot of people who ask the same question as Rachel.

"What are you going to do?"

I usually give the same answer I gave her: "I'm going to make sure that this doesn't happen to anyone else."

There are many ways of accomplishing that, and many of them are completely nonviolent. In the case of a Tall Deer, however, there's only one option.

The first friend on Rachel's list was another young woman who I also won't name; let's call her Lucy. She wasn't very hard to track down, and we met at her house; after hearing my identity and my intentions, she agreed to take me to the site of the attack the next day.

We drove out in the morning, eating a haphazard breakfast of bagels and fruit in the car, and arrived at the site of the attack before noon. Of course, the exact spot where the group had found Rachel unconscious was off-trail, and Lucy refused to go there, or even leave the trail at all. I was actually grateful for this, since now I could work without being watched. I passed Lucy the thermos of coffee we had brought along, told her to stay where she was, and went to examine the site.

Almost immediately, I picked up Tall Deer sign; it wasn't hard to find. High branches and tree limbs in one area had been snapped and pushed aside by the creature as it had charged at Rachel, and a lot of leaf litter and small ground plants had been flattened beneath its immense weight. I found only one reasonably clear track in the mud: an enormous deer's hoofprint, deep and well over a foot long. Just the sight of it was enough to make my breath catch in my throat as I realized how massive this monster had to be: 10 feet tall, at the very least.

I took Lucy back to the trail entrance and said goodbye, then got back to the attack site in the evening. It was too late to start tracking, but I camped overnight at the nearest suitable spot, and just as the sun started to rise, I got started on following the cryptid's trail. This was unexpectedly difficult, because despite its size, the monster left surprisingly little sign; now that it wasn't in open attack mode, it hadn't pushed over trees or torn up the ground like I had been hoping.

It was late afternoon when I found the body, or what was left of it. I came upon a tiny stream, and I might not have noticed the dead animal on the bank if there hadn't been a Tall Deer print right next to it. I crouched down to examine the remains; it looked like a bobcat, but it was hard to tell, since all that remained of it were a few splatters of dried blood, some small chunks of bone, and little pieces of tissue and hair. I couldn't be positive, but judging by the tracks, it looked like the poor guy had been seized while drinking at the brook. Bobcats are wary and speedy, and it was tough to imagine that the Tall Deer had been able to grab it before it ran away. I took a look around, but there were no obvious places where the monster could have approached the water unseen.

Something wasn't adding up here, but I had to keep moving. Maybe the bobcat had been hard of hearing and hadn't noticed the Tall Deer in time, or maybe it had been old or injured and unable to escape. Whatever the case, the Montana woods had just suffered another casualty.

I got up and continued to follow the Tall Deer's trail. After another hour or so, I lost the trail on some rocky ground. I had to take an educated guess at where the Tall Deer might have gone, and eventually wound up going west. After a little while, I stepped out of the trees and...onto a hiking trail. This made me pause. Had the monster really come this way? Then my heart skipped a beat as I realized what was going on. Hiking trails led to campsites. And for a Tall Deer, campsites were a buffet. The monster was probably following alongside the trail, waiting for unwary hikers. And if it didn't get anybody on the trail, then it might even attack a campsite. I mentally kicked myself for not picking up a map of the trails at the entrance to the area. Now I had to make another guess. Which way would the Tall Deer have gone? I took a moment to look for more prints, but on the trail itself, there were only tracks of hikers and campers, and alongside the trail, there were only a few marks that didn't indicate much of anything. With no real clues to go on, I just started walking, heading down the trail in a mostly random direction; I kept heading west, continuing the way I'd been going earlier and hoping that the Tall Deer had gone that way as well.

My instincts turned out to be good. After less than an hour of walking, the trail led me straight to a campsite. It was little more than a big clearing in the woods, with a few garbage cans and a pair of tents already set up there. Two women and a man, all middle-aged, sat around a burnt-out campfire, talking and laughing. When I came up to them, they all seemed a bit shocked; after all, most people don't go casually hiking with rifles and a combat tomahawk. I greeted them as nonchalantly as I could, even though I was also trying to keep an eye on the trees. From Rachel's encounter, it seemed that the Tall Deer didn't seem to like groups of people, but you could never be too safe. I asked the trio if they'd seen anything unusual, but they hadn't. One of them asked what I was doing and if I was a park ranger or going hunting. I was tempted to lie so I wouldn't give myself away, but I just said something along the lines of "I'm doing an investigation". Then I showed them my badge and asked for their cooperation. They instantly agreed, although they were visibly unsettled. Sometime around then, I got an idea. I reassured them as much I could and said that it would be best if they just kept going about their business, but didn't leave the campsite. They said that they hadn't been planning on leaving until the next day anyway, and so I thanked them and went back off towards the trail.

I had a plan. Hopefully no other hikers would show up, and hopefully the Tall Deer used its vision and its hearing more than its sense of smell. I looped around the campsite, putting the tents between myself and the three people as much as possible. There was a small slope overlooking the area, and I decided to take up a position there; from this vantage point, I could see the campsite, the trail, and the surrounding treeline, and hopefully the campers hadn't noticed me. It was getting dark, so I pulled out a power bar and ate while I did some journaling and waited.

Thankfully, no other campers showed up the rest of that day, and for that I was grateful. My plan probably wouldn't work if there were too many people at the campsite. To say it straight-out, I was using these three campers as bait, essentially. I wasn't going to let them get hurt, not by any means. But I *was* hoping that the Tall Deer would come to this campsite so that I could deal with it here. I had a feeling that it would see these three people as a potential meal, and when it showed itself, I would strike. Again, before you get mad at me for having these campers nearby, believe me when I say that I truly did think this through. I would never actively put people in harm's way; these three campers were going to be a target with or without me. These letters all tell you about my thought process and mental calculations I go through as a Hunter.

First, when I got to the campsite, it was already nearly evening; there was no way these people would be able to get to safety or even another campsite before dark. You can obviously imagine why being out hiking after sundown would be a bad idea in any situation, much less one with a Tall Deer roaming the woods. Next, I didn't want to go off and camp by myself either! I probably tasted just as good as the campers, and being alone would actually make me a more tempting target. Or worse, what if I left the campsite and the Tall Deer wound up attacking it while I was away and wasn't there to protect the campers? Lastly, I remembered a piece of invaluable information from Rachel's story: the Tall Deer had run off when her friends had come to help after hearing her scream. This indicated that the cryptid could be deterred by large groups or people who it couldn't catch off-guard; perhaps this was some sort of holdover instinct from its deer identity. And if this held true, then even if I couldn't kill the monster, I could likely hurt it or scare it enough to drive it away, keeping the campers safe.

It got dark eventually, and the group lit their fire again. They had a game of cards and cooked dinner, then ate and spent some more time talking. Soon, the man and one of the women went into one of the tents, leaving the other woman by herself by the fire. If the Tall Deer was going to strike, it would be soon. I drew my rifle, my eyes trained on the treeline around the campsite and my ears perked for any hint of noise.

After I had waited for a little while, the woman who remained by the fire stood up, picked up a pail of water that she had nearby, and began to put out the flames. The campfire hissed loudly as it was extinguished, and dark gray smoke rose into the air as it died. It was nearly a full moon, so the light without the fire was still decent. It was then that I heard a low groaning sound, like a tree creaking in the wind, but with more bass to it and a slight, unnatural echo. I couldn't pinpoint the exact location of the sound, but it had definitely come from the opposite side of the campsite. The woman must have heard it too, because she froze and looked around, clearly spooked. The noise came again, and this time I was sure that it was coming from somewhere between my 9 and 12 o'clock. I raised my rifle and looked through the scope, peering through the moonlit darkness to where the groaning had come from.

I couldn't see anything there except for the trees, swaying slightly. And yet there was no wind. Then it became clear why the bobcat had been caught off-guard, and how the Tall Deer was able to move without being noticed. Those weren't trees. I was looking at two enormous, trunk-like legs, slowly advancing through the forest. I lifted my scope to see the full figure of the Tall Deer, 12 feet tall and lumbering straight towards the campsite. As I took aim at the skull that was its head, two pinpricks of crimson light flared to life in its hollow eye sockets. With no other warning, it charged.

I squeezed the trigger, readjusted my aim, and squeezed again. The Tall Deer lurched, then gave a roar that shook the whole forest: half screaming deer, half screaming man, and all fury. In the campsite, the woman was frozen in place, but my shots had cut the cryptid's charge short about 50 feet from her. The Tall Deer whipped its upper half around, searching for the source of the gunshots, and I took the opportunity to fire again, still keeping my crosshairs on its skull. The round must have missed as the creature moved its head to look for me, until a second later, its hollow red eyes found me. With another enraged bellow, it rushed me, taking massive strides across the campsite, apparently intending to eliminate the threat rather than flee from it. I began backing up to keep distance between us, firing as I did, and although the Tall Deer flinched as my shots struck into its chest and neck, it simply raised its arms to shield itself as it closed in. I was burning with the desperate urge to turn and run, but my head was still in the game; I couldn't outrun this monster, and I wasn't going to abandon these people.

The Tall Deer pushed out of the campsite and into the treeline again, smashing through branches and trampling over smaller foliage completely as it stomped up the slope towards me. At some point, my rifle clicked empty, and rather than reloading, I discarded the gun and drew my combat tomahawk. Things always seem so much larger up close, and as the Tall Deer reached me, its sheer enormity again nearly drove me into fleeing. Instead, I put the energy of that impulse into repositioning myself, diving to the side as the monster raised one enormous hand over its head. There was an audible whooshing sound and a rush of air went over me as the Tall Deer swiped through the empty space only a foot or two away from me, and my dodge took me right next to one of the beast's tree-like legs. I swung out with both hands, and I felt the resistance as my tomahawk bit deep, cutting through the dark fur and into the flesh beneath. The Tall Deer gave a low groan and dropped to one knee, supporting itself on its uninjured leg.

Still keeping the two-handed grip, I slashed into the same leg once more. Neither strike drew blood; Tall Deer might not even have any remaining in their bodies. The monster had lowered its head, and I was about to step in for a slash when it reached down and snatched at me with one enormous hand. I backstepped, but its claws still raked across my shoulders and chest, tearing my jacket and shirt and leaving shallow cuts that immediately filled with blood. The other hand came swinging around a moment later, throwing me backwards as it smacked me dead center in the chest. I hit the ground hard, the wind knocked out of me, and a piercing pain went through my lower right side as something there cracked. I struggled for breath, managing to slide away as the Tall Deer balled its hands into fists and began pounding downwards at me. The pain was still sharp, but I didn't let it stop me from rolling away and getting back up to a crouching position once I had gained some distance. Louis' advice came back to me just then: I had to hit this cryptid in the head. And to do that, I had to knock it down again.

Staying low, I stepped towards the Tall Deer as it reached out to grab me, just barely ducking beneath its claws to wind up almost directly between its legs. Without stopping, I chopped into the leg I'd already injured, eliciting a deep bellow that made my ears ring. The cryptid collapsed backwards onto its wounded leg again, and as it fell, its head sunk down, giving me the best opportunity yet. I drew back my tomahawk with both hands and swung with every ounce of strength my muscles could muster. The blade cleaved down between the Tall Deer's antlers and into its skull, practically splitting it in half. The creature didn't even scream; it just groaned again, shaking the ground like an earthquake. Then it dropped backwards onto the ground completely and shuddered a few times before going limp. I fell to my knees beside it, panting, shaking, and trying to ignore the pain.

When I had recovered somewhat, I went back to the campsite and made sure that everyone was okay. The pair who had been in their tent had never left, and the woman who had initially been charged had retreated into her tent as well. All of them were shaken but still able to communicate, and they let me take one of their maps to locate the nearest ranger station, which was surprisingly close. I told them to stay where they were and that everything was okay now; they were safe. Despite the darkness, the trail to the ranger station was completely flat and clear of obstacles; it would have been an easy hike if not for the fact that every step sent waves of pain through the lower right half of my body. But I was able to push through it and arrive at the station very quickly. There, I found a phone and got in contact with a Hunter cleanup crew, and the rest is history.

I had my claw wounds treated at a nearby hospital, and although they left some pretty nasty scars, they weren't too bad. Worse were the two fractured ribs and bruises that I had gotten from being swatted; those took longer to heal, and I was out of commission for almost two months while I recovered and then took some time to relax. Whenever possible, Hunters try to kill things from afar; most cryptids don't have ways to hurt you at a distance, so if you can take them down before they get to you, you'll be okay. But close combat is where Hunters get injured and die. I was lucky to only get these wounds; encounters with Tall Deer can be much, much worse.

Anyway, that's about it for wendigo and Deer People, pecifically Tall Deer. As always, I hope you learned something from my stories and the information I gave. These were two monsters people asked about a lot, so I wanted to talk about them. And hopefully now you won't get them mixed up! Next time we'll talk about something else. If you have any suggestions or questions, feel free to leave them in the comments and hopefully I'll see them. In the meantime, use your common sense. Stay on the trail, bring a friend, and all that good stuff; you know by now if you've been listening to my letters so far. Just be safe in the woods, especially up north, and be safe in general during these crazy times. We'll talk more soon. This has been Sam White Owl, signing out.

LETTER 6 – THUNDERBIRD

U.S.A. (WASHINGTON, WYOMING)

Written August 2020

Hey, everyone, it's Sam White Owl again. I've been a little busy lately, helping my nephew who I talked about at the beginning of my last letter. He's been trying to do more jobs here in the States, and we've been training on and off for a while now. I don't think he's entirely sure where he wants to go yet, so I've been exposing him to as much as I can, so that he has options. Maybe I'll bring him along on whatever my next case is. If we wind up having any crazy, or at least interesting, experiences, those might be a story to tell in the future, but for now, let's get to the cryptid for this letter. Since a lot of people asked about them, we'll be talking about thunderbirds this time around. We've also been talking a lot about humanoid cryptids, so I figured we'd deal with something else this time around.

Thunderbirds are found in the stories of many different Native American peoples, and they may once have called most of North America home. Nowadays, however, thunderbird populations are found mainly in the Great Plains and the Pacific Northwest regions of the United States; you can find them in other places too, but most of them live towards the northern and western parts of the country. They're important beings, usually holy ones, in many Indigenous beliefs from these areas; like their eagle and hawk relatives, thunderbirds carry messages to and from the heavens, and as representations of power, righteousness, and protection, they often show up in legends to battle other creatures, especially evil ones. And as you might have guessed from the name, *thunder*birds are also said to have control over storms.

Size-wise, although male ostriches can occasionally get a little heavier, thunderbirds are easily the largest species of bird in the world, even if conventional science doesn't acknowledge their existence: fully-grown adults have a wingspan of 25 to 30 feet. I didn't fully realize just how huge that was until seeing it for myself; that's nearly the length of an average bus. When standing on the ground or perched, thunderbirds are easily 7 feet tall or more, and their eggs are the size of a small backpack. In appearance, these cryptids resemble a cross between a vulture, a condor, and an eagle, and over three times larger than any of those. Their necks are a little long, and they have heavy beaks that hook downwards at the end to more easily tear the flesh of their prey. Babies are a light ash gray in color, but as they grow up, their feathers darken until becoming jet-black. A mature thunderbird has entirely black plumage, except for a mane-like ruff of white feathers around their shoulders and the base of their neck, and a few streaks of white feathers down their breast; funnily enough, the white chest markings actually resemble lightning bolts. Thunderbird tail feathers form a wedge shape, which allows them to have better control of their movement while flying.

Besides their enormous size, the most famous feature of thunderbirds is their supposed ability to control storms. Their wingbeats are said to create lightning and powerful winds, and in the stories, they battle their enemies by hurling thunderbolts, often from their *eyes*, almost like Superman! Is this true? Well, I'm not going to say yes, but I'm also not going to say no (...although the "lightning vision" part is a little tough to wrap my head around). Thunderbirds certainly tend to show up wherever storms are, but it's not clear if they actually control the weather; still, they fly around inside of storms completely without fear, which is incredible enough on its own. I've never seen a thunderbird shoot or throw lightning, but I *have* nearly been struck by lightning while attempting to bring one down. But we'll get to that.

My first experience with a thunderbird was when I was around 11 or 12, hiking in Washington state with my father. It's funny, because my dad was never a capital-H Hunter, and yet he still had several cryptid experiences of his own. Some people say that once you have one encounter, you're bound to have more. I don't know if that's true, but my dad certainly knew what to look out for, at least. He didn't go out to purposefully find monsters, but when he came across them, he knew what they were. My mom had taught him a lot, so he knew a bit about how to protect both himself and me; usually he at least carried a revolver when hiking on far-off trails, and when going off-road, he took a hunting rifle. This particular day, we were hiking in a high-elevation area, just my dad and I, having some father-son time out in the woods. We were on a trail that took us up into a rocky area with lots of cliffs and crags, which I now know is ideal thunderbird habitat; they prefer mountainous areas that are rocky and open, so that they can see prey and build their nests.

My dad and I were walking along when we heard a loud whooshing sound from a rocky outcropping off to the right. Both of us stopped in our tracks and looked over to see an enormous black bird soar out from the rocks. I saw the white ruff on its neck and I remember my voice cracking as I gasped out something like "Thunderbird!" I only saw the creature for a few seconds, because it quickly flapped its wings and swerved around a big boulder; when I followed it to the other side, it was gone. It probably took off over the trees, and I'm not sure what it was doing, but it was amazing more than scary. It was awe-inspiring just how *big* the bird was, but more than anything, I was so grateful that it had shown itself to us. On our way back down the trail, it started to rain. Now, it rains all the time in that part of Washington, so I don't know if the thunderbird caused it, but it certainly made the whole experience live up to the legends.

That was far from the last time I'd see a thunderbird. Years later, when I was 27 and spending time in Colorado, I was contacted by Sergio about some strange happenings one state over, in Wyoming. Two cattle ranchers had been reporting that their animals were being killed; these cows were being slaughtered and eaten, in numbers that were more than most predators would cause. I remember that my mind went straight to a dogman being the culprit, and I asked why Louis wasn't handling it, since he was a bit closer to the area and far more experienced with dogmen than I was. Sergio had bad news: Louis was recovering from being in critical condition. Apparently a wolfman had nearly ripped off his arm, and he was out of commission, potentially forever. For a couple of days, I beat myself up for not keeping in touch with Louis more closely; I might not have been able to assist on the hunt, but there had to be something I could do to help his healing process. To flash forwards in case you're concerned, Louis was eventually fine, although his damaged arm prevents him from being an active field Hunter anymore, and from that point on I made sure to talk with him more frequently than before. Based on how he and I had handled the two wolfmen in Utah, it seemed like I might be able to handle this job with the ranchers in Wyoming. I agreed to the task, and soon enough I was headed up to check on some cattle.

When I got to the first of the two ranches early in the morning, the owner greeted me and immediately led me to the area where most of the cattle killings had taken place. There was a small ditch in the cows' pasture that filled with water when it rained, and the rancher told me that on two separate occasions, he'd found dead cows near this watering hole, with the last killing having occurred only a few days ago. Unfortunately, he'd already disposed of the remains, so I couldn't do an autopsy, but as we walked, I asked him for more information on the state of the bodies. They had both been eaten to the point where he couldn't tell how exactly they'd died, but his guess was that they'd succumbed to blood loss. Their eyes had been missing, and big strips of flesh had been removed from their sides and backs.

I still believed that a dogman could be responsible, so I asked about any wounds to the throat, stomach, or groin; like wolves, coyotes, and other canines, wolfmen target these vulnerable areas when taking down larger prey. No dice: the rancher said the cows' undersides had been entirely untouched. Skeletal damage would have been the next clue; when both killing and eating, dogmen will often snap or shatter their targets' bones, like I had seen with the bison in Utah. But the rancher hadn't seen any broken bones either, although he wasn't looking out for that. This was a little weird, but I believed what the man was saying, and he seemed quite sure of it. Again, it would have been extremely helpful to take a look at the bodies, but my only remaining option was to inspect the site of the cows' deaths.

When we arrived at the little water-filled ditch, nothing seemed out of the ordinary at first. The spot was just a grassy field, with a few cows grazing in the distance and rolling plains beyond; gorgeous scenery, but nothing unusual. A few yards away from the ditch, I found some dried blood on the grass, but not much, meaning it couldn't have been pooling. Then I noticed the flattened grass where one of the cows had been laying, and a heap of upturned dirt immediately nearby where the rancher had buried some of the most recent remains; interestingly, nobody had come along to scavenge them. There was some more flattened grass where the rancher had pushed the body to the hole, but besides his own tracks and a few other cow hoofprints, I found no other evidence. I spent a while puzzling over this, but I was pretty stumped.

Sergio's briefing had mentioned pigs, so I asked the rancher if he'd had any other animals go missing besides the pair of cattle. He said that one of his pigs had indeed vanished, and completely without a trace to boot. We went to check out the pigpen, but I couldn't turn up anything there either; no bloodstains, no body, no prints. The pig had just disappeared, like it had been snatched out of existence (and as you know, this concept wasn't too far off). I think this is when I started considering that a thunderbird might be responsible here, but that was far from a guarantee. I thanked the rancher and left to head to the next property, hoping to get some more clues there.

In the late afternoon, I arrived at the second ranch, where I was met by the second rancher and his teenage son, who we'll call Lee. They invited me inside for a drink, which was really nice of them, but I declined as politely as I could; it was important to get to the site of the cow killing before we lost the light. They had a horse waiting for me, and thankfully, I've been able to ride since I was pretty young. One cow had been killed at this ranch, but it had been a week since then, which didn't give great prospects for gathering evidence. But as we rode to the kill site, Lee told me a completely new story that was worth more than any pawprint or piece of fur.

When I asked them to describe how they had come across the dead cow, Lee explained that it was him who made the initial discovery. He was just doing his daily morning check of the animals when he'd found the cattle herd a few hundred yards away from their usual hangout spot and clearly in distress, mooing and milling around, eyes wide with fear. Lee started to approach in order to calm them, before spotting something in the distance. One of the cows was lying dead on the ground, and on top of it, ripping off pieces of meat with a hooked beak, was the biggest bird he had ever seen. When he rode closer, it had lifted its head and looked at him with one piercing yellow eye, before tearing off a huge chunk of the cow with its talons and flying away with the meat in its grasp. Once the shock had worn off, Lee raced home and told his parents, who, as you might imagine, thought their son had gone off the deep end. But Lee was a good kid, and he knew what he'd seen, so after showing his parents the dead cow as proof and engaging in almost an hour of back-and-forth with them, he managed to convince his dad to at least help in reporting the incident to local wildlife authorities. Of course, this was a report of a cryptid, with a teenager as the witness, so he'd basically been laughed off; the authorities told him that his eyes were playing tricks on him and that he'd just seen a very large eagle eating a cow that had died of old age or sickness. So, Lee and his dad were both surprised and grateful when I had shown up.

To make sure this was a thunderbird, I asked Lee for more details about its appearance. He described the wingspan as over 20 feet and the feather coloration as jet-black, with white markings on the chest, neck, and head. That was more than enough to confirm the monster's identity, but to make sure that I had all possible info, I still took a look at the kill site. Besides a few tufts of downy gray feathers, there wasn't much, but at least the mystery had been solved; this was clearly a thunderbird, and now it was just a matter of tracking it down.

I asked Lee what direction the bird had flown off to, and he pointed to the northwest, where, a few miles away, a line of jagged green and grey mountains rose up. The thunderbird's roost had to be somewhere up there. I thanked Lee, his dad, and the horse they'd lent me, then hopped back in my car and set off towards the mountains.

For obvious reasons, tracking birds is a lot more difficult than tracking earth-bound animals; flying creatures leave far fewer footprints or other traces on the ground, and they aren't hindered by difficult terrain either. But everything leaves sign, especially something as large as a thunderbird. It also had to sleep somewhere, although I didn't know if this one had a true nest. When I got near the base of the mountains, it was already dark, but with my truck, there was no need for a full campsite; after some journaling and a quick, cold dinner, I slept across the back seats.

I woke up early the following morning and used my binoculars to look at the mountain peaks. Thunderbirds are known to nest up high, so I figured that my chance of finding this one would get progressively better the further up the slopes I went. I noticed some bare, rocky cliffs in one particular area and set that as my first destination, but before departing, I took some time to concoct the proper dosage for my tranquilizer darts. Thunderbirds usually aren't very dangerous to humans, and this one hadn't been either, so relocating it far away from any farms or ranches seemed like a good option; of course, birds can travel great distances with ease, but there were many areas where food was plentiful without having to go after domestic animals like livestock. Based on the wingspan that

Lee had described, I mixed up a few possible doses of tranquilizer and loaded each dart appropriately. I also grabbed one of the trackers that I generally carry in my supplies. These are identical to the devices that you may have seen other organizations use: little electronic boxes that can be attached to straps or cords and then wrapped around part of an animal's body to transmit information, mainly location data, to a computer program. After tranquilizing cryptids that are going to be re-released, Hunters usually attach trackers to them in order to keep tabs on them in the future. With the darts and the tracker ready, I grabbed the rest of my usual supplies and headed out.

The trek along the mountains and the search for the thunderbird wasn't very exciting, so I'll spare you most of the details. Mostly I just hiked up through some very pretty forest, aiming for the rocky cliffside that I had seen earlier. There were a few small animals along the way, as well as some deer sign, which made me wonder why the thunderbird had resorted to attacking cattle; deer are much smaller and weaker, and there seemed to be plenty of them nearby. Maybe it was the terrain; such a huge bird wouldn't be able to navigate very well through the forest, and the deer had probably learned to hide further in amongst the trees if a thunderbird approached.

A couple days later, I reached the cliffs near dusk. I wasn't going to risk any sort of night investigation, especially not on a cliffside hundreds of feet in the air, so I camped out and set off again in the morning, looking for any possible sign of the world's biggest bird. The cliffs sloped sharply down to my left, the south, and rose more gradually to my right, the north, as I walked westwards along the slope. It was a sunny day with a few clouds, and since it was getting into autumn, there was a slight chill in the air, especially this high up. I kept my eyes mainly on the sky, hoping to potentially catch the thunderbird flying. A full-grown thunderbird needs quite a bit of food per day, probably around 15 pounds; they have to hunt, and like all birds of prey, they do so from the air. The cliffs gave excellent visibility over the landscape and the mountainside, so if anything flew by, I would probably see it...except that said visibility dropped drastically sometime in the afternoon, when the sky became dark gray and it started to rain. At first it wasn't too bad, but soon enough, it began to pour. I threw on my jacket and continued forwards; most of my supplies were waterproof, but we all know how miserable it can be to get rained on in the cold, and very soon, both I and everything I had were wet. I tried to keep my rifle as dry as possible, and mostly managed it, but it was a hassle.

Stupidly enough, I didn't make the connection between the weather and my mission until a few minutes had passed. At first, I just figured that the weather had changed like it always could. Then it hit me: it had been a clear and sunny day, and I hadn't seen a single raincloud. I looked to the sky and saw only dark gray, but I could just feel that the thunderbird was close. A rumble of thunder came from nearby, making me suddenly realize that it likely wasn't safe to stay out in the open. There was nowhere nearby to take shelter, though, and I was afraid that if I did, I'd miss the thunderbird. One of the cardinal sins of any trip or outing is not being prepared, and I was a complete idiot for not expecting a storm; how had that not occurred to me when I was going after a creature with the word *thunder* right in its name? At a loss, I simply scrambled for a large boulder nearby and crouched down; it didn't do much to keep me out of the rain, but at least it was something to lean on while I decided my next move.

Thunder boomed again, closer this time, and off to my right side. Then I had a thought: what if the thunder was traveling *with* the thunderbird? I looked in the direction the sound had come from and waited, until after a minute or two, there was a flash of lightning. In the brief instant that the bolt lit up the sky, I saw the shadow of a massive bird swirling through the clouds. The majesty of the sight was quite literally heart-stopping. I'd found the thunderbird, and although it was still far out of range, I loaded my rifle with a tranq dart.

The wind began to pick up, and a second bolt of lightning zigzagged through the clouds, illuminating the thunderbird again. Now it appeared to be veering to the north, my 3 o'clock, closer to the peaks, but not quite to my position. It looked like it might be landing soon, so I set down my pack and began moving quickly across the rocky ground, heading towards the spot on the mountainside where the great bird looked like it was flying to. As I got closer, the air almost began buzzing or tingling, charged with electricity; it definitely made my heart beat faster, but it wasn't totally unexpected, so I kept going. Never mind the fact that I was holding a rifle that would probably act like a lightning rod; metal doesn't actually attract lightning, but it does *conduct* it. But this was probably my best, and maybe only, chance at catching the thunderbird.

The rain blew hard into my face as I ran, almost blinding me, and soon the thunder was practically on top of me, making me flinch every time it boomed. At some point, I slowed down to catch my breath, and a bang of thunder exploded above me. Lightning crackled overhead, highlighting everything with a purplish glow. That was when I saw the thunderbird clearly, only a few hundred feet away and slowly circling over a big rocky outcropping that I hadn't paid attention to before. The rock formation was a large, raised ledge that jutted out over the landscape; if you've ever seen The Lion King, this ledge looked a lot like Pride Rock, where the lions live in that movie. It was off to my 2 o'clock, so I changed direction to head straight towards it. With any luck, the thunderbird would land on top of it and offer me a good, clear shot.

As I approached, the wind started to intensify even more. I looked up and saw the dark form of the thunderbird hovering in place and flapping its wings back and forth, churning up the air and increasing the speed and power of the wind. I would definitely have to adjust my shot to compensate. The thunderbird might have seen me around that time, because it gave one of the most powerful sounds I've ever heard in my life. I wish I could have recorded that screech, because it was incredible; I felt it in my body and nearly dropped to my knees. It sounded like a deeper, more powerful version of a red-tailed hawk's cry, with an almost metallic reverb that cut the air. I suddenly felt like I was facing down a tidal wave; it wasn't just that I was powerless, but that on a basic level, I was completely insignificant next to such might. It made me want to turn and run, but I was here for a reason, and I put the energy of that impulse into raising my gun and targeting the thunderbird.

My first shot went much too wide as the wind swept it far off course. As I reloaded, the thunderbird swept down towards the ledge, knocking me backwards with a tremendous gust as it landed on top of it. I stumbled back a few feet but managed to regain my footing and raise my rifle for another shot. Right after squeezing the trigger, thunder crashed overhead, and everything was instantly blinding white, like the world's biggest camera had flashed right in front of my face. I felt an electric rush go through my body and I staggered back, dropping my rifle and flinging up my hands to shield my head and face. I dropped into a crouch and stayed there, stunned, as my vision slowly began to clear. Eventually I looked up and saw a dark black patch on the rocks, probably no more than 15 or 20 feet away from me, where it looked like a lightning bolt had just struck. I don't know why I wasn't hit; maybe electricity near a thunderbird doesn't behave normally? Thankfully, not only had the direct bolt missed me, but I'd also escaped being roasted by any ground current. Ordinarily, I would have stayed there in shock for a while, but then I heard the thunderbird screech again, and I rushed forwards. A white blur still clouded my vision because of the lightning flash, but I could see well enough to grab my rifle.

The thunderbird was jetting towards me, moving almost too fast for an animal of its size. As it came, I loaded another dart, and the bird was nearly on top of me when I lifted my gun to fire again. I don't even remember aiming; I think I just pointed the rifle straight ahead, pulled the trigger, then dove to the side. One huge wing collided with me and knocked me backwards, but I'd avoided getting slashed or grabbed by the bird's talons. I fell onto my backside, fortunately missing a direct landing on my tailbone, then quickly stood up and turned to face the thunderbird, which was wheeling around for another pass at me. Through the pouring rain, I saw the bright red plume on the butt of a tranq dart sticking out of the bird's left shoulder area. I'd hit it, and now I just had to wait for the tranquilizer to do its work.

I spun around to face the rocky outcropping where the thunderbird had landed before; maybe that would offer me some shelter while the tranquilizer kicked in. I took off at a sprint for the rocks. When I was about halfway to the ledge, I took a single glance behind me and saw that the thunderbird was almost on top of me again. With no way to get to shelter in time, I threw myself to the ground, covering my head. As I dropped, pain suddenly erupted across my back as the thunderbird's talons sliced through my clothes and into my skin. Then I was yanked upwards, my feet skidding across the ground as those same talons hooked into my clothes and started to lift me up. I remember crying out and trying to somehow grab the ground with my boots. I had to be too heavy for the thunderbird to pick up...right?

As it happened, I wouldn't have a chance to find out. Just as my feet left the ground, the thunderbird abruptly relaxed its grip, dropping me. I landed in a heap, hitting my knees and one of my shoulders hard, but I scrambled back onto my feet and continued my sprint towards the rock formation for shelter. Behind me, the thunderbird gave a short, sharp shriek, which rang my ears but lacked the full power of its previous cry. I turned around again to see the thunderbird shakily veering off to the side, wings beating slowly and just barely keeping it aloft. It was gradually sinking, and after a few seconds, it stopped flapping its wings. The massive bird tilted to the side as it went down, landing on the rocky ground on its stomach and sliding to a stop. I had a hard time staying upright, and my heart hadn't stopped pounding, but that was it.

I paused for a moment to recalibrate and allow the remaining white haze over my vision to fade a little more. The wounds on my back stung from the rain and the cold, but they didn't feel deep; evidently, my jacket had protected me from the worst of the thunderbird's talons, although it was still crazy that they'd pierced all the way through to my skin. I needed to get some sort of bandage, and fortunately I remembered the general area where I had dropped my supplies earlier. I made my way there and tied a spare shirt tightly around my shoulders where my injuries were, then brought my stuff back to the thunderbird. Approaching the enormous animal so closely certainly made me tense up, but it was securely sedated, and after I stood next to it and felt its damp feathers with shaky fingers, I was able to breathe a little easier. The tagging process was simple. I took out the tracker and attached a tailor-made leather strap to the back of it, then looped the strap around the cryptid's neck and fastened its metal clamp shut. The device now sat on the back of the thunderbird's neck, secured tightly but comfortably.

Before going, I put a hand onto the black feathers of the thunderbird's head and took a moment to breathe in sync with it. I couldn't tell if it was a male or a female, but it was beautiful. There are a lot of different ways to give thanks to the world and its inhabitants, often through prayer and ceremony; even though I don't usually do any full-on rituals for hunts, I do thank the ancestors for protecting and guiding me and my companions, and, like in this case, to the creature I hunted for teaching me and ultimately providing a different way of being. Sometimes it's through a standardized format, like a memorized prayer, but often it's more freeform and organic, giving thanks in a way that fits a particular situation. That thunderbird remains one of the most majestic creatures I've ever encountered, and although it could have killed me as easily as swatting a fly, it taught me a lesson instead, a lesson in the grandeur of existence beyond tiny young Sam. I sat there with the thunderbird in the rain for a little longer, before grabbing my rifle and starting back the way I'd come.

The tranquilizer serum would last at least until I got back down the mountain, to the nearest ranch, and to a phone; plus, even after the thunderbird woke up, it would be too weak to move for a long while, much less fly. That gave me plenty of time to contact a cleanup crew and give them the rundown of the situation, as well as the tracker information. Then they could trace the bird's location with the tracker and pick it up, reapplying any tranquilizer as needed. The thunderstorm eventually stopped as I descended the mountain, and I arrived back at the ranch sometime very late that night. Lee and his dad were overjoyed to hear that I'd dealt with the thunderbird and let me use their phone to call in the crew. A bit later, once I'd had the chance to do some research and speak to Sergio and some other Guides, we decided where to bring the thunderbird. The rest went exactly how you'd expect. The crew picked up the thunderbird without a problem and brought it to the location we'd decided. Then Canada had one more thunderbird, and I had one more successful hunt under my belt.

So that was the first thunderbird hunt I ever went on. There are some stories about thunderbirds trying to take human children, but that almost never happens. Thunderbirds don't really seem to attack humans unless they're threatened, but if you do encounter one, just try to take shelter if you can; that will protect you both from the bird itself and from any lightning it might bring with it. But as always, if you absolutely *need* to fight, bring a high-powered weapon. Flying animals tend to be a bit more fragile than ground-dwelling ones, so if you can hit the thunderbird enough times, high-caliber bullets will be sufficient to bring it down. But you really shouldn't ever be in this situation. Thunderbirds are powerful and magnificent, and they're among my favorite animals. Most of the time, you'll just catch them flying overhead. If you're lucky enough to see one, you might understand their beauty and grace, and why they've been so sacred for thousands of years.

And that's pretty much all I have for this letter. Hopefully you found this an informative or at least entertaining look into a cryptid that's more cool than scary. I know a lot of you have been asking about thunderbirds, so I wanted to devote a letter to them. Next time, I think we'll probably talk about some aquatic creatures. And since I've gotten pretty comfortable with these letters by now, I feel like I'm ready to introduce you guys to Heather, one of the most important people in my life. You'll probably get to meet her next time. And as usual, if you've got any questions or other cryptids you'd like to hear about, please don't hesitate to ask! I'll do my best to respond to you guys. I really appreciate your support and your interest, so I'll keep the stories coming. But until the next one, stay safe, stay well, and stay home if you can. We'll talk more soon. This has been Sam White Owl, signing out.

LETTER 7 – BUNYIP + MAKARA

AUSTRALIA, INDIA

Written September 2020

Hi there, everyone. Sam White Owl here once again. It's hard to believe that this is already the seventh letter. It's crazy how far these experiences have gotten in such a short time. All thanks to Swamp Dweller, and to you guys! You have no idea how much your support means. But we can move on from the sappy stuff, at least for now. There will be more coming soon. Let's get into this letter, which I should point out will be a little more personal than usual. But cryptids were involved, I promise! It's also another long one, so maybe grab a drink or a snack before you settle in.

We'll actually be talking about two rare cryptid species for this letter: the bunyip and the makara. I mentioned makara in a previous Q&A, but only very briefly, so no worries if you don't remember. We'll discuss them more in the last part of the letter, so let's begin with bunyips.

Bunyips are found in Australia, and they may be the most well-known cryptids from that continent. Humans pushed them to near-extinction at the end of the 1800s, and most people nowadays believe that they're purely fictional. But although bunyips are rare, Aboriginal people knew about them and have been dealing with them long before Europeans came to Australia. These days, the Hunters mostly leave bunyips alone unless they pose a threat, like in the story I'm about to tell.

Bunyips are aquatic mammals, and apex predators in their ecosystems. If you ask around or go online, you'll find a million different visual interpretations of what bunyips look like, from shaggy water cows to scaly Creature from the Black Lagoon-type monsters to weird walking octopus things. You might be disappointed (or maybe relieved) to hear that they look far less alien than any of these. They're about 10 to 15 feet long, not including their tails, and weigh 700 to 1000 pounds. They have heads that are similar to dogs or seals, with small ears and two huge canines that resemble shorter versions of the teeth of a saber-toothed cat. Bunyips' thick necks can contract and extend; when they need to grab prey more easily, their necks can stretch up to 3 feet long. Their bodies are long, with long tails that help them swim swiftly and four legs ending in paws that look a bit like flippers. Their entire bodies are covered in somewhat shaggy, water-resistant fur that's black or brown in color. Bunyips live in freshwater areas, from creeks to swamps to rivers, and are commonly found in billabongs, which are like Australian ponds; however, they can absolutely walk on land too, and this is how they travel between different bodies of water. Bunyips will eat practically anything that moves, but their diet is mainly fish and crayfish, along with certain aquatic plants.

My first and only experience with a bunyip was in 2003. Australia has a pretty active Hunter community, including my friend William, who I mentioned all the way back in my second letter, the one about crawlers. He's a really nice guy, around my age, and he's served as my main contact in Australia ever since we first met. Unlike a lot of Hunters, he actually has a sense of humor and fun, which makes working with him a nice experience. He's white, with light brown hair and brown eyes, and nowadays, he has a prosthetic leg; he lost the bottom half of his right one to a Blue Mountains cat, a type of big feline cryptid native to southeastern Australia. But at the time of this story, both of his legs were still intact!

In late 2003, William called me, saying that he had taken on a task that he thought might involve a bunyip. He wanted some backup, but all the local Hunters that he knew were already on jobs in other countries around Oceania. William and I had worked together before, though, so I guess he decided I was the next best option. I quickly agreed, and soon enough, I was outside the private airfield of the airport in Sydney, waiting for William to come pick me up. I should note that these days Hunters almost always take private flights, both to draw less attention and to transport our equipment with less hassle. Around the time of this story, however, the whole private flight system in Australia, Asia, and Oceania wasn't super well-integrated, for reasons that are above my paygrade to know; because of this, I was on public airlines for the two tasks I'll be talking about in this letter. I didn't have to wait at the Sydney airport for long, because after a while, William pulled up; I don't remember what kind of car he had, honestly, but it was a big black SUV. He hopped out to greet me, and that's when I saw another person get out of the car. She was a woman probably about my age, with midnight-black hair and stormy gray eyes that instantly met mine and held my gaze. This, as William introduced me to her, was Heather.

I'm not going to try to hide the fact that I immediately found Heather attractive; you'd be insane not to. But more than anything else, her eyes are what caught my attention. She's always had beautiful eyes, but that's not entirely what drew me in. It was the way she looked at me. It was just...powerful, and when her eyes locked with mine, there was an energy there; I almost felt like I should be bowing rather than shaking her hand. I know, I know, this is over the top, but it's just how it was! It was not an intimidating or off-putting feeling, though; it felt pleasant and sophisticated and warm, and I didn't want to look away from her. She smiled at me, we shook hands, and when I introduced myself, she nodded excitedly with a big and genuine grin, then immediately started helping to put my bags in the car. After we had loaded up, we all hopped in and headed off to our destination.

As we drove, Heather explained a bit about herself. She was from Ireland, and a long bloodline of Hunters; in fact, even though both of our families had been dealing with cryptids for centuries, her ancestors had joined the Hunter organization way before mine had, which is saying something. Ever since Heather was little, underwater life had fascinated her, and so as she grew up, she started to focus on aquatic cryptids, which is why William had called her for help on the bunyip as well. This got me interested, because although I love learning about animals and monsters, I don't know as much about the underwater world. I asked her a question that I honestly can't remember now, and her answer started the first of many incredible conversations. I quickly realized that Heather really knew what she was talking about; she was incredibly smart, or at least it seemed like it. I could have talked with her for hours, and I did, at least until we arrived at our destination. Neither of us wanted to stop the conversation, but we'd have plenty of time to get to know each other later; right now, we had an investigation to kick off.

We left the car and followed William to the bank of a small river, which he had been called to a few days earlier. A local farmer had been grazing his sheep on the pastureland around the river when he'd heard a loud splash from the water, followed by one of his flock bleating in distress. He rushed over to find one of his sheep thrashing in the river; assuming that it had fallen in, he'd been preparing to pull it out when he noticed the churning water turning from white to red, and the sheep's struggles quickly lessening. Shocked and unarmed, the farmer had been unable to do anything but watch as something large, black, and furry rose up from the frothing current, forced the sheep underwater, and dragged it downriver, leaving a trail of blood in its wake. Terrified, the farmer immediately rounded up the rest of his flock and returned home; later he had apparently reported it to the authorities as a crocodile attack, but as they had told him, crocodiles don't even live in that part of the country. And when William showed up to do an interview, the farmer had clearly described seeing something furry. That led to the bunyip possibility, and now we were here.

We started by seeing what we could find at the attack site. I asked if it had rained since the farmer's encounter, and William said it hadn't, which was good; with any luck, the tracks from the day of the encounter might still be around. The ground was mostly bare dirt and sand, with some patches of grass here and there, which also meant that any tracks would be easier to see. The three of us split up to look for clues. It was easy enough to find the prints from the farmer's flock of sheep, but I was more interested in what I might find on the riverbank. There were some river plants and some sparse grass growing on the bank, but it was mostly dried mud, which is good for finding sign, mainly tracks. It took a while of walking down the river, examining the edge of the muddy water for anything out of the ordinary, but before long I found a haul-out spot.

A haul-out spot is a place where a creature that lives in the water comes up, or "hauls out", onto land. Otters, crocodiles, seals, and more all have haul-out spots, and fittingly, bunyips do too. This haul-out spot looked like a big drag mark, a disturbingly wide slick of mud where the bunyip had emerged from the water to drag the sheep away. Right next to it, I could see where the struggling sheep had churned the mud up before being yanked fully into the river.

I quickly called Heather and William over to see my discovery, and I was rewarded with approving nods from both of them. Before continuing, I should quickly point out that, even with a good memory and in-depth journals, I can't remember every gesture or bit of conversation exactly as it happened, so I'm just recreating some of that stuff for you.

"Keen eye, Sam," Heather told me, and suddenly I felt pretty pleased with myself.

"Yeah, good find. Definitely looks like bunyip sign. We should keep going downstream, see if we can find anything else," William said.

We did just that, and although we didn't find any more tracks or prints, we did come across something more organic. A few minutes' walk away from the haul-out spot, William pointed something out on the opposite bank of the river: a big clump of fluffy brownish-white material and some long reddish objects. I had no idea what we were looking at, and I initially thought that maybe it was some trash that someone had thrown out. We needed a closer look, but for that, we'd have to cross the river. Then I saw Heather emptying her pockets.

"You're not going to swim across, are you?" William asked.

Heather just laughed and gave a wild grin. "It's no trouble. Sun's up, so I'll dry off fast. Be back soon!"

She leapt into the water and started her swim, with William and I watching in disbelief. Soon enough I saw him turn to me out of the corner of my eye, although I was still watching Heather, and he elbowed me in the side.

"I see you, Sam! You'll be cracking onto her soon enough!" he said, quiet enough for Heather not to hear.

I distinctly remember my face flushing completely and William practically cackling as I shoved him lightly. "No! I'm not...I mean...Maybe? A little bit." We'd only been together for a few hours...Had I really been that obvious?

"Well, don't let me get in your way. Good luck and godspeed, Mr. White Owl. Godspeed," William said.

The river was only about a hundred feet wide where we were, if that, so Heather soon reached the other bank and picked through the objects there, before grabbing a few and heading back across. She put them on the ground, giving us a nice, clear view of the remains of the unfortunate sheep.

"Looks like some pieces of wool and a few bones. I think the bunyip must have vomited them up, like a shark or a bird will do with undigested material," she explained. Looking at the bones a little closer, they were marked with slight indentations that were definitely tooth marks. Did bunyips chew their food?

"How old do you think these are?" William asked.

It was tough to tell, but there were still some dried blood marks on some of the bones, and they hadn't been entirely dried out by the sun. They couldn't have been sitting on the bank for any more than a day or two, meaning that the bunyip was very likely still in the area.

"That's good. But how do we track it down? It probably swims faster than we realize, and we don't know where it is," I said.

"We could use bait. Try to lure it out," William said after a moment of thinking. I remember laughing as I pictured us sitting in lawn chairs with beers and fishing rods waiting to reel in the bunyip; the term "bait" is familiar to all Hunters, but typically not in the context of water.

"That's not a bad idea. We need to get it into shooting range. We're going to tranquilize it, yeah?" Heather asked. We had been considering it but hadn't decided yet; although I didn't know bunyips like the other two, I wasn't against that plan.

"Should work. I know a lake we can move it to. I also know a place we can get some bait. We know it likes sheep, so I'll pick up some blood and meat. Anything else?" William asked. Heather and I shook our heads, and William gave us a mischievous grin. "Right, well, I'm off to go grab the bait. Why don't you two stay here, set up camp, get to know each other, relax a bit?"

I tried to act nonchalant, and honestly, I probably didn't play it off very well...William went out a few minutes later, leaving Heather and I to get settled. We set up the big 4-person tent that William had brought and then sat around on the dusty ground. After discussing our respective lives and careers for a long while, the sky eventually started to get dark. As we watched the sun set together, I told Heather that I found talking to her to be a really nice change of pace. I usually didn't have much time to relax and truly have fun on the job, and neither did most Hunters that I knew, unless there was alcohol involved. Most of us don't drink or do drugs while actively on a task or in the field, but it's unfortunately a little too commonplace among Hunters when they're not working. I'm very lucky that I never fell into that trap; I limit myself to a few beers or a glass of wine every so often. Some Hunters use drinking or doing drugs as a pastime, but many do it as an escape, and we all know how slippery that slope is; I've seen the problem of substance abuse on reservations, but it's everywhere else too, and we all know someone who's struggled with it. But Heather was different. She didn't go to drinking or drugs to numb herself or drown out trauma, and she told me that she didn't even need that to have fun. I respected her so much for that; really, it made her that much more charming.

It led to the question of what she did for fun, then, and she answered that she used to be interested in Irish dancing, especially step dancing. I'm not personally a big dancer, but I asked if she could show me a bit herself. At first she was a little reluctant, saying that she didn't have the right shoes, the right floor, or even music, but I just shrugged and said that it was okay. Honestly, I didn't really care about any extra stuff; I just wanted to see her dance. At this, Heather hopped up with a big grin, and soon she'd turned into a stamping, spinning whirlwind of steps and kicks. She might be a Hunter, but I could tell by the ease of her movements and the smile on her face that she could have made a great dancer if things had gone differently. Her moves were precise and graceful, and I gave her a round of applause when she was done. She took a mock bow, laughing a bit.

"That was great. I wish I could dance," I told her, and she reached out a hand to me.

"Let me teach you," she said.

I took her hand and she pulled me closer, then started to show me how to stand and how to get ready to do some of the steps. Pretty soon, it started getting too dark to see each other, so we continued the impromptu lesson by the light of a campfire. It was the happiest I'd felt in a long while. Being a Hunter generally means being alone for long periods of time, and that solitude can really start to ache. But being close with someone else changes that, and interacting with Heather just made me feel *good*. We were both so caught up with each other that we didn't notice the headlights of William's car until he honked the horn, making us both jump and laugh.

"Well, well, well. What is *this* I see?" William asked as he jumped out of the car.

"Just a little dance lesson, you moron. What did you get for us?" Heather asked.

We walked over to the back of the truck, and William pulled open the trunk. A sheep hopped out onto the ground, giving a short, confused baa as it looked at us. I immediately realized what was going on.

"Is *this* the bait?"

William nodded and grabbed the end of a rope that was tied around the sheep's neck. "Damn right it is. Better than a hunk of meat and a bucket of blood, right?"

Heather and I frowned at each other, before she knelt down and gave the sheep a gentle scratch on the head.

"Hello, little one. Don't you worry. We'll have you well looked after. We're *not* going to let you get eaten," she said, looking pointedly to William at the last bit.

We tied the sheep to a small tree near the riverbank, and attached another length of rope to the one already around her neck, allowing her to move around about 20 feet away from the water's edge. Next, we all grabbed our rifles and collectively decided on proper tranquilizer dart dosages, based on Heather's knowledge of bunyip size and weight. After loading up our tranq darts, we took up our positions. There were some bushes near the tree where we had tied the sheep, so William and I hid in those, while Heather swam across the river again and laid down in some reeds on that bank. Hopefully the bunyip would be active enough at night to take the bait; the key was to shoot at the right time, before it grabbed the sheep, but after it showed itself sufficiently. There was no wind to throw off our shots or carry our scent, but it was only a half-moon, so we didn't have much natural light. We all had headlamps, though, which we turned on and used to illuminate the water; Heather said the light wouldn't deter the bunyip as long as we didn't flash or move it too much. I remember it being pretty chilly, so I put on a windbreaker and settled in the bushes to wait.

At some point during the night, I must have dozed off; the course of the day and the time zone change had me pretty exhausted (or "wrecked", as Heather would say). But I was jarred awake by a sudden, entirely unfamiliar sound. A low, booming roar was coming from downriver, echoing through the night, and despite not being particularly loud, it still made me want to cover my ears. Something about the call sounded less like an animal and more like some kind of small explosion; still, I could somehow tell that it was the roar of a predator. I looked at William, who nodded, and I gripped my gun a little tighter. The roar came a few more times from the same spot over the next few hours, but eventually it went quiet for the rest of the night. Later, we determined that the roaring was likely territorial behavior: the bunyip was advertising how strong and powerful it was, both to scare off opponents and to declare its ownership of this area.

As the sun rose the next morning, I felt myself having trouble keeping my eyes open, and when Heather came back over to us, she looked very similar. William saw this and told us to head into the tent to get some sleep while he watched the sheep for a while. Heather and I thanked him, and soon we were both clocked out and snoring alongside each other in the tent. And before you ask, no, nothing *inappropriate* happened between us; we just got some much-needed sleep.

For the rest of the day, all three of us took turns watching the sheep and sleeping in the tent, with a few rounds of cards and conversation here and there. All you kids out there, learn from this story: you might have a surprisingly good time if you actually talk to others *in person*! Like before, Heather and I passed the time quickly, telling stories and facts about the monsters we'd hunted and the experiences we'd had. William and I had some good conversations too, and I learned a bit more about him as well. That evening, Heather got interested in the charms that I wear and carry, the special and sacred objects, so I showed her some of them and explained the significance of each one. While telling her about one of them (I can't remember which one exactly), we heard the bunyip's booming, rumbling roar again, this time from probably less than a mile away. William came running out of the tent, rifle in hand, and we all rushed to take up our positions from the night before. Heather crossed the river quickly, and William and I crouched down in the bushes by the tree. I think the sheep knew that something was wrong, because she started to bleat and pace around nervously; maybe that would actually be more appealing to the bunyip.

Pretty soon, night fell. The sheep was still nervous, and we were still watching the water closely with our headlamps. After a while, William pointed downriver, to our left, where the water was moving in a slightly odd fashion. I looked where he was pointing and saw what appeared to be a dark black log floating on the surface of the river; if it hadn't been moving upstream, *against* the gentle current, I might never have thought anything of it. As the so-called "log" got closer, the water shifted slightly. A small black hump emerged from the water ahead of the log, and the light from our headlamps reflected off of two glowing white eyes on the front of it.

"There. Now," I told William.

We both raised our rifles, poking the barrels out of the bushes, and when I'd found the bunyip's head in my scope, I pulled the trigger. William's shot wasn't far behind mine, and after a second, I heard Heather's gun go off too. I guess maybe I had missed, because it wasn't until William and Heather fired that the bunyip gave any reaction. Its head raised up from the water, and it gave a startled, angry *BOOM* sound. In the light of my headlamp, I saw the water dripping from the fur of its black, doglike head and its long saber teeth. I fired again, and this time my dart sunk squarely into the side of its neck. With a short yelp, the bunyip dove into the water, and I saw its dark silhouette heading back downstream, its long tail lashing back and forth to propel it through the water.

William was on his feet instantly. "Come on, we gotta stay on it!"

We all jumped up and began running downstream after the bunyip; we had lost sight of it in the water, but soon, there was a loud splash from somewhere ahead of us. We slowed down, and then heard the bunyip rushing through the darkness on Heather's side of the river. William and I both turned to see the huge beast burst out of the reeds, running on all fours. It swiped its head to the side, hitting Heather's legs and knocking her down, before standing up on its hind legs and swiping downwards at her with its front paws. She rolled out of the way as it came down, and I dropped my rifle and drew my revolver, which was loaded with live rounds rather than darts. I had hoped not to use it, but if there was any situation that called for it, this was the one. As I raised my weapon, I gave a loud shout to draw the bunyip's attention. The cryptid turned to look at me, and I could tell from its eyes and its swaying on its feet that it was getting woozy, giving me hope that I wouldn't have to shoot it down after all. Heather took the opportunity to sprint off into the shadows while the bunyip was distracted, and surprisingly, it didn't look at her; instead, it roared another loud boom at me, opening its fanged mouth wide. I started backing up, hoping that it might chase me, and William raised his own pistol to cover me. The bunyip took a step forward and slipped in the mud, before giving a low groan and collapsing onto its side. I gave a whoop of triumph.

When Heather returned a little while later, she crouched down next to the bunyip, and even from that distance I could somehow tell that she was smirking at me and William. "Right, so...Looks like some of us are gonna have to swim."

William and I both sighed and grumbled, but it wasn't like Heather was going to drag the 800-pound bunyip over to our side of the river. Reluctantly, we took off our outer layers of clothing and crossed over to join our teammate and the snoring monster. William had a tracker, and Heather and I lifted the bunyip's head so that he could tie the device's cord strap around the beast's neck. Then we walked back upstream and swam across to our camp. As we dried off by the fire, William pulled out a map and showed us the lake where he'd been thinking of relocating the bunyip; Heather and I had approved of his choice, although that was mostly a formality, because we didn't know the area and were simply trusting William's analysis and reasoning. Then we decided to pack everything up into the car and head right back to civilization. I was asleep for most of the car ride, but I do remember stopping briefly at the closest building so that William could put in a call to the cleanup crew; at another point along the way, he also made a stop somewhere to drop off the sheep, who was just fine. By sunrise we had checked into a hotel, where all of us got to work, by which I mean taking warm showers, cleaning up, and settling in for some well-deserved sleep.

I spent a few more days with William and Heather in Australia, mostly seeing some of the local sights and hiking around the outback. I'll spare you all the touristy details, but Australia is a beautiful country with lots of great environments to visit. But eventually, it was time to go home, and so I found myself back in the airport in Sydney. Heather and I were catching flights that were close together to head back to Ireland and the US. We said goodbye to William and hugged him farewell outside the airport, then went inside to go to our separate departure gates. Of course, when it came time to say goodbye, neither of us wanted to leave. We stood outside of some random airport restaurant, and eventually Heather scribbled something down on a piece of paper, which she handed to me; it was a phone number.

"Please call me. I don't want to lose touch," she said.

I put the paper in my pocket and smiled. "Of course. We decided we're going to go on our next job together, right?"

"Right! Plus, we've got to finish our dance lessons...I'm going to miss you. Have a good and safe trip home. We'll talk more soon...Bye, Sam." She leaned in and kissed me on the cheek, lingering there for a moment before pulling back, giving me another wave, and disappearing into the crowd.

It was about then that I think I really fell for Heather. Fell for her *hard*, I mean. We may have been a whole ocean apart, but that didn't stop us from talking to each other just about every day. Our calls lasted for hours, and they became the part of my day that I looked forward to the most. We discussed everything from cryptids to history to culture to music, and I felt like I got a little bit smarter with each talk. It was great being able to speak to somebody on a regular basis, but I also loved that it was thoughtful, meaningful conversation; I could teach Heather some things, and, oh boy, did she teach me! It was wonderful, but also painful, because I wanted more than anything to be with her in person. We had made a promise in Australia that we would invite each other to help out on our next jobs, and before long, the opportunity arrived. I was roped into it when Heather called me one night, sounding pretty excited.

"You're never gonna believe this...We're gonna go after a makara!"

I think I almost dropped the phone; I had heard of makara enough to know that they were rare and enormous, and it was crazy that they'd even found one, let alone that they were going after it.

Makara are huge marine cryptids that live mainly in the Indian Ocean; they're mammals, but they aren't cetaceans like whales and dolphins. They look pretty weird, kind of like a cross between an elephant, a crocodile, and a whale or fish. They have long bodies with two front flippers that look a bit like crocodile feet, and heads with long, flexible, trunk-like snouts and mouths filled with teeth. The back half of a makara's body ends in a long, heavy, whale-like tail, complete with a fleshy, horizontal fluke; on their backs, they also have small dorsal fins. Like other marine mammals, makara breathe air, but they don't have blowholes like cetaceans; instead, they have two nostrils on the sides of their long snouts. Makara are enormous, ranging from anywhere between 65 to 85 feet in length, which is bigger than many whales, and 100 to 140 *tons* in weight, making them some of the biggest animals in the world. They seem pretty intelligent and often get mistaken for whales.

Makara are carnivores, eating squids, turtles, dugongs, dolphins, rays, all sorts of fish, and occasionally even whales. Because they're so gigantic, they have no natural predators besides orcas (and even then, only multiple orcas at once), making them pretty much the top predators of their ecosystems. They're very wary of humans, for good reason, and usually stick to deeper parts of the ocean to avoid us. Beyond that, makara are very rare, with a total population of no more than a few hundred, if that; they reproduce very slowly, and pollution and overfishing have killed off some of their more reliable food sources. Because they're effectively an endangered species, and because we want to make sure they don't come into conflict with any watercraft, the Hunters have set up a system to tag and monitor any makara that we find.

Heather told me that there had been several recent sightings of an untagged makara in the Indian Ocean. Her help had been requested by the South Asian arm of the Hunters, and she'd agreed to be part of a task force with the job of taking a boat out to locate and tag the monster. Because of the sensitive nature of the assignment and the various conditions that come with being on a ship, Heather had asked whether I could come along for the job, and fortunately, the Hunter's Indian branch had approved the request. I thanked her for thinking of me and giving me this chance, and after confirming the task with Sergio, I was on my way to India. I arrived at the airport in Kerala, where Heather was already there to greet me. We practically jumped into each other's arms, giving each other a long, tight, and much-needed hug.

When we finished, a big man came up to join us, and when I say big, I mean it; this guy stood almost 7 feet tall and had arms that looked as thick as small trees. He was definitely Indian, and probably in his 40s, although his beard maybe made him look older. I introduced myself, and he shook my hand and said that his name was Dak, short for "Daksh". He wasn't a very talkative guy, but he was really polite, and more importantly, a good Hunter. He and Heather helped me get my stuff into an old, beat-up truck, and then we began the drive to the port.

The ride was pretty short, although traffic was ridiculous, and soon we were all aboard our ship. I don't know much about boats, so you'll have to excuse me if I get some lingo wrong. Our vessel for this job was much larger than I'd expected, somewhere around 150 feet long, with a thick metal hull and all the features you'd imagine from a ship of that size; just to be safe, I won't give you the name of the boat, but I will say that I thought it was kind of cool. When Heather, Dak, and I boarded, I felt like we were the walking setup for a bad joke, like "An American Indian, an Indian Indian, and an Irishwoman all walk onto a boat..." But one of the best parts of being a Hunter is having such a great variety of coworkers; our organization is global, and I've been fortunate enough to meet, work with, and befriend all types of really cool people.

The captain, who we'll call Hamid, made things even more diverse: he was from Eritrea, and although he wasn't a Hunter himself, he had been working with us for a long time, typically by lending his ship and his services to Hunters who needed to work in the Red Sea or the Indian Ocean. Hamid and his crew were happy enough to keep our secrets, and I have to imagine they were well-paid to do so. It was dark when we arrived at the docks. Hamid himself came to greet us when we climbed the ramp onto the deck, and he assigned one of his crew to give us a tour; there were all the usual boat fixings, so I won't bore you with the details. The really interesting part came when Heather grabbed me by the hand and took me to the edge of the deck.

"Have a gander at *that*," she said, pointing over the railing to where a large object was attached to the side of the ship. Although it was partially submerged beneath the water, I could make out enough detail to tell that it looked like a huge drum, with its face pointed away from the ship, out to sea.

"Okay, interesting...What is that?" I asked.

"It's a reverse hydrophone. Like a big speaker. We're gonna play whale song off it, and everything for kilometers around will hear. You know makara like whales for some reason. Maybe because they sometimes eat them? That's how Hunters have been luring them in for ages now. They play the whale song and the makara come, and then they put the trackers on them. Simple, yeah?"

Classic hunting tactics, just scaled up tremendously; the hydrophone would become a gigantic game call. We weren't going to find the makara; it would be finding us.

Not much happened that night. I was exhausted from traveling, so I just headed to my (very small) room below deck and went to sleep. We must have cast off sometime that night, but I was so tired that I didn't fully notice the ship moving. The next morning, Heather knocked on my door and very eagerly told me to come up on deck. When I emerged, still sleepy, the ship was fully out to sea, with no land in sight. We were in the Indian Ocean, of course, but I had no idea where.

Heather gave me a good morning hug, which helped wake me up, then took me to the edge of the boat where the hydrophone was. Dak and two other crew members were already there, and in the daylight, I now saw that the hydrophone was hanging from some thick metal cables, which in turn were hooked up to a big winch, like a crane. When Dak turned a big wheel that was attached to the winch, the cables extended, lowering the hydrophone slowly into the water. Heather sat nearby beneath a makeshift sort of tent, under which sat a computer screen and some other electronic consoles that had thick wires running from them to the hydrophone. Heather operated the computer, and I watched her click on something that threw sound wave diagrams onto the screen, along with a GPS display and what looked like a map fused with a radar scanner.

"Wow. Lots of information. What am I looking at here?" I asked. You probably know that I'm not very tech-savvy, and I also wanted to let Heather do her thing and teach me.

She just laughed and started showing me around her makara-tracking software. The sound waves were a visual of the whale song currently playing from the hydrophone. The radar-map hybrid displayed our boat and any objects in the water around us; we'd be able to see anything large that came close to the ship, from rock formations to schools of fish, pods of dolphins, and, hopefully, hungry makara. Finally, the GPS showed our location on a larger scale, as well as those of the other makara that had been tagged with trackers in the past. After explaining all this, Heather said that the next step was to go to the last reported location of the makara we were aiming for; if everything went according to plan, when the monster came to us, we would tag it with a tracking device.

In order to avoid attracting every single makara around, our speaker system was designed to project the whale song only about 20 miles out from the boat; that meant we'd have to be pretty close to our target for our plan to work. So we spent the next couple of days sailing around, going to each place where the untagged makara had been spotted and waiting there for the whole day. In the morning, just after sunrise, we would lower the hydrophone into the water and start up the whale song; then at dusk we would turn off the speaker and bring it back up. On one afternoon, some of our ocean-dwelling cousins paid us a visit: a trio of short-finned pilot whales, small (for a whale) gray animals who evidently wanted to meet a new friend. As you might imagine, they seemed pretty confused by our supersized metal whale, but they were interested enough to hang around for 10 or 15 minutes to check us out. We let them do their thing and just watched from the deck as Heather told Dak and I a bit about them. Soon they moved on, and I was grateful that we hadn't thrown their lives off too much. Other than that, there was a lot of waiting. The water was definitely pretty, but the view did get a little stale after a while.

What *didn't* get stale was Heather, and she and I spent pretty much every day together. Sometimes we would talk, sometimes we would read, and other times, yes, we would dance. Heather seemed pretty determined to teach me a basic piece of Irish step dancing, and I got the feeling she'd been preparing her lesson for quite a while. She honestly wasn't very good at teaching, but I didn't really mind; it was enough just to spend time with her. Plus, the dancing happened to be a great workout, especially underneath the hot sun. After one particular lesson, we sat down underneath her tent in front of the computer screen, both drenched in sweat and breathing hard. Heather asked how I was feeling, and I gave her a thumbs-up and a grin. She smiled back, and then scooted one of her hands over to hold mine. I squeezed it gently, and for a long moment we just sat there, feeling happy together.

Dak came over after a while and said he'd seen us dancing. We told him about how Heather was teaching me, and he thought that was nice. When he said that it was always great to learn from people from different backgrounds, that led to Heather asking him about makara and their place in traditional Indian culture and Hinduism. She had seen them before in some paintings, and Dak nodded and told us that makara are portrayed a good deal in Hindu art and sculpture, often with the head of an elephant or a crocodile and a body resembling a lion, fish, or seal. A few Hindu gods are actually supposed to ride on makara. Then Dak mentioned that the makara is the patron animal of Kamadeva, the god of love and desire, and both Heather and I immediately got really awkward about that. Looking back on it now, it was actually a little funny, but in the moment, I couldn't stop thinking that Dak had meant to embarrass us. Or maybe he was trying to point something out. A question came to my mind, and I decided to ask him when we had a moment without Heather around. I got my opportunity after dinner that night, when I found him in one of the hallways and opened by asking if I could run a question by him.

"Of course, my friend. What is it?" he replied. I can picture myself running a hand backwards through my hair, which, ironically, Heather and many other people have told me I often do when I'm nervous or flustered.

"Well...It's Heather. I'm sure you can tell that...well, I'm into her. And I'm wondering if there's any, you know, any kind of rule against that? You've been in the Hunters for a while, right? Is there anything that says that you can't have a relationship with another Hunter? My mom never told me about such a thing, but I'm trying to make sure," I said. Dak actually laughed, which I remember well because it was the first time I'd heard him do so.

"There's no rule that I know of. Go ahead. Just be careful, Sam. You both know how dangerous this job is. I would try not to get too attached," he answered. That last part made me a little frustrated; how was I supposed to control my feelings like that? I knew he was right, though, and I just hadn't considered it before. Maybe it was better to keep my distance. Dak had given me good advice to think on, so I thanked him and headed off to bed.

The next day, I was a little more conscious of getting closer to Heather. I kept thinking about what Dak had said, which I couldn't believe I hadn't thought about until our talk; I guess I just had tunnel vision for Heather. The last thing I wanted was for something bad to happen to either of us. But every time I talked to Heather or even just *looked* at her, it got harder and harder to stay away. I'm sure some of you have been in similar situations. I spent a lot of time trying to figure out what the right thing to do was. There wasn't long to mull it over, though, because sometime that afternoon, as I was reading in my small room, there was a loud knock on the metal door. I opened it up to find an excited-looking crew member who told me that the makara had been sighted.

I instantly dropped my book and went racing up to the top deck. At the bow (the front), there was a whole clump of people clustered up on the railing of the starboard (right) side, looking out ahead of us. I quickly found Heather in the crowd, and she pulled me up to the railing, pointing out over the fairly calm blue sea. At first, I didn't see anything, but after waiting for a few minutes, a massive, dark gray hump rose out of the water, several thousand feet away. It came up maybe about 5 feet above the waves, stayed visible just for a second, then sank back below the surface. I could hear Heather laughing, maybe in excitement or maybe at me, because I couldn't stop staring. I'd barely caught a glimpse of the animal, but I knew that we'd only seen just a tiny fraction of its body; this creature was larger than anything I'd ever seen before or since.

"Holy crap, that animal is gigantic," I said. That was the first time I'd seen Heather get her excited, slightly crazy glint in her eyes, and I remember it so clearly.

"Yep, that's our girl out there. Let's hope she stays close to the surface," she said.

Hamid ordered the engines to be shut off, and soon the ship came to a stop. A moment later, Dak came over carrying a large crossbow. He had a few darts for the weapon, but they weren't meant to kill or hurt anything; they each had a small metal head, yes, but attached to the edge of each of those was a tiny black cylinder, only about two inches long. These were the trackers, which Heather had explained worked almost exactly like the devices I was familiar with, except that these were designed to be inserted into the makara, instead of tied onto it; Dak would shoot a dart into the makara's layer of blubber, which would hopefully stick and implant the tracker on the dart. According to Heather, this is sometimes what scientists do to tag whales, and the Hunters had just co-opted the system for our own needs.

"Want to see how it works?" Dak asked me, and I nodded.

Dak, Heather, and I all climbed up onto the very end of the ship's bow. In the distance, I saw the makara's short, gray dorsal fin come up for a moment before submerging again. Eventually, I saw the shadow of its body just beneath the calm surface of the water as it slowly approached our ship. Even from that distance, it was clear again just how enormous this creature was; it must have been longer than two school buses put front-to-rear. This huge, dark shadow drifted closer, eventually turning a little bit to come around to the port (left) side of our boat. As it passed the bow, Dak had an easy angle for his shot. He fired the crossbow almost straight down, and the dart sunk into the water. But the makara didn't react. Dak grumbled and shook his head, reloading as he motioned for me and Heather to follow him.

"What happened?" I asked.

"It wasn't close enough to the surface for the dart to hit. We may have to wait until it comes up for air," he answered.

We headed to the port side, and the crew began to follow. Pretty much everyone was on deck at this point, gawking at the makara and crowding us; Dak pushed through the crowd just with his enormous size, and Hamid helped out by ordering his men to back up and give us some room. We eventually made it to the port side railing and saw the makara's shadow almost right up against the side of our boat. From here, I could actually see through the water and get an idea of the monster's color; its skin was a grayish, almost green color. It seemed to be inspecting the hydrophone, which was still playing the whale song.

"Pull the hydrophone up a bit, so it comes closer to the surface," I suggested.

Heather snapped her fingers in agreement and raced over to the big wheel that controlled the winch that the huge speaker was mounted on. I ran over to help; maybe Dak could turn the wheel by himself with his tree-trunk arms, but Heather and I would definitely have to work together to move it. Even with our combined strength, it was still pretty heavy, but soon the hydrophone began to rise, slowly but surely lifting up from beneath the water. When it was about halfway out, we stopped and ran back over to the edge of the ship. The makara slowly began to rise as well, and after a few seconds, the top of its back broke the water. Immediately, Dak fired a second shot, and I clearly saw the dart sink into the makara's skin.

"Got it!" Dak said, and the crew all gave a cheer.

I held my hand out to Heather and she slapped me a high-five with a wide grin. As I went to pat Dak on the back, the mood quickly changed when the whole boat suddenly tilted to the side. Had we just been *pushed*? I looked back over the edge of the ship again, and my eyes went wide: the makara was gone.

"Uh-oh. Where'd it go?" somebody asked.

The ship lurched again, and this time, I knew for sure that we had been jolted by the makara. Somebody yelled something like "It's under us!" Looking over the edge again, I saw the cryptid's shadow emerge from beneath the ship. It turned so that it was parallel to the boat, and then its huge, greenish-colored tail fluke emerged from the waves and smacked into the side of the vessel. The force of the hit pushed the ship to the side, knocking me and a few of the people around me over onto the deck; we might have been able to stay upright if we had been bracing, but this caught us all by surprise.

Dak helped me back up and immediately turned to Heather. "What is it doing?"

"I think she's basically sizing us up," Heather responded.

Hamid was shouting orders, and I heard him yell something about guns. Guns? Sailors began to rush back and forth, and there was a loud splash as the makara sunk back under the water. The monster's massive shadow disappeared as it dove deep, to the point that we lost sight of it. A few moments later, a group of crew members raced up to where we were at the edge of the boat. Two were carrying pistols, and the rest were holding big assault rifles.

"What is this? Hamid, are you out of your mind?!" Heather shouted at the captain. I'd never seen her angry, and let me tell you, it was scary. Hamid looked frustrated, but even he took a small step back.

"We won't fire unless absolutely necessary, but I'm not going to let that thing sink this ship. If it comes back, we start with flares, and if that doesn't work, we use bullets," he said. Heather looked almost like she was about to punch him across the face, but I ran up and grabbed her by the hand.

"He's just trying to keep us safe," I told her, and she gave an angry growl before turning away from Hamid and going back to the railing.

Shortly afterwards, there was a loud splash from the starboard side, and the ship jolted under the impact of another strike. We all rushed over to see the makara's enormous shadow right alongside and parallel to us again. The huge monster rammed the side of its body against the boat, and Hamid gave the order to shoot a few flares at it. The men with the pistols shot several times down into the water, and although the flares extinguished pretty much as soon as they hit the surface, they still made a bright light and a lot of noise. The makara's shadow held still for a moment, and then it dove again, disappearing into the depths.

"Is it gone?" someone asked after a tense moment.

Then there was a huge sort of blowing noise from near the bow, as if a giant had sneezed out a big breath through a pipe. Pretty much everyone started running to the bow, and there we saw the makara's face clearly for the first and last time. A massive head, shaped like a crocodile's but with smooth skin and a long, flexible nose, rose out from the water and gave a snort from its nostrils, then turned to look at the ship with small black eyes, flicking its nose back and forth a few times. After staring at us for a few moments, it gave another snort and sank back beneath the waves. Then its enormous shadow turned and began to swim away from us. The crew all started applauding and cheering, and I gave a sigh of relief; it looked like there was no need for bloodshed. I turned to look at Heather, and saw that she had happy tears running down her face.

"Pretty cool, huh?" I asked her as she wiped her eyes.

"Yeah. Thanks for being here to see it with me," she said, and reached out for a hug, which I gladly gave her. Right then,

I wouldn't have wanted to experience that moment with anyone else.

With our job done, we headed back to shore and said goodbye to Hamid and his crew. That left us Hunters to our own devices. Dak was nice enough to invite us to his hometown in Tamil Nadu, and so we took some time to go there. It was beautiful (but crowded!), and we wound up staying there for a few days as he showed us around and introduced us to some of his family and friends. I wish I had visited some of the more famous locales of India, but maybe I'll go back there someday. In any case, Heather and I had a great time there, but before long, we were back in the airport to go home. Heather's flight to Ireland was before my flight to the US, so Dak and I went to drop her off (again, we had to take public airlines this time). When we'd gotten inside to the check-in area, Heather gave us both a hug and then turned to look at me. We stood there in silence for a moment, before I got a sudden urge, and without really thinking, I spoke up.

"I don't want you to go. Because I like you, Heather. A lot," I said, and she started laughing. I might have brown skin, but in that moment, my face must have been completely red. Then Heather reached out and touched my cheek.

"I like you too, Sam. A lot," she repeated with a grin, and without even thinking about it, I took her face in my hands and brought it to mine, kissing her hard. Heather returned the kiss just as forcefully, but after a while, we both had to come up for air, so I rested my forehead against hers and looked into her gray eyes.

"Please come with me. To the US. I really want to be with you."

She seemed to think for a second. "Well, if you're offering...I suppose I'll cancel my flight, then."

All I could do was kiss her again. And yes, this did actually happen in the middle of an airport, and it was just as wonderful as it seems in the movies. Reality doesn't always match fiction, but here, the universe made an exception for us.

So Heather and I flew back to the US together, but when we arrived at my house in the very early morning, both of us were far too tired after everything to do much besides clock out straight to bed. We both woke up sometime in the early evening, which was when I got a great idea. As a kid, there was a pond by some woods near my mother's house that I would often visit and play around by; I still remembered where it was, and I figured it would be a great place for what I guess was our first official date. Heather took me up on the offer, and we drove over with a bunch of blankets and some food; I don't remember what we ate, but that was the last thing on my mind. Afterwards, we talked for a bit while we watched the sun set over the hills, turning the sky orange and red and purple. Heather said she'd never seen a sunset like that before.

Soon the stars came out, and both of us wrapped up in one of the blankets, holding hands and looking at the sky. Neither of us were very good at identifying constellations, but we did our best. At one point there was even a shooting star! Eventually I hugged Heather tighter and thanked her for coming with me.

"Of course...You *did* seem a little lonely," she replied, before kissing me. I could feel heat practically steaming off of her, and I tangled my fingers in her hair to return the kiss.

"Yeah...I just need to be near you," I breathed out after a moment.

"*I* need more than that," Heather said against my lips.

And then things started moving very fast all of a sudden. The world became just the two of us, and, well, I'll spare you the graphic details. It was well past dark by the time we decided to just snuggle up in the blankets and fall asleep right there on the grass. And it was some of the best sleep I've ever had. Well, Heather snored a bit, but you know what I mean. It was kind of crazy that it had taken so long, but it was very different to be with someone else after such a long time alone. I just felt *good*.

Anyway, as you've probably realized by now, there's no more cryptids for this letter, so we can leave things here. Heather and I had a lot more adventures together, so this time I figured it was important to tell you how we met. I also feel comfortable enough now to talk about some more of the personal stuff. Heather was part of one of my most important hunts, so I wanted you guys to get to know her a bit before I tell that story a little later.

I know this letter wasn't all that scary or intense, but hopefully it was at least interesting. For next time, we'll definitely talk about one of my hunts with Heather, but I'm not sure which one yet. Probably one of the scarier ones! Maybe the chupacabras and the so-called "Battle of the Tall Grass", which we kind of became famous for. We'll see, but for now, feel free to keep leaving your suggestions and comments for me to check out! I've really been enjoying what you guys have to say, and the positivity has been amazing to hear. So keep it up, and stay healthy and happy and safe, everyone. We'll talk more soon. This has been Sam White Owl, signing out.

LETTER 8 – EMELA-NTOUKA

REPUBLIC OF THE CONGO

Written September 2020

Hey guys, it's Sam White Owl again. I hope you're all doing well and staying safe, because these are pretty crazy times. I know it can be a lot to handle, so don't forget to take care of yourselves. Maybe Swamp Dweller's channel is one place where you can do that, and if so, then I'm happy to pitch in with my stories. Every little bit counts! For me, writing my experiences out has allowed me to process the past more, both the good and bad parts. I've kept a lot of intense things to myself or in my journals, and it's been good to get some of those out and heard. My family and friends and community definitely help out by lending their ears, but it's very different when *thousands* of people are hearing me too! Teaching also makes me happy, so hopefully you guys are also learning something from my rambling. But I'm not done yet, so I hope you're ready for more!

This time, we're going to be talking about the emela-ntouka. Unusual name, I know; it comes from the Bomitaba language, which is spoken in the Republic of the Congo, in Central Africa. In English, the name "emela-ntouka" has a chilling translation: "elephant killer".

Emela-ntouka live in the western part of Central Africa, primarily Cameroon and the Republic of the Congo; despite being reptiles, they're similar to rhinoceroses when it comes to appearance and behavior. Emela-ntouka have thick skin covered in small, rough, lizard-like scales which range in color from sandy tan to light gray to leafy green. Structurally, their bodies are long and thick, supported from underneath by four sturdy legs, with muscular tails that stretch behind them for balance; on the opposite end, emela-ntouka have rectangular heads with beak-like mouths that resemble the jaws of a snapping turtle. On either side of these heads are two leathery flaps that slightly resemble miniature elephant ears; Hunters call these "frills", and they're for display and communication purposes rather than hearing. Emela-ntouka flap and lift their frills to indicate certain emotions or intentions, and to enhance the effect, they can flush their frills with blood to turn them different shades of red. The most distinctive feature of an emela-ntouka is their horn, which sticks up vertically from the nose, just like a rhino's. Each emela-ntouka has a single large horn that they use for self-defense and display; their horns grow throughout their lives and usually get to between 3 and 4 feet in length. Speaking of which, emela-ntouka are enormous: adults stand between 7 and 8 feet tall at the shoulder and measure about 25 feet long, including their tails. Still, they're not quite as tall as African forest elephants, as some accounts claim.

Overall, emela-ntouka pretty closely resemble the dinosaurs known as ceratopsians, with the main differences being that these cryptids have longer bodies and lack the bony shield-like frills and upper horns at the base of the skull. In fact, some Hunters actually believe that emela-ntouka are direct descendants of these dinosaurs, who survived up until the present day. However, as far as we currently know, ceratopsians didn't ever live in the area of the world that's now Africa. Then again, I guess they would have had 65 million years to move. I personally think that emela-ntouka most likely evolved on a different path from dinosaurs, but who knows?

In terms of behavior and lifestyle, emela-ntouka are similar to modern African rhinos, the other animal they resemble physically; African rhino species mainly live in open savannah and scrubland, though, while emela-ntouka stick almost exclusively to swampy, forested areas. This is one of the biggest reasons these big guys are so elusive, despite their size; it's just not easy to get deep into the parts of the jungle where emela-ntouka live, not to mention the on-and-off warfare that's cropped up in the broader Congo region over the past several decades. Like many cryptids, we know more about emela-ntouka physicality, as in their anatomy and physiology, than about their ecology, meaning their lifestyle and how they exist in the world. Their diet is pretty clear, though! Being browsers rather than grazers, they go for fruits, shrubs, and occasionally roots and fungi; every so often they'll even stand on their hind legs or knock over whole trees to eat the higher-hanging leaves and fruits.

Emela-ntouka are almost exclusively solitary. In fact, even going through the Repository, the Hunters' database, the largest group I could find on record only had 4 members; there are a couple reports of pairs or trios, but every other account (from Hunters and otherwise) is of loners. On the rare occasions with more than one, it usually seems to be a mother and her young; Hunters have also observed males fighting, but this doesn't seem terribly common. The breeding and reproduction habits of emela-ntouka are unknown, but since there don't seem to be many of them, they probably don't give birth very often and might only have one or two offspring at a time; we don't even know if they lay eggs or not, although they probably do, like other large reptiles.

Like rhinos and ceratopsians (a name which literally means "horned faces" in Greek), people mainly know emela-ntouka for their horns, which they use for display and, of course, for combat. Also like rhinos, emela-ntouka have an incredibly short fuse and will attack almost anything with very little warning or provocation; they have better vision than rhinos, but that doesn't change their tendency to charge first and ask questions later. And once an emela-ntouka has started a charge, there's not much that can survive the impact. Even African forest elephants, who have no predators besides humans, are not immune, so the name "emela-ntouka" is no exaggeration; these creatures can indeed be elephant killers.

And that's why, in late 2005, Heather's Guide, a man named Callum, contacted her about some strange events in the Republic of the Congo. Heather and I had moved in together only a few months after starting our relationship; although I'd been more than willing to pack up and move to Ireland, it eventually wound up that she came to live with me in Oklahoma. It was just us, and between hunts, we did a little bit of everything: lots of hikes, visits to my family, travel, movies, and time alone whenever we had the chance. It was before going to sleep one night that I first told Heather I loved her. Although I was probably close to knocking out, I wasn't asleep yet, and I definitely meant it. And you can probably imagine how I felt when she said the same thing to me. It wasn't like we started planning our lives together then and there, but I would be lying if I said that the idea didn't cross my mind. I was 32 and Heather was 34, and lots of people get married much earlier than that. But I wasn't planning on giving up Hunting anytime soon, so when Heather got the call from Callum about the Congo, I was ready to go.

Heather and I had been on a bunch of hunts together by then, and, without exaggerating, we made a damn good team. I had been to Africa twice already, but the eastern part of the continent; the Republic of the Congo is in the western central portion, hundreds of miles away, with a very different climate, wildlife, and cultures. Heather, on the other hand, had been through the broader Congo region pretty extensively in the past, conducting aquatic monster research on some of the large reptiles that inhabit the area's many rivers and marshes.

According to Callum, there had been disturbing reports coming from a couple teams of regular (as in non-Hunter) scientists in the western portions of the Central African rainforests: dead animals were turning up in their study areas, in quantities and from species that normally don't just get killed off. They had come across the bodies of adult African forest buffalo and forest elephants in alarming numbers, despite these animals having no real predators besides humans in the locale. But the dead elephants still had their tusks, so this wasn't ivory poaching, and neither elephants nor buffalo had been eaten, so it wasn't bushmeat hunting either; besides, no rational human goes after such large and dangerous animals for food anyways. Disease or old age might have been responsible, but all the dead animals had been healthy, and most were young adults, with the oldest being middle-aged. But some of the reports noted puncture wounds on the corpses, and that's where the Hunters took notice.

Emela-ntouka are rare and powerful, and we don't want any hyper-aggressive ones roaming the forest and threatening other vulnerable species like elephants. Worse, if there really was an aggressive emela-ntouka in the area, then the researchers would be in danger as well.

So pretty soon, Heather and I were on the ground in Brazzaville, the capital city of the Republic of the Congo. It was the peak of the rainy season, and when we stepped outside from the airport, I immediately felt like I'd walked into a hot shower that had just been turned off. I've never enjoyed heat or humidity, and this was some of the most intense I've ever experienced. We were nearly on the Equator, so I had been expecting this sort of climate, but it's different when you're actually in it.

"It's too hot," was all that I could say, and Heather just laughed.

"You're gonna love it even more when it starts raining," she replied. This was baffling. Heather was from *Ireland*, of all places; how was she handling this climate better than me?

Our car arrived a while later, and we were greeted by a lean but muscular man who introduced himself as Kembo. He was a little younger than us, and he wasn't a Hunter; instead, he worked with the group of researchers that we were going to visit. For the sake of safety and privacy, I can't tell you what institute or organization these scientists were from, but they were a mixed group: most were from West and Central Africa, and a few came from further away and overseas. Their job was mostly to study local elephant populations in the northern part of the country; again, I'm not going to tell you exactly where, but we were headed there because it was the site of the most recent killings.

The plan was to do some interviews and get as much information as possible from the researchers, then go out on the hunt; the weather and terrain would definitely make it rough, especially without someone who knew the exact location firsthand, but I was confident that Heather and I would get through it. In addition to information on the case, the scientists could give us suggestions on the environment and travel, which Heather also knew a good deal about, and although it's not any sort of substitute, we had also read up on the general area and spoken to other Hunters who were from here or had spent time here before. Even if it wasn't my home turf, I had also worked in other rainforests, and a lot of outdoor survival knowledge and skills are useful just about anywhere. And with a sturdy tent, plenty of food and water, high-caliber guns, and all the usual supplies, we were as well-equipped as possible in terms of gear as well as knowledge.

We helped Kembo pack our stuff into his jeep, and then hit the road heading straight for the research base. It was a long drive, since we practically had to cross the country; Brazzaville is all the way in the south, and we needed to go much further north. The jeep bumped steadily along, and although I managed to keep my eyes open for an hour or so after leaving the big city, it wasn't long before Heather and I were both out cold, leaning against each other in the backseat. I woke up a little while later to find it getting dark, and soon afterwards, we were driving through thick tree cover. Eventually we pulled up to a clearing in the forest, and Kembo told us that we had arrived.

The research base was mostly an assembly of big canvas tents on the clearing's edge; these were very large, semi-permanent structures, like the kind used for military field hospitals. There were also two shack-like buildings made of wood and an open pavilion with a stone floor and a thatched straw roof. Everything was well lit with electric lanterns and portable lights, but it didn't seem very busy. A few people were sitting underneath the pavilion, talking and eating dinner, but I assumed most others were in their tents.

Kembo took us to the pavilion and introduced us to the people there. One of them was the team leader, and since she didn't want to be named here, let's just call her Eva. She was from the nearby country of Gabon, and she welcomed us to sit with them for dinner; Heather and I had been ready to do our own thing, but Eva insisted that we eat with her and the other researchers. You guys know me: I'm kind of shy and not a huge fan of big groups. And especially in this sort of work context, I had wanted to keep some distance to avoid being asked a ton of questions. But Heather quickly accepted the invitation. Now, look, it's not like I'm the stoic black man or the stone-faced Indian, and she's not the happy-go-lucky Irish lass all the time, but the introvert-extrovert lines certainly went down that way!

While we ate a meal of mashed plantains and chicken with the scientists, Eva told us that we could ask her anything. I mainly used the chance to get an idea of the land and the different environments around us. As expected, we were pretty much surrounded by forest; there were some more open savannah-type areas to the east, but in almost all other directions, the terrain was thick jungle. Heather asked about swamps, and apparently there was indeed some marshland to the north; that could certainly be where an emela-ntouka would hang out. The researchers asked us a bit about ourselves, which we answered as politely as we could without saying too much, simply telling them that we were from a global organization and were here to look into the recent animal deaths. Most of them seemed a bit concerned and even suspicious, but they had every right to be; even if Sergio or Callum may have contacted them before our arrival, Heather and I still weren't giving them all the details. At the same time, I knew that once we dealt with the emela-ntouka, they would feel a lot better, even if they didn't know exactly what took place. That's just the nature of our job: most of the time, Hunting is thankless work, but we're all okay with that.

When Heather and I brought up the dead animals, the scientists all got very quiet and very serious. We were finished eating by then, so Eva took us into the biggest tent of the camp, which was set up as a command center or headquarters, with lots of desks, shelves, cabinets, and papers. There were also a few computers, and Eva pulled up some images on one of them for us. They were aerial GPS maps of the study area, marked with little dots and corresponding coordinates; I quickly noticed that most of the points were clustered together in a place that was north of the base.

"These are the locations where the bodies were discovered. All of the casualties have been either buffalo or elephant, and each was somehow killed. We know this because we found distinctive wounds on the bodies," Eva explained.

When we pressed, she said that each of the bodies had at least one large puncture wound somewhere, usually a vulnerable spot like the stomach or the chest; one elephant had even been gored through the neck. Eva emphasized that the stab wounds were very large, as if made by a big pole or even a tree branch. She and the other researchers were baffled and very concerned; elephants and buffalo are huge and powerful, and they don't just get randomly stabbed to death. I asked Eva if she had any tracking experience, and she said that although she knew a bit, we should really talk to Kembo, since he was one of their lead trackers. After making a mental note of that, we asked if she or anyone else had noticed anything unusual, especially in the immediate area around the bodies. She had personally seen many footprints in the area, but that didn't mean much; both elephants and buffalo are social animals, so their companions or herds would have left plenty of tracks if they had come over to investigate or grieve.

Heather and I figured that was all the info we'd get from Eva, and we were getting tired, so we said goodbye to her and went to find Kembo. He gave us a few more details about some of the specific dead animals, along with the news that a struggle had clearly taken place around most of the corpses: the ground in the vicinity had been churned up, leaving many footprints, few of which were clear. If they had been charged, then the elephants and buffalo could certainly have tried to fight back. Kembo also noted that most of the killings took place in and around the swamps to the north, something that we had seen in the GPS printouts. Finally, he had found sign: trails in the marshes that might have been elephant pathways, but were different somehow. He described seeing frequent gashes on trees, which elephants sometimes leave with their tusks, but not as often as this; he compared these to the marks made by a rhinoceros horn, but he knew very well that rhinos don't even live in the country in the first place. Unfortunately, the ground of the wet environment shifts so quickly that Kembo hadn't found any footprints, but that was almost irrelevant; all of the other datapoints were just more evidence of a rogue emela-ntouka, so we thanked Kembo and told him that we would search the swamps tomorrow.

Heather and I unloaded our stuff from the jeep and set up our tent off to the side of the clearing, a couple hundred yards away from everyone else. Before we went to sleep, Eva came over and handed us a few printed copies of the marked GPS images. I had been thinking about getting a fuller map in the morning, but Eva said that this was the closest thing they had. That was fine; Heather and I had our own GPS systems, so we could use those to get to the labeled coordinates. We said goodnight to Eva and settled into the tent for the night.

It was hot and muggy, so we left the tent flap open, screening it with a mosquito net Heather had brought. By the light of our headlamps, she and I marked up the printouts even further as we planned our approach. We were headed into the bush, as wilderness areas are called in Africa, Australia, and some other places that British colonists saw as being untamed; there would be no manmade trails or roads, so we'd have to make our own way to the swamps, our first main objective. The images included some data on elevation and tree cover, and we used that to draw a route that went through the lowlands and the clearings in the forest as much as possible. That way our progress would be faster, until we'd have to veer off into the thick jungle and marshy areas. When we finished laying out the plan, we went to sleep. All around us, the calls of frogs and insects were loud, but they made a great lullaby.

The next morning I woke up while it was still dark, a little restless from not being adjusted to the time zone change yet. Heather was still asleep, but I let her be and sat on the grass outside to catch up on taking notes and journaling; I also went over our makeshift map one more time. At some point I looked up across the clearing and saw a few large shapes in the darkness. Cautiously, I brightened my headlamp to see four big antelope staring at me with eyes that reflected whitish-green from the light. They all had spiral horns and gorgeous patterns of white stripes on dark brown fur, and after we had looked at each other for a while, they turned as one and walked off into the shadows. These antelope are called bongos, and it was cool to see some local creatures. Soon the sun came up, turning the whole forest gold; it was beautiful, and I took a few moments just to admire the quiet of the jungle in the morning. If it wasn't for the heat and humidity, I could see myself really loving it there.

Eventually, things in the camp and the jungle started to get lively. Birds began to call, and the researchers began emerging from their tents. Heather woke up too, and we started breaking down our tent and getting our supplies in order. Soon, Eva invited us over to the pavilion to have breakfast before we set out, and we were in the middle of eating when it started to rain; it wasn't coming down terribly hard, but it was enough that it would noticeably affect our progress. Despite my asking, nobody could really tell when it might let up; this was the *rain*forest, after all. Heather and I consulted and decided that it would be best just to go. We would move slowly and stay careful, but at least it was only a couple miles to the swamps. As always, we had made sure to bring gear and clothing that was waterproof, so our stuff would be fine in most cases less than a flood.

We said farewell to Eva, Kembo, and the other scientists, who all wished us good luck, before setting out for the swamps.

We started off trekking in a general northerly direction, using our solid boots to cross the now-muddy clearing. I won't bore you with the entire step-by-step journey, but it was actually more pleasant than I had been fearing. It was still hot, but the rain cooled things down significantly. After about an hour and a half, the rain stopped, and the sun and the heat returned with a vengeance, only for us to escape an hour or two later when we crossed the last of a few clearings and entered the jungle.

If you're not very familiar with tropical forests, they're one-of-a-kind places. Unlike the cartoons, you won't find super bright rainbow colors all over the place, because things in tropical jungles are mostly just green and brown; there are splashes of different colors here and there from fruits or flowers or fungus, but it's mostly brown bark and dirt along with green leaves and vines. There are thousands of plant species, including some absolutely gargantuan trees, whose broad leaves and branches block out the sun so completely that you can usually travel in complete shade for miles. So Heather and I were spared from the direct sunlight, although the heat and humidity weren't going anywhere. Thankfully, there weren't a ton of flies or mosquitos, although that was unfortunately bound to change as we approached the swamps. In a few parts of the forest, walking turned out to be easier than I had expected. Because the huge trees prevent almost all of the sunlight from reaching the forest floor, there isn't always a ton of ground cover in the understory; mosses, shrubs, and smaller leafy plants never disappear entirely, but it's more open than you might think.

There's also a ton of animals, of course; I've heard that half of all the world's species live in tropical forests, and if you go there, you can see for yourself. A tiny brown antelope called a bay duiker spotted us at one point and went bounding away through some nearby brush. A few minutes later, Heather spotted a green flap-necked chameleon on a branch, close enough that we could have grabbed it. The air around us was filled 24/7 with birdsong and insect calls, sometimes soft and distant and other times almost right in our ears. Sunbirds flitted through the air, and once we even noticed a perching hornbill with black and white feathers. We spotted some weaverbird nests too, which, yes, are literally woven from grass and reeds and hang down from the undersides of tree branches. That first day we could also hear grey parrots squawking off in the distance; these are the big, chatty kind that a lot of people have as pets, but here in the rainforest is where they come from and where they truly belong. You might also find it amusing that we got into a stare-off with a pair of gray-furred, white-nosed guenons called greater spot-nosed monkeys. The curious little guys were young, maybe siblings, and they followed us through the branches for a bit until an older one, maybe mom or dad, came up and pulled them away with a growl, which made Heather and I laugh. We saw so much just in those first hours, but I think you get the picture.

We eventually made it to the edge of the swamps, to a place where the ground started getting moist and muddy, and the amount of undergrowth and brush ramped up. Things were going to get more difficult from here. We tried to check our

GPS coordinates against the map, but as expected, the signal was practically nonexistent within the thick tree cover. Still, we had a good idea of where we were, and this was where we really needed to be on the lookout for emela-ntouka sign; any that we found was unlikely to be fresh, especially after the rain, but this wasn't exactly the most stealthy of animals.

On the way to the first kill site, I brainstormed two strategies for finding the emela-ntouka if we had trouble tracking it. The first would be to locate some elephants or buffalo, or maybe even hippos. If we stuck close to these animals, one of them might eventually do something to get on the emela-ntouka's nerves, and when the monster struck, we could strike back. The second idea was much riskier, at last for me and Heather. For this strategy, we could go to a spot close to many of the kill sites and make our presence there very obvious by making a lot of noise and putting up lots of bright colors. If this lure worked as intended, then the emela-ntouka would come to shut us up.

"That might just be insane enough to work," Heather said after I told her the second idea.

"I'll take that as a compliment, I guess," I replied, and she ruffled my hair with a laugh.

The lure idea would be more dangerous, but probably faster, and it would keep the animals out of harm's way much better. So the decision was made: if we couldn't track the emela-ntouka down, we would try to lure it in. Going forward, we searched for clues at different kill sites marked around the edges of the swamp. As I've said before, technology and I usually don't get along very well, so I let Heather deal with the GPS; she picked up our coordinates when and where she could, usually in clearings, and between the GPS and our makeshift maps, we were able to make our way to various destinations. Unfortunately, we couldn't turn up much; most of the killings had happened at least a few days ago, and between humidity, rain, and scavengers, there were few remains or tracks left. The skeletons were largely intact, and we also found some buffalo horns and small pieces of elephant tusk, but no footprints or scat. There were some fallen saplings and crushed undergrowth, however, which left no doubt of the cryptid's recent presence.

On the second night we camped on the edge of the treeline, alternating on watch as usual. Initially things were uneventful. I heard quite a bit of movement in the trees nearby at one point, but it didn't sound like anything very big. After being silent and holding still for a long time, I caught sight of a small sounder of giant forest hogs moving through the undergrowth, surprisingly quiet except for some soft snuffles and grunts, and the shifting and crunching of the foliage as they went by. I thought about waking Heather up to see them but ultimately decided against robbing her of precious sleeping time.

I think it was about two or three hours later that we first heard what might have been the emela-ntouka. I was asleep in the tent when I was awoken by a distant bellow, fairly high-pitched and lasting only for a second. I can't describe it very well, but it sounded a bit like the sort of bellowing roar that a cow or bull makes when angry or in pain. Heather came over to find me already up, and we waited to see if we'd hear the sound again. There was a ton of snapping and crashing in the trees, maybe a mile or more away, although trees and elevation can make it hard to gauge distance purely off of sound. A couple seconds later, the bellow came again, and both the calls and the sound of the rainforest getting torn to bits continued for about 10 minutes longer, before stopping for the rest of the night. It might have been an elephant or hippo, but I'd never heard either of them make that sort of vocalization; to be fair, I don't know all of their different sounds, but I just had a feeling that it was something else. Heather wasn't ready to rule out the possibility of the call being something other than a cryptid, but we both agreed that the creature seemed to be in a state of heightened emotion, maybe scared or angry or hurt.

Neither of us were able to sleep after that, so we stayed awake on watch together, until starting to pack up as the sun rose. In the orange light of dawn, a herd of 6 buffalo came to graze on the other side of the clearing, eating their breakfast as we were eating ours. While breaking down camp, Heather and I both agreed that we should head northwest, in the general direction of where we'd heard the noises during the night.

We walked that way for a while, and before long we came upon a place where it looked like a giant had taken the world's biggest weed-whacker to the jungle. There were trampled plants and broken branches all over the place, and huge chunks of soil had been torn up and scattered around. There was also an odor that didn't seem to come from anywhere in particular, like a mix of wet earth and rotting fruit; it wasn't intense, but it still made us wrinkle our noses, and at full strength it probably would have been enough to send us running.

"Christ, look at this!" Heather said, which I remember very well, because evidently her discovery hadn't been at the level of a full "Jesus, Mary, and Joseph". But it was certainly worth a curse word of my own, because the fallen tree Heather was pointing at had to be over 20 feet tall, with a trunk at least 5 feet across.

"If it knocked over something this big, then it was making a point," I said after we had looked at the tree for a bit.

Several smaller trees had been toppled too, with their roots and vines strewn around in a tangled mess. And on the edge of this brand-new clearing, two tree trunks that had been left standing were scarred with raw vertical wounds, colored pale yellow against the dull brown bark and gouged out by a single horn.

This amount of damage was tragic, but it also seemed seriously out of the ordinary. It was possible that the emela-ntouka had been displaying, and maybe marking its territory; many animals advertise their presence and their power by making lots of noise and causing damage to their surroundings, and sometimes mark their territory in similar ways. We didn't know if emela-ntouka were territorial, but it would make sense, and this could be evidence of that. But for reasons I can't quite explain, I just had a feeling that this cryptid was more likely to be sick. Even though emela-ntouka are notorious specifically because of their temper, extremely violent behavior like this can indicate both physical and mental illness. Heather wasn't so sure, but whatever the case, we needed to find the creature. Fortunately for us, it had left behind a clear trail, but it was a grim one.

We followed the swath of broken branches and trampled leaves, all while the underbrush grew thicker and the ground grew muddier. Soon we were well into the swamps, hopping and slogging from one patch of dry ground to another. The bugs were everywhere, which was the most annoying part of this whole journey; mosquitoes, gnats, and flies have an important role in nature, but that doesn't mean they aren't horrendously irritating. At least we had malaria medicine and vaccines for things like yellow fever and dengue.

After a while, the sounds of running water became audible ahead, and soon we emerged from a cluster of bushes onto a sunny embankment alongside a slow-moving stream. The opposite bank was covered thickly in brush and reeds, but the side we were on was more open, allowing us to get a good look at a group of big grayish-black blobs lying no more than a couple hundred feet away. For a second, I thought that we were looking at some big boulders, but then I noticed a few wiggling ears. Before either Heather or I could say or do anything, one of the "boulders" stood up on four short legs and turned towards us, opening a wide mouth with two enormous saber teeth.

We had walked right up onto a group of sleeping hippos, and one of them didn't seem to appreciate visitors.

"Back up, right now," Heather said quietly, and we immediately did just that.

The hippo that had gotten up started to step towards us, giving deep, loud grunts with its mouth still open, so we picked up the pace, and once we'd gotten back into the treeline, we turned and bolted in the opposite direction. We stopped after a while, and when we'd caught our breath, Heather burst out laughing; after a few seconds, so did I. It's always a good day when you aren't chased down and mauled by an angry hippopotamus. And if you think I'm joking, I'm absolutely not: hippos have enormous fangs, can weigh over 2 tons but still run as fast as a tractor, and kill more people than lions every year. Besides leopards and the emela-ntouka, hippos were probably the most dangerous thing to Heather and I in the area. But their presence gave us an idea.

It seemed that the emela-ntouka might come to that stream to drink, and when it did, the hippos were bound to react. We could stake out the trail that we had been following and attempt to lure in the cryptid; if it didn't come before nightfall, we could just camp there and take turns on watch as usual. And all the while, the hippos would act as an early alarm system if they saw our target.

But first, we had to make sure that the hippos wouldn't come our way when they got up to feed at night. We looked around, but it didn't seem like there was too much nearby that was good for hippos to eat; they'd probably head downstream to get food, south of us, so we wouldn't have to worry too much about any hippos crashing into our camp in the dark (could you imagine? What an absolute nightmare, even worse than the emela-ntouka...). Next, we found a spot with good visibility and two sturdy, climbable trees with big branches that overlooked the emela-ntouka's trail (unfortunately, I can't remember what kind they were). Heather and I both climbed each of the trees to test if they would support us and if we'd be able to shoot down from their branches. We would run to these trees and climb them if we had to make an escape.

We then took out the most colorful stuff we had. It wasn't much, because we always pack clothes that can blend in with the natural world and the environment where we work, but we had a few things that were bright red or yellow, mainly underwear and T-shirts, plus some assorted bandannas and rags. We fastened cords between the trees to form makeshift clotheslines, then tied on the items to hang in a way that they would stick out even at a distance; hopefully the artificial colors would be bright and out-of-place enough to get the emela-ntouka's attention.

We finished putting up the clotheslines in the afternoon with plenty of daylight left. The next step was to make a lot of noise and wait for the emela-ntouka to come to us. We seemed to be right in the middle of the monster's apparent range, so sooner or later, it would have to notice us, and hopefully respond aggressively (weird thing to hope for, I know). I found myself wishing that we could have set some traps, which was when I got an idea. The ground was too wet and soft to dig any kind of sustainable pit or trench, but we could put up some stakes. I had brought my combat tomahawk along, and although it's made for fighting, it does serve as a decent woodcutting axe and general tool. There were plenty of trees and logs all around the swamp, so while Heather set up our tent and kept watch over the camp, I started gathering some wood.

We alternated singing as time went on; neither of us have great voices by any means, but it was a fun way to keep entertained and create more of a disturbance like we wanted. Heather mainly sung a bunch of traditional Irish stuff, which I thought sounded beautiful, but I'm obviously biased. She'd also introduced me to U2, who had quickly become our favorite band, so we had a singalong together from some of their albums for a while. At one point I did an award-winning rendition of the Star-Spangled Banner, which I could barely finish because we were laughing so hard at how horrible it was. The whole time I chopped up a bunch of the sturdiest branches and logs I could find, sharpening the ends to make stakes. We placed the stakes at a few key points along the trail and around the area, including some at the bases of our two escape trees. Heather and I would be able to swerve around them, but there was no way the emela-ntouka could. We didn't expect the stakes to be lethal, but they could definitely do some damage and slow it down.

Eventually the sun began to set, with no sign of the cryptid. Disappointing, but we just planned to do the same thing the next day. Before dinner, we made a quick trip to the river to see if the hippos were still there, which they were; I guess they'd been able to tolerate our horrible singing. Once we had checked on our roly-poly friends, it was back to camp for the night. Everything was calm until sometime early in the morning, just as the sky was starting to turn red. I was standing watch, and from somewhere to the south I heard the hippos start to go *nuts*. Hippos make a ton of noise, especially when they're angry, upset or scared, and there was a whole lot of honking, wheezing, and squealing coming from the river. It could have been a crocodile, or even just a fight, but my senses were telling me otherwise. I went to wake up Heather, but she was already out of the tent and grabbing her rifle. A new sound reached my ears, and I took a few steps out from the camp. Something was moving through the foliage far away...something *big*, and headed straight for us.

"Okay, let's get ready to run for the escape trees. Something's about to be on us," I told Heather.

I've joked about her skin being so pale that it practically glowed in the moonlight, but this time it allowed me to see the determination on her face. She nodded, before grabbing me and kissing me hard; after all, every fight could be our last. "I love you, Sam. We can do this."

"I love you too. We can. We've got this," I replied, and I meant every word.

We looked back at the trees to the south, where it sounded like a freight train was nearly on top of us. What happened next was very fast, but here's how I remember it. First, a baby and an adult hippo came crashing through the trees in front of us, probably a mother and child, eyes glowing red in the light from our headlamps. They slowed down upon spotting us, and then the full-grown one quickly swerved to the side, west towards the river; the baby stumbled, righted itself, and splashed through the mud after the adult. But behind the hippos was the true freight train, a 7-foot tall silhouette barreling through the rainforest directly towards us.

The emela-ntouka came into full view a second later, its huge, copper-colored frame thundering out of the trees a few hundred feet away. It glared straight at me and Heather, and its ear-like frills flapped out on either side of its head, flushing red with blood as it gave a low rumble. Heather and I fired in unison, aiming for the emela-ntouka's small, black eyes. It flinched and staggered backwards with a surprised grunt, then, with zero hesitation, lowered its enormous horn and charged. We turned and sprinted for our escape trees, weaving between the stakes to put them between us and the monster; the ground shuddered underfoot, and behind us we could hear the emela-ntouka's breath pumping like an enormous pair of bellows. It would have overtaken me if I had stayed on the ground for much longer, but thankfully I reached my tree a few seconds later; climbing is hard when you're carrying a rifle, but I had practiced this.

The emela-ntouka let out a deeper version of the roar we'd heard several nights ago, and right as I hauled myself onto a big branch where I had perched earlier, the entire tree shook as the monster rammed into it. Gunfire cracked out from Heather's tree, and the emela-ntouka rumbled angrily. A second later it hammered into my tree again, producing the last sound I wanted to hear: splintering wood. I looked down to see that at least two of the stakes were sticking out of the monster's scaly hide, but it seemed completely unfazed. It backed up a few steps and looked up at me with a huff, before lowering its head and rushing forward again. This impact nearly flung me off of my branch, and now the wood began to groan as well as snap; I had thought this tree would hold up, but I was quickly beginning to reconsider my assumption.

I adjusted my grip on my rifle and fired down at the back of the emela-ntouka's neck, causing it to bellow and step backwards, tossing its head up and down. That hit should have killed the monster, or at least dropped it, but evidently I didn't have a clean shot on any of its vulnerable areas. Heather fired a few times before making a long, piercing whistle to get the emela-ntouka's attention; although it looked like a couple of her shots made it flinch, it didn't even look back at her. Instead, it charged my tree again, and this time I felt the whole thing tilt beneath me; with one or two more hits like that, it was going down.

I continued firing until I had to reload, still aiming for the monster's neck. Between the bullet wounds and the stakes, the emela-ntouka's light brown scales were drenched red with blood, and even in the heat of the moment, it made my chest hurt to see how much pain it was in. For both its sake and ours, this needed to end quickly.

The emela-ntouka rammed my tree one final time, and the whole thing lurched to a nearly 45-degree angle from the ground, forcing me to grab onto the trunk as the branch beneath me went vertical. Then the monster reared up onto its hind legs, pressed its front feet against the trunk, and started to push. I finished reloading and tried to get off another shot at the monster's head and neck, but the entire tree was collapsing, and me along with it. I braced myself against the bark, and when the trunk was only about 5 or 6 feet above the forest floor, I jumped off. The muddy ground cushioned the landing a bit, but my legs still went numb for a second from the impact; it hurt, but I pushed through the pain and started running in Heather's direction. I might not be able to climb up to her, but she would have a better shot if I lured the cryptid that way.

I spun around and saw the emela-ntouka still thrashing through the branches of the toppled tree about a hundred feet away, tossing leaves and dirt into the air with its horn. It must have lost me after I jumped, and now was our best chance. I aimed my rifle and gave a loud shout of "HEY!" The monster whipped around, flaring its frills, and again, Heather and I fired as one right at the creature's eyes. The emela-ntouka made another high-pitched squeal and staggered to the side. It brought down its horn, but only a few swaying steps into its charge, it gave an exhausted groan and collapsed onto its side. Mercifully, it didn't get up. Still catching my breath, I walked over to Heather's tree, where she had already clambered down and now started checking me for wounds or injuries.

"I'm okay. Just a little shaken. I'm fine," I told her.

She looked noticeably relieved when I said that. "You're sure? Can I give you a hug?"

I nodded, and we squeezed each other in a tight hug for a moment, before going over to the fallen cryptid. The emela-ntouka was massive, and we measured it as nearly 26 feet long from nose tip to tail tip. Aside from some slightly darker patches, its scales were a uniform light brown, the shade of coffee when it's been mixed with milk; when I don't have a tan, my own skin tone is about the same color. And also like me, this emela-ntouka had quite a few scars across its body; many were long and broad, possibly made by elephant tusks, hippo teeth, or even the horns of other emela-ntouka. Speaking of which, this one's horn was almost 4 feet long and covered in dents and scratches from all the damage it had done over the years.

It can be tough to determine the sex of many reptiles, and it's the same with emela-ntouka. But from what we could see, this was a male, old, angry, and venting his rage on anything that got on his nerves; he could have been sick, as I had suspected, or maybe a younger and stronger emela-ntouka had even pushed him away from a better territory or mating opportunities. While I was doing the usual short prayer, I made sure to apologize to him for causing him so much pain. Heather and I were both pretty dismayed about not being able to finish the fight faster; unfortunately, that isn't always possible, especially with such an enormous creature. But he must have been very unhappy, and whatever the case, he wouldn't be hurting anyone else anymore.

We retrieved our bullets from the body where we could, took a few chips of horn and patches of skin for analysis by our Guides, and then decided to just let it be; between the climate and the scavengers, the jungle disposes of remains quickly.

Back at the research base, there was a working phone line that we used to contact the nearest Hunter cleanup crew; they were to the north in Cameroon, but we gave them the coordinates of the body and the fight scene. Eva, Kembo, and the scientists were concerned about me and Heather, but we reassured them that we were fine and that, more importantly, the animals would be too. They seemed too wary to ask for the full details, but that was for the best; we had helped them out, and that's what counted.

Both Heather and I would have liked to stay in the rainforest for a while longer, because despite the heat, it was really cool there. Unfortunately, we'd probably overstayed our welcome with the scientists, and I doubt regular camping is allowed in that area (not to mention that rogue cryptids are far from the only dangers in the rainforest). So we said goodbye to everyone, and Kembo drove us back to Brazzaville. We went around the city for a little bit before heading back to the US, and that was that. I would definitely love to go back to the Republic of the Congo sometime, because it's a gorgeous place with a lot to experience.

Anyway, that's about all I've got for you guys this time. We're nearing the end of these letters, and I've got a big one planned for next time. It's probably going to take me a long time to finish it, but I think it'll be good for all of us for me to share it. For now, I'm just enjoying reading your questions and thoughts, so thanks again for all of your comments. I'm excited to hear more! We'll talk more soon. This has been Sam White Owl, signing out.

LETTER 9 – WECHUGE

CANADA

Written November 2020

Hey, everyone, it's Sam White Owl again. First, I'd like to apologize for the long delay in getting this ninth letter to you guys. I suppose I owe you a bit of an explanation, so here's what happened. In mid-September I got invited to be a leader for a sort of training seminar. Most capital-H Hunters get their training as apprentices to more experienced members, and although some places have group lessons for this purpose, there's no Hunter academy or anything like that. But recently, some older Hunters in the western US got interested in establishing a more formal training program. They arranged for us to do an extended wilderness training seminar, where my job was to help teach and supervise the students.

We did all sorts of lessons, from tracking to advanced survival skills to weapons training. We did lots of book work too, going over case studies, field reports, and post-action writeups; a lot more paperwork than you might think goes into being a Hunter, although our Guides handle most of it. We even brought out a psychologist to talk about and prepare for some of the more abstract aspects of capital-H Hunting; as you might imagine, lots of Hunters struggle with mental illness and psychological conditions as a result of our work, and although I don't talk about it much, I've struggled a lot in this area as well. I wish we had done more to address this stuff earlier, but it's great to see the organization making a more active effort now. That's part of what this letter will be about, actually.

We also had a very interesting and pretty troubling encounter while we were out there, which I can tell you about some other time. In any case, we were pretty much off the grid for this training. That was part of the goal: to get the students more acclimated to the types of environments and conditions where they'd often be working for extended periods. So no beds, Internet, or cellphone signal for the duration of the training, just like how it usually is on a task. That's more or less why I've been gone for so long. But I don't expect any more big holdups like that. However, this is the second-to-last letter that I agreed upon with Swamp Dweller. So as sad as it may be, you'll probably only have to wait for one more after this.

With that being said, let me start this letter off by addressing a specific viewer question: Have I ever been on a hunt that I regret? Only one, and that's the story I'm going to tell now.

This time we're going to be talking about one of the rarest and most dangerous creatures on the planet: the wechuge. There aren't many creatures in this world that I actively dislike, cryptid or otherwise. But I make an exception for wechuge, and I fear them more than almost any other monster. Like with the word "wendigo", the plural of the word "wechuge" is the same as the singular: there's no "s" at the end. The similarities between these two go way beyond naming conventions, though. Both are creatures from the traditions of different Indigenous groups of the northern United States and Canada. Both are living representations of ice, cold, hunger, and starvation. And both have an insatiable appetite for flesh, especially that of humans.

For the Dane-zaa people, a wechuge is the end result of a human who was possessed by one of the great spirit animals and became overwhelmed by their power, growing "too strong". I don't know if this is true or not, but the Hunters have no other definitive answer as to the origins of wechuge; as with many other cases, the old tales are the best source of information here. Whether their roots are human or not, wechuge certainly have a humanoid body structure. They stand between 8 and 15 feet tall, with disproportionately long arms ending in hands with immense claws, and feet that simply resemble larger versions of humans', much like with wendigo. Unlike wendigo, however, wechuge are covered with fur, several inches long and usually gray or jet-black in color; this fur grows longer around their necks, shoulders, and arms, flowing out like a mane. Wechuge heads are oversized versions of the skulls of predatory mammals, typically wolves, but some have also been seen with bear and lynx skulls. The upper canine teeth on these skulls are typically oversized, and these enormous fangs are a wechuge's primary weapons, along with their claws and their immense strength, speed, and cunning.

Wechuge seem to be active only in the winter, traveling with the snows and storms of Canada and very rarely the northern US. This climate provides them one more natural method of both attack and defense. In addition to claws and teeth, wechuge seem to have some affinity for ice itself, often appearing with layers of it coating parts of their bodies or with enormous icicles protruding like spines from their fur. Ice from a wechuge is supernaturally durable, and they use it as both armor and weaponry. In most cases, fire is the only strong countermeasure to this.

Wechuge ecology is very much like those of wendigo or Tall Deer. They're permanently ravenous predators, with an existence that seems to revolve entirely around hunting, killing, and eating. Hunters have only ever observed wechuge on the attack, striking out from blizzards and snowstorms to slaughter and devour their victims. They'll eat anything with a heartbeat, and frequently go out of their way to seek out humans in particular. The Hunters have a kill-on-sight mandate for wechuge; their very existence relies on nonstop, indiscriminate slaughter on a scale that can destabilize entire ecosystems. As brutal as it might seem, it's to protect humans, cryptids, any other living beings, and the environment as a whole that we don't hesitate to slay wechuge. It's far from easy or pleasant, but there is no mercy when it comes to these monsters.

I learned this lesson for myself in the winter of 2008. Around this time, jobs in Canada had been increasing in number, and lots of them had made a big difference and been pretty lucrative and fulfilling for me and Heather. To get closer to the action, we decided to move way up north to a spot in Washington state, just off the Canadian border. We also weren't too far from where my dad lives, so it was nice to still be close to family. I've always liked Washington a lot, and it was exciting to introduce Heather to my dad and show her around some of the areas I'd visited in the past.

Our house was also great, being situated on a high woodland slope, with mountains in the distance and a lake pretty close by. It was a beautiful place, especially in the fall when tracts of the forest became yellow and orange and red like wildfire. One of those autumn days I thought about taking Heather to this one particular ridge that overlooked the lake and asking her to marry me. I never did. I think it's because, honestly, taking that extra step never felt necessary to either of us. We knew that we loved each other, and that's always been enough. I think I've always been a bit scared of such a permanent contract too. Like Dak had made me consider back on the Indian Ocean: when you're a Hunter, it's so easy to lose everything in an instant.

So I never proposed to Heather at the ridge over the lake, although from time to time I still think about it. It's a pretty magical spot. We spent lots of time there and in the other parts of the woods around our house in our free time. There were no cryptids in the area, at least not that we ever found, and there were no trails either, so nobody ever interrupted our time alone or otherwise bothered us. All in all, it was a great place to rest, recuperate, and de-stress in between tasks, which is really the best you can hope for in a home when you're a field Hunter.

Heather and I had been living there for quite a while when winter of 2008 rolled around, and along with it, an urgent request from Lodge administration in Saskatchewan. When Sergio informed me of the distress call, I remember getting genuine physical chills. It was just like the situation with the wendigo a few years earlier, and if you've heard my previous letter about that, then you'll know it was *not* a fun experience.

And this case seemed to be shaping up to be even worse: several dead bodies of both large animals and humans had been found in the woods, their deaths coinciding with heavy snowfall and high winds. There were hardly any actual bodies to speak of, though; the remains were little more than gory scraps of clothing, fur, or the occasional bone, accompanied by gallons upon gallons of blood splashed across the rocks and trees. Each of the victims had been completely devoured. This manner of death could have been the work of a few types of monster, including wendigo. But the relationship to weather patterns suggested something even more alarming: wechuge.

To be frank, when I heard this, I was hesitant to take the job. I thought back to my wendigo hunt and got a sick, shaky feeling. This time we might be going after something even more dangerous, and instead of Zack, it might be me, or Heather. Ever since my earliest training days, my mom has told me repeatedly that there's no shame in turning down a job if you truly aren't prepared for it. And I have indeed turned down cases in the past, whether it was due to lack of experience, lack of knowledge, lack of preparation, or whatever else. Here, however, there were so, so many other lives on the line besides mine. There was Heather's, and those of any other Hunters who might answer the call for help. And yet there were also the lives of all the other people and animals that the wechuge would take if it wasn't taken out as soon as possible. Having to weigh lives like this is a terrible burden, but Hunters have to do it with every job. In this case, I'm still not sure if I made the correct choice.

I told Sergio that I would get back to him ASAP, and then sat down to talk things over with Heather. We had always been very open about our thoughts and feelings to each other, and we'd had this same conversation before other jobs too, but it was never easy. So we sat on the couch in the family room, and I don't remember who spoke first, but Heather felt the same way I did. We had a responsibility both to each other and to everything we protect as Hunters. We held hands and sat in silence for a minute, before calling Sergio back and telling him that we were going to take up the hunt.

Soon Heather and I were in a remote hunting lodge in the Saskatchewan woodlands, and when I say "remote", I mean it: the only way to get there was to fly in on a float plane or seaplane, landing on top of the lake where the lodge sat. In the winter when these lakes freeze over, the planes exchange their floats for skis and touch down on the ice, which is how we arrived. There were no roads for miles, much less towns, but a group of reckless winter hunters (the regular, lowercase kind), had recently gone missing in the area. Combined with a recent snowstorm near the lodge and close proximity to the other kill sites, this seemed like the perfect place to rendezvous and begin the hunt.

By the time Heather and I showed up, there were already two other members of our organization at the lodge. They introduced themselves as Phil and Dana. Phil was an older guy, tall and lean, with broad shoulders and a dark beard that was mostly gray. Dana was much younger, probably even younger than Heather and I, with blond hair and a ton of tattoos. Both were Canadian Hunters from the general central region of the country. Nakia arrived just a bit after me and Heather. She visibly had at least some First Nations blood, but I never asked which tribe she was from. Nakia was the last one who had responded to the distress call, so soon as she arrived, we got going.

Each of us grabbed one of the maps that the lodge had; they had been updated within the last 2 years, so we expected they should still be accurate. The missing people had last checked in from somewhere to the east, the same direction from which the snowstorm had initially come, before it had veered south and disappeared into the woods there. With that being our best lead, we all agreed to start by heading south.

To cover more ground and increase our chances of finding sign, we decided to split into two groups. Heather and I would be one, and the remaining trio would be the other. To stay in contact, Dana and Heather carried matching radios. In the forest, they would have a clear signal up to around 3 and a half miles; any further than that and the connection would get spotty. The hunting lodge also had a satellite phone, which are standard equipment for Hunters these days, but weren't very common back then. Phil essentially commandeered this one, which would allow us to communicate with the outside world without having to get to a landline or somewhere with cellphone signal. If the wechuge continued to head south, it would eventually come to towns, and that was what we were going to prevent.

We set out from the lodge in the late afternoon, immediately splitting into our two teams. I'll cut out some of the more boring day-by-day details and just say that Heather and I were the ones to come across the first clue. And it was a big one: a stretch of ruined forest, with tons of downed trees and broken branches, to the point where it looked like a bulldozer (or an angry emela-ntouka) had come through. We radioed the others and met up to follow the tragic trail as it plowed southwards. After a half mile or so, thankfully, the damage to the forest decreased steadily, and the snow covering the ground thinned. Walking became easier, and before long, a trail of enormous human-like footprints came into view ahead of us. We did a brief examination but didn't linger; we were on the right trail and we didn't want to lose time.

Our pace was good for as long as the light was, but as the sun started going down, we made camp rather than trying to push it. The forest was quiet except for the creaking and rustling of the trees in the wind; this is completely normal for this environment in the wintertime, but it was more than a little creepy with the knowledge that the wechuge was out there somewhere. The atmosphere in camp was tenser than on almost any other hunt I've been on. Nobody joked around or told stories, and we hardly even talked beyond what was necessary. It could have been that Phil, Dana, and Nakia were just quiet by nature, but I'm certain that we were all at least a little on edge.

I don't remember having either dreams or nightmares that night, but it was a rough one. We didn't bring individual tents; instead, we built one big circus tent-style shelter from tarps that we tied together and lashed to trees. We each had our individual sleeping bags beneath the shelter while one of us kept watch outside, and just about the only nice part of the situation was that divvying up watch duty between five people gave each of us a good amount of time to sleep. It was warm in the shelter despite being freezing outside, so I was physically comfortable; mentally, however, I couldn't get my brain to stop running through everything I'd heard about wechuge. I was able to use some of the breathing techniques I've learned over the years to settle myself, but then I would look over to Heather's sleeping bag in the dark and it would all start up again. I did manage to get *some* sleep, but it was crappy, and when we woke up early the next morning, I still felt tired.

It might sound weird, but it was actually a relief to get going on the trail again; I usually feel better having something to do, and I quickly got in the zone by continuing to track our target. Sometime in the early afternoon the trail led us to a cavern in the hillside, with an awful scene at the entrance. The snow was churned up and splashed red with sickeningly large puddles and streaks of blood. Clumps of brown and black fur were scattered all around, and here and there, chunks of ice stuck out of the snow. Brown bear and wechuge footprints were muddled up and scattered around, but only one set of tracks left the area, and I'm sure you can guess whose. Even woken up from hibernation, a grizzly bear is one hell of a fighter, and yet the wechuge hadn't left even a single bone behind. I don't know if any of us were really surprised, but it was still disheartening.

After assessing the area, we moved on, and eventually the wechuge's trail led us to a frozen river that we walked along for a few more hours, keeping the water to our right, the northwest. At some point along the trek, there was suddenly a huge commotion from somewhere on the other bank: through the trees came barking, yipping, and crying that I instantly recognized as wolves. Wolves that were absolutely terrified.

"Guns up!" someone shouted (I think it was Phil), but I had already gotten the memo.

I whipped out my rifle and aimed at the treeline across the water, squinting in the fading light to catch any hint of movement. The wolves were still barking at something, and a few seconds later we heard what it was. The wechuge's cry started out as a high-pitched shriek or scream, before deepening into a bestial roar that rattled my chest and the ground underfoot, even from a distance. The roar lasted for what seemed like forever, but was probably about 10 seconds, followed by wood crashing and snapping as the monster rushed through the trees. The wolves yelped and cried out, and their calls faded away into the distance. After a few seconds, everything was silent.

"We need to move," Heather spoke up after a moment.

Shaken but motivated, we picked up our stuff and continued down the river, moving fast. By the time we found a ridge to camp on, the sun had almost completely vanished. We put two people on watch instead of one, but none of us really slept well anyways. I kept having the same nightmare on repeat, where an iceberg ripped the shelter open and the massive arm of the wechuge came reaching in with long, clawed fingers. Every time, I would snap awake and roll over to look for Heather, who was of course in the same spot, lying quietly next to me in her own sleeping bag. The last time this happened, she was awake, and she just reached out a hand to hold mine. After that I slept a bit better, at least until Nakia burst into the shelter in the dead of night.

"It's snowing," she said, with fear audible in her voice.

We all armed ourselves and stepped out to where Nakia and Phil were standing, looking out into the dark. The wind had picked up significantly, and its whooshing and the rattling of tree branches blocked out most other sounds. The fire had nearly been snuffed out entirely, and since the moon was covered by clouds, the only other light came from our headlamps. And true to Nakia's word, snow had begun to fall. At first, I could see the individual flakes, but in what felt like seconds, it was coming down practically in sheets, smothering both sight and sound. Phil took a few steps out towards the treeline, fiddling with the night vision goggles on his face.

"Can't see a damn thing, even with night vision. Snow's too thick. I don't like this," he said after a minute.

"Bad weather doesn't necessarily equal an attack," Dana said, but that didn't make things much better.

"Let's stay quiet and keep listening," Heather said, and I felt proud when everyone followed her suggestion.

I don't know how long after this it was that Phil got hit, but I would guess that it was only a minute or two. I just remember us all waiting, trying to see anything through the storm. Then something moved in the darkness and there was a low thumping sound. Phil collapsed into the snow and the rest of us immediately opened fire in the direction of the movement. A distorted howl echoed out over the gunshots, and for a brief moment, our incendiary rounds lit up the silhouette of a colossal figure as they impacted. Then the blizzard swirled again and the wechuge vanished. I glanced over to Phil to see him still collapsed, blood soaking into the snow around his crumpled form.

"Keep your eyes up! I'm checking Phil," I called.

I crouched next to Phil, but almost recoiled when I saw what had happened. An enormous icicle, maybe 3 feet long, had been thrown like a javelin and speared through the lower portion of his chest cavity, going in through the front and emerging in a bloody spike from his back. His breathing was wet, ragged, and wheezing, and from the position of the icicle and the amount of blood drenching his clothing and the snow around him, it was painfully clear that there was nothing I could do besides say "I'm sorry". Phil started to reply, but between the wind, his gasping, and the blood leaking from his mouth, all I could make out was the word "finish" before he stopped talking. After a few more choking gurgles, he went silent again, and this time, he stayed that way.

"Phil's dead," I stated, standing shakily and taking a look at everyone. All of us were still wound up, and Dana specifically looked like she was in shock.

"What's our next move? Wait for it to come back?" Nakia asked.

"It might come back for Phil. Or it might still be wary of our guns," Heather said.

We had to stop and think. I remember looking at my watch and figuring that we had a few hours until daylight. Based on the timing of its confrontations with the wolves and the bear, our target didn't seem to prefer the day or the night; it was likely just as active no matter what time it was. In any case, it was still dark and snowing, and there was no way to move safely in these conditions. Where would we even go? And yet we couldn't camp without the protection of a fire, a shelter, or our sleeping bags. And on top of all this, we didn't know where the wechuge was.

"We might try ambushing it," Nakia finally suggested. I wasn't sure, so I looked to Heather, who shrugged.

"We could move Phil to the hollow at the bottom of this ridge. The wechuge will have to be down there to get him. We lay low on the ridgeline and fire on the bastard when it comes," Heather said.

It sounded like the best plan we had, so we took it. While Heather stayed with Dana to soothe her and get her moving, Nakia and I half-carried and half-dragged Phil down the ridge and into the hollow. I felt sick, and I resolved that I wouldn't let the wechuge set a single claw on him; it seemed like the least I could do for him. We laid his body a few hundred yards into the hollow at the bottom of the ridge we were camped on; the only reasonable way to get to it would be to come through the entrance of the hollow, straight in. Once we were finished positioning Phil, we regrouped with Heather and Dana. I was still getting over what I'd just had to do, but I was still in fighting shape, and luckily Dana was looking better, so we put her with Nakia as her partner. The two of them stayed on the ridgeline where our camp was, in the trees overlooking the hollow. Heather and I went to the other side of the area and positioned ourselves on the opposite ridgeline. We couldn't see our partners, but we could see Phil and the entrance to the hollow. We all had clear shots; when the wechuge came, we'd be ready.

I'm used to waiting in silence for long periods, but that night, I was tensed up the whole time. I felt like the wechuge might hurl another icicle at any moment, spearing another one of us like it had impaled Phil. I felt like a total rookie. But I did my best to keep breathing, and every so often Heather and I would squeeze each other's shoulders or hands. Never once did

I see any trace of fear in her eyes or body language; I knew that she had to be scared, though, so maybe she was trying to reassure me. But she'd always been the better Hunter, and that night I could see it.

After what felt like hours of waiting, the wechuge appeared at the entrance to the hollow below us. The light was horrible between the falling snow and the lack of moonlight, and since we had our headlamps turned off to remain hidden, all I really saw was a slightly darker patch of shadow move behind the curtain of snow. Heather tapped me right as I saw this, and we both readied our rifles. Maybe about a minute later, two glowing yellow lights came into view through the dark, more than 10 feet above the ground. Slowly, the eyes moved forward and the shadowy form of the wechuge came with them. It moved silently as a ghost, and I could only guess that the wind was drowning out its sounds. Slowly and deliberately, it walked towards Phil's body, and when it had gotten nearly directly across from me and Heather, I raised my gun. Just as I put my crosshairs on the head of the silhouette, either Nakia or Dana fired first from the other side of the hollow. The wechuge took a quick step backwards, whipping around to search the opposite ridgeline. Heather and I squeezed our triggers, and gunfire rang out from both sides of the hollow. For a brief moment, flames from our incendiary rounds burst out across the wechuge's chest and neck. The firelight gave me a glimpse of glistening ice and black fur, and saber teeth on a gigantic wolf's skull. An instant later, the cryptid vanished back into the snow, and I heard its pained howl come from somewhere off in the trees. Heather and I sprang up and turned on our headlamps.

"It's going to be light soon. I say we follow it," I stated. Ordinarily, between the snow and leaving our supplies behind, I wouldn't have suggested this. But the wechuge was seriously injured, and we had it on the run. We could end this.

Heather seemed to think for a second before replying. "Are you sure?"

The question made me briefly second-guess myself. Like I'd been thinking earlier, she *was* the better Hunter. But something inside of me was shouting that we needed to press our advantage. We were too close to lose our target now.

"Yes. This is our chance," I answered, meeting Heather's gaze under the shine of her headlamp. She was silent for a moment before she nodded.

"Right then. I'll radio the other two and we'll track this thing down," she said.

The sky started to brighten significantly as we began following after the wechuge. A few minutes was all it took for Heather and I to find the cryptid's trail; the footprints were deep enough that the wind and snowfall wouldn't wipe them out for some time. After radioing this over to Dana and Nakia, we made it a few hundred feet before the wind picked up heavily, blowing clouds of snow into our path. In a matter of seconds, it was a total whiteout, with nothing visible past a few feet or so. I stopped dead in my tracks, my mind suddenly screaming that I had made the wrong choice. I felt my heart thumping a million beats per minute and my stomach sinking. Heather's voice rang out in my ears.

"Listen!"

I strained my ears to pick up anything besides the howling of the wind. For what felt like forever, there was nothing else.

And then from my 1 or 2 o'clock, I heard the unmistakable crunch of snow. Heather and I immediately turned, guns raised, and as I spun around, something slammed into the back of my left leg, stabbing into my calf. I dropped to my knees in the snow, literal ice-cold pain shooting through my leg; I didn't even need to look to know that I'd been hit by another icicle that the wechuge had thrown. Doing my best to ignore the freezing pain, I fired a few shots in the direction we'd heard the noise come from before. Heather had already done the same, and then I saw her aiming in a different direction out of the corner of my eye. Branches snapped from off to the left, and Heather and I both hit the ground to avoid any icicles. But the wechuge was finished with ranged combat.

In one impossibly fast moment, the snow whirled and the wechuge burst out on all fours from the white emptiness to my right, a completely different direction than either Heather or I were expecting. We whipped our rifle barrels around to take aim, but in that moment, I realized that we were just too *slow*. It happened too fast for me to fire. Too fast for me to make a difference. The wechuge stood up to its full height, Heather fired a single shot, and then the monster swung one enormous, clawed hand. Heather was thrown backwards into the snow at the base of a tree, but my gaze didn't even follow her. Every one of the countless times I've replayed these few seconds in my mind, it always happens in slow motion. And I can't believe that even my eyes were too slow to follow Heather as she fell. But like I said, it just happened too fast for me to act. Too fast for me to save her.

Heather's blood splashed across the snow, and I closed my eyes and fired. Heather's last round had knocked the wechuge off-balance; she'd given me a perfect opening, and I took it, squeezing the trigger again and again, as if shooting my rifle was the only thing I knew how to do. My first shot staggered the wechuge, and by the third or fourth, it was screaming a high-pitched cry. The sparks and heat from my rounds lit up the creature's long mane like a torch, and before I ran empty, my last shot chipped bone off of the monster's skull. Its right eye went dim, the yellow glow guttering out to leave only a black socket. Then the wechuge was gone, its shrieking and the glow of the flames vanishing into the snowstorm. I didn't even think about following it. I feel like a bad Hunter saying that now, but at the time I wasn't thinking purely like a Hunter. I was thinking like a human.

Before I reached Heather, I knew what I was going towards. I was hoping with everything I had that I was wrong, that maybe some miracle had occurred, but I think I knew what I was going to find. I limped to the tree where Heather had impacted to find her struggling to sit up against the trunk. I helped her do so and realized that she was still clutching her rifle somehow. I put the gun in her lap, then looked up at her and confirmed my fears. Heather's lower torso had been slashed by the wechuge's claws, and blood soaked her clothing and the snow around her. The wounds weren't even terribly deep, but they were long, and there was no way we'd be able to stop the blood loss in time. There was nothing I could do to save her.

I think Heather already knew this too, because she just looked into my eyes and lifted her hands to hold my face. I think she was too weak to say anything, and for my part, all I remember saying were the words "Heather...I'm sorry..." over and over. At some point, she put a finger to my lips, and I stopped speaking. She took my face in her hands again, and I could see in her face and in her eyes that she was calm. I think she wanted me to be calm too. I nodded, and she gave me a sad smile. Then her storm-gray eyes drifted closed and her hands fell from my face, leaving only her blood on my cheeks. I gave her one last kiss on the forehead and hugged her to me. I didn't care about the blood soaking through my jacket and my pants. I just didn't want to let her go.

I don't know how long I sat there holding Heather, but at some point the blizzard must have died down, because I heard Nakia and Dana come rushing up. They said something to me, but I don't remember what. I don't even remember crying. I was just in a daze, lost, and I stayed like that for a long time. As much as all the details before this point are engraved into my mind, all the details for quite a while afterwards are essentially one big blur. Somehow, someone took Heather from me, and I found my way back through the forest to the lodge we'd flown into. Later on, I learned that Nakia and Dana had tried to track the wechuge down, but even though it was grievously wounded, they had eventually lost its trail and pulled back. It was gone.

I returned to the US, but not to Washington. I didn't want to deal with the memories there. Instead, I went all the way back to Oklahoma and showed up on my mom's doorstep in the dead of night. I didn't have to say much for her to know what had happened, and after cooking me some chicken noodle soup, she put me to bed in my old room. Sometime that night, I woke up to go to the bathroom. When I was walking back to bed, I think my brain expected to see Heather laying there. But she wasn't, and she never would be. That was what opened the floodgates, and for the first time since Heather's death, I cried. I spent the rest of the night sitting there on the floor, sobbing until the sun came up and I finally, mercifully fell asleep.

Like I said earlier, much of this time is just hazy in my memory. Sometimes the brain just covers up experiences that are traumatic or hard to handle, and I've definitely blotted a lot of this out. For a long time, I spent most days sleeping, crying, or just staring into space. The hardest part was the memories that came back to haunt me constantly. And not just the memories of Heather's death or of the wechuge hunt, although those were certainly there too. But *all* the experiences Heather and I had once shared kept coming back to me, good and bad: when she'd taken me to visit Ireland, or when we'd argue over what movie to watch, or when we'd nap together in the woods. It all kept surging back into my head, bringing waves of emotions that sent me deeper and deeper into a pit. I could have tried doing something else to distract myself from these memories, and eventually I did just that. But at first I could barely get out of bed, and even the *idea* of doing much more than that was unimaginable.

It wasn't just the grief and the loneliness that were destroying me either. It was the fact that, on some level, this was my fault. Heather and I were both raised as Hunters. We had each been taught for as long as we could remember about the dangers of our job. We knew that each task might be our last. We knew when we began our relationship that we both could lose each other any time we went into the field. But none of this made the loss any less painful, especially knowing that I was partially responsible for it. *I* had chosen to go after the wechuge after we'd ambushed it in the hollow. And I couldn't stop thinking that if I'd just been a little less stupid, Heather might still be alive. Even today, over a decade later, that thought still crops up in my head sometimes.

Remember at the beginning of this letter when I talked about how I wish the Hunters had more mental health support? Well, this experience is what really made me think about that firsthand. Because you can't just go to any random therapist to talk about the problems that Hunters face. And it's not like our organization has mental health professionals that work for us full-time. So almost the only people I had to talk to were my family. And many Hunters can't even turn to their own families. I'm lucky that I was able to turn to mine, and that they understood me and did everything they could to help.

Over many conversations, I eventually managed to explain what had happened during the wechuge hunt to my parents, my older sister, and some of the community elders. And over many more, they all helped me to realize that Heather's death was not entirely my fault. After all, Heather and I had made all our decisions together. We had both agreed to go on the hunt in the first place, and we had both agreed to keep chasing the wechuge after the ambush. Yes, maybe if we had chosen differently, the outcome might have changed. But we had done the best we could at the time. That's what all these different people told me, and that's what I tell myself when I start thinking about whatever mistakes I might have made. Heather and I did the best we could. To hope for anything more would be unrealistic and foolish. And sometimes things just don't go the way we plan. Thinking about all this made me feel a little better, but it still took a lot of tears and a lot of time to process Heather's death. I think I'm probably still processing it, honestly.

The next big step along this road came in the winter of 2009, just over a year after Heather's death. I hadn't been on a single hunt for a cryptid in that entire time; I'd told Sergio that I needed a break and that I would get in touch with him when I was ready to start back up. Luckily, we Hunters are paid well, and I had more than enough funds saved up to live comfortably while I recovered. In all honesty, I was considering giving up my role as a Hunter. I'd spent close to 10 years doing my job with Heather at my side, and the prospect of going back to it alone was lonely and even a bit scary. If it hadn't been for Sergio calling me towards the end of 2009, I don't know what would have happened. But call me he did, and as much of a surprise as that was, it was what he told me that really made my heart race.

The wechuge was back. And this was not some other member of the species, as I initially suspected; no, this was the same creature that we had found in Saskatchewan more than a year ago. This was the same monster whose eye I had put out. This was the being that had killed Phil...That had killed Heather. This time, it was in the woods of Quebec. First, a team of environmental scientists had reported losing some of their data in a freak snowstorm. Then a lone capital-H Hunter had come across the wechuge itself near an empty cabin in the high forest. He'd taken refuge in the building, where there was a working phone that he'd used to report his encounter to the Lodge, just before going missing. In his report, he'd distinctly mentioned that the creature's skull was charred and blackened, and that one of its eyes was no more than a dark socket. Sergio called me as soon as he got the news.

I try to never personalize hunts, but this was different. This was my chance for revenge. This monster had taken Heather and made me suffer more than I ever had. This was my chance to make *it* suffer. A lot of the stories I was told growing up have lessons in them about how revenge and hatred are bad things to carry around inside of you, how they can destroy you from within. A lot of those lessons came back to me as I thought about facing the wechuge again. But this was a literal monster, a being which only knew how to cause suffering and pain. I had to stop it from doing that. At the very least, I had the chance to stop it from taking anyone else like it had taken Heather. And if I got my own personal revenge while doing so, then that would be even better.

I responded to Sergio with one request: I would hunt the wechuge again, but only if I had the chance to do so alone. Any other Hunters who responded to the case could be nearby, even on standby, but I wanted to be able to face the monster alone first. I wanted the opportunity to kill it myself. I knew the foolishness of my request; what I was asking for was reckless and selfish at best, and potentially suicidal at worst. But if I was going to die, I couldn't think of too many better ways to go down. And I was hoping that maybe revenge would make things hurt even the slightest bit less.

Initially, Sergio obviously tried to talk me out of it. He even yelled at me, which he's never done before, telling me that doing this wasn't going to bring Heather back to life, even if I succeeded. But I had made up my mind, no matter how irrational and selfish I was acting. Eventually, I think Sergio just took pity on me.

"I was debating whether I should even offer you this job," he told me.

"I'm glad you did," I responded.

"I'm sure you are. I can't believe I'm doing this, but fine. I'll ask if you can go ahead solo. At least this way you won't get anyone in trouble but yourself," he replied.

I knew the higher-ups in the Lodge probably wouldn't accept my request, but you never know if you don't try. Soon enough, Sergio got back to me: by some miracle, the Lodge had approved my request. The only condition was that the rest of the Hunters who had answered the distress call needed to be within half a mile of me at all times, ideally forming a defensive perimeter if possible. I was fine with this, and even if I wasn't, I doubted I'd be able to negotiate. A half mile was honestly a generous distance; I'd have plenty of room to work, and to fight. I took the job and didn't even give my family the details. All I said was goodbye and that I loved them. I didn't consult the elders either; I just thanked them for their help, and after that, I headed north once again. I was fully committed: this time, it was going to be either the wechuge or me.

Upon arriving in Quebec, I immediately went to rendezvous with the other Hunters who had taken the task. We chose to meet at the cabin where the lone Hunter had called in the wechuge sighting and then gone missing. When I arrived, I found 3 others waiting for me a short distance away from the cabin. I was surprised to find Dana from the previous wechuge hunt; I hadn't expected her, but then again, she wasn't from very far away. The other 2 Hunters were named

Eric and Francis, both muscular white guys with long hair and beards who I later learned were also Canadian. To be perfectly honest, I don't remember them much, which I'm a little ashamed to say, because I ordinarily try to get to know my teammates at least a little. This time, though, my thoughts were focused almost totally on the hunt.

We started by investigating the cabin. The front door had been knocked off its hinges and was lying on the floor inside the tiny foyer. A few windows had been cracked or shattered, maybe from the force of the wind or flying debris. The inside of the cabin was generally clean and well-furnished, so it was probably somebody's summer home. That explained the working phone that the missing Hunter had used to make the report; there was no cell coverage in this area. As for the Hunter themselves, their fate was quite clear. Dried blood was caked all across the walls, the furniture, and the carpeted floor of the living room, and there was far too much red for any human to have lost and survived. It was possible that some of the blood was the wechuge's, but we didn't need that to track it down; when we left the cabin, the cryptid's trail was plain to see. Just like Saskatchewan, an obvious trail of collapsed trees and snapped branches led off to the east through the forest. You couldn't have asked for a better trail.

I won't walk you through every detail of the days we spent following the wechuge, but the basic format of how we traveled was pretty much in line with what I had expected to do. During the day, I traveled ahead of everyone else, tracking the wechuge on my own. Even though the others were only a half mile behind me, I still left them markers to follow my trail in case they lost it. As it had last time, the trail of damaged trees eventually stopped, and I had to follow the wechuge mainly by finding its prints in the snow. By drawing arrows in the snow or cutting obvious marks into conspicuous tree trunks, I was able to mark the trail for my fellow Hunters. Before the sun began to set, I would stop and let the others catch up to me, and then we would all camp together for the night, taking turns on watch. Then as it began to get light in the morning, I would eat quickly, grab my things, and head out to start tracking once more.

This whole process repeated for a few days as we followed the target through the forest and down into a large valley. Several times, I came across the site of a kill or a chase, where the wechuge had ambushed or run down some unfortunate animal. I never heard or saw any of the attacks occur, though, and I always arrived to the same scene: blood and feathers or fur all over the snow, with the wechuge and its victim both long gone. Each time I found this, I got a little angrier and a little more disheartened. I wasn't getting any closer, or at least it didn't feel like it.

At some point I began to notice something disturbing about the wechuge's trail. If I was remembering the landscape correctly, I was starting to make a circle. The wechuge had begun to loop around, counterclockwise. I was pondering this when I thought of a frightening possibility, based on something I had learned long ago. African buffalo are known for being highly aggressive, and they're said to sometimes do something similar to what I was observing with the wechuge. When I was in Tanzania, I had been told that if a lone buffalo encounters a predator, they may initially drive them off, then make a huge circle to come around and hit the threat from behind when they least expect it. I don't know if this is true, but it jumped to mind when I noticed the path the wechuge was taking. Something in my gut told me that I was onto something, and that I needed to turn back.

I did exactly that, retracing my steps and meeting up with Dana, Eric, and Francis. When I told them my realization and my explanation for it, Francis actually laughed in my face. Dana and Eric were more willing to consider the possibility, though; Dana knew firsthand how fast this creature was and how quickly it could get around behind us if we weren't expecting it. I had a plan, though, and as the sun began to set, I laid it out.

I had the rest of the group head back the way I came from so that we switched places; now they were further ahead on the wechuge's trail than me, and I was behind them. This meant that if the wechuge was going to circle back on us like I predicted, then it would come to me first; I was the first one the cryptid would encounter, and that was exactly what I wanted.

A lone target without a fire would be more attractive prey than a trio of armed humans with a fire and a shelter, or so I hoped. I found a good spot in a clearing that sat along the edge of a little wash; a wash is a small ravine or gorge where water flows, and this one was maybe 5 feet deep and filled about halfway with frozen water. On the opposite side of the clearing from the wash was a little ridge, and I decided to lay in wait there. I placed my ground tarp, sleeping pad, and sleeping bag right in the center of the clearing, making them as obvious as possible; I even took branches, pine needles, and fallen leaves and stuffed them into my sleeping bag to make it look like I was laying inside. I was hoping the whole time that the wechuge wasn't somewhere nearby watching me; if it was, then this would all be for nothing. By the time I finished setting up, the sun had disappeared. I think I briefly considered lighting a small fire to attract the wechuge's attention, but then realized that might provoke it to attack from afar with its icicles. I couldn't have it pitching projectiles; I needed it to come in close. So without making a fire, I took my weapons, left my pack by my sleeping bag, and went up the nearby slope to settle in and wait.

Visibility was good, with the crescent moon giving off some light to the area. There was a slight breeze at first, and I hoped the wechuge didn't operate by smell; based on its habits of hunting in blizzards and the fact that its physical biology didn't really seem to have a functional nose, I felt reasonably confident that it wouldn't pick up my scent. Everything was silent except for the occasional rustling of pine needles or leaves in the wind. My ears strained to hear anything out of the ordinary, and even though I couldn't see very well at a long distance, my eyes were peeled for any unusual movement as well. My thoughts kept veering back to Saskatchewan, to Texas, to Libya and a dozen other hunts where I'd been in this same sort of situation, but with Heather by my side. I missed her a lot on that night, but each of the many times I thought of her, I did my best to turn my focus back to the present by concentrating on my breath and my five senses. After a while, my efforts were rewarded: I heard the crunch of snow from somewhere off to the right side of the clearing. I took a deep breath and turned to see the pinprick of a single yellow eye, glowing well over 10 feet above the ground in the shadows.

No doubt now. This was the one.

For a moment, the wechuge appeared to just stand there, observing the clearing and probably calculating its next move. I could have fired at it then, but I wanted it to come out into the open before I shot; I needed to be sure I had it. A few moments passed, and then the height of the wechuge's eye lowered several feet; it was crouching. Then it sprang forwards on all fours, faster than seemed possible. It made no cry or roar as it leapt forwards, snapping through branches and kicking up snow. In only two or three bounds, it was on the sleeping bag, crouching over it and mauling it with rapid swipes of its clawed hands. Then it picked up the biggest piece of the bag in both hands, raised it to its mouth, and bit down on it, driving the saber teeth of its wolf skull head completely through the polyester and insulation. Then it froze, going entirely still for an instant. This must have been when it realized what was going on, because a moment later it opened its jaw impossibly wide and gave a howl of rage that sounded partially human. It raised the ravaged sleeping bag over its head in both hands and began to repeatedly smash it into the ground, beating and pounding the snow with enough force that I felt it vibrate through my body. It was acting like a child throwing a tantrum, and that made me feel a strange mixture of revulsion, anger, and even pity, somehow. But I knew my chance was coming, and so I continued to wait.

After about a minute of raging, the wechuge tossed the scraps of the sleeping bag away and stood up to its full height and cried out the same vocalization I had heard it give a year before: a high-pitched shriek that deepened and became an earthshaking roar. Then it paused for a moment, and I knew it was time to strike. With the wechuge's head in the sights of my rifle, I fired. Plumes of flame burst out across the monster's skull, lighting up the darkness, and it stumbled backwards, trying to bat out the fire that was already spreading across its upper half. I stood up as I got down to the last few rounds in my rifle, and for a split second the wechuge's lone yellow eye met my gaze. The creature stepped towards me, its mane and torso still blazing, and I saw it reach up and snap off a huge icicle from one of its shoulders. I dove to the side, feeling a rush of air go whooshing past my face as the makeshift javelin missed. I made another dive back the way I came and snapped my rifle barrel up to see the wechuge rushing me. My rifle had nearly run dry, but I managed to hit the wechuge's face with the last rounds, and somehow, one of those shots stopped the monster dead in its tracks. Its remaining eye went dark, and it raised its hands to its face, screaming another partially human cry. It was still burning, and now that it was blind, this was the best opportunity yet to end this.

I dropped my rifle and picked up my shotgun, which I had been waiting for a moment just like this to use. The blinded wechuge was staggering aimlessly, swatting at the flames that roiled across the upper half of its body. As I approached, it thrashed out at me with its claws, but I was too far away. I could have finished things from a much greater distance with more rifle rounds, but I wanted to be close. I wanted the wechuge to *burn*.

As I got closer, close enough to feel the heat of the flames, I raised my shotgun and pulled the trigger. The dragon's breath ammo sent a jet of flame rushing out from the barrel, igniting the monster's legs and lower half. It screamed again, a high-pitched, bloodcurdling sound, and this time, it kept screaming. The sound made my stomach turn, and I felt sudden, frigid tears rolling down my face as I pulled the trigger again and again. Each flaming shot further fueled the inferno that was consuming the wechuge, until finally the creature's screams died out and it collapsed into the snow, heaving and twitching a few more times before falling still.

I dropped my shotgun and took a few aimless steps before crumpling and bursting into tears. I was exhausted and relieved, but I still can't tell you exactly why I started crying on that night. Maybe I was crying for the monster I'd just killed, which may once have been human. Maybe I was crying for Heather, who wasn't there to appreciate victory with me. Maybe I was crying because Sergio was right: getting revenge didn't bring Heather back. And I still miss her.

It's now been over a decade since I killed the wechuge, and thankfully I've never had to hunt such a being again. I went back to my family in Oklahoma and told them about this second hunt in full detail. As you might imagine, they were angry at me for basically running away and acting alone, even though they understood why. I acknowledged my behavior as having been selfish and risky, and I apologized extensively. Everyone forgave me eventually, although it took a few years before my mom did so.

To say that I didn't gain anything from my revenge mission against the wechuge would be silly and false. I gained revenge, and the satisfaction of destroying the thing that had destroyed such a huge part of my life. But at the same time, it didn't give me what I really wanted.

Heather is still dead, and nothing will change that. Killing the wechuge made her loss a little more bearable, but it was still a *ton* of effort and a ton of danger for only a little personal payoff. At least I helped to protect a lot of innocent lives, but I could have done it in a safer and less self-centered way. As I've said before, every type of being has teachings we can learn from, even something as destructive and dangerous as a wechuge. Think before you act, everyone, and use your head as well as your heart. It might not be a matter of life and death, but it might just make a big difference.

And as cliche as it might sound, the future really does hold a ton of possibilities. If you've listened to my previous letters, you may have already noticed that I've mentioned having a girlfriend. Her name is Serena, and I met her a few years ago now. She's a veterinarian, and no, she's not a Hunter. I guess I have a thing for women who work high-stress jobs that are all about saving lives! Serena listens to these letters and proofreads them for me along with my nephew before I send them in to Swamp Dweller. She's incredibly intelligent, with a will of steel and the kindest heart you can imagine, and I love her a lot. Serena is a lot like Heather, but she's not Heather. And I've learned to accept that, because that's perfectly okay.

Anyway, that's enough sappy stuff for one letter, I think. Well, one last thing. This story has been a lot about my personal experience with grief and depression, and to be completely honest, those are issues that will probably affect you far more than any cryptid. Mental illness can be just as dangerous as claws or fangs. I didn't really have any professional psych help with my struggles, but obviously things are different for us Hunters. For you guys, there's a lot of help available if you just reach out. If you're struggling, ask for help. You might be surprised by the outcome.

That's all for now, though. The next letter will be my last, so if you have any final questions or comments, be sure to speak up so that I can see what you have to say! As always, I'll be reading everything, even if I can't address it all. Otherwise, stay safe and stay healthy, everyone. We'll talk more soon. This has been Sam White Owl, signing out.

LETTER 10 – CAMAZOTZ + MACHA

BRAZIL, IRELAND

Written January 2020

Hey, everybody, it's Sam White Owl, back again. This will probably be the last time I say that, which is kind of sad! In case you weren't aware, this is the tenth letter that I've sent in to Swamp Dweller, and it's the last one that he and I agreed upon doing together. Writing this feels pretty surreal. It doesn't quite feel like the end yet. And actually, I suppose it's not, because we still have the whole rest of this letter to go! So let's get into it. I'll save most of the sappy stuff for the end, but I did want to briefly say up top that I really, really appreciate all of the warm wishes and condolences that you guys gave me on the last letter. As I've said, it was a difficult one to write, and reliving those memories definitely hurt. But you guys keep reminding me of the positivity and the light that there is in the world, and I can't thank you enough for that. Much love from me and Serena to everyone who brought good energy and support to that last letter. You each mean a lot.

Anyway, with that said, let's get into the actual stories for this letter. A few episodes back, someone asked about the monster known as the Camazotz, and I've briefly mentioned them during part of a Q& A where I was discussing cryptids from Mexico. I didn't go into much detail on them, though, so don't worry if you missed it. Here are the details. Camazotz are flying creatures that live throughout Central and South America, from central Mexico down to Chile and Argentina. On a few occasions, they've been reported by people in the southwestern United States, and even in the Pacific Northwest, but it's incredibly rare for them to go so far north; generally, they're found from the Mexico-US border southwards. Camazotz can tolerate drier climates like deserts, but they mostly prefer subtropical or tropical environments, which is where they're found all over Central and South America.

The name "Camazotz" itself comes from Mayan mythology, and in the K'iche' language, it literally means "Death Bat", which is what Hunters call Camazotz. In the epic myths and stories, the Camazotz were vicious bat creatures or spirits that lived in the underworld, and the Hunters just applied the name to the similar species of cryptid.

It's not entirely clear what exactly Camazotz are. In appearance, they seem somewhat humanoid, and although they're considered mammals, they also have some reptilian characteristics. The most basic description most people would probably give a Camazotz at first glance would be "bat person". They stand slightly shorter than most humans, between 4.5 and 6 feet tall, with two human-like legs. These legs end in five claws, four on the front of the foot and one on the heel; the claws primarily serve to grip onto things like perches or prey, but they can also slash and tear. Just like bats, Camazotz don't really have arms; instead, their hands have developed into huge wings, with their elongated finger bones forming a framework that web-like skin stretches over, identical to bat wings. In fact, bats are some of the only creatures to have evolved this unique type of wing structure, so it seems possible that Camazotz are related in some way. Unlike bats, however, Camazotz have long, prehensile tails that end in a sharp spike of bone; they use their tails to grip things, but also as weapons, stabbing out with the spikes like spears. Their heads somewhat resemble a furry crocodiles', but with oversized bat ears sticking up from the skull and massive, circular, yellow-orange eyes; their long snouts are lined with sharp teeth which they primarily use to chomp and tear. Apart from their wings, most of a Camazotz' body is covered with short fur that ranges in color from tan, russet, or brown up to gray and black.

It's tough to learn about Camazotz social systems, especially because they fly over such large distances, but they're typically seen in groups that Hunters call "flocks"; most flocks number between 2 and 20 and make their homes in very deep and remote areas of the forest, roosting in the highest cliffs, the deepest caves, and the tallest trees. Throughout the day, Camazotz rest in these hidden locations, before awakening as the sun goes down and flying out to find food. Large flocks tend to split up into smaller bands when hunting, mainly into what seem like sibling or parent-child groups.

Although they resemble bats in many ways, diet is one of the biggest differences. Whereas most types of bats eat insects, Camazotz prefer much meatier prey. Some Hunter research indicates that they like to have their lairs near bodies of water for easy access to fish and waterfowl, and they also go after other birds and small mammals like monkeys and rodents.

Camazotz will fly far in search of food, though, and this is where they usually become threatening to humans. They're known to have raided villages and small towns in the past, taking domestic animals, livestock, and occasionally even people. Using their tail spikes, claws, and teeth, Camazotz can be ferocious, especially in numbers; despite their size, they can also fly surprisingly quietly, and unless you're looking upward or actively searching for them, you may not know they're nearby until it's too late. Because of their aerial mobility, nocturnal lifestyle, and remote, hidden roosts, not a lot of humans ever see Camazotz or encounter them. But for the unlucky people and creatures who fall victim to a Camazotz attack, it's never pretty.

I've been on a couple Camazotz hunts, but the first was in Brazil. It was a strange one in some ways, first of all because it wasn't exactly planned. I didn't even prepare for it in advance; in fact, I was actually on a bit of a vacation when I got caught up in it. Things started when my friend Ray called me and invited me to his home in Brazil. Ray is actually from Venezuela originally, but he moved to Brazil as a young boy, where he learned Portuguese and started working as a field guide and forest ranger in some of the dense, remote portions of the Amazon rainforest. He developed close relationships with some local Indigenous groups in the northern jungles and learned a lot from them. But didn't put much stock in many of their myths and stories until he saw the remains of some illegal loggers who had been killed by a pair of iara, the ferocious, faerie-like water women of many Brazilian waterways. Soon, a capital-H Hunter showed up from the city to speak with the cryptids, and Ray was guiding her through the forest when the iara ambushed them. Luckily, both Ray and the Hunter were armed, and together they killed the attacking monsters. Impressed by Ray's gun skills and environmental knowledge, the Hunter submitted him as a candidate for the organization, and when we offered him the position, he took it.

Ray and I met at an interesting event. It's not often that the Hunters hold communal gatherings or events for the lower-ranking members who aren't part of the Lodge, but there was one time that we had a big seminar-type event in the Mexican desert. A bunch of us were tapped to give lectures and lessons, some of which were about how important it is to follow the knowledge and wisdom of indigenous people around the world, which for us specifically is invaluable for learning and understanding various contexts for cryptids.

My mom was lucky enough to be selected as a speaker, and my sister Erika and I tagged along with her. Ray was also giving a lesson there, which I found to be both interesting and informative. I'm not a great talker or a big social butterfly, of course, but Ray and I got along well and quickly got to know each other. He invited me to Brazil so that I could meet some of the Indigenous folks from the Amazon who he knew. I thought he was just making the offer out of courtesy, but I accepted, not actually expecting anything to come of it. Then around a year later, Ray got in touch and extended his offer again, which was a pleasant surprise. I wasn't busy at the time, and you guys know that I always love to travel and learn, so soon I was visiting Brazil for the first time.

Ray met up with me at the airport with his usual smile, wearing sunglasses, jeans, and a well-worn bucket hat. He looks like the typical South American mestizo: brown skin, a little lighter than mine, spiky black hair, and a lean build that's on the shorter side. Besides the vicious scars on one side of his face and neck, he would probably seem just like a totally average Latino guy. He gave me a big hug and helped me get my stuff into his red pickup truck; I don't know if I've ever met a Hunter whose main vehicle was *not* a truck. Trucks mostly just have a lot of room for things, such as guns, some of which I had brought with me; Ray had recommended that I take some weapons, partially because he wanted to check them out and partially because we'd be going into the home area of both jaguars and cryptids. It was unexpectedly fortunate that I'd followed his advice.

I won't tell you exactly where I landed, but you probably won't find it on most maps; I'll just say that it was a small airfield in the northern part of the country, a few hours away from Ray's house. We went there to spend the night before heading out to the forest the next day. Ray lives on a big plot of land in a rural area, where he actually runs a small farm. This was pretty surprising since he has to be out Hunting so much, but he says he loves the farmer lifestyle, and he pays a few field hands and a manager to help him out, especially when he's away on a case. The whole setup actually seemed to work out pretty well!

Hanging out at the farmhouse was nice, but early the next morning we hit the road for the rainforest; Ray's house is pretty close to the edge of it, so it wasn't long until we were driving amongst some serious jungle. The trees and foliage quickly became tall and broad, pressing in close on either side of the road. If you've listened to my eighth letter, about Heather and I battling an emela-ntouka in the Congo, then you'll probably have a good idea of what this forest in Brazil looked like; even a whole ocean apart, these environments have a ton of similarities. We drove for maybe about an hour, although I'm not sure, until reaching a point where the bumpy dirt road came to a stop. Ray told me to wait in the car while he went to the village we were going to visit and let them know we were coming; when visiting more rural communities, especially Native or indigenous ones and/or ones that aren't used to visitors, having someone they know give them a heads-up is always a respectful and helpful thing to do. After a couple hours, Ray came back and said that I was welcome.

The people we were visiting were members of the Yanomami, one of the bigger Indigenous groups from the Amazon region. They have a bunch of communities in the northwest part of this area, and Ray has spent many years getting to know them. The village we visited consisted mainly of one big building called a shabono; this is essentially a huge U-shaped roof and back wall made out of leaves and reeds, supported by big logs that act as dividers between different sections. Almost the whole village lives in this communal house, and it sits around the edge of an open patch of jungle.

When Ray and I walked up, most of the villagers were in the clearing surrounded by the shabono or sitting in the house itself. Photos and videos usually show indigenous Amazon people without much clothing, wearing only loincloths made of bark, with their faces painted red, black, and yellow. And while it is true that a whole bunch of the Yanomami were dressed like that when I visited, there were also quite a few wearing T-shirts or sneakers. Most of them don't leave the forest, and if they ask him, Ray sometimes brings them this kind of clothing; they get outside clothes from other Native groups too, so that was one way many people in this community had some Westernized, "mainstream" customs.

I got a lot of curious looks when I walked into the village; they get visitors, but not a huge number. Ray introduced me in Portuguese, which quite a few of the Yanomami speak nowadays; unfortunately, I only know a handful of words and phrases, so I had to rely on Ray to translate. After he introduced me and I repeated my name, the villagers seemed more at ease. Some of the younger kids, maybe 4 or 5 years old, seemed really into my wide-brimmed, camo-patterned hat, so I took it off and knelt down to give it to them. They immediately started battling over it, which was pretty amusing to the rest of us, but a couple adults immediately shut things down; generosity is a core value of Indigenous cultures, and although we all have things that are our own, a hat is something that you can share. Some of the adults and the other kids seemed pretty surprised by my hair, which is a lot curlier than theirs; Ray told me that they were saying that I didn't look Indian, so I had him explain to them that I was only half, and that most Cherokee look very different from Yanomami folks.

After a while, the initial energy started to die down, and I noticed that a good number of people had been standing back from the crowd. They looked unusually serious, and when I turned my attention to them, things got very quiet. I quickly sensed that something was off, so Ray and I stepped over to the group. One of them, a young woman, stepped forward, her eyes flicking between Ray and the ground. When she got close, she began to talk in a halting, quiet voice; from her frequent pauses, it sounded like she didn't speak Portuguese very well, but her voice was also trembling, and her eyes were watering. When she finished, a few tears had run down her face, but she never lost her composure. Ray turned to me, his expression gone dark.

"She says that she lost her daughter...to monsters," he told me.

My first reaction was confusion. "What do you mean? Like cryptids?"

Ray turned back to the young woman and asked her something. She responded, hesitating a lot and gesturing with her hands to help her explain, I think mostly for my benefit; at one point, I clearly remember her raising her hands up and down, a very clear pantomime of the beating of wings.

"OK. She says she was out getting some vegetables from the crops, four days ago. It was getting dark and her little girl was nearby playing with friends. The kids must have been spread out. She heard a scream, then saw four enormous bats. She says two of them picked up her daughter with their legs. The children started screaming, and then the bats and her daughter were gone over the trees," Ray explained.

"Camazotz," I said, and Ray nodded.

Names are very important in Yanomami culture, to the point of holding so much power that they aren't even spoken in almost all settings. Even if we did know the little girl's name, there's no way I would repeat it, so we'll call her Yarima, a known Yanomami female name. Ray continued to translate for Yarima's mom. Apparently, some of the village warriors, of whom there were quite a few, mainly older men, had gone out after the Camazotz; some Yanomami and other Amazon Indigenous communities fight with each other, although it's become far less frequent these days, hence why most of these warriors were in their 40s at the youngest. They had returned empty-handed, unable to track down the flock. The woman had been hesitant to ask, but with Ray here, she ultimately decided to go for it: knowing what Ray did as a Hunter, she was now asking him to go after the Camazotz and bring her daughter back.

Ray explained to me that this was incredibly important, even though the woman knew that Yarima was probably no longer alive. In Yanomami culture, the souls of the dead are only put to rest when their mortal remains are given a proper funeral; usually this involves cremating the bones of the dead, but obviously, in order to do that, you need said bones. There are extremely similar beliefs in practically all cultures; we all have funeral ceremonies, and everybody knows the concept of the restless spirit who can't be at peace unless they're given the proper respect and closure. For this woman, and the whole community, Yarima would never find peace for all eternity unless her remains could be recovered. Even though this particular community had some more Western cultural influences, the Yanomami usually don't even *talk about* the dead, so the fact that this mother was sharing her dilemma with us was huge.

"What do you think?" I asked Ray.

"We need to do something. Not just for this woman either. These Camazotz are eating children, for God's sake. They're aggressive," he answered. I agreed, but there was just one problem. I'd studied up on Brazilian monster species before coming, but...

"I've never hunted a Camazotz," I said.

To my surprise, Ray just shrugged. "There is a first time for everything."

Our first step was to gather more information. Mainly, we had to figure out where the Camazotz were roosting. But we faced the exact problem as the warriors: we couldn't track the cryptids directly back to their roost, given that they could fly. We considered setting out bait to lure the Camazotz in, but even if that did work, we'd most likely only get a portion of what could be a larger flock, since Camazotz split up to hunt. Ultimately, we started by asking around, beginning with the rescue party that had tried to go after Yarima.

After the warriors of the party had gotten together, Ray and I spent a long time talking with them. As it turned out, only about six had actually gone out to chase down the Camazotz; the other twenty or so had been too wary of the monsters or simply unwilling to risk their lives and make matters worse. The small band that *had* gone to the rescue followed the advice given by Yarima's mother and traveled east, the direction in which she'd seen the Camazotz fly off. But soon it had gotten too dark to continue and they had been forced to stop. The next day they pressed on, but as they had feared, there was no trace of either Yarima or the death bats. These men were extremely skilled hunters and trackers who knew those jungles better than anyone; if they couldn't find any sign, there was no way in hell Ray or I would. I was at a bit of a loss until I started thinking more broadly.

"They said the Camazotz flew east. What's over there?"

Ray relayed my question, and a few of the warriors answered, using pantomime to fill in the linguistic gaps. After a few follow-up questions, he turned back to me.

"It sounds like there's actually a cave in the east. Some of them believe that the Camazotz may live there, but I think they're afraid of that area. They say their search party turned back before going that far," Ray explained.

It was a bit frustrating to me that the warriors hadn't gone further, but I couldn't blame them; even the bravest people can't do everything, and they deserved credit for simply being willing to go after massive predatory cryptids in the first place.

"What's so bad about the cave area?" I asked.

Ray's translation was quicker this time. "They say it's just a bad place. Dangerous. I think they're talking about bad magic. I don't remember the word in English."

"Cursed?" I suggested.

Ray snapped his fingers. "Yes, that's it. Cursed. They didn't say that, because they don't want to talk about such bad things, but I think they meant something similar. That cave could be where the Camazotz have their nest."

If the Camazotz truly did roost there, it would make sense for the place to be understood as cursed or off-limits, and some of the men said that they did in fact believe that was where the death bats lived. Rules are made for a reason, but Ray and I decided to start our search there. The Yanomami made it very obvious that it was a stupid idea, which they were certainly right about, but since nothing forbade me and Ray from it, we were hopefully in the clear.

Indigenous people are not stupid or weak, and the Yanomami knew exactly what the deal was; digging in for defensive action was smarter than a direct assault on the cave. The Yanomami know the rainforest like you might know your house or your office, but they had no idea how big the Camazotz flock was, and they would have to enter an explicitly off-limits region to follow it. When they got there, they would have to fight almost exclusively with bows and spears, although they also had a pair of bolt-action rifles. They could have rounded up more men from other communities, but the majority would still be way past their fighting prime, and all trained and accustomed to fighting humans, not cryptids. More deaths were virtually a guarantee; even the entire rescue party could be killed. And if even a single life was lost, it would be yet another tremendous hit to a small, close-knit community where everyone is so highly valued and loved. Losing Yarima was devastating enough, but is it really the best course of action to have an indefinite number of other people go into a potential massacre?

The difference here isn't that we were smarter or wiser or braver than the Yanomami, but that we were just in a different position. Battling monsters is our way of life: our weapons and gear were explicitly designed to take on creatures like Camazotz, and we'd done it dozens of times before. The Yanomami are extremely hardcore, but they're far from heartless, and Ray was a valued friend; evidently some of them had actually tried to stop Yarima's mom from requesting our help at all, because they didn't think it was right to ask us to go into such danger. The Yanomami didn't want us to walk into this fight, but we had a good shot at handling it.

By the time we finished getting info from the villagers, it was almost evening. We hiked back to the truck, where Ray always kept a spare set of camping supplies and gear, as do most Hunters; among other things, this included a tarp, a little single-person tent, and some food and water. I had brought my pack as well, which mainly held my food bag and a water bladder. And of course, we both had weapons. Since I had come to Brazil intending to show Ray some of my arsenal, I had combat gear still in his truck: this time it was my standard loadout of rifle, pistol, combat tomahawk, and a pair of knives, plus a shotgun. Ray was equipped with a rifle, a pair of matched pistols that I think were some kind of Taurus, a couple of knives, and one absurdly sharp machete.

After taking stock, we determined that we had enough supplies to get going in the morning. We would head back to the village at dawn to request a guide; hopefully someone would be willing to take us at least partway to the cave, which they had said was actually quite close, maybe a few miles off.

That night we set up camp next to the truck and discussed our approach to handling the Camazotz themselves.

Tranquilizing would be nearly impossible given that there were at least four, and we didn't have anywhere to bring them without potentially endangering even more people. And they had already proven to be aggressive to the point of attacking settlements directly. So unfortunately, we decided that we would have to kill them. Afterwards, we would get in touch with our Guides to inform them of the situation and submit our reports. With that grim decision made, we settled in for bed; I slept across the back seats of the truck while Ray got into his tent. After an uneventful night we woke up at first light, had something to eat, and then packed up and set out for the village again.

When we got there, most of the Yanomami were already up and about. Many of them came over to greet us, but both we and especially our weapons got lots of wary or even angry looks, which I could certainly understand. Luckily, we weren't planning on staying long. Ray talked to a few of the old women and some of the warriors we'd spoken with yesterday. After some bustling around and discussion, a group of about ten of the village men was assembled. Most were dressed in only small loincloths, with faces painted with black lines and dots; each of them carried a short bow and a quiver made of bark and stocked with arrows, and a few also held short, fire-hardened spears. Although most of them were hunters rather than warriors, and all of them were probably under 5-and-a-half feet tall, and, these were hardcore guys, and it was inspiring that so many of them were here.

"They'll show us to the cave," Ray said once we had assembled.

"Great. I'm guessing they're not coming the whole way?" I asked.

"Correct. The cave is on the river nearby, and they'll take us as far as the water's edge."

With that clarified, we set off. Food is part of how the Yanomami celebrate and bond, and in another situation, maybe we would have had a group meal before leaving. But we needed to use the daylight as much as possible, so we were given a gift of cassava to go; even without any sort of toppings or accompanying food, the taste was solid, and it was definitely energizing. At first, our route took us down a cleared dirt path that led to the community crops; these were a set of fields of different vegetables and plants, all located in a big clearing about the same size as the one that held the shabono. The warriors led us past the fields and into the jungle beyond, where our progress immediately slowed among the roots, rocks, and ground plants. With our heavy packs and gear, obviously Ray and I were nowhere near as fast as the Yanomami, most of whom were in loincloths and knew exactly where they were going. Three of them followed behind us, though, and when the men in front of us always waited for us to catch up. The ground was fairly even for most of the journey, with a slight downward slope as we went. The trees and bushes rose high all around, and every so often the green and brown surroundings would be punctuated by a splash of color from a piece of fungus or a bright poison dart frog.

The jungle was filled with noise, from the wind in the leaves to the nonstop songs of birds and insects. Once, the barking roars of howler monkeys started up from somewhere off to the south and didn't stop for about ten minutes. At another point, one of the Yanomami ahead of us pointed out the furry form of a tamandua, or tree anteater, as it clambered up a tree trunk in the distance. Not too long after that, we spotted of the blue and black beak of a channel-billed toucan in the branches overhead. And at some point, we stepped over a line of leafcutter ants, carrying dead bugs and pieces of plants as they marched in single file along the trunk of a fallen tree.

After several hours, the trees suddenly parted, and we found ourselves on the muddy banks of a dark, slow-moving river. A flock of scarlet macaws took flight from the treetops across the water as Ray and I approached. The Yanomami stopped at the edge of the treeline; this was where they left us. Ray exchanged a few words with them, and then they all raised their weapons to us in a silent salute. Ray turned and motioned for me to follow as he started to walk upstream.

"They say the cave is a short distance this way. They'll wait here for us until we come back, or until 3 days pass," Ray told me.

"Let's make sure we *do* come back, then," I replied, already feeling on edge now that we were on our own; the Yanomami knew better than to walk into this.

We continued on, and the river slowly dropped into a small valley or hollow where we had to duck back into the trees and the brush. After about half an hour, we rounded a bend in the river and came to a canyon-like area where huge, dark boulders rose up on either side of the water. On the same bank as us, a black gap was visible in the cliffs, maybe around 25 feet above the ground. I pointed the it out to Ray, who immediately spat out something in Spanish or Portuguese that sounded like a curse.

"They might have told us we would have to climb," he said in English. I chuckled at his reaction and took a closer look at the cave entrance. It was taller than it was wide, and although it was narrow and high up, it looked like there were quite a few handholds and footholds leading up to it.

"We can definitely get up there," I told Ray.

He grumbled. "Yeah, okay. But not without something to eat first." he replied.

With that, we stopped where we were to have a quick lunch. We didn't light a cookfire, in case the scent of the food spread and attracted the Camazotz. At first, attracting them actually seemed like it might be a good idea, to get a sense of their potential numbers. But we didn't want any of them flying away, so in the end, we again decided against luring them; they were all probably in the cave asleep, and that's where we wanted to keep them. Ideally, Ray and I would climb up to the cave mouth and blast the Camazotz there; it felt gross to do so, but it would be safer than letting them fly out. It's crucial to have respect for all beings, but that doesn't mean making unsafe concessions, especially in a true life-or-death situation. As I'm sure you've realized by now if you've listened to any of my letters, neither Hunters nor monsters fight fair. We fight for survival.

After we ate, Ray and I selected our weapons. Since we'd have to climb, we'd be leaving our packs and most of our gear right there at our lunch spot. I settled on my shotgun, since close quarters stopping power would be important in this sort of situation. Flying beings also tend to be less resilient and resistant to injuries than other creatures; even minor damage to their wings can often compromise their flight capabilities. I hoped that if any Camazotz got into the air, then I'd be able to bring them down with a well-placed burst of buckshot. I decided to leave my tomahawk behind in favor of my knives; although they didn't give me much range or power, I might not even have room to swing my tomahawk. Ray also exchanged his rifle for his pistols and his own knives instead. We hung our food from a branch to keep it at least somewhat away from animals, then secured the rest of our supplies to a tree trunk and covered them with a tarp to protect them from rain. Then we started toward the cave.

When we got to the base of the cliffs, it was surprisingly easy to find a climbing route up to the cave; the rocks were uneven and offered plenty of gripping points and footholds. I slung my shotgun on my back; not the safest gun etiquette, I know, but it left my hands free to climb. As quietly as possible, I began scaling the cliff face, with Ray right behind me. We made quick progress, but about three-quarters of the way up, a nasty stench hit us. It had undercurrents of blood and the heavy odor of something dead, which is difficult to describe. But the main smell was almost like rotting fruit, a scent that I hadn't experienced for a while; for some reason, my mind flashed back to my grandmother's kitchen, and I had a hazy memory of when I'd found some bananas that had gone bad in the trash there. The odor wasn't overpowering, and I'd smelled worse, but it still made me wrinkle my nose. It grew more intense the higher we went, and before long, I had gotten level with the cave entrance, hanging onto the rocks to the right side of it. There was no ledge either above or below the entrance, so after taking a deep breath, I jumped across the rocks, landing at the bottom of the cave mouth and gripping at the walls to steady myself. The entrance and the few yards directly beyond it were tall enough for me to stand up straight, but it looked like the cave dropped rapidly into pitch darkness beyond that. The odor was strong, and it seemed fresh.

I motioned for Ray to secure a rope to the rocks to help us get down more easily. Once he'd done that, I signaled for him to wait a second while I strapped on my headlamp. This would be a pitch-perfect (no pun intended) scenario for a good pair of night vision goggles, but unfortunately, I didn't have mine, seeing as I didn't come to Brazil knowing I'd be chasing death bats into caves. I had to rely on my headlamp, so I put it on, offloaded my shotgun, and flicked the light on. The white beam illuminated the dark brown stone walls of a wide tunnel that continued ahead for a short distance. Dark blotches and bloody drag marks were scattered across the cave walls and floor, and a single yellowed shoulder blade lay discarded partway down the tunnel. But there were no Camazotz, so I stepped back and motioned for Ray to come over.

Once Ray had made the jump, he took up a position beside me with his pistols drawn. The tunnel was wide enough for us to walk side by side, so we continued deeper in like that. I felt like my heart was beating with the force and volume of a bass drum, and I was dreading that any second, we might be mobbed by beating wings and tooth-filled snouts. But the beams of our headlamps didn't light up any eyes, and no roars or screeches burst through the quiet. We reached the end of the tunnel, where it took a sharp bend to the left and dropped down a few feet. The cave walls narrowed significantly here, leaving room for only one of us to pass at a time. Anxiety made my chest tighten at the sight of the narrow passage, and alarm bells started going off in my mind. I've never liked tunnels or other confined spaces; I'm not even particularly claustrophobic, but this type of area makes me uneasy, especially on hunts. There just aren't many ways you can move. And at that moment, the tight and narrow path ahead seemed like a deathtrap.

I took a deep breath to steady myself, then looked at Ray, who gave me a reassuring nod. After a moment, I stepped down into the tunnel ahead. The walls closed in around me, leaving only a couple inches of space to either side. The same foul odor was thick now, and as I moved forward one step at a time, my headlamp revealed more bloodstains and yellow and white bones on the floor. I kept an eye out to see if any of the bones were human or if there were any scraps of clothing around, but I didn't turn up anything. The darkness in front of me seemed to swallow the light of my headlamp, but I kept my gun raised and my senses on alert as I advanced.

After what felt like forever, the tunnel opened up surprisingly suddenly, and I found myself in a much larger cavern. Stalactites hung from the ceiling and stalagmites rose from the floor among ledges and small piles of stone. Water dripped steadily down from above, where a few small cracks and openings in the ceiling let in some isolated shafts of sunlight. A huge pool of water occupied much of the cavern floor. Ray later told me that cave pools like this are called cenotes in parts of Central and South America. They often serve as swimming pools for tourists, but I would never even think of touching the water in this one, which was murky brown and probably full of guano (that's the word for bat poop, if you didn't know).

To be fair, the cavern would have been quite beautiful if it hadn't been for some other details. First, the air was heavy with that stench of rotten fruit and blood. Second, the floor of the place was revolting: piles of dark guano, bloodstains, fur, feathers, and bones of all shapes and sizes lay scattered everywhere across the damp stone floor. And third, hanging from the ceiling amongst the stalactites were the sleeping forms of nine Camazotz. Like gargantuan bats, they grasped the stony cavern ceiling with the claws on their feet and hung upside-down with their wings and tails wrapped snugly around their bodies. They were all at least 30 feet overhead, but even from that distance, my powerful red headlamp revealed their dark fur, long snouts, and huge, pointed ears; thankfully, their eyes were hidden beneath their wings, so they didn't notice the light.

As I stepped into the cavern and took all this in, the sight of the Camazotz made me freeze. I put out a hand behind me to tell Ray to stop, then took a few cautious steps forward. My gaze switched between the ceiling and the floor, alternately watching for any movement from the Camazotz and any obstacles on the ground. Aside from a few ear twitches, none of the monsters moved or seemed to realize that I was there; Camazotz have much better eyesight than most bats, so their hearing may not be as sensitive, which I was very thankful for in that moment. After a few more quiet steps, I motioned for Ray to come forwards.

Once Ray was in the cavern beside me, we counted the Camazotz again and noted their positions. Through careful pantomime and lip reading, we silently agreed to go back the way we'd come and pull back into the small tunnel behind us if things got too heated. Then we selected our targets. Hopefully, if we shot fast, we could possibly gun down two Camazotz each before things got too chaotic. Ray picked out a pair of creatures on the right side of the cavern, and I chose two on the left. Mine were only a few feet apart, both dark brown in color and hanging at a similar height. I got as close to them as I felt I could, then looked over to Ray, who gave me the signal to start counting down from 10. I started counting in my head and put the leftmost Camazotz in my sights. As I reached 0, Ray and I both fired.

The gunshots were deafening in the cavern, and almost immediately, they were joined by the sound of beating wings and screeching, chattering cryptids. I didn't even watch to see if my first shot had killed my target; as soon as I pulled the trigger, I flicked my barrel over to the second monster I'd picked out and fired again. After that second shot, I distinctly remember seeing that Camazotz go plummeting to the ground, but I didn't trace its fall. The rest of the flock had taken to the air now, flapping around the cavern faster than I'd expected. I picked out another Camazotz and fired at it a few times, but I didn't manage to hit it squarely until it latched onto one of the cavern walls and held still for a moment. As I saw it drop, I took a moment to reload and reassess. At least three Camazotz were still flying, and one of them started flapping towards me, lashing its tail. I jumped backwards to give myself more space as I finished reloading, and I had to duck as the bone spike at the end of the monster's tail whipped out to spear me. I raised my shotgun and let off one more quick shot before breaking for the tunnel entrance.

Ray was backing up into the tunnel, firing as he went, and as I approached, he turned and leapt inside. A second later, I dove in after him, and we both spun around to face back towards the cenote cave. A big gray Camazotz thrust its snout into the tunnel, snapping its yellowed teeth only a few inches away from my boots. It staggered backwards as Ray sent several shots into its glowing yellow-orange eyes, and I fired a pellet into its face for good measure. Blood and chunks of flesh and brain matter went spraying across my face, my clothes, and the surrounding stone, and what remained of the Camazotz lurched backwards into the cavern, jerking and writhing. I felt sick, and I couldn't hear anything except for sharp tinnitus ringing in my ears. I kept my gun trained on the mouth of the cave, but I couldn't see any movement on the other side. Soon Ray tapped my shoulder, and we pulled back deeper into the tunnel. Turning to face him, I motioned to my ears to indicate that I couldn't hear, and he nodded. We stood there for a second before the ringing in my ears started to die down.

"I killed at least three. Maybe wounded more. What about you?" I asked, my voice sounding muffled in my ears.

"The same. So we may have three left. Are you hurt?" Ray asked.

I shook my head and was about to ask him the same question when I caught a glimpse of movement in the darkness behind him. The light of my headlamp reflected off a pair of glowing yellow eyes. I grabbed Ray's shoulder and pulled him towards me, but the Camazotz behind him gave an ear-piercing screech, hooked the primary claws of its wings into his back, and yanked him out of my grasp. I jumped after it, because there was no way to get a clear shot: Ray was in between me and the monster, and my shotgun pellets would spread anyway. Subconsciously realizing this, I dropped my gun and drew my oversized combat knife from my hip. The Camazotz had begun to force Ray to the ground, and I saw it raising its tail for a stab. I lunged in and used my free hand to grab at the cryptid's tail while I thrust my knife upwards at its neck. My blade punched through fur and sunk into the flesh and muscle beneath, and the Camazotz gave a gurgling yelp as its hot blood rushed over my hands. Its tail thrashed around like a hairy python and whipped out of my grasp before stabbing outward at me. The spear-like bone at the end of the tail pierced my upper left arm, but I twisted aside and the spike pulled out before it sunk very deep.

The Camazotz drew its tail back and snapped out at me with its crocodile-like snout, but then Ray's pistol rang out from underneath it. The cryptid fell aside, its huge leathery wings flapping out and smacking into the sides and floor of the tunnel. I saw it moving to stand up, and I stepped closer to ensure that it didn't have the chance. One leathery wing whacked me a second later, and I stumbled forward, falling to a crouch beside Ray and the Camazotz's head. The monster bit at me again, but it was too far away to reach. I leaned in over its jaws, reversed my grip on my knife, and rammed the weapon into the top of the Camazotz's head, pushing through the resistance of its skull to drive in the blade as far as I could. Once the cryptid had gone limp, apart from its twitching wings, I got shakily to my feet and helped Ray to push the corpse off of him. Standing up beside me, he cursed under his breath as he reloaded his pistol.

"My God...That was too damn close," he said after a moment, his voice still muffled in my ears after the sound of the gunshot. The Camazotz shifted on the floor, arching its tail, and Ray whipped out his machete lightning-fast and hacked into its neck, which made it fall still again.

"How badly are you hurt?" I asked him.

"Doesn't hurt too bad. Check for me," Ray said, turning so I could examine the wounds on his back and shoulders. They were bleeding, but not too heavily, and they weren't deep.

"Not too bad. We'll get to them after we're done here, if you can manage," I told him.

"I can hold on. Can you?" Ray asked, pointing to my left shoulder where I'd been stabbed by the Camazotz's tail. I took a moment to pull out a rag and tie it around the wound.

"It can wait. It didn't get me too deep," I answered.

"Then let's finish this. Only two Camazotz left. Maybe less. But how did this one get behind us?" Ray asked.

I didn't know, but the only possibility was that there was another exit from the cenote cave. We decided to go back into that main cavern, hoping to find the remaining Camazotz there. We weren't disappointed. The cavern floor was strewn with the corpses of the flock, and a single survivor stood amongst the carnage. The lone remaining Camazotz had black fur and was hunched over a dead one with brown fur, its snout buried deep into the corpse as it ate its own flock member. The scene churned my stomach, and my head swam with the stench. As Ray and I entered the cavern, the surviving Camazotz raised its head to look at us and then made a chattering noise and turned to flee. Its right wing was bleeding heavily, but it bounded forwards with its powerful legs and used its left wing to pull itself along the ground in an awkward hopping scramble. I couldn't help but pity the cryptid on some level; gross as it might be, it didn't want to die. But we couldn't let it go. Ray ran up and fired into the back of the monster's skull twice, causing it to crumple to the floor, where he finished it off with his machete.

"All clear, then. Let's count the bodies," I said after taking a short moment of silence.

There were eight dead Camazotz scattered across the cavern floor; along with the one we'd killed in the tunnel, that was the entire flock. Ray and I had done it. After taking care of our wounds, our next step was even more grim: Ray and I started to comb the whole cavern in search of Yarima's remains. I remember hoping the whole time that they hadn't fallen into the waters of the cenote; if they were down there, there was next to no chance of recovering them.

As we moved towards the rear of the cavern, Ray pointed out a large crack in the wall which was really only visible if you looked at it from an angle; it was about 10 feet up and definitely big enough for a Camazotz to fit into, if it folded its wings in. Although there wasn't much point in climbing up to check, both Ray and I agreed that the crack likely led to another opening to the outside, which must have been how the Camazotz in the tunnel got out and flanked around behind us.

More importantly, we found what we were looking for at the rear of the cavern. There were bones everywhere, but the first human one that I came across was a small femur, still stained red. My stomach dropped at the sight, but I crouched down to the damp floor and found some small chips of bone nearby, held together by dried flesh. As I took a closer look, I realized that the smaller pieces were the remnants of a foot, and my heart sank; I hadn't expected Yarima to be alive, of course, but this was still gut-wrenching. I called Ray over and together we continued scouring the area.

In the end, we found almost all of Yarima's body, except for some of her teeth, fingers, toes, and pieces of her skull, which the Camazotz had broken open; we even found a lot of her hair and parts of her clothes. All the bones were almost entirely stripped of flesh, and handling them felt so immensely wrong. We still had a bit of daylight left by the time we brought the first of the remains to the cave entrance, and over the course of a few trips, we brought them all down from the cave and put them in a separate bag. Then we returned downriver to the party that had led us here.

It was just before sunset when we got back to our guides, who were sitting around a fire talking with each other. They seemed surprised to see us back so quickly, but their expressions hardened and grew solemn when they heard and saw our results. Ray and I brought up the bag with the remains, and the Yanomami built a little sort of shelter out of leaves and branches for us to put it beneath; unfortunately, this didn't do much to block out the smell of the cavern that still hung over the bag.

We camped nearby for the night, and made our way back to the village in the morning. Yarima's mother was one of the first to meet us, taking the bag from us with tears that must have been a mixture of grief and relief. She kept repeating a phrase to us that Ray told me was a Yanomami expression of deep gratitude. The villagers invited us to stay, but Ray and I declined; we had to get somewhere with a phone to make a report and call in a cleanup crew. So we bid farewell to the Yanomami and headed back to Ray's farm. I stayed there for a while longer, and we paid the Yanomami a couple more visits in that time. And fortunately, none of those trips were nearly as eventful as our first.

I've been on one other Camazotz hunt, which I mentioned in an earlier letter as being the largest I've ever been on, in terms of the amount of Hunters that were actively involved. But that's a story for another time. This hunt in Brazil with Ray was my first experience with Camazotz, and it was a grim example of how dark and grisly Hunting can be sometimes. It can obviously get far worse, as I've talked about in letters like my previous one, but that still doesn't change how it felt to kill those Camazotz or find Yarima. In the end, though, Ray and I did our best to keep people safe, and that's what counts.

Now, I've got one more story before I go, because I'd like to share one of my more meaningful experiences with cryptids. Like my Camazotz hunt in Brazil, this was a situation that was brought on by circumstance and chance more than anything else. Also like that hunt, this one was concerned with the afterlife, and the eternal peace and restfulness of a spirit. In this case, it was Heather.

This happened in 2010, only a few months after I'd killed the wechuge in Quebec. At that time, I had put a lot of the trauma of those events behind me, especially after Heather had been buried on her family's big plot of land in the Irish countryside, alongside many of her Hunter ancestors. I won't tell you where in Ireland her family lives exactly, but it's in the north, immediately adjacent to a large tract of forest and a big pond. The graves are toward the south of the property, and not too far away is a big mound, which Heather told me was the home of some local daoine sídhe, a.k.a. faeries.

According to Heather's family stories, this group of fae had inhabited the area long before the arrival of humans, as is the case in countless other parts of Britain and Ireland. When Heather's ancestors had come to the area, the daoine sídhe had initially tried to drive them away, but upon realizing that the humans were capital-H Hunters, they proposed a deal: in exchange for leaving the mound, forest, and pond alone, and for protecting them against more aggressive members of both fae and humankind, the daoine sídhe allowed Heather's ancestors to settle on the land. So her family had lived on that land for a couple centuries, running their farm and helping to protect the local faeries if they were threatened by either cryptids or humans. I can't tell you how much of this is true and how much is legend, but Heather's family certainly does have a relationship with the faeries that live on their property. To this day they refuse to touch the woods, the pond, or the mound. Evidently none of Heather's surviving family members had ever personally seen or spoken to the daoine sídhe, but they all knew of their presence and followed the agreement that their ancestors had supposedly made with them.

As it happened, this was part of the reason why Heather's uncle and her Guide, Callum, contacted me in early 2010. Her uncle would rather remain anonymous, so let's just call him Finn. He was a former capital-H Hunter who hadn't really been cut out for the job; after a few hunts, he'd decided to leave the organization and take over the management of the family farm, the same one that I just talked about. Finn had lived there with his wife and their children for many years, and none of them ever saw or dealt with the daoine sídhe on the land, up until shortly before Finn and Callum called me. As they both explained to me, a malevolent and potentially dangerous faerie had recently appeared on the farm.

Finn told me that he hadn't seen anything at first; he had only felt a disturbing sensation whenever he'd venture near the forest or the nearby gravesite. Usually these were places of calm and peace, but then Finn had begun to get the feeling that he was being watched when he would go there. Apparently, this was a normal feeling in those areas, given that faeries do indeed live there, but now the sensation had become dark and sinister, like there was something *else* observing Finn. Something besides the normal faerie inhabitants of the land. Something that Finn called "evil".

The feelings of being watched by some dark presence had eventually escalated into full-on dread, making Finn's heart race and his muscles tense. He described feeling like the air had grown heavy and started pressing in around him, and a few times he'd flat-out turned back to the house. But he was determined to get to the bottom of whatever was wrong. One gray and rainy afternoon he went back out to the graves, pushing through the sensations of dread and danger that intensified with every step he took. As he got closer, he saw a red light in the distance, which he soon realized was coming from the mound: the little hill was emanating a blood-red glow, and Finn knew somehow that it was a warning. This spooked him enough to abandon his goal. As he turned back, he heard a booming owl's hoot from the woods, and he looked to the forest to see an enormous owl watching him from the top of a tree. According to Finn, the bird was nearly as tall as an adult man, with spotted brown, black, and red feathers; its eyes glowed an eerie orange, nearly red color, and Finn said that he could feel malice in its stare. He immediately recognized that this was the presence that had been watching him, and he broke, running back to the house and immediately calling Callum.

The two had determined that the owl was a type of faerie known as a Macha. The name "Macha" actually refers to one aspect of the Morrigan, an ancient Irish goddess associated with war, battle, fate, and death; in her form as Macha, the Morrigan is associated with birds like crows and owls, which is why the Hunters call these owl-shaped daoine sídhe by her name. In appearance, Macha faeries appear as gigantic owls or as owl-headed humanoids with feather-covered bodies. As with Finn, the presence of a Macha can cause feelings of extreme dread or even terror, and they seem to drive off other faeries. Macha are drawn to sites of death, and are usually seen at cemeteries, tombs, and other burial sites, anywhere from days to years after someone has been laid to rest there. Although it may sound silly, the locations of their appearances have led to the belief by many people that Macha devour the souls of the dead.

Before leaving for Ireland, I prepared as much as I could for what could very well be a fight against a hostile faerie. This consisted of two main things. First, I paid a visit to my weapon maker contacts from the Smith branch of the Hunters, who I've mentioned in previous letters. They were able to resupply me with plenty of new ammunition for my guns, all of which they had integrated with iron. The daoine sídhe hate iron; its touch burns them, slows them down, and prevents them from doing things like producing light or shifting their appearance. The second key ingredient in battling faeries is salt. Similarly to an experience I once had, which you may remember if you've listened to my letter about skinwalkers, salt can act like a barrier to the daoine sídhe; they usually can't move past it if it's scattered on the ground or in an entryway like a door or a windowsill. Although salt doesn't slow or suppress faeries like iron, it does burn them too, so I dunked all of my new iron bullets and buckshot pellets into a bucket of salt before I headed out. I also made a few "salt bombs", which were basically just little plastic pouches that I could throw or slam; upon contact with something solid, the bombs would split open and scatter salt in a small radius.

With all these preparations already made when I arrived in Ireland, I had Finn pick me up from the airport and take me right to the farm. As we drove, I asked him to update me on the current situation. Not much had changed, though. The red light from the faerie mound had faded, and the night before I'd arrived, there had been a thunderstorm that had shaken the house. Finn said that on several occasions he'd glimpsed the Macha's glowing eyes or its huge shadow near the house through the rain. It hadn't hurt anyone physically, but Finn said that he and his family were all experiencing the feelings of dread and anxiety consistently now, even inside the house; he'd felt scared just walking to the car from the front door. He actually started to tear up when he told me all of this, and although he didn't mention Heather or the graves, I knew he was terrified about their wellbeing too. I made a silent promise to myself that I would not give up on this mission, no matter what.

It didn't take long to reach the farm. When we arrived, it was still pretty early in the evening, but the sky overhead was almost pitch-black; it almost looked like the middle of the night, just with no stars or moon. It was raining lightly, and before I even stepped out of the car, I could already feel what Finn had described. The air felt too heavy and close, like it was pressing in on everything, and more than that, something just felt off, *wrong* somehow. The sensation of being watched hit me soon after that, and although I know it well, it still made me shiver.

"What do you think?" Finn asked quietly after I had stood outside the car for a moment.

"I don't like it. But I'll do my best to stop it," I answered, telling the truth as best as I could.

I started to grab my stuff from the back of the car; Finn moved to help, but I waved him off. I was going to get started immediately, and I had a sense that this wasn't going to take very long. In hindsight, I should have accepted his offer to go inside first; I was hungry and tired, and it would have been smart to get something to eat and take a nap before heading out. The house was also surrounded by a circle of salt, so it was a safe place to rest. But I just had an overwhelming instinct that I needed to get going right at that moment.

My pistol and shotgun were the firearms I would be bringing, but I wasn't expecting to use them as normal; I had packed all my ammunition in a box of salt, alongside my tomahawk and knives, and along with the salt bombs on my belt, these would be key to fighting any of the fae. Once I was geared up, I started off towards the graves, leaving behind anything that wouldn't be necessary for combat or basic wound treatment. It wasn't long before the woods rose up on my left side, with some of the trees just starting to grow their leaves again after the winter. I took a second to peer through the rain in that direction, but although I definitely felt that something was there, I didn't see anything.

Continuing on, the feeling that something was wrong only intensified, and the pressure in the air got heavier. Eventually, I caught sight of the mound in the distance; it was little more than a shadow through the rain, but I knew what it looked like from previous visits. My head started to spin at the sight of it, but I kept walking. The rain had turned the path underneath me from dirt to mud days ago, and each step made it just a tiny bit harder to slog through the watery muck. But soon I was rewarded with the sight of the graves, not too far away from the foot of the mound. The gravesite is simple, just a collection of maybe sixty tombstones surrounded by a low wooden fence. The few times I'd been here before had all been to visit Heather's grave, so I knew where hers was located.

Very quickly, after only a few more steps, it became noticeably harder to breathe, and I started to feel like I shouldn't be there. It was probably the Macha's presence causing this, but the urge to turn back soon grew almost overwhelming. I stopped walking and tried to take a deep breath, but I was physically unable to, and a feeling of utter helplessness washed over me with a full-body chill. Then I thought of two things.

First, I remembered the promise I'd made while driving to the farm with Finn: I had told myself that I was not going to give up on this mission, and I wanted to hold to that. And second, an image came to me. It was the memory of Heather's eyes in the moments before her death. Her eyes had been so calm, just like she herself had been throughout all our hunts. If she could be like that only moments away from the end of her life, then I could at least try to replicate it. Even today I do my best to channel that level of tranquility and peace.

I don't know much about spirits or souls or the afterlife, but I and most of my family believe that they exist in some form or another. In fact, one of the sacred objects that I wear on my hunts is a little ring of red glass seed beads passed down to me by my grandma; it was painstakingly and lovingly created and kept from decades ago as medicine for healing and protection in hard times, and it's also a direct line of connection to our ancestors. I know they're with me, because I've felt them, and on that day, I could also feel that, wherever they are, they had brought Heather to watch over me too. I actually have a special charm from her too, a little stone engraved with an Irish Sailor's Knot, a symbol of unbreakable love that was worn to safely bring sailors back home to their partners and families; as a knot, for us, it also represented the interconnected nature of everything outside of us as well. I keep these two items right next to each other, and I guess all of them got together to help me out. Suddenly, it was almost like Heather and I were on a task together again, and I had to protect her, like I couldn't do before.

After that, my ability to breathe and move returned, and I smiled and said a quick "Thank you" as I pressed on. Soon I was opening the door in the fence around the gravesite. When I stepped inside, the weight in the air lightened dramatically, like a literal load dropping off my back, and I actually breathed a sigh of relief. After taking a quick look around, nothing seemed out of the ordinary, visually speaking. Ever since personally encountering the Macha, Finn had been unable to bring himself to go back to the graves, so he hadn't salted around the area. I totally understood, and in fact, that might actually be beneficial for me. I wanted to draw the monster out, and I had a sense that the graves would be the best place for that; I doubted that the Macha would risk approaching a human with a firearm if there was also a barrier of salt in the way. Finn had seen the Macha at the edge of the treeline, and instinct told me that it was still somewhere in that direction. I felt anxious, but ready, so I took up a position at the entrance of the gravesite to wait.

Because of the black sky overhead, there was no sunlight to indicate the passage of time. I mostly remember keeping a surprisingly level head. Sometimes I can get lost in my thoughts or feelings during the long periods of inactivity on hunts, although over time I've gotten better at being in the moment and focusing on the present. On that day in Ireland, I remember keeping very calm while waiting for the Macha. A million different emotions and thoughts came up, of course, but I didn't let them derail me. I was sad and scared and I missed Heather tremendously, but more than all that, I felt determined. I was going to see this through.

After what must have been a few hours, the sky had gotten even darker, and the rain had intensified a bit. There had been a few rumbles of thunder, and I had seen lightning in the distance a couple times. At some point, the weight of the air around me started to increase noticeably. And then I heard a series of owl's hoots from the woods to the east. I've always found the sound of owls hooting pretty cool, for lack of a better word, and it is related to my name, after all. But the call of the Macha was just unearthly; it was much too deep in pitch and boomed like a drum. A few seconds after the sound, I saw a pair of orange-red eyes flare into view at the top of a tall, dead tree. The Macha's body seemed to fade into view a moment later. Finn's description was accurate: the faerie appeared just like an enormous owl, its feathers speckled in various shades of brown, black, and red. Two feathery tufts stuck straight up from the sides of its head like horns, and I could practically see the danger and dark intentions in its eyes. The Macha and I stared at each other for what might have been nearly a minute, before eventually I chose to make the first move.

Most of the daoine sídhe are very intelligent and are usually just as smart as humans, if not more so. Most can also speak. Faeries mainly speak to each other in their own languages, but many of them are able to communicate with humans in English, Gaelic, and other human languages. This means that, much of the time, faeries can be negotiated with; in fact, the Hunters who specialize in dealing with the daoine sídhe usually act much more like diplomats than warriors. With all this in mind, I decided to try talking to the Macha. Maybe that was stupid, but I always try to avoid bloodshed if at all possible, and I figured there was a good chance that the Macha would at least understand me. Not breaking eye contact, I stepped forward. I felt a little silly as I began speaking, but I didn't stop.

"Hello. My name is Sam White Owl. I am a Hunter. My duty is to keep balance between humans and beings like yourself. The people of this place have an agreement with the daoine sídhe who live here. I'm here to uphold that agreement and protect all of them," I said.

The Macha didn't respond, and again I felt ridiculous. What was I even doing? Then the Macha flapped off of its perch. Tendrils of mist and rain streaked from its feathers, trailing behind it as it moved. I held my ground, ready to raise my shotgun, but the monster didn't attack. It swooped down and landed on top of the fence about 50 feet away, shaking the wooden posts. It locked eyes with me again, and for a second time, I tried talking to it.

"I don't know why you've come, but I won't let you hurt anyone, living or dead. Please, go. I have no desire to fight you, but I will if I have to. Go. Go, and we can all live in peace," I said, trying not to raise my voice any further.

The Macha spread its wings wide, revealing streaks of rust-colored feathers on the undersides. It didn't open its black beak, but I very clearly heard three words:

LEAVE THIS PLACE.

The faerie's tone was calm but cold. But I couldn't do what it said.

"I can't. You know this. I'm sorry. I don't want violence. Go. Please," I repeated, already bracing myself.

The Macha was silent for a moment, then opened its beak and gave a raspy, ear-splitting screech. I winced and nearly dropped my shotgun to cover my ears, and then, with a single flap of its massive wings, the Macha surged forwards at me. I immediately took aim, and just a second later, when the faerie was almost on top of me, I fired. In the instant before I pulled the trigger, the Macha veered to the side with an almost incomprehensible speed, dodging the shot completely. I swung my barrel and turned, trying to get back on target. Just before the Macha hit me, I caught a glimpse of dark feathers and fired once again, and the cryptid let out a cry of pain as it crashed into me.

I went tumbling backwards, feeling the Macha's sharp talons shredding through my jacket into my forearms, but I'd thrown off its attack, and the wounds weren't deep. I hit the ground on my back, keeping a tight hold on my gun, and then the Macha was over me, trying to grasp my arms with the vice-like grip of its talons. It almost succeeded, but I managed to jerk one hand free and reach for my belt. The enormous beak snapped down at my face, but I leaned my head to the side to avoid it, then smashed a salt bomb right into the side of the owl's feathered head. The package burst open, spraying grains of salt across both my face and the Macha's, but of course, this only hurt one of us.

The Macha flapped backwards, battering me with its wings in the process and letting out loud, booming coughs as it jetted into the air. Like the reaction of walkers to blessed ash or werewolves to silver, the salt had burned the faerie: clouds of whitish-gray smoke or steam were billowing out from the side of its face. Ignoring the pain in my arms, I raised my shotgun and started shooting. The Macha was flapping erratically, moving in unpredictable bursts both horizontally and vertically, so I never landed a direct hit, but I did see a few more plumes of smoke erupt across its wings where a few of my iron buckshot pellets hit. After one of these shots, the cryptid gave a short screech and went down, falling to the side and hitting the ground with an audible thump.

A tombstone stood between me and the huge cloud of smoke that was fuming up from where the Macha had landed. The cloud had eliminated my line of sight, and the tombstone blocked me from getting a shot, so I ran to the side to get a better angle. As I moved, the steam billowed and shifted, and as I stopped to take aim, the Macha rushed me again. It had shifted forms inside the cloud: now, instead of a huge owl, it was in the shape of a lean humanoid figure with an owl's head and a body covered in feathers; its hands and feet both ended in huge talons, and its wounds still trailed smoke as it moved.

I had been expecting the Macha to come around either side of the tombstone, but instead it leapt straight over the obstacle before I had time to adjust my aim. My first shot went wide, and my second went off harmlessly into the air as the Macha reached me and yanked the gun barrel aside with one taloned hand. It was stronger than its relatively lanky new shape appeared, and it grasped my gun with both hands and tore it away from me with seemingly little effort. I sprang backwards, grasping to pull my tomahawk out of the sheath on my back. Either the Macha didn't know how to use a shotgun or its talons prevented it from doing so; whatever the case, it moved in on me fast, swinging the gun by the barrel like a club in one hand and slashing with the talons of the other.

One of its unarmed swipes just barely caught me across the face, slicing shallow gashes across my cheek and temple, but I managed to duck its next swings and pull out my tomahawk. The Macha's attack was unrelenting, keeping me on the defensive. I used the handle of the tomahawk to block the faerie's makeshift club, and each time I caught one of its strikes, the collision sent a shockwave through my arms. There was no opening for me to retaliate, and I was tiring fast. Just then, there was a bright flash of white light from behind me. I realized that it had come from the mound, and it was so bright that it temporarily blinded me; if I had been facing it, I have no doubt that it would have taken out my vision for far longer.

Judging by the Macha's screech, it was blinded as well, and when my eyesight returned, I saw it stumbling backwards; it had been facing the flash, and with the keen vision of its owl's eyes, its sense of sight must have been completely shot. The faeries of the farm had helped me, and this was my chance to repay them. I stepped in on the Macha and swung my tomahawk as hard as I could with both hands, aiming squarely for its neck. I landed the hit exactly, slashing through the Macha's neck in a spray of blood and smoke. Then I pulled the tomahawk free and the Macha's steaming corpse toppled to the muddy ground.

I took a deep breath as I stepped back from the fallen faerie, waving smoke out of my face. The white cloud of fumes totally enveloped the Macha's whole body, and only at this point did it strike me that the steam had no real smell; maybe the rain was dulling whatever scent it may have had. In any case, I watched as the smoke cloud began to rise, and with it, an eerie, beautiful sight. A soft blue glow slowly came to life from within the cloud, and then a very distinct orb of this light slowly rose from the Macha's fallen form. I blinked a couple times, and one of these times, I swore that I saw a pale silhouette of the Macha's owl form, clutching the ball of light in its talons. An instant later, the image was gone, but the sphere of light remained, continuing to float slowly upwards.

When it was about 10 feet above the ground, the light stopped, and I got the feeling of being watched again. This time, though, there was none of the dread and hostility I'd felt earlier; now, the sensation just felt neutral. Then I heard the Macha's voice again, as clear and calm as it had been the first time. Now, however, it seemed almost approving.

WELL FOUGHT, WHITE OWL.

Then the orb of light darted forward, sailing overhead. I watched as it soared towards the mound, circled it once, and then plunged down into it, vanishing from sight. I felt the weight in the air lift, and all the prior feelings of fear and darkness lifted with it. The sky was still black, and the rain showed no signs of stopping, but I could feel that I'd done it. The farm and everyone on it, living and dead, human and monster, were safe.

I still don't know the meaning of the blue light that I saw rise from the Macha's body. I've told quite a few people about it and made sure to note it in my report on the situation. Similar things have been reported before with other types of daoine sídhe. The general conclusion that people seem to come to, which I agree with, is that the light was some kind of intangible representation of the Macha's very being; you might even call it a spirit, or a soul. As for why it flew into the faerie mound, I think only the inhabitants of the mound know for certain. My best guess is that what was left of the Macha integrated itself into the population of the daoine sídhe that live on the farm; maybe it felt like it owed them, or maybe it had nowhere else to go. Whatever the case, Finn says that to this day, everything is calm on the farm, so it looks like everyone is all getting along.

Right after I saw the light, I went over to the fence and leaned on it to bandage myself; all of my wounds were pretty shallow, but it took a while to stop the bleeding. I was shaky and a little light-headed, but before I staggered back to the house, I did two things. First, I turned to the faerie mound and bowed my head to it, before calling out to whoever might be listening there.

"You saved my life. Thank you for protecting me as I try to protect you."

There was no response, but for some reason I felt like my words had been heard. I waved farewell to the mound and went to do the second thing. Slowly, I moved to the back of the gravesite and found the thin vertical rectangle that was Heather's tombstone. I knelt down on the wet grass in front of it and took my usual moment to breathe and connect before I started speaking. To be completely honest, I don't remember exactly what I said to Heather on that occasion; I think I got emotional and didn't write much about it in my journal afterwards. But I know that thanked her for continuing to guide, inspire, and strengthen me, especially on all of my hunts. I gave her a quick life update and checked in with her about my feelings, and I expressed my gratitude for being able to protect her from the Macha; it didn't make up for failing to protect her from the wechuge, but I was doing my best, which I know she understood.

Finally, when I was done, I took a moment of silence before saying goodbye the way we used to end our phone calls, the same way I end these letters for you.

"Thanks, Heather. I love you...We'll talk more soon."

I took one more moment to be silent and feel the warmth and peace of connecting with Heather again. Then I stood, picked up all my gear, and made my way back to the house. Finn called Callum and a cleanup crew, and he and his wife started to help fix me up. I stayed passed out on the farm for a couple more days, but eventually I recovered enough to bid them farewell and return to the States. After that, you already know some of the rest of my story. Eventually I met Serena, started to help train my nephew, and haven't stopped hunting since, although I will say that I am getting pretty damn close to calling it quits.

As I get close to that point, it's been good to look back on where I've been. Coming to Swamp Dweller has offered me a unique chance to do that, and both he and every single one of you have been vital in helping me to share my stories and information. It's had a far bigger impact than I ever expected, so I want to thank all of you from the bottom of my heart for making that happen. I hope that what I've shared can help keep you safe, or inspire you, or at the very least gave you a bit of enjoyment. It's truly been a pleasure sharing with you. I've got plenty more stories, but at least for now, this is goodbye. So thank you again, and much love to you all. Please continue to stay safe from cryptids, pandemics, depression, or whatever else. I hope we'll talk more soon. And this has been Sam White Owl, signing out.

Q&A – DOGMAN

- What is the most dangerous cryptid?

This is a difficult question to answer, because pretty much all monsters can be dangerous in their own right. But some are naturally more aggressive or threatening to humans. The wendigo is one such monster. Yes, they are real, but they're incredibly rare nowadays, and very difficult to kill. No, wendigo do not have antlers; the antlered creatures you might see are usually called Tall Deer by Hunters, and they're also rare and threatening. We can talk about both of these cryptids in another letter. The aswang of the Philippines is, to put it super simply, a vampire-type monster, and although they're strong and fast, their stealth is what really makes them dangerous; most aswang victims are dead before they even have a chance to fight back. And if you're stupid enough to get on the bad side of a troll or a thunderbird, then they will squash you like an ant, even though they normally don't go after humans. All in all, though, this is a bit like asking what the most dangerous animal is. Hippos, lions, tigers, vipers, elephants, or even mosquitoes could all be valid answers, not to mention humans.

- What do you think about Missing 411?

I've gotten a couple comments talking about the Missing 411 series. I only know a little about it, but if I understand correctly, it's all about real-life unsolved disappearances in the wilderness. I can definitely say that a lot of missing persons cases have cryptids behind them, but I'd have to look into it more to tell you exactly what types I think could be involved in specific instances. That being said, there's usually a far less mysterious explanation, and I know for a fact that a lot of people exaggerate, omit, and/or flat-out make up facts, sometimes to sensationalize events or promote one particular theory, and sometimes out of negligence and bad research. More people than you might like to admit go missing for very mundane and often very tragic reasons. It's not like there's thousands of serial killers stalking the woods constantly, but dangerous people do sometimes use the wilderness as cover. And unfortunately, a lot of people actually *want* to disappear, and go out into the woods to do it.

- Are there any places that people should stay away from in order to avoid cryptids?

This is funny, because cryptids can be pretty much anywhere. There are even quite a few that look like humans or have a human form. This makes it tough to avoid them entirely. However, many of the most dangerous monsters live in places that are relatively far away from human settlements: far northern tundra, isolated areas of the forest or jungle, or the deep ocean. In these places, even if you aren't expecting cryptids, you need to be extra aware of your surroundings, and probably bring a friend, a weapon, or both. Being in a group reduces the chances of being attacked by a wild creature (or dangerous person, as I just mentioned), and of getting lost or stranded somewhere; honestly, both of these are much more likely than running into a cryptid.

- Are there any animals that we thought were extinct but are still alive today?

Sort of, but not in the exact forms you might recognize. For example, there are quite a few dinosaur-like cryptids, but they're likely not *direct* descendants of the dinosaurs. And if they are, they're certainly not identical to their ancestors; they've had to go through 65 million years of evolution and major environmental changes. Others, like the Loch Ness Monster, don't seem to exist. Sorry, Nessie fans. But birds are classified as dinosaurs, so maybe you can be happy with that. There are some other relict creatures too, but again, they're not one-to-one identical to their ancestors.

- Have I hunted a gamer?

Ha ha, very funny. But I have had to fight people before, which is a dark and upsetting story that I'm not going to tell right now.

- What do I know about vampires?

Quite a few people asked about vampires, and yes, they are real. They don't shapeshift or have any "magical" powers, but they are very strong and very fast, and they live for hundreds of years. Like some other monsters, they look basically identical to humans, and some were actually humans originally. Our two peoples get along just fine, and there are actually a few Hunters, mostly in Europe, who are vampires themselves.

~

We'll end the question-and-answer section of this letter by addressing some international listeners. This time, I saw comments from South Africa, New Zealand, and Canada.

- Canada?

I've been to Canada many times, since it's right next to the US and our countries share a good deal of monsters. There are a bunch of Canadian Hunters, all very active. In the big picture, you'll find crawlers in the south, Sasquatch and Deer People all across the country, and more dangerous cold-weather creatures like wendigo further north. A few monsters that live mainly in Alaska, like kushtaka and amarok, range east and south into Canada too.

- New Zealand?

New Zealand has a lot of Hunters too, although not as many as Australia, along with some really unique monsters. Among the most dangerous are the Maero, who are similar to Sasquatch; you can find them in upland alpine regions, but their population is small. Some of New Zealand's smallest monsters are the Patupaiarehe and the Ponaturi, who are a lot like fairies or goblins; they're also very rarely seen, and usually pretty peaceful. Every so often, Kiwi Hunters may have to deal with a taniwha, which are huge aquatic reptiles; most taniwha were killed off long ago, but there are a few left, and the Hunters keep close tabs on them. Tons of animals like kiwis and kakapos also used to be considered cryptids.

-South Africa?

There's a decent-sized Hunter population in South Africa, including some who come from the Zulu and Sotho traditions. Perhaps the most dangerous South African cryptid is the Impundulu, also called the Lightning Bird; many Hunters believe that they might be related to the North American thunderbird. Then there's the Tikoloshe, little gremlin-like beings who don't have nearly as many magic powers as in most of the stories. You've also got Inkanyamba, which are like huge eels, and Grootslangs, enormous cave-dwelling serpents very closely related to pythons. And no, Grootslangs do not have elephant heads, but they do have tusk-like fangs and weird little flaps that look like ears.

Hopefully some of those last answers gave a decent glimpse into the wider world of cryptids. There are monsters and Hunters pretty much everywhere. I would guess that most of you guys are from the US, so it's important to keep in mind that the world is a big place, and our experiences are actually a small minority of the greater whole!

Q&A – SKINWALKER

- Are some cryptids vulnerable to silver?
Yes, and I can personally confirm it. I mentioned in my previous letter that I've dealt with a werewolf in France, and I was advised to use silver bullets, which some European hunters swear by. So I commissioned some rounds infused with a silver alloy, and when I shot the giant wolf with them, the wounds actually appeared to smoke or steam rather than bleed. It was bizarre, but it worked. Other creatures are vulnerable to different substances, like iron; the fae of Britain and Ireland can hardly stand the touch of it. Is copper a reliable substitute for silver? I'm not sure; I've never tried it. But a bullet between the eyes usually does the trick no matter what metal it's made out of.

- Is it possible for crawlers to group up and hunt bigger game like humans?
I guess so, but I can't find any records of it. Crawlers seem to be very solitary, but there are a few accounts of pairs being spotted. They obviously need to get together to reproduce, and I imagine that young ones probably stay with their parents for a little while. I highly doubt that they'd ever come together to hunt in groups, though. It's such a tragedy that so much of this knowledge must have been lost in the extermination effort I mentioned.

- How many Hunters normally go on a job together?

It very much depends on the situation. I'd say that I mostly work alone. But as you see in most of these letters, I usually try to link up with at least one local Hunter whenever I'm dealing with a new monster or traveling somewhere I don't know well, especially international locations. The largest number of Hunters I've worked with at once was five, when we were going after a group of Camazotz in southern Mexico and Guatemala.

- How did Hunters bring down monsters in past centuries if such heavy firepower is required to kill cryptids?

Well, the old-fashioned way: a lot of effort and a lot of manpower. Old stories and records show that Hunters used all sorts of weapons: swords, spears, bows, axes, halberds, harpoons, hammers, and just about anything else you can imagine. As it's always been, they usually made kills by striking hard enough in the right places, usually the head, eyes, and chest. An arrow in the eye or a hammer to the skull can be just as effective as any modern bullet. It was incredibly risky, though, since Hunters usually had to get up close to do damage. It was brutal and vicious work. Hunting in our own era is dangerous and horrific, but it's got nothing on how things were in the old days.

Q&A - WENDIGO + TALL DEER

- Are dogmen vulnerable to silver?

I'm not sure, actually. Unlike with werewolves, I've never tried using silver on wolfmen. However, if the theory of these two monsters being related is correct, then I guess silver might be effective on both. But as you may have seen in my third letter, you don't need silver to bring dogmen down.

- How did my family get involved with monster hunting?

Well, I wish there was some elaborate origin myth, like some superhero story, but there's not. I think my mom's side of the family, the Cherokee one, has just been dealing with cryptids for generations, trying to help people and monsters coexist in peace. In our community, we were often the ones who people came to when there were problems with beings like Sasquatches or dogmen. Then at some point, one of us got the attention of the Hunters, and our family joined up. The first formal record of any of my ancestors being enrolled comes from 1753. He was named Matthew Drum, and I'm sure he's one of the main guys who's been watching over our family ever since.

- What are my weapons like?

I know some of you guys are really into guns, and I got multiple questions about my choices. Almost all of them are custom-built, not officially manufactured by a company. The Hunters who craft our gear, especially weapons and armor, are known as Smiths, capital-S; the name comes from "blacksmith", because that's always been their role in our organization. There are different Smiths all over the world, and many of the best in North America are in the Deep South of the USA. I won't give the exact names of the guys I work with, but they make great (and often pretty weird) weapons.

Most of my firearms are made from some combination of parts from standard guns, along with components specially tailored for my personal needs and preferences. For example, the regular, publicly available Taurus Raging Hunter (ironic naming, I know) is a revolver, but my version has been rigged very differently. It takes some parts from the Raging Hunter, mainly the barrel, sight, trigger and trigger guard, and a bit of the hammer. The rest, however, is all custom-made in order to accept a magazine rather than a cylinder. These custom parts are balanced out to work with all the others, and the Smiths did such a smooth and seamless job making this pistol that you might never realize it's kind of a Frankenstein's monster. I had it made because I really liked the feel and shooting of the Raging Hunter, but I preferred a magazine over a speedloader; I'd need to have one of those two options, since on hunts, there's often no time to reload each chamber of a revolver individually. It might seem unnecessary (and might actually be illegal), but the result is definitely worth it.

- Can I confirm any Creepypasta monsters?
I actually didn't know what "Creepypasta" was until I saw

some comments talking about it! What a wacky name. But "online horror stories" is too long, and lacks the goofiness factor. Having looked into some stories a little more, most of what I've seen is fictional, but some things could be genuine. For example, the Rake monster is almost certainly a crawler. Others are definitely fictional, like the Slenderman and whatever the hell a Kazatrapp is.

- More importantly... do cryptids take huge poops?

You bet! The bigger the monster, the bigger the poop. Everyone poops, after all.

~

Let's respond to some of the people from outside the US. This time, I'll get to commenters from Japan, Brazil, Russia, and Eastern Europe. As usual, all of these places have monsters and active Hunter communities.

- Japan?

Japan in particular is home to lots of very strange and very terrifying creatures, some of which are unlike anything else on the planet. The most well-known among the Hunters might be the kappa, small amphibious humanoids with beaks and turtle-like shells; they're mischievous more than anything else, so they typically aren't too dangerous. Also mischievous are the multi-tailed fox-folk, known as kitsune in Japan (they're the same as the huli jing in China and the kumiho in Korea). All of the fox-folk are shy and very rarely seen, but they're highly intelligent, with a rich, very mysterious culture and some shapeshifting and other "magical" abilities. More dangerous cryptids include creatures like the tsuchigumo, giant cave-dwelling spiders that are becoming increasingly rare, and spectral beings like the yuki-onna, a.k.a. "snow women". There are countless other types of monsters that call Japan home, far too many to name here, but like everywhere else, the populations of many Japanese creatures are decreasing steadily as cities and urban areas expand.

- Brazil?

Brazil also has a ton of cryptids, although the Hunter community there has gotten a bit smaller in the past few years. As in other countries, most Brazilian monsters inhabit rural and wilderness areas, and in this case, the Amazon rainforest has always been home to many of these. You may have heard of the mapinguari, a giant humanoid that might be related to the North American Sasquatch. There are also the caipora, who are small human-like creatures who play tricks on people in the jungle; just like the stories, they ride on small rainforest pigs known as peccaries. A few enormous serpent cryptids also make their home in Brazil, with the largest being the aquatic boiúna, who share the rivers with the mermaid-like iara.

- Russia and Eastern Europe?

I got many questions about Russia and too many countries in East Europe to go over individually. These regions have a lot in common, though, although Russia is far, far bigger and has a lot of other unique monsters too. The most famous would certainly be the vampire, which likely originated in what's now Hungary or Romania, although we're not entirely sure. As I mentioned in an earlier letter, vampires are essentially humans with increased physical capabilities who need to consume blood to survive. Then there's a variety of giant humanoids, who are closely related to each other and probably to Sasquatches. These guys live in the mountains, and humans call them many different things across various regions and languages; "Almas" and "Abnauayu" are two common names. Because of the hostile northern environment where most of them live, they can be very difficult to learn about.

Werewolves are common across Europe as well, including the eastern parts. There are also a few human-like cryptids who dwell in the lakes and forests, most of whom resemble stereotypical elves (think Lord of the Rings); there are many groups with many names, like the vila, rusalka, or samodiva. None of them have all the spectacular powers that they do in the folktales and myths, but they can do some truly incredible things, like start fires out of thin air or call animals directly to them. Without exception, they're extremely secretive and incredibly hard to learn about (unless you can earn their trust, which is apparently very difficult). Lastly, a variety of reptilian monsters inhabit Eastern Europe as well, mainly in the mountains and seas. There are also too many of these to name individually, but they include the ala and the kulshedra, two types of gigantic, winged serpent-like cryptids that sometimes grow multiple heads and seemingly influence the weather. You might even call them dragons!

Q&A – THUNDERBIRD

- What do I know about aliens?

Not much, really. Statistically speaking, it seems likely that they exist, and there's too many reports to just dismiss. I think they could certainly be out there somewhere, but I've never had a personal experience with them. Pretty much all of the creatures that Hunters deal with seem to originate from this planet. But I'm always up for learning more and broadening my horizons.

- Speaking of aliens, have I ever encountered any black-eyed children?

This is something that I had to look up, actually! They're supposedly strange children with pale skin and pitch-black eyes, often suspected to be extraterrestrial somehow. I had no idea what these beings even were, and there are no official Hunter records of them, but maybe I can ask around. Again, alien stuff really isn't my thing. So even if these black-eyed children are real, I unfortunately don't know much about them.

- Why do cryptid sightings and encounters seem to be more common in the past 10 to 20 years?

There's a lot of possible reasons for this. Humans have been encountering cryptids pretty much forever, but as urban areas expand and we push further into so-called "undeveloped" land, we encounter all sorts of creatures more commonly, including monsters. Wilderness activities, and travel in general, have also become much easier and safer; more people are going to more places, so they're more likely to encounter more monsters. Also, even though sightings and encounters have indeed become more frequent over the past couple decades, there's also been an increase in people actually coming forward with their stories. Modern technology like cellphones and the Internet have also allowed people to share their experiences much more widely, including made-up ones! So on that front, sightings and encounters are also being *reported* more frequently.

- Are faeries real, and have I ever encountered them?

Yes and yes. Faeries are also called the fae or the daoine sídhe, and there are many species of them, most of whom are not the stereotypical Tinkerbell pixies that float around your garden. They're endemic to Britain and Ireland, with very few anywhere else. This is mainly why I haven't dealt with them much, since I haven't done a ton of jobs in that part of the world. But I have had a few experiences with the daoine sídhe, and my nephew has handled a lot of cases involving them, so I can ask him more about it. The main job of some British and Irish Hunters is to deal with the fae, so I might contact some of them too. Maybe I can even do a letter focused on faeries sometime down the line.

- Root beer or cream soda?

I'll say root beer, but only because I've never really tasted cream soda. I love a good root beer float.

- Do I think the US government has done any experiments involving cryptids?

I don't know. I certainly hope not, although I wouldn't be surprised, unfortunately. But I can guarantee that cryptids did not originate from any sort of human experiment. Most of them have been around since ancient times.

- What types of non-human creatures are allowed to join the Hunters?

I'm not involved in recruiting, but this is an interesting question. As far as I know, we don't have rules about what species can or cannot be members of our organization. As long as they agree to our mission and our purpose, we'll probably accept them! Of course, they also have to be qualified for the job, just like any human would have to be. Some of us are faeries, vampires, and werewolves, just to name a few. Just like in any community, however, there's certainly racism within the Hunters; I've experienced it myself, and I'm sure that non-human Hunters have to put up with very similar problems. But we usually make arrangements and treaties with different cryptids, rather than actually take them into the organization itself; it's a lot easier to just cooperate with different cryptids than it is to recruit them all into the Hunters. I could write a whole essay about this, so we'll leave it here for now.

~

Now it's time for some cryptids from around the world. This time I saw comments asking about India, southeast Asia, and the Netherlands.

- India?

India is one of those places that has an enormous amount of cultural diversity packed into a single area, and many of its local monsters are spread over surrounding regions too. A few comments mentioned specific cryptids, so I'll hit those first. The infamous Monkey Man of Delhi was indeed a hoax (essentially just some guy in a suit, as far as we know), but there are a few primate cryptids in South Asia that are real. The Mande Barung is an Indian relative of the North American Sasquatch, and of course the Yeti, the lovely Abominable Snowman of the Himalayas, is related to both as well. At the most basic level, they're all large, hairy humanoids.

Then there are the rakshasas, who aren't quite as powerful as in the myths, but are still very strong. Some of them take on a demon-like appearance in their human forms, but they're best-known for changing shape into a few different animals; like skinwalkers, it's often predatory beasts like tigers and wolves. I'm not sure where rakshasas come from, but they usually take a form that's nearly indistinguishable from humans, and some choose to live alongside us, generally in big cities; they're just as intelligent as us, and our species usually get along perfectly well. In fact, the average rakshasa is pretty shy, but they're mighty, and some can certainly pose a threat...just like humans. There are also some dogmen and vampires in different parts of Asia, and Indian Hunters have records of both, although they're pretty rare. India also has some reptilian monsters, like some truly huge unrecognized (by most non-Hunters) types of snake, and the giant, semi-aquatic monitor lizard known as the Buru. Offshore, there are also the very rare makara, enormous sea mammals that resemble crocodiles and fish combined; they don't have elephant heads like in the myths, but they do have long trunk-like snouts. I've met a makara before, so maybe that'll be for another letter.

- Southeast Asia?

This is a massive region, with far too many cryptids to go over here. We just mentioned the Indian rakshasas, who are spread across much of Southeast Asia as well. There are also lots of primates, like the Batutut, who live on both the mainland and the island of Borneo, although they're mostly found in Vietnam; the infamous "Rock Apes" that American soldiers encountered during the Vietnam War were Batutut. Interestingly, they're more closely related to gibbons, the so-called "lesser apes" (although I hate that term), than to Sasquatches, chimpanzees, and humans, the "greater apes" (an equally terrible term). A closer Sasquatch relative is the Orang Gadang, who lives in Indonesia. Also from Indonesia are the Siwil, small humanoid beings who are very shy and similar to the Little People of North America, and the golden, leopard-like cat known as the cigau. I've mentioned aswang, the terrifying vampire-like monsters of the Philippines, in a previous letter. The highlands and oceans of the Philippines are also home to the Marcupo, gargantuan snakes that are massive enough to be thought of as the sea serpents from old legends.

- The Netherlands?

There aren't too many cryptids here, because it's such a small area, but there are some. Probably the most unique are the Kabouter, little gnome-like creatures that live in woodlands and under hills. They're nowhere near as helpful to humans as they are in the fairy tales, though; in fact, they don't really like to interact with us at all, and usually run or hide if we show up. And no, not all of them wear red hats and have beards, although some do. A few Dutch waterways are home to a small number of nixies, mermaid-like beings; no, they can't shapeshift, but they are just as intelligent as in the stories. Unfortunately, because of water pollution and increased human population, nixies are incredibly rare in the Netherlands nowadays. Then of course you have your werewolves and vampires, which are common in most European countries.

Q&A – BUNYIP + MAKARA

- Are there any cryptids bigger than a Sasquatch or dogman?

More than you might want to believe! I've already mentioned a bunch, such as thunderbirds and several kinds of reptile. But if you're wondering specifically about bipedal creatures, trolls easily have you covered. They live in Scandinavia and can stand a whopping 50 feet tall; the largest on record was supposedly over 100 feet tall, but if that's true, then I think the ones that got that big have probably all died out, unfortunately. Any troll, but especially those really enormous ones, truly would have been known as "giants". Interestingly, the laws of physics and thermodynamics should make it impossible for a creature this tall and with this body structure to even exist, but you should know by now just how many rules get broken when it comes to monsters. If King Kong or Godzilla can do it in the movies, I guess trolls can try their best to keep up!

- What do I know about dragons?

So, if you're talking about the standard Western European dragon image, the kind with four legs, wings, and flaming breath, then no, they don't really exist. However, there are a few kinds of similar large reptiles that Hunters sometimes refer to as "dragons". Most of them resemble winged snakes, although some have a single pair of legs, and they mainly live in Eastern Europe these days, in mountain ranges like the Balkans and large bodies of water like deep lakes, coves, or seas. On a related note, you might find it interesting that apart from a few cryptids, there are essentially no vertebrates (creatures with a backbone) that have six limbs. The classical Western dragon would be an exception to the rule, with four legs and two wings; a wing is just a different type of limb from an arm or a leg.

- What do I know about the Goatman?

Well, we should probably be saying Goat*men*, because they're likely a group; among the Hunters, we use the plural term, and they aren't well-understood. They're not common either, but the few that we know of crop up in places all over the United States, rather than a smaller, localized region. A lot of the popular stories are just urban legends and nonsense, but the mimicking voices is true, and absolutely bone-chilling. Strangely, this has all been in fairly recent times; almost all the encounters and reports of goatmen are from the 1950s at the earliest, including among the Hunters. Unlike with Sasquatch or dogmen, there hasn't been any long-standing interaction between humans and goatmen in North America, at least none that I know of. Unfortunately, all this means I don't have much info on them, but they have been aggressive in the past, so just like any other wild creature, you probably want to just leave them alone.

- What happens to monsters after Hunters deal with them?

In almost every case, we call in a cleanup crew after tranquilizing or killing a target. Hunters who make up the cleanup crews are sometimes called Undertakers, with a capital-U; that name sounds very grim, and it certainly can be, but like most Hunter titles, it comes from an earlier time, when extermination was always the end goal of a hunt. Nowadays things are different, but an Undertaker's job is still to deal with whatever situation might be left after a hunt. For sedated and captured cryptids, they're in charge of transporting and relocating them to locations that Hunters and capital-G Guides pick out. For dead cryptids, I've heard that the crews usually burn them, occasionally bury them, or take them back to a facility for research. Again, that's just what I've heard; I really don't know for myself exactly what happens to the bodies. Cleanup crews also...well, clean up a location if needed, often to conceal aspects of Hunter activity. That frequently entails cooperating with Guides and interfacing with community leaders or local government and law enforcement, usually to secure a location and/or manage PR stuff. But an Undertaker's main priority is the actual monsters.

- How many licks does it take to get to the center of a Tootsie Pop?

You know, I think I once tried counting this, but I must have given up eventually. It's really hard! So I can't give you an exact number, but it has to be at least a couple thousand, right?

But some cryptids have rough tongues, so for them it would probably take far fewer.

- If wendigo are always hungry, then why would they capture people to transform them?

This is a very insightful question! I can't give you one certain answer, and neither can the Hunters in general, but there are some ideas. I think it must have to do with the innate drive that every creature has to continue their bloodline; in this case, transforming humans into other wendigo would serve a similar purpose to traditional reproduction, although (presumably) without the usual sharing of genetics. Somehow, wendigo must be able to balance this with their constant need for food. Maybe they only capture people if they have another readily available food source? I've also only ever heard of people being captured by wendigo when they're in groups; the monster kills and eats most of them, then takes one or two survivors away to be transformed. So I would guess that they really prefer to *eat* humans, but will capture them if there's access to other food. In any case, I'm not entirely sure, but there's my best guess, and it's a very good question, although a dark one.

- What do you do when you track a cryptid?

Well, hopefully from my stories so far, you've gotten a decent idea of this, but I'll get a bit more specific. Now, I could write whole books on this, but here are some of the fundamentals. Tracking a monster is usually a lot like tracking any other animal, and to be successful, you should have a good idea of their habits, behavior, and way of life. Of course, you also need to get clues, which are called "sign". Pretty much any trace of a creature's presence is considered sign: footprints, pieces of hair, dung, broken branches, shifted rocks, and so on. Every living being leaves sign, so it's just a matter of finding some. Once you have, then you can try to follow whoever left it. And to stay one step ahead of a creature, you need to know how they think, behave, and interact with the world around them. So research, investigation, and observation are always important. Sometimes bait can also be helpful to lure a creature, as you'll see in both parts of this letter. And you need to stay hidden; the most important things you can do are stay out of sight, stay upwind of any potential target, and stay quiet. Again, it's like hunting other animals. To mask your scent, you can also sprinkle urine, fat, or other leavings of a creature over yourself and your clothing. It's also important to think about what senses your target relies on the most. For example, Sasquatches mostly navigate the world with their senses of sight and hearing, just like humans, but of course they can smell things too. So it's crucial to think and plan ahead. In the end, hunting and tracking, of monsters or otherwise, really comes down to one of the most ancient principles of the world: know your quarry.

~

Our international comments this time were from Mexico and the UK, and I'll throw Ireland in there too, just because it has a lot of the same monsters as Britain.

- Mexico?

There are quite a few different cryptids in Mexico, the most famous of which is almost certainly the chupacabra. These little guys live primarily in the arid desert areas of northern Mexico and the southwest United States, but they also live in tropical climates like the Caribbean (they originated in Puerto Rico) and down further into Central America. They suck blood and attack livestock, but they're generally not very aggressive towards humans...for the most part. Mexico also has shapeshifters known as nahuales, who are very similar in many ways to skinwalkers. Further south, mainly in jungle areas, live the winged bat-like cryptids known as Camazotz, who I've had some wild experiences with. Throughout Mexico you can also find the small humanoids known as aluxes or chaneques, who are very similar to the Little People to the north; they don't have all the magical powers that they do in the legends, but they shouldn't be trifled with or offended. There are also some Sasquatch relatives that range into Mexico, as well as dogmen. Mexico is a big country with a diverse range of monsters, but these are some that came to my mind first.

- Britain and Ireland?

These islands are home to far more monsters than their small landmass might suggest. Many are faeries, who are also called the fae or the fae folk; the Hunters often refer to them by one of their names in the Irish language, "daoine sídhe". There are many different groups of fae folk, and most have a pretty human-like appearance, although some, like sprites and brownies, are very small, and others, like spriggans and púca, can change form; a few, such as the badger-like buggane, appear much more animalistic. The daoine sídhe tend to be mischievous rather than violent, although there are exceptions, such as the Black Shucks, huge dogs that are otherwise known as barghests or hellhounds. But openly dangerous fae are rare, although unfortunately, the populations of all types of faerie have declined more and more as humans expand their settlements, populations, and infrastructure. Some faeries have managed to establish themselves in urban environments, though, and a rare few have even integrated into human society. There are non-fae cryptids in the region too; for example, the most mountainous regions of Scotland are home to the Greymen, which are extremely rare Sasquatch relatives. And, of course, vampires and werewolves are common across Ireland and the UK.

Q&A – EMELA-NTOUKA

- Have you ever thought about writing a book?

Ever since I started sending my letters to Swamp Dweller, somebody said that I should write a book about my experiences and knowledge. I think it might be a good idea. I don't know much about how to get published, but I'm sure I could figure it out with some help. On the other hand, I'm not sure how the Hunters would respond. I don't think the organization would completely block my book, but there would certainly be resistance. There's been some pushback against these letters, in fact. But writing for someone who reads stories on YouTube is different from publishing a book. Anyway, this is certainly something to consider!

- Are there any peaceful or docile cryptids?

Yes, of course! Monsters are mostly like animals. Some are more aggressive than others (although, also like animals, pretty much any cryptid can be aggressive if need be), but many, maybe even most, are actually pretty peaceful. In my very first letter, I talked about Sasquatch and how they're mostly quite gentle (but this is far from universal). Many of the more intelligent humanoid cryptids are not inherently hostile, including faeries, some groups of the Little People, and more. Even some otherwise predatory creatures don't tend to attack humans, like makara. Check out the previous letter to learn more about them. And then some monsters just don't really pose any real threat to us, like the veo of Indonesia; these guys look much like the animals called pangolins, and although they're very big and maybe a little scary-looking, they never attack humans. I just happen to tell you guys about the dangerous cryptids because they're the ones that combat Hunters like me usually have to deal with. Plus, some of the most popularly known cryptids are the dangerous ones, and I know people would like to hear about them. I'd also just hope to help you guys keep safe.

- How do Hunters deal with guns being illegal?

I imagine you who asked this are not from the US, because this issue rarely comes up here. But I don't say that as a good thing, because our gun laws are honestly insane, and actually extremely problematic. I think it's okay for people to own weapons, but with common sense rules; you can get away with *far* too much gun-related stuff here. That being said, racial profiling is a sad reality, so people with darker skin like me do have to be more careful and more aware; it's not like I constantly get stopped by the police, but it's just an extra reason to be mindful and smart. I have been detained and questioned before, though, and in those situations, I was able to show my Hunter badge and move on without further trouble. I also usually only carry about 3 guns at a time, so it's clear that I'm not illegally selling mass quantities of them or something.

I'm pretty sure that Sergio and other Guides call ahead or otherwise notify law enforcement in the areas where Hunters are assigned, but even if they didn't, Hunters are usually able to use the badge and other documentation of our organization to deal with police and law enforcement all over the world; like I said, the whole gun issue comes up primarily outside the US. We often ship our guns or fly privately into other countries to avoid the usual security hassles, although that's only really been an issue for the past 20 years or so. With all this being said, wherever Hunters go, our jobs are usually far away from the places you'd normally encounter law enforcement, so most of us don't often cross paths with them anyways. Travel is where the big problems are. Good question!

- How are the Hunters organized?

Pretty loosely, if we're being honest. I've talked about some of the different groups or "departments" within our organization, like the Smiths and the Undertakers, but I think you were asking more about the leadership structure. I can't give away too much, but this is another good question, so I'll share some of the less confidential details. As far as I know, the highest level of our organization is known as the Circle, with a capital "C"; that sounds odd, even a little silly, I know, but as always, the name comes from centuries ago and just never changed. The Circle has nine members, and although I can't tell you who they are (I actually don't know all of their identities myself), they come from all over the world and work together to oversee the organization. They're kind of like a board of directors. I don't know the whole process of how Circle members are appointed, but the parts I'm aware of are more democratic than you might expect.

Beneath the Circle is the Lodge, with a capital "L", again, named after old European hunting traditions. There are various roles in the Lodge, but mostly the head honchos are the capital-K Keepers. They're like regional managers, with each overseeing a very big geographical area, similar to the ones the United Nations divides the globe into; for example, there is a Central Australian Keeper and a Horn of Africa Keeper. Below the Keepers are the capital-T Tenders, who oversee major subdivisions of various countries, such as states, provinces, or smaller regions; for example, there's an Alberta Tender and an Argentine Patagonia Tender.

In practice, the Lodge doesn't have too much effect on the day-to-day operations of any single lower-ranking Hunter, like how the leaders of many countries usually don't affect the average citizen's everyday life as much as local governors or town officials. In this way, Lodge members are mostly responsible for putting together large-scale policy and regulations; they make sure that the Hunters are collectively acting in the best interests of humans, monsters, and the broader environment. A Tender might interface with individual Guides or put out a call for assistance (like I mentioned in my wendigo and Deer People letter), but when it comes to the average Hunter's daily job, we pretty much have free rein to work with our Guides, unless we do something that goes against the rules or seriously threatens anyone's safety. Phew, that was a long answer. But hopefully now you have a better idea of the Hunters beyond rank-and-file folks like me.

- Scandinavia?

As you might imagine, there are a whole bunch of different monsters in the Nordic countries; they're so sparsely urbanized, with so many forests, caves, mountains, and coastlines that offer great habitat for all sorts of wildlife, including cryptids. The most iconic Scandinavian creature is probably the troll. These big guys live way off in the wilderness, and their favorite foods seem to be large mammals and fish; however, their biology is extremely bizarre, including a metabolism and anatomy that allows them to do crazy stuff like digest entire trees. There are numerous subspecies of troll, but none are known for their intelligence or their manners: unlike the folktales, they don't wear clothes, they don't speak any human language, and they don't care what religion you subscribe to. The largest trolls can be well over 50 feet tall, and that would be the closest thing you'd find to a "giant", which some Hunters called them in the past. There are also lots of creatures in the Scandinavian waters. The coasts and fjords are home to several enormous snake and fish species. The näck or nøkk is the Nordic counterpart of the nixie, although in Scandinavia, they seem to be mainly male rather than female. Näcken inhabit freshwater locations like rivers, lakes, and waterfalls; they're much more common in Scandinavia than other parts of Europe, because of the far lower levels of water pollution, but they're still very secretive and poorly understood, even by the Hunters. And of course, werewolves and vampires can be found in the Nordic countries too. I think those are the big ones, but there are many more.

~

Now I'll talk a little bit about some specific monsters which you guys have mentioned but aren't the topic of this letter. When Swamp did a T-shirt giveaway along with my thunderbird letter, leaving a comment was part of the criteria for entering the contest, so on that video in particular, you guys mentioned a *ton* of different cryptids you'd like to hear about. As I'm writing this, there are apparently over 800 comments, and most mention at least one type of creature! Obviously, there's no way I can get to all of them, but here's some super quick info on a few that seemed to be the most popular or commonly mentioned.

- Feline cryptids from South America?

Well, there aren't many of these, largely because most feline monsters that get reported in Central and South America are misidentified jaguars or pumas. The large, semi-aquatic Water Cat does call South America home, though. They're sometimes called Water Tigers, but the Hunters use the former name, since, just like sabertoothed cats, Water Cats aren't actually tigers at all; they also have several local names in various languages, such as "aypa" and "yaquaru". They're close relatives of the jaguar, but you can easily distinguish them with a quick look: Water Cats don't have any sort of spots, and their tails are skinnier and end in tassels or tufts; they also have long fangs that resemble the classic canine teeth of sabertoothed cats, but about half as long (there's something very weird about so many aquatic cryptids having saber teeth, but we can talk about that later). Like basically all felines, Water Cats are solitary and secretive, but they have populations all over South America.

- Stick Men?

Like skinwalkers, it's taboo to speak of these among many Indigenous communities. The name "Stick Men" or "Stick

Indians" is an English invention, but it's how the Hunters usually refer to these beings; they have multiple Native language names, but much like walkers, it's considered especially taboo to speak these. To try and keep a reasonable distance, I'm not even going to talk much about these creatures in general. To simplify drastically, these are essentially malevolent forest dwellers. One type is very tall, and the other is very small, but in overall appearance, they mostly resemble unmixed Indigenous folks from the northwestern United States; I should point out that the small kind of Stick Men are not the same as any of the various groups of Little People who live across North America. Stick Men live in the western half of the US, particularly the Northwest, and thankfully, they're very rare nowadays. Hunters have fought and killed some, although this is apparently very difficult. Although Stick Men sometimes play relatively harmless pranks on campers and travelers, on other occasions they lure people deep into the woods; sometimes these victims will die of exposure, thirst, or starvation, but other times Stick Men will drive them mad, psychologically destroying them with illusions and tricks. Occasionally Stick Men flat-out kill people physically; they're horrifyingly fast and strong, and they wield weapons more skillfully than many humans. I've never met one, and I hope to keep it that way.

- The hideous Kardashian cryptid?

I can't say I know much about this particular monster! I don't follow modern pop culture much; Hunters have to deal with enough nonsense and insanity already.

- Banshees?

A.k.a. Wailing women, these ladies are found all across Ireland. They vary in size from very tall to very short, but usually they're slightly smaller than adult humans, and they always appear in a floor-length white or occasionally black dress. They aren't human ghosts, but one of the many groups of fae folk, almost identical to the Scottish caoineag. Banshee appearances have fallen dramatically over the centuries, and they're very rarely seen nowadays; this is probably connected to the overall decline in populations of faeries and most cryptids worldwide from the 1850s onward, caused by the spike in human population, expansion, and destruction that the Industrial Revolution enabled. Banshees' unearthly screams are what make them famous, but they only unleash them when provoked in some way. Normally, banshees cry, wailing death lamentations in various ancient and medieval languages as they float through the night, visiting the families of people who have recently died or who are about to. But even though banshees are connected with death, they aren't malevolent; in a really tragic way, they actually seem to grieve along with the families of the dead (although many faeries are well-known for having different thought processes than humans, so this interpretation could definitely be incorrect). They're very mysterious, since they only appear to most humans at such specific times, and other daoine sidhe are oddly hesitant to discuss them. In any case, banshees aren't directly dangerous or aggressive, and you'll probably never see one. Be thankful if you don't.

Q&A - WECHUGE

- Have I ever encountered any cryptids that act as guardians over a particular area?

Yes, I have. Many faeries fall into this category, with a ton of them being extremely protective of certain groves of trees, bodies of water, and especially hills and mounds. I've also mentioned nixies in the past, who are water beings connected to specific rivers and streams, which they often defend quite aggressively. Little People and Sasquatches also tend to have specific areas to which they act as guardians. And of course, many cryptids are just plain territorial, defending a certain stretch of land or a home range.

- What do I think the Mothman actually is?

To tell you the truth, I don't know much about the Mothman, and neither do the Hunters. There are only a few recorded sightings in our files, and never any close encounters. There appear to be a few different individuals, though, not just a lone entity. I'm mostly on the side of them being worldly creatures, especially because there are some other powerful winged humanoids who aren't demonic or supernatural. But I'm open to being mistaken! Mothman (I guess Moth*men*) could be related to owls somehow, but who knows? In any case, this is definitely a weird and interesting being, but since it doesn't appear to be actively dangerous, combat Hunters like me put our priorities elsewhere.

- Have I ever had any experiences with shadow people or demons?

Demons, no, and I can't say if they even exist in the Judeo-Christian form you're probably imagining. But shadow people, yes. I actually saw one at my school when I was a teenager. Nothing very exciting, though, as far as these things go; there was just a human-shaped, adult-sized shadow that walked across a room from one side to the other. Millions of other people have seen them too, and I tend to believe that they're a common form of ghost. It's hard to deal with something intangible, and since shadow people don't seriously harm humans on a large scale, we often focus our efforts on more physical beings. However, there are some Hunters who specialize in dealing with intangible creatures; I've never really been involved with those guys, so I don't know much about that whole world, but I can certainly reach out and try to get some more information.

Q&A - CAMAZOTZ + MACHA

- Is there a way to build bonds with certain cryptids?

I'm a bit hesitant to answer this question, to tell the truth; this isn't "How to Train Your Cryptid". However, it is an important thing to know, so I'll be honest. Yes, there are ways to form bonds with certain monsters. If you've listened to my third letter, you may remember that I helped a mother Sasquatch and her baby fight off a dogman; after that, the Sasquatches left a perfect circle of river pebbles on my front porch, which I think was an expression of gratitude. I would consider that a bond. Many monsters are just animals, so you can bond with some of them just like you would with other animals. Of course, cryptids with a more human-like nature, such as faeries and werewolves (who are actually just a different sort of human), are easier to form connections with, since most of the time interacting with them is a lot like interacting with a human. I'll go into this topic a bit more with my second story in this letter, so stick around to hear more.

- Do I have any suicidal thoughts after losing Heather?

Yes, I certainly did, even though I didn't talk about it explicitly in my previous letter. Heather's death was the hardest experience I've ever had to go through, and there were many, many times where I didn't want to carry on living without her. However, as I explained, I came to realize that her death wasn't wholly my fault, and that there was more to life beyond her. And things did get better eventually. So I'm glad that I never gave into those urges. If you're in that boat yourself, please, *please* reach out for help. The world is a better place with you in it.

- Have I ever had to deal with rogue Hunters or Hunters gone bad?

Yes, and I think I referenced this once in the past. It's a dark story, and I'm not going to go into it now. I'll also add that there is a special group of Hunters whose primary job is to act as enforcers and keep other Hunters in line; they have different names in different places, but the ones I met in Chile were called the Watchers. Usually they prevent incidents like the one I mentioned.

- Why don't Hunters wear armor?

This is a super logical thing, but I hadn't really thought about explaining it to you guys! In the old days, some Hunters in different parts of Eurasia used to wear metal armor, especially before guns were invented or when they weren't readily available; every so often there was wooden or padded armor in Africa and North America too. But armor limits mobility. My mom often told me that the best way to take a hit is to not get hit in the first place, and the vast majority of Hunters operate by this same principle. Not to mention that much of the time, armor simply doesn't stand up to the claws, fangs, and other natural weapons that monsters have: the weaponized blood of a zabraq will melt straight through bulletproof vests, and if you get pummeled by the fists of a

Sasquatch, it's not going to matter what you're wearing. Some Hunters who deal with smaller or weaker cryptids might put on some Kevlar or leather protective pieces, but it's incredibly rare that people actually go out in a full suit of any material. I've personally worn arm and leg guards against little guys like chupacabras, but for the vast majority of monsters I've faced, armor doesn't do much except slow you down. This was a good question!

BONUS LETTER – TRAINING TROUBLE

U.S.A. (UTAH)

Written September 2024

Hey, everyone. It's Sam White Owl, back once again. It feels good to say that after such a long time! As of my writing this, it's been over 2 years since I last spoke to you. If you're back with me now, thank you. This bonus letter is something I'm including specifically for this book; unlike my others, this one was never put onto YouTube and read aloud by Swamp Dweller. I wrote and edited it with Elías Ramos, my nephew who I've explained is helping me out with this book project, so it's brand new! I wanted to include something fresh for those of you who have previously listened to the YouTube series, and of course those of you who are just joining will get something extra out of this as well! I also find it really fulfilling to write these letters, and I hope *you* find it fulfilling to read and listen to them. I've really missed them.

This time around, we'll be talking about some of the most recent stuff I've ever brought up in these letters: this took place in 2020, and I've mentioned it before, because it's the main reason why I took a break for a couple months between writing my emela-ntouka and wechuge letters (numbers 8 and 9). To better understand what happened, I would highly recommend reading Letter 4, where I speak about skinwalkers, as it has a lot of background information that will help you understand this story a lot better.

Speaking of background, Serena and Elías both helped me realize that throughout all my letters, I've hardly ever talked about what it's like to train as a Hunter and learn the different skills that you see in my stories. A bunch of other people have asked about this too, and it ties directly into the 2020 experience I'll be telling you about. This is going to be one of those supersized letters that you guys have enjoyed in the past, so grab a snack or a drink and settle in!

As I've mentioned in the past, most capital-H Hunters learn how to do our job by studying as apprentices to older, more experienced members. I didn't know about this until recently, but we have all sorts of different names for new Hunters: "newbies", "rookies", "greenies", "puppies" (that one's pretty great), or my personal favorite, "Hatchies", or "Hatches", short for "Hatchlings". Maybe I just like that last one because of my own name, but it's what I've been used to saying, and I've always imagined it with a capital "H" as well. The Hunters are a pretty informal organization in many ways, and we don't have formal ranks or a set career progression path. It's purely up to your mentor when you get to graduate from being a Hatch (although they'll probably always think of you as one. You'll always be your parents' baby, after all).

If a Hunter recommends an outsider for membership in the organization, then they often personally take the new Hatch under their wing (pun fully intended). Other times, Hatchies get taught by older Hunters who live in their general area and are generous enough to volunteer as teachers. There are some veteran Hunters, especially retired ones, whose main role in the organization is to serve as mentors for Hatches. Usually it's a one-on-one thing, master and apprentice; that way there's no worry about multiple students having drama or different styles and speeds of learning. Every so often, there's a case where a teacher takes on multiple Hatchies, but it's rare.

My situation was much the same, with the twist that I had been in consideration as a Hatch from day one, ever since I expressed the interest and the aptitude. That's because, like many of my colleagues, I come from a family of capital-H Hunters. I've told you guys about this ever since my very first letter, but here's a short quote from a Q&A section with a little more detail:

Well, I wish there was some elaborate origin myth, like some superhero story, but there's not. I think my mom's side of the family, the Cherokee one, has just been dealing with cryptids for generations, trying to help people and monsters coexist in peace. In our community, we were often the ones who people came to when there were problems with beings like Sasquatches or dogmen. Then at some point, one of us got the attention of the Hunters, and our family joined up. The first formal record of any of my ancestors being enrolled comes from 1753. He was named Matthew Drum, and I'm sure he's one of the main guys who's been watching over our family ever since.

Many Hunters, maybe even most, also have family history in our line of work, whether as part of the organization or not; I doubt many of them can trace as far back as 1753, but a ton of families have been members for at least a few generations. However, as I've always tried my best to make clear, most people simply aren't cut out to be mainline combat Hunters. To get there, you have to show the right talents and traits, including courage, willpower, stability, and competency in all of the on-the-job skills like observation, tracking, shooting, and more. You also need a good heart, and the ability to responsibly balance life and death. Being a combat Hunter is not for the faint of heart or unprepared, and no matter how ready they think they might be, most people just don't have what it takes.

However, fighting and actual "Hunting" is only a small part of what our organization does; in fact, combat Hunters like me are probably a small minority of the organization. Many of us have completely different responsibilities, some of which don't even require you to go outside. There are multiple different sub-groups of the Hunters, which have names that likewise start with capital letters and originate from the roles that they played in earlier times.

I've mentioned the Smiths, as in "blacksmiths", who craft and tune our weapons and gear. The Guides gather intelligence, interface with non-Hunters, and arrange tasks for us combat Hunters. The cleanup crews, a.k.a. Undertakers, take care of the mess that hunts usually leave behind, mainly by relocating or disposing of dead, captured, or sedated cryptids. The Surgeons, like my sister Erika, work in various laboratory-type positions, such as doctors, physiologists, and chemists. There's also tons of behind-the-scenes bureaucracy, communications, and paperwork stuff, like collecting reports and write-ups, consolidating information, and coordinating operations. The Tenders and Keepers, for example, are kind of like regional managers; they oversee all the lower-ranking field Hunters in certain geographic areas.

Research is also a vital part of our work. Some Hunters go out in the field, like you see in my letters, but rather than combat, they focus on all sorts of studies, observations, surveys; that entails following tracks, studying behavior, assessing data from tagged monsters, and more. These are just a few other jobs that Hunters perform; there are a lot more, and each takes a different set of skills and qualifications. So there are plenty of opportunities for non-combat Hunters or people who just want to stay indoors.

My mom, however, was a combat and field Hunter, and she taught me to be the same. Many of us wind up apprenticed to family members, and I was my mom's Hatch. When I was about 5, she and my dad divorced, and I spent most of my childhood growing up in Oklahoma with her. I've always loved being out of the house and in nature, so my mom taught me all sorts of outdoor survival skills from a very early age, and my dad did the same whenever I went up to Washington state to visit him. But it wasn't until I was about 11 or 12, in middle school, that my mom really started teaching me the more intense stuff.

I always had expressed interest in following in her footsteps, but it wasn't until then that she started to seriously consider it. For a long time (and still today sometimes), it frustrated me that she didn't start earlier, but as I've grown up, I understand why she would just want to teach me the fundamentals and observe me over time before deciding that I might have what it takes. She made it crystal-clear that there was no guarantee I would make it to the position of a combat Hunter; in fact, my older sister Erika had already "flunked out" before me, although her talent and interest in chemistry meant she wound up making a good capital-S Surgeon. But I was determined to succeed, so I gave it everything I had.

I've always loved my job, which was a big help, rather than simply wanting to prove myself to my mom. I mean, I love my mom, but I wouldn't have worked my ass off to follow in her footsteps if I didn't genuinely want to. Plus, she never pushed me to even take after her in the first place. Being a combat Hunter is a deadly serious job, in the most literal sense, so this isn't like parents pressuring their child to join the family company or study to become a lawyer or doctor. But my mom was a great teacher, and I hope that I was even half as good during the story I'm about to tell. But we'll get there. Thanks, Mom!

Learning any profession can take years, and in many ways, it never really ends; like other jobs, Hunters are always picking up new information and skills with every task we take on. Of course, I can't explain every bit of what our training entails, but here's some of the stuff people have asked about. All this mainly applies to field Hunters, meaning those of us who go out to directly deal with monsters, conduct research, gather data, and so on.

The most basic things Hunters need to learn for fieldwork are natural extensions of the various outdoor and survival skills that a lot of us are exposed to from a young age. Some Hunters work primarily in urban and suburban environments, sticking to cities and towns for their tasks, but the vast majority of us operate in what you might call the countryside, the wilderness, or the bush. We're usually out there for extended periods, ranging from a few days all the way up to a few months; some research Hunters even do studies that run for multiple years (sometimes without a break, which is really hardcore). Most of the time my jobs take at least a few days, but I've never been in the field for longer than a couple months. When you're away from stores and supply stations for that long, you need to know how to find food and water for yourself; hunting, fishing, trapping, and gathering are vital to sustain yourself if you run out of your provisions and resupplies. In an ideal situation, you won't have to go this far, but things can and do go sideways; thankfully, there haven't been many times I've personally been there.

Hunts frequently take us over long distances, and we usually wind up traveling for at least a few miles on a daily basis. This obviously means you need to be in shape, but you also need to know how to find your way around. Navigation skills, like reading different types of maps, GPS, and a compass are fundamental, but sometimes you won't be able to fall back on those tools, so you'll have to rely more on your environment. Interacting with the world around you means knowing how to read it: noting landmarks and orientation, tracking the sun to manage your activity while you have daylight, identifying paths that will save you energy and resources, picking up on clues that can lead you to water and food sources, and more.

You also need to know who you share your environment with, from plants to fungi to animals. In addition to teaching big life lessons, these beings can give specific survival instructions. Animals in particular can tell you so many things if you watch and listen: if an area is safe, where you might be able to travel, where food and water might be, and so on. Tracking is a whole discipline all on its own, from identifying prints to reading them to determine how fast or in what way an animal was moving and how recently it passed by, or looking for snapped branches or nibbled shrubs or flattened grass beds, and more. I'm not joking when I say that there's a real science to examining scat, a.k.a. poop; you can find out what left it, what it was eating, how recently it left the poop, why it pooped in a certain space, and so on. Plants can point you in the direction of water, different elevations, or good camping sites. Wood is especially crucial, and you need to know what types of wood are flammable and good as fuel for fires (these characteristics don't always overlap!), what types are sturdy enough to build shelters, and what types are workable enough to use for tools or even just to carve and whittle to pass the time. And of course, certain berries, leaves, fruits, roots, mushrooms, and other plants and fungus can feed you or help with health issues.

There are countless other active skills that field Hunters (and really everyone!) should know: hand and bow drill for fires, shelters for different conditions and lengths of time, different types of knots for different purposes and materials, collecting and filtering water with sediment and debris, knapping a stone or shaping a bone for a blade or scraper, and a million more. Modern gear allows us to skip over much of this, but tools break and wear out and get lost, and when they do, you need to be prepared to do things the hard way.

Long ago, our ancestors knew how to do all of these things like the backs of their hands, because it was necessary for survival. But urbanized modern-day Western culture has completely forgotten almost all of it. Relearning this serves practical survival purposes, but it also lets you connect with ancestral, long-held practices, and helps you gain an understanding and appreciation for how all of us once lived and just how resilient, intelligent, and adaptable humans are. This stuff is often spoken of with derogatory terms like "primitive" or "savage", but just consider how much thought, knowledge, creativity, and strength they actually require!

A lot of this might not be super exciting, and I rarely spend time talking about putting it into practice; I don't want to bore you, and I also can't reasonably cover all of these details. However, so much it is present in the background of all of the different hunts and experiences I tell you guys about.

So every field Hunter needs to know the outdoor survival part, but with combat Hunters, people always ask about, well, the "combat" part, and I know some of you guys love this stuff. Every hunt and every cryptid calls for a different arsenal, so combat Hunters have to be experienced with all kinds of weapon, whether that's small arms, big guns, or all sorts of melee weapons. Shooting a pistol is very different from a shotgun, which is different from a bolt-action rifle, and so on. We typically use high-caliber ammunition, the kind of stuff designed for elephants or bears; in a battle, there's no reason to pull punches. We often use hollow point rounds, more rarely tracer rounds, and occasionally, as you can see in my wendigo and wechuge hunts, incendiary rounds, or "flamers" (usually for their effectiveness against monsters of ice and cold). Sometimes we also get the Smiths to make our ammunition out of specific materials and alloys that cryptids are vulnerable to, like iron for faeries and silver for werewolves. A combat Hunter should be familiar with all the major sorts of firearms and ammo, even though we all have our favorites.

My mom was really thorough, and she even taught me how to use much more old-school weapons. I've practiced countless times with bows, crossbows, slings (not sling*shot*, although I have used those too; I'm talking about the ancient weapon that you whirl around and cast), and even javelins (often with an atlatl, a long shaft to throw a spear farther and harder). I can also throw bolas (a pair of rocks attached by a rope, which is great for tripping up anything with long legs), and I have a pretty good arm with a boomerang, if I do say so myself! Learning all these is probably overkill on some level, but I'm glad for the knowledge, and I actually have had to use them more than once; maybe I'll tell you about some of those occasions another day.

Finally, it's equally important for any combat Hunter to know their melee weapons. As I've said before, you *never* want to engage in close combat, but sometimes there's no choice. A Hunter's primary melee weapon is usually the knife; they're versatile, lightweight, and double as indispensable tools outside of combat. Lots of monsters are just plain big, so most of us carry at least one bear knife or something similarly long and oversized; it's probably more accurate to call these things "daggers", because some have blades that are over a foot long. A bunch of Hunters, especially in South and Southeast Asia, carry a kukri, a curved Nepalese knife or short sword that's both a fantastic all-purpose tool and a deadly weapon. In thick forest and jungle, especially the Caribbean and Latin America, any good Hunter carries a trusty machete, another weapon-tool combo. Every one of us carries at least one knife or another blade; because it pays to have extra, I have two on me during any given job, one on my chest and one on my belt.

You've probably also heard me mention my combat tomahawk, which is designed for fighting but can serve other survival purposes if need be. Unlike a knife, my tomahawk requires some room to use effectively, but it lets me fight at a farther and therefore safer distance. Other Hunters also like different types of axes, hatchets, or sickles. Less commonly, some Hunters have more purpose-built weapons, and every so often you'll hear about some brave, foolish, and/or deranged Hunter who goes out with something like a sword or a hammer. In niche cases, some Hunters have used ice picks or climbing picks as weapons in a pinch, which my friend William has actually done once (if you're familiar with the experiences I recount in my later 9 letters, you may remember that he saved my life like this when we were being swarmed by amikuk in some Alaskan ice tunnels). But these are all last resorts.

Phew, that was a ton of information! I hope that answered some of your questions and gave you a better idea of what Hunter training is all about. But just like any of my letters, this is a tiny peek of a gargantuan iceberg; you could very literally fill entire libraries with everything there is to know about our job (we've actually done exactly that; I talk about the Repository in my later letters). But now that I've given you this overview, I'll tell you that story from 2020.

For a long time, there have been on-and-off conversations about establishing a standardized Hunter training program, with some of the wealthier people and higher-ups even throwing out ideas about creating schools or academies, but nothing's ever taken off in any big way. I never really paid much attention to this big-picture education stuff until I was approached by my friend Louis, who you may remember from my dogman letter.

Louis is a Hunter from Utah who's probably 15 or 20 years older than me. Utah isn't super far off from Oklahoma, so our paths have crossed more than a few times, and he's taught me quite a bit during our hunts together. It turns out that he also wants to pass that knowledge down in a more formal capacity, so he got together with four other veteran Hunters and arranged a training seminar, for which he invited me as teacher #6.

I've trained my nephew extensively, but I'm not his main mentor, and I was a bit hesitant to accept Louis' offer; I'm kind of shy, and I also didn't know how exactly to teach in a group setting. Thankfully, these Hatchies weren't complete novices; they knew the basics, and we would mainly be helping them improve and providing different perspectives than their usual mentors. Louis had even made a whole miniature syllabus to guide us! I won't give you all the little details of how it worked, but our group of 12 would stay out in the Utah wilderness for a few months, trekking through different areas of a stretch of high desert that Louis knew well. We would go through a bunch of lessons, and by the end, all of the kids would have built more advanced skills in everything from climbing to sharpshooting. Additionally, none of them had ever been out in the field for more than a month at a time, and never more than a few days alone, so this would be excellent practice for basic solo survival. Once Louis had explained all of this, I felt pretty good about the idea, so I agreed to help out.

Before long I was out in the Utah high desert in September, accompanied by the five other veteran Hunters and our six Hatchies. Twelve people is a lot to remember, and not all of them want to be identified anyway, so I'll just bring up the pertinent folks as we go. You already know me, and Louis is just the same as in my dogman letter, although nowadays his left arm only has about 40% of its original function, and his beard has gone completely gray; he's white, with a tall and stout build, and always wearing a cowboy hat. Each of us teachers had one main Hatchy who was like our temporary apprentice; they all learned with different teachers from day to day, but we were responsible for taking care of our specific Hatch and checking on their progress throughout the program. In some ways this was kind of like a hardcore summer camp, which was nostalgic; I only ever got to go to summer camp for a few years, because after that the summers were entirely devoted to training with my mom.

My one-on-one student was a 20-year-old girl named Mei, who was from a place in northern California that I obviously won't specify. She's from a Chinese family, which I learned because I was able to speak to her in Mandarin with a few of the phrases that Serena has taught me; that really surprised her, but pleasantly so, which I think got us off to a good start. And overall, Mei was an excellent Hatch!

When it comes to physical strength, I fully admit that I judged her unfairly at first. I wasn't sure how far she'd be able to go relative to the male Hatches, but I was glad to find that I had nothing to worry about. Mei wasn't as strong as the boys, of course, but she had no problem with any of our strength and stamina-based activities; when we practiced close combat skills, she outperformed the only other female Hatch, and when I let all six of them take a crack at using my tomahawk, Mei actually had a better swing than two of the boys as well. She was also the group's best climber, and always light and nimble when it came to movement-based drills. It's never a competition, but I say all this to show that Mei could more than hold her own with the physical stuff.

She's not the best shooter or tracker, but she has a real knack for reading the environment, with an especially good eye for plants. We also did a good amount of bookwork in this program (that may be surprising, I know, but Hunters have to do a lot more paperwork than you might think!), and Mei showed that she has a great memory and recall ability, maybe even better than mine, and she performed very well in almost all of the tests and quizzes. I feel like I'm writing a school report to give her parents here, so although both she and they should be very proud, I'll stop here so I don't embarrass her any more than I already have!

Now, you've probably already recognized that we were off the grid during this program: no established campgrounds, cellphones, or Internet. To make sure that we weren't entirely isolated from the outside world, though, we had radios and a pair of satellite phones, although they were mainly for emergencies. There were also four ranches nearby, but our training area measured a couple hundred square miles, with very few roads, so getting anywhere meant taking a nice long hike. Louis knew all of the ranchers, and we were in the area with their permission. None of them knew anything regarding the Hunters, though; in their minds, Louis was just running a regular wilderness survival course.

We also had a seventh Hunter on standby watching our backs, a local friend of Louis' named Pine (which I thought was a cool nickname). He was a lanky redheaded guy in his 30s; I don't think I ever saw his eyes, because he was always wearing one pair of Aviator sunglasses or another (they were all pretty nice, though, I have to say). Pine drove around in a massive truck full of extra emergency supplies; normally he followed a couple miles behind us, but occasionally he went off to check the conditions in an area or set up things like climbing gear ahead of time for us. At one point, he also brought out Amy, a psychologist who talked to us about some of the mental and emotional challenges of being a Hunter. We were fortunate to have Pine around in general, but if it wasn't for him specifically, the madness at the end of the training could have gone a lot worse.

We got our first bit of foreshadowing about a month and a half into the program, when we were in a small canyon doing some climbing practice. I was with Louis and the four other teachers at the base of a cliff, with the six Hatchies scaling the rock face above us; they had harnesses, but they all knew the importance of caution and were taking their time. At some point, we all heard a car engine in the distance; since we were the only human beings out there, this sound always meant that Pine was nearby. As always, this is my best recollection and recreation of events. One of the teachers took out his radio and stepped away, before returning with a frown.

"Pine needs us to see something he found. Says we might have a problem."

Most of the time, Pine kept to himself, and we kept in touch with him via radio; every day we did a check-in in the morning, afternoon, and night, but it wasn't too unusual for us to have in-person meetings. Still, Pine was a really laid-back guy, so for him to say that something might be wrong was a little concerning. Soon, we heard his car stop at the mouth of the canyon, and he came walking out of the bushes. The teachers all gathered around him, while still keeping one eye on our Hatchies.

We shared the training area with a variety of animals, including some large herbivore species: deer, pronghorns, and occasionally wild or feral horses, along with domestic cattle that the neighboring ranches often allow to roam around during that time of year, before the snow begins. There are some natural bodies of water here and there, but this is the desert, so many of them dry up in the summer and even into this period of September. To reliably sustain the cattle, the ranchers keep a bunch of water stations throughout the area, from big troughs and pools to smaller pipelines and water mains. Our group took advantage of these every so often, as do the other animals...including predators.

A few hours earlier, Pine had been filling up at a big metal water pool when he'd noticed some disturbed foliage and muddled tracks in the scraggly trees nearby. Even before looking closer, he got the distinct sense that something wasn't quite right. He decided to investigate, and in only a few minutes, he came across some dried bloodstains on the ground, more than enough to indicate a recent kill. There are black bears, coyotes, and cougars in that region of Utah, and although our group size alone made us very safe, it would still be good to know if any of those animals were around.

The clues led Pine to a dead pronghorn antelope; although pronghorns technically aren't antelope, people still call them that, and they do look almost identical. They're beautiful, and well known for their incredible speed and stamina: a sprinting pronghorn can hit nearly 60 miles per hour, making them some of the fastest runners on the planet. Cheetahs are just about the only mammal that can outrun them, and it's actually often theorized that, potentially, a big reason for pronghorns evolving to be so incredibly fast is that during the Ice Age, their main predator was the American cheetah; yes, you read that correctly! American cheetahs weren't actually cheetahs; they're much more closely related to cougars, but that name is just so crazy that I like to bring it up. And you should keep it in mind, because although American cheetahs have been extinct for thousands of years, their cougar cousins are still alive and well, and have taken up the crown as one of pronghorns' top predators. It's not at all unusual to find pronghorn antelope that have been killed by cougars, wolves, or coyotes, but the pictures Pine showed us were especially strange. I have to go into some pretty upsetting detail, but I'll try to keep it as clean as possible.

This pronghorn's stomach and rear end had been partially eaten, but there wasn't a single clear single deathblow; instead, the antelope had been mauled, with gashes torn open all across its back, neck, and sides. This sort of thing isn't unheard of; you might see it with a young predator that hasn't learned to kill effectively yet, or in a situation where the prey manages to put up a good fight. But what Pine showed us was so severe that it almost seemed malicious, as if the predator was going out of its way to cause the antelope pain. But even more disturbing and perplexing was the fact that the pronghorn was missing its head.

"What the hell?" somebody asked as Pine pulled up the photos of the poor animal's bloodied neck stump (the actual question was a lot more colorful; you can use your imagination).

"You ever seen a predator take a critter's whole head off?" Louis asked the group. Nobody said yes.

There isn't an easy explanation for why a predator would decapitate a kill like this and yet leave much more accessible meat untouched. The stomach area is the softest and easiest to reach, but apart from some parts of the hindquarters, this pronghorn had hardly been eaten. Cats can be picky, though (as you might know from personal experience), so they sometimes get selective about their food; animals can have a taste for specific organs like livers or hearts, and eyeballs are a top pick for many creatures, especially birds. Skulls, on the other hand, are thick, and it takes effort to crack them open to get to the brain within. And none of this explained why the *entire* head would be missing.

"Where *is* the head?" I asked Pine.

He just shrugged. "I couldn't find it. And I looked for a while, too."

Someone suggested the possibility of a dogman, but Louis shook his head. "Don't think so. I've never seen a single monster around here. It could happen, but I doubt it."

There was also no reason to jump to the conclusion that this was a cryptid when it was more likely to be another animal. Still, we didn't rule out any possibility. Pine had found a few tracks around the pronghorn, but nothing clear, and he hadn't turned up any other sign. But his photos and videos were extensive, and the long, closely grouped wounds across the pronghorn's body were certainly claw marks, rather than bites. That meant that the culprit was almost certainly a mountain lion. This was concerning, because they're a much bigger threat to humans than coyotes or black bears, the only other large carnivores in the area.

Even though we were armed to the teeth and in a large group, we still decided to just play it safe. The original plan had been to wrap up the program by sending each Hatch out by themselves for a few days, to prove their solo abilities. Now, though, we gave each of them a partner, making three pairs. Additionally, we teachers would also be in three pairs, trailing our one-on-one students at a distance and ready to help if anything went sideways.

A few more days went by where we trekked up into some low mountains with thicker tree cover, then down into some flatland where we did some shooting practice. We started by giving the Hatchies stationary targets: rocks, stumps, and junctions between branches, and so on. They were more than used to this, so after assessing their skill, we began ramping up the difficulty. We gave them multiple targets at once and timed how quickly they could nail them, and gradually they all grew snappier and started achieving shorter times. As I mentioned earlier, Mei wasn't an amazing shot, but she was solid, and her results were consistent, especially with a revolver. We didn't judge the Hatches against each other much; it was more important that they improve upon their own performances.

After a while we progressed to moving targets, typically by hanging a stump or rock from a branch and pushing it to swing back and forth. Most of the Hatchies were already well-practiced with this too, and they proved to be more than capable of hitting their marks. By working together, we could set up multiple moving targets at once, and the Hatchies progressively got better at our new timed exercises as well. Coming into the program, the kids all had a solid baseline experience and skillset, and it was clear that, day by day, they were refining and improving their abilities.

Tracking was easy enough to set up, given that there was plenty of wildlife around us. On different days, we would have one of the six Hatches lead us on some sort of trail we discovered, starting with easier targets like deer or wild pigs before moving to tougher creatures like raccoons, jackrabbits, and ringtails. Some of the kids turned out to be excellent trackers, and although Mei struggled with some of the smaller animals, she definitely improved after being given some pointers and advice. The last challenge was to have Pine or one of the other instructors go out on their own, sometimes leaving intentional clues here and there, before we had the Hatches lead the rest of us to track them down about six hours later.

Since each teacher knew our own Hatchy best, we would act as their particular quarry on the day when it was their turn. Like many people, Mei had trouble tracking over rocky ground, so I intentionally crossed over a few of those areas to challenge her. At first, I purposely disturbed patches of pebbles or left scratch marks here and there, but I gradually stopped, again in order to increase the challenge. Maybe after a few months of training specifically focused on tracking, I might not have done this, but Mei still had a way to go. Even so, I wasn't making it too easy for her.

After four or five hours of walking, a bit before noon, I stopped on a scrub-covered cliffside and radioed the teachers to let them know that Mei could start tracking me. I sat down on a rock and took another look at my map, which was when I noticed something interesting. Most of the maps Louis had given us were standard topographical ones, showing elevations, bodies of water (there were few of these, and some were dried up), and roads (of which there were even fewer). Important points like mountains and streams were labeled already, but Louis had also marked all the copies he'd given us, highlighting some of the area's places of interest. He'd marked the locations of all those cattle water stations I mentioned earlier, some of the cool rock formations, a burnt forest, and even an actual ghost town, which I really wanted to visit.

When I looked at the map at this point, I found that I was near an interesting location. When I had left camp early that morning, I had traveled based on what would make a good exercise for Mei, with no particular destination in mind. But now I saw that I had just happened to end up near Louis' label of "Petroglyphs". Petroglyphs are rock art, often carvings, and Louis had previously told me that these ones were left by Native people many centuries ago. I wanted to check them out, partly because they were Indigenous-made, but also because it's not every day that you get to see ancient rock carvings that are still visible! They were close by, but if I went there right then, it would probably give me too much of an indication of where I was. So I decided to wait until she found me at my current position, then suggest that a visit to the petroglyphs.

Mei just about met my expectations, and maybe even did a little better. The other teachers could have given her a hand if she had trouble finding my trail and got too far off course, but that never happened! With only a few hiccups, she led the group directly to where I was, arriving just before dusk. The first thing I did was hold up a hand for her to give me a weary but elated high-five.

"Did you go easy on me?" she asked.

"Only a little. Did you need any help?"

"Not even once," she answered, with one of the proudest smiles I ever saw from her.

"Your girl did good," Louis said, patting Mei on the shoulder.

Each of Mei's victories was wonderful to see, but something about this particular one hit me in a different way. I mentioned earlier than I've trained my nephew on and off as a Hunter, and for those of you who have listened to some of my later letters, you may also know that I now have a daughter. About two years after the events of this letter, a friend of mine, an Australian Hunter named William, passed away. He had a daughter named Rain, who Serena and I wound up adopting. That's all a story for another time, but I bring it up to say that now I know firsthand what it's like to be proud of your kid when they accomplish something big. If you yourself have children, you probably know that this is one of those feelings that, although you can come close, you can't *fully* understand until experiencing it. This moment, being a proud teacher for Mei, was very much like that. It was also a moment when I felt very connected to how my mom must have felt while training me!

After celebrating with a quesadilla dinner (Mei's favorite), we headed up to the petroglyphs the next morning. They were surprisingly difficult to reach, because they were situated on some cliffsides. When we made our way up to them, it was a great experience. There were many geometric and stylized designs, like circles and spirals, plus a few that looked like elongated human-like figures. In several areas there were even some remnants of yellow and red pigment left on the rock. According to Louis, this was once a gathering place, and we went under a big overhang that was colored black, possibly from the smoke of ancient fires. Underneath were more spirals and shapes, maybe representations of celestial bodies for astronomy purposes. It was incredible stuff, and I only wish that I had been with someone who could have told me more about them; I could guess, but I wanted a better idea. I'm not from Utah, and the Cherokee are originally from the other side of the continent, but it's still meaningful to see stuff that your distant relatives did, especially things as important as these carvings must have been to their creators.

After spending a few hours there, we started to head back down the cliffside. When we were nearly at the bottom, clambering down some big boulders, one of the Hatchies directly ahead and below me, a tall blonde 22-year-old named Tom, abruptly keeled over. It was like he'd been hit on the head or knocked out, because he suddenly and completely went down entirely out of nowhere. He actually tumbled a short way down the rocks, but thankfully, it wasn't far to the ground, and he just barely missed landing in some thorn bushes. The rest of us all climbed down as fast as we could, and by the time I arrived, Mary, Tom's one-on-one instructor, was already by his side. I noticed bloody scrapes on his shin and elbow, but for some reason, he was clutching his skull and grimacing in pain, even though I hadn't seen him hit his head in the fall.

"God, it feels like somebody just shoved a spike right through my brain," he groaned through gritted teeth.

"Have you been drinking enough water?" Mary asked. Dehydration is always a concern (yes, for all of us, even for you, dear reader!), but especially out in the desert, where your body constantly loses much of its water and heatstroke is an ever-present threat.

"Yeah. This just came out of nowhere. It's getting better now," Tom answered.

While Tom and Mary attended to his scrapes, the rest of us checked in and made sure everyone else was feeling alright. This was strange, and I had the sense that not everything was as it seemed. I wondered if it had anything to do with the petroglyphs. Although I don't personally believe in all the old tales, I still try to respect them, and I've personally seen more than enough to confirm some of them that otherwise defy what we think of as "reality". I didn't really think that the petroglyphs would have somehow caused Tom's condition, but there was no harm in looking into it.

Later that night, I asked Tom and the people who had been nearby if he had somehow treated the carvings badly, such as touching them or making fun of them, but it didn't seem like he had. That was good, but something told me that there might be more to this story, and a couple of the other teachers agreed. Around that time, Mary came up to me while I was journaling off to the edge of the campsite, as I usually do. Mary is a blonde Texan lady, probably around my age; she's stern and no-nonsense, but she and Tom definitely got along well. As I've said before, the dialogue in these letters is mostly my memory and recreation, but this first bit is pretty much exactly how it happened.

"Listen, Sam. You're our resident Indian, so I'm coming to you," Mary said.

"Uh, come again?" I asked. Mary and I weren't very close, but even if we were, most people usually don't say stuff like "resident Indian" unless they're joking. But Mary seemed completely serious as she crouched next to me.

"I...have a weird feeling about things right now," she said, and I remember her going silent for an uncomfortably long time.

"Okay. Me too, a little. What are you thinking?" I asked her.

"I'm not sure. Do you know...anything?"

Then Mary gave me a look that told me what she was getting at. She was clearly aware of the superstitions and guidelines: the name "skinwalker" shouldn't be spoken out loud, especially not at night. In fact, just discussing these beings in the first place can be risky. As I mentioned earlier, I highly encourage you to read my fourth letter to get a clearer picture of this topic. But to give an extremely reductive summary for this story, skinwalkers are witches from the lands of the Navajo, or Diné. They take on the forms of animals and wreak havoc with abilities that can only be described as supernatural. They are very real, and put bluntly, they are the very definition of evil.

"No. I don't know anything. I've dealt with them before, and our situation right now doesn't seem the same," I told Mary, wanting to shut down the conversation.

Honestly, I had briefly considered this possibility earlier, but there was no need to go there. I'm also no expert on skinwalkers by any means; even though I had done a couple jobs out west that directly or indirectly involved walker activity, we Cherokee don't deal with these beings like Southwest Natives like the Diné, Hopi, or Ute have to. I think Mary came to me just because I'm Native and she might have thought that all of us know about this stuff. Fortunately, I do, but our different nations and tribes are all very different, so she got lucky.

"You don't think this could be...I dunno, some type of dark magic or something?" Mary asked.

"We have a weird pronghorn kill and a Hatch who got a temporary migraine. Not nearly enough evidence to jump to that conclusion, especially when Louis says he's never seen a cryptid here and the ranchers haven't had any problems," I replied.

"Maybe." Her tone of voice was clearly unconvinced, so I tried to come up with something we could do.

"I really think it's alright. But just in case, we can burn up some ash and do some prayers. That might help," I suggested.

These countermeasures wouldn't guarantee complete protection from a walker, but they would help, which seemed to make Mary feel better. I wasn't going to talk any more about the matter during nighttime, but I honestly wasn't very worried about it. Not only was there no definite indication that there was any walker nearby, but Louis and Pine had also vetted the whole training area way before we'd arrived. On top of that, we were also a good distance away from the Navajo Nation, which is where almost all walkers live. As I say in my letter on skinwalkers, many beings derive their power from the land, often specific geographical regions; in the case of walkers, they're tied to Dinétah, the Navajo homeland. The modern boundaries of the Navajo Nation reservation are located within Dinétah, but the region extends beyond that, with four sacred mountains roughly marking its borders. The farther away from Dinétah a skinwalker is, the weaker their abilities become, and there were at least 30 miles between there and the training area.

Nonetheless, Mary and I brought up the matter with the other teachers early the next morning. I think Mary was the only one who was truly concerned about the walker idea, but we all figured that there was no harm in taking precautions. My previous letter has much more information about walkers, but just like back then, I'm intentionally refraining from diving super deep here. We started by giving the Hatchies a basic rundown on what they needed to know about the subject, even though most of them already knew a bit. Next, I took us all through some of the ceremonies that are necessary to confront walkers; I'm no medicine man, so I could only do so much, but I have learned a bit from the Diné over the years.

A core part of many ceremonies worldwide is praying. I direct my prayers to the universe and the earth in general, and often my ancestors or the beings that I interact with, rather than any specific god or deity. I say some before setting out on any hunt, although I don't talk about it much in these letters; it's a bit personal and, unlike with walkers, usually isn't explicitly connected to the letters. In all these cases, I usually do a combination of different prayers that my mom taught me, along with more fluid ones that I create or change around for different situations. They're mostly in English, but some are in the bits of Cherokee that I know.

The more walker-specific aspect of the ceremonies was the preparation of white ash. We did this by creating a separate, special firepit and burning sage, juniper, and cedar; you can use other types of wood or plants for this, but these ones were readily available and have a ton of sacred properties that I won't get into here. It's important to treat this with respect and intentionality, and it was great to see that everyone was very careful in preparing the fire and collecting the plants, and stayed very serious and purposeful throughout the ceremonies. Once the white ash was ready, I walked everyone through the proper patterns for applying it to key parts of the body (men use one sequence, and women use the inverse). This is to shield against walkers. Lastly, we sprinkled the ash over all our gear and coated our weapons and ammunition with it, being careful not to interfere with the functionality of our guns. This gives weapons the ability to hurt, and even kill, walkers. Finally, we smudged ourselves with sage, and I said some of the prayers I have been taught over the years, both in English and occasionally in Cherokee. Without a specially trained medicine person, this wasn't perfect, but it was what we could do. Plus, it was a good call to at least educate the Hatchies. A *very* good call.

For a few days after the petroglyph incident, I occasionally spotted Tom looking out over the hills or into the campfire with a thousand-yard stare, and I can't blame him. One morning, I overheard another Hatch, Jason, telling Tom that we had nothing to worry about from a coyote that might give us a cold. Instinct kicked in, and I immediately shut down the conversation to drive home the point that this was no laughing matter. Irritation and concern led me to raise my voice, which I instantly began to regret when I saw the boys' frozen, wide-eyed, "deer in the headlights" reaction. I've always been taught to never react purely out of emotion, so I gave an awkward

"I'm sorry" and stepped away. I was kicking myself for the next half hour, but at least nobody else had witnessed the interaction. Or so I thought, until I spotted Mei talking to Tom and Jason later that evening. I couldn't help but wonder if she was talking trash, sticking up for me, or something completely different, but it didn't matter; I'd simply made a dumb mistake. And soon Mei came over to grill me about it.

"You know that Jason was trying to cheer Tom up, right?" she asked after I had explained things from my perspective.

"Yes, but I didn't want them making light of the situation," I answered.

"Sure, but now Tom feels like you proved him right. He's still anxious," Mei replied. Rather than angry, she just sounded disappointed. "Why did you react like that?"

I had to really think before answering. Even though it had been a minor incident, I don't normally lose my cool so easily. "I got mad. I don't want any of us getting cocky just because we're not necessarily in danger. I just worry about you guys. Sorry."

"Well, how about telling them?" Mei asked.

For decades, I've been reminded countless times that the duty of a Hunter is to protect others, and Mei was able to very patiently show me how I might do that better. It was the kind of thoughtfulness I would have expected from my mom or Louis, so to hear it from a Hatchy was pretty crazy. I went back to Jason and Tom and apologized again, explaining my intentions and assuring them that we were safe. They both understood and appreciated where I was coming from, and after I thanked both them and Mei, we all wound up sitting next to each other during a game of cards later that night. I don't think any of us won a single hand, but spirits enough after our talk earlier.

As the seminar went on and the Hatchies continued to improve, we eventually decided that it was finally time for them to go out on their duo voyages. This was the final test of their skills. There hadn't been any more signs of potential predators or walkers, but we still stuck with the plan we had decided on before: the kids would go out in pairs, three groups of two, and the one-on-one teachers for each pair of Hatches would follow roughly half a mile behind them. All the different groups would be spread out over a wide distance, but Pine always had his truck, and all six pairings of teachers and Hatchies had a radio and a GPS locator and beacon. For shorter-range communication, all of us also had whistles which we could blow in specific patterns to call for help, signal that we were stopping or starting to move, and so on.

Mei was paired up with the only other female Hatchy, a 22-year-old Black girl named Aliyah who was also from California. That meant that I would be with Arturo, a lean middle-aged veteran Hunter whose family was originally from Mexico, and who was an expert in many of the skills that Aliyah needed to improve upon. Every pair of teachers had picked out a certain location in the training area that we would direct our Hatches to travel to. We gave the Hatchies enough food and water for about a day and a half, but after that, it would be up to them to provide for themselves. They were more than skilled enough to do this, but they could always call for help, and we made sure to choose destinations for them that were near water sources that could be found on the map. If you're anything like me, then you might enjoy the location that Arturo and I picked as the goal for our Hatchies: I mentioned earlier that I really wanted to visit that ghost town, so soon enough, Mei and Aliyah were on the way there, with Arturo and I following behind.

It took a few days to get to the ghost town, and although Arturo and I couldn't help but be a little worried about the Hatches, we were still confident that they could handle themselves. We heard a gunshot at one point, which Mei and Aliyah later told us was them bringing down a grey fox. That's not the best meat in the world, but it is a lot, and more than enough to last them for the rest of the journey when combined with the food they had initially been provided. It was impressive that they'd gotten such a fast and stealthy creature, and I was very proud of Mei when I later heard that she had been the one to take the shot. Between the fox, some assorted lizards and bugs, and prickly pears, the Hatches did a good job keeping themselves fed. I know that this stuff doesn't seem very appetizing, but when it comes to survival, you take what you can get. For thousands of years, Native people in the region ate this sort of stuff. If it makes you feel any better, you can make just about anything taste at least halfway decent with enough flavoring and cooking! And it's not like everyone eats bugs all the time (although if more people ate insects, we would be well on our way to solving world hunger). In any case, Mei and Aliyah were fine on food.

A few days later, we finally arrived at the ghost town early in the evening. It was set in a wide hollow, and I was a little surprised at how small it was: five or six mostly intact buildings and several others that were little more than skeletons or stubs of wood sticking out of the sandy ground. There were also multiple large boulders, some scraggly shrubs, and a few stands of small trees here and there amongst the ruins. This terrain made the following events...interesting. Overall, it was a very cool place. Arturo and I arrived on a ridge overlooking it, and far below we could see Mei and Aliyah slowly walking through the ruins.

We radioed the girls and congratulated them, and it was great to hear them give relieved, satisfied laughs in response. Since it was getting dark, and everyone had been on the move all day, we decided that the Hatches could stay in the town tonight while Arturo and I made camp on the ridge, before we would all catch up in the morning to celebrate and explore. Arturo and I high-fived, which I imagined the girls were also doing, and just like earlier, that feeling of teachers' pride hit me deeply. Unfortunately, the good feelings were not to last. An hour or two later, as the sun was setting, Louis' voice came across the teachers-only radio channel.

"We got a problem, y'all. Everyone needs to get to their Hatches, right now." His tone wasn't panicked, but it was more urgent than I'd ever heard it.

About three hours earlier, Louis and his companion teacher had come across one of the herds of ranchers' cattle that roam through the training area. Their pair of Hatchies had just passed by the water station where the herd was clustered, but when the teachers got there, Louis had noticed that the cows seemed much more skittish than normal. The herd had even fled from the teachers, running off at a quick pace at their approach. Louis got a strong sense that something wasn't right, so he called Pine on his personal radio, asking him to drive over and scope out the scene while the teachers continued after their Hatches.

Around the watering pool, Pine discovered a mess of muddled tracks and other sign. He took his gun and followed the sign until he got to a dry creek bed, where he started to pick out small patches of dried blood on the gravelly rocks. He followed the blood trail, which only got larger as it went on, until it led him to a patchy grove of trees. Dragged beneath one of the trunks was the carcass of a huge bull. Cows are big animals in general, but these specific cattle were enormous, with the bulls having nasty horns; any predator in its right mind would go after a deer or a wild horse rather than risk tangling with one of them. Nevertheless, this bull had been utterly brutalized: although its head was still attached, it had been quite literally torn apart, just like the pronghorn from weeks earlier.

And it didn't take long for Pine to identify the culprit.

"These were the biggest cougar prints I've ever seen. Damn near 8 by 6 inches," he stated over the radio. For the first time in a while, genuine chills went down my spine; those tracks were bigger than an African lion's. Mary may have been right.

"This is either the biggest panther the West has ever seen, or we got a walker out here. Get to your Hatches ASAP. Make sure you've got your white ash applied, and we'll pray it works," Louis said.

The skinwalker might not have been actually going after us at that exact moment, but we weren't going to take any chances. Immediately, we all agreed that keeping the kids safe was our first priority, and our plan was simple. First, all of the teachers needed to reunite with their Hatchies; doing so would put us into three groups of four people each. Pine was closest to Mary's group, so he would pick up the four of them and bring them to Louis' group, where he would exchange Mary and her partnered teacher for the two Hatches who were with Louis. Once Pine had those four Hatches, he would come to my group last and retrieve Mei and Aliyah, who were all his truck had room for. Then he would drive all six kids to the safety of the nearby town. This whole evacuation process would take a matter of hours due to the distance between our different groups, and because traveling on foot at night is dangerous even without a roving monster in the area, we would all shelter in place while we waited for Pine to reach us. As you may have guessed already, this was the right call.

Arturo and I radioed Mei and Aliyah and instructed them to stay where they were. While we hurried towards their position, we considered what exactly had brought the walker to the area, and Arturo threw out the possibility that maybe we had attracted their attention. Walkers are just as intelligent as any normal human, and if this one knew about the Hunters, maybe from another of their kind, then perhaps they wanted to use this opportunity to go after us.

It wasn't long before Arturo and I reached the ghost town and reunited with the girls, who had set up camp outside a big, mostly intact wooden structure; I'm not sure what purpose that building might have served once, but it looked like a barn or storehouse, so we'll just call it a barn. The sun had gone down by then, and with only a crescent moon, headlamps, and lanterns, visibility was going to be low. We dug out an oversized firepit, which provided additional light for the campsite, but this was primarily for conducting a new ash blessing ceremony. Ever since the ceremony we had done after the petroglyph visit, when we had first put the white ash on our bullets and weapons, we had each been carrying a pouch of that ash with us. I didn't know if it would still hold the same power, but reestablishing the spiritual protection of the ceremony would be helpful regardless. We reapplied the older ash to our equipment and our bodies, then sprinkled the rest on the ground in a wide perimeter around our camp; fortunately, we had just enough left to make a complete, unbroken barrier. After that, we did some prayers and started a fresh fire using juniper wood we gathered from around the area. Since this new ash wouldn't truly be white until it had laid out for a while, I wasn't sure how effective it would be versus the old stuff. For that matter, I wasn't sure how effective *any* of this would be without the knowledge of a trained Navajo medicine person, but we had no better option.

"Can we go inside?" Mei asked, pointing to the barn right next to us. Her voice was shaky, which reminded me that she had never encountered any sort of monster before. Arturo and I figured that it would be best if the two of us stayed by the fire, but we told Mei and Aliyah that they could go into the barn as long as they tested the sturdiness of the structure beforehand.

"I got you, Mei," Aliyah said, rubbing her on the shoulder as they stood up from beside the huge fire. They were the only two female Hatchies, which was one reason they had been paired up for this journey, and they had bonded over the course of the training. They weren't best friends, but it was good to see them just being there for each other.

While the girls checked the stability of the building, Arturo and I agreed that we would both try to stay awake; however, if it came to it, we would alternate shifts on watch, so one of us would be up and ready at all times. This was mainly for sentry duty, but also to keep the fire stoked with all the juniper wood we could find; you can generally keep a fire burning overnight by just throwing a thick log or two on it, but we wanted as much flame and ash as we could get. The Hatchies said that the barn was sturdy and safe, so after a little while, we took some of the new ash and extended the perimeter barrier around the building. Then all we could do was wait.

Our various groups kept up intermittent but consistent radio contact to monitor everyone's status and location. This also made it less lonely, but it could only do so much to ease the tension. For the first time, I was seriously concerned about the safety of the Hatches. Could you imagine what it would be like if your first extended outing in the wilderness, even just a long camping trip, ended with the possibility of being jumped by a skinwalker?

I can't recall exactly what time the nightmare *truly* started, but it was at some point when Arturo and I were on guard, sitting across from each other on either side of the fire with our heads on a swivel looking out into the dark. The fire made it difficult to use night vision gear effectively, so we just had headlamps. Suddenly, Arturo's head whipped to the side, as if he'd just seen something out in the shadows. Instantly, I had my rifle readied and my eyes scanning the area, waiting for Arturo's report. There was a light wind, but the desert was silent, and I did *not* like that one bit. But after a long while, maybe about half a minute, Arturo still hadn't said anything.

I didn't take my eyes away from the darkness as I prompted him. "Hey, what is it?"

Still no answer. I risked a glance at my co-teacher. He had his revolver in one hand and was slowly lifting it, raising his arm almost straight up over his head so that the gun was pointing towards the sky. For a moment I didn't know what was going on, until I looked at Arturo's face. His gaze was still locked on the darkness beyond the fire, and his expression on his face was completely blank. If you've ever heard the phrase "the lights are on, but no one's home", Arturo's eyes were the very definition of it. It was like his body had suddenly become uninhabited, and my stomach turned as I realized what was happening.

"Arturo!" I shouted. He didn't make a sound as he started to bend his arm inwards, bringing the revolver's barrel towards his head.

I lunged forward and grabbed his arm, dropping my own gun as I tried to tear Arturo's away from him. He seized it in a vice grip with both hands and tried to pull away from my grasp, and I realized that although Arturo was smaller and slightly older than me, he could more than match my strength. Our struggle took us to the ground, and while we wrestled, I got a glimpse of his eyes; they were still missing the light of full consciousness, but his pupils were shuddering madly, almost like something inside of his eyes was trying ferociously to escape.

If you've read or listened to my skinwalker letter, then you may remember that one of the many abilities of these beings is what Hunters call "persuasion" or "influence". By making extended eye contact with a target, a walker can speak to them in a voice that only they can hear and command them to do whatever they're told. Once somebody has been touched by a walker's persuasion, they can try to resist it, but only trained medicine people or other spiritual practitioners, or the most strong-willed of people, can even *hope* to break away. The good news is that if a walker doesn't reestablish eye contact with the victim, their influence will gradually weaken and eventually wear off completely. The bad news is that this can take anywhere from a few minutes to an hour, depending on the strength of the walker's abilities. Until then, the victim is trapped.

Disconcertingly, Arturo remained completely silent as we fought, but Mei and Aliyah must have heard my shout, because they immediately came rushing out of the barn. Although it would have been nice to have some help with Arturo, I needed the Hatchies to watch our backs.

"Look to the east, tell me if you see anything!" I told them.

Aliyah ignored the directive and ran straight over to us. "Arturo! Wake up!"

I've never seen or heard of anyone successfully freeing a victim from a walker's influence by simply telling them to "snap out of it", so I was shocked when Arturo's eyes suddenly went wide and he stopped fighting against me.

"Aliyah!...Sam?" he asked. His voice was shaky, but the light had returned to his eyes.

"Arturo, can you hear me?" Aliyah asked. I turned to her, and I admit that I snapped at her. It was good that she'd seemingly broken Arturo out, but I had still told her and Mei to watch the darkness; Arturo could only have been influenced if he'd made eye contact with the walker, meaning that the cryptid was still around.

"Aliyah, get back and help Mei! I've got Arturo!" I shouted, causing her to jump. I didn't intend to startle her, but she quickly nodded and hurried off.

"Good God, it got me," Arturo said.

"Are you with us? Are you hearing its voice?" I asked. I wanted to release him, but I needed to be sure he was completely free from the persuasion.

"I'm okay. I can control myself," he answered, shakily but confidently.

I was grateful, although it was still hard for me to believe that Aliyah had truly dragged him out of the influence. But neither of us had much time to consider this, because right as I had finished helping Arturo to his feet, I heard Mei shout "East-northeast, 2 o'clock!" and fire her rifle. At almost the exact same time, Arturo grunted and collapsed as if he'd been knocked unconscious. I only saw him go down out of the corner of my eye, because I was already looking in the direction that Mei had called out. In the shadows, I caught a glimpse of two glowing red eyes on a shadowy shape that was much too big and much too fast to be any animal I'd ever seen. With no time to pick up my rifle, I drew my revolver and opened fire alongside Mei and Aliyah. I don't know how many of our rounds landed, but clearly not enough.

The creature swerved around to our 11 o'clock and leaped, completely clearing the barrier of white ash and aiming right for Aliyah. She managed to dodge a direct collision, but the monster still knocked her to the ground as it passed, overshooting her and landing with a thud. The skinwalker took the form of the largest cougar I've ever seen, bigger than a male African lion and colored dark gray with a russet underbelly, instead of the usual tan and white. It whirled around with a snarl that shook my chest, and my heart stopped dead as it dug its claws into Aliyah's leg and lunged for her throat. I'm so thankful that the Hatches were on their game, because all our bullets, especially Aliyah's, went right into the walker's head and neck. It sprang backwards, screaming; all cougars have a cry that sounds like a screaming woman, but this one had an *actual*, unmistakably human female voice beneath the cougar's. Crazily enough, she tried to jump back and grab Aliyah again, but none of us had let our fingers leave the trigger; the gunfire was too much, and the walker sprang back over the ash line to the 9 o'clock direction of the camp and dove into one of the nearest clumps of trees.

As soon as the walker disappeared, I told Mei to check on Aliyah while I rushed over to Arturo, who hadn't moved from where he'd fallen. He was laying on his side, and almost as soon as I reached him, I saw what the problem was. While confirming that he still had a pulse, I could see that he was breathing, but only just; his eyes were frozen wide open, and I also noticed his fingers and the muscles around his mouth twitching occasionally. Arturo was paralyzed, but entirely conscious and attempting unsuccessfully to move; if you're familiar with the horror of sleep paralysis, this was very similar. Carefully, I scanned his body until I found the culprit: sticking out of the base of his right shoulder blade was the tail end of a walker's bone dart.

Unlike many creatures, walkers have numerous ways to attack from a distance, and one of their favorites is by hurling bone darts. These projectiles are a few inches long, shaped roughly like thick needles, and weighted for throwing. That's dangerous enough, but the real threat is that they're crafted from hollowed-out human bone; walkers fill the darts with corpse dust and other toxins which they infuse with some kind of curse or darkness that allows them to paralyze and poison. They fling these darts with great speed and accuracy; although this is usually to hurt and terrorize, this was a life-and-death situation, and this dart had probably missed a lethal hit to Arturo's neck or spine.

I hurriedly grabbed a rag and covered my hand with it for protection as I gently removed the dart from Arturo's back. Maybe it was just nerves, but my fingers tingled slightly underneath the rag, and I swiftly dropped the dart into the fire and took a deep breath. I needed to move Arturo, but before doing so I checked in with the Hatches. Aliyah's legs had been torn up pretty badly, and her voice was unsteady as she said that she would need help walking. I wanted to curse, but I tried not to let the girls see me too openly upset.

"This walker could come back any second. Mei, are you okay?" I asked.

"Yeah, just a little rattled," she answered.

"Okay, good. Both of you go inside the barn, quick, and radio a sitrep to the whole group channel. I'll bring Arturo in. And good shooting. We'll be alright," I told the Hatchies, squeezing their shoulders and giving them the most encouraging nod that I could.

While the Hatches made their way into the shelter of the barn, I went back to Arturo, scanning the perimeter as I did. There was no sign of the walker, but I still moved quickly. I apologized to Arturo before picking him up and slinging him over my shoulder. As I ran him into the barn and laid him down, he made a soft groaning noise, which was a big relief; that meant the paralysis was already wearing off. Equally as importantly, it meant that Arturo was resisting the longer-term toxins. Whenever a walker uses a tool or weapon for their rituals and abilities, they corrupt that object on a spiritual level, and coming into contact with it can be just as lethal as the walker themselves. Being made unclean, especially through injury like Arturo and Aliyah, will flat-out poison you, and without a purification done by a professional, your days will be numbered. Arturo and Aliyah might have been fine for the moment, but we needed to get them this type of help ASAP; the same went for me and Mei, although we were better off.

I radioed in a follow-up communication to the one that the girls had already given the group, but there wasn't much that the others could do; based on where all of our groups were, it would be impractical to deviate from the rescue plan we'd already set up. While we held our ground, the most immediate concern was tending to Aliyah's injuries. She and Mei had already started the process, and I kept an eye on the outside as I came over to help. The wounds weren't deep, but they were bleeding a lot, and for now all we could do was pressurize, stitch, and bandage them. Thankfully, we had made sure the Hatchies were all up to date on their field medicine, so they knew how to deal with Aliyah's injuries without my constant supervision, and it was a tremendous load off my back.

Once everybody had been mostly stabilized, both physically and psychologically, I had Mei cover me while I assessed the scene of the fight. Quickly but carefully, I searched the ground and the air for any indication that our bullets had done any real damage, which would give an idea of how effective our other type of field medicine (no pun intended) had been. Walkers bleed, and injuring them with properly prepared materials also produces a gas that resembles dark smoke or steam. Unfortunately, I hadn't seen either when we had been shooting. That smoke has a really vile scent that's difficult to properly describe, but I didn't smell it, and I only found a few drops of dark, maroon-colored blood here and there. That wouldn't be enough to stop the walker, at least not for long. These monsters are resistant to all injuries, but even shots to the head and neck hadn't brought her down. That was very disconcerting, especially to a Hunter who's used to instantly killing things in that exact manner.

But the bullets had clearly caused the walker pain, and even if it was only a little, we *had* been able to hurt her.

The line of ash on the ground had been completely ineffective, but maybe that was because the walker had simply jumped over it. Leaving it in place couldn't hurt. Although we also had to abandon the fire, we took a bit of fresh ash with us into the shelter of the barn; it wasn't much, and the color was darker than I would have liked, but hopefully the ceremony had successful.

The inside of the barn was empty and large, probably 30 by 20 feet; this allowed us to keep well away from the entrance and the walls, which the walker would now have to break through to reach us. I had laid Arturo on the remnants of the wooden floor in the center of the space, and the Hatchies stayed by his side, occasionally asking for guidance or confirmation on treating Aliyah. Meanwhile, I rotated around the walls, where there were plenty of cracks and holes in the planks where I could observe the shadows outside.

Every so often I talked a bit to the Hatches to keep their spirits up and reassure them. Even though I was fully aware that they weren't babies, I was still in charge of them, and that's a big enough responsibility even under normal circumstances. It really helped that they were such troopers. Mei kept constant watch on Aliyah and Arturo with a level of vigilance and caring that I had never seen from her; anytime either of them needed water or a hand to hold, Mei was there before they had to ask. For her part, Aliyah was sweating and shaking, but she hardly even cried out during the whole night, and never once complained. She kept her head and stayed completely in the moment, even when she had to cry for a bit. She might not have been my Hatchy, but damn if I wasn't proud of her too.

Steadily, and quicker than I expected, Arturo regained control of his body. He was able to talk before he could move, although his voice was strained and soft at first. There wasn't much to be said, so we just told him to stay quiet and save his energy. Knowing that I would have his assistance made me feel a lot better, especially when we started to hear voices from outside the barn. First, it was Mei's, softly asking for us to step outside "just to talk". It sounded just like her, but the tone was too flat, and it had a sort of lo-fi quality to it, almost as if it were coming out of a speaker. I've heard this before, and I hated it even more now; mimicking voices is one of walkers' favorite forms of psychological warfare, but we weren't going to let it get to us. I told the Hatchies that they could cover their ears if they wanted to, but neither of them took me up on the offer. They sat and listened as the walker circled the barn for what must have been close to half an hour, switching to my voice, then Aliyah's, then Arturo's, asking us to come outside, to give up, even to kill ourselves, and worse; you can use your imagination. It almost physically hurt to listen to this, to the point where I found myself gritting my teeth and practically choking my rifle. At a certain point, I wanted to flat-out order the girls to cover their ears, but ultimately, despite a few tears, they kept their cool the entire time.

As this went on, I tried to follow the walker, going to whatever side of the barn it was outside of. The darkness outside was thick, but a few times, I thought I glimpsed movement. You always have to be careful not to jump at shadows, literally, so I wasn't going to act unless I was sure. I heard sand shifting on multiple occasions, and I'm positive that at one point, I saw a woman's silhouette flicker from left to right through the shadows between some branches. Every time, though, the walker moved away before I could even take aim.

Shortly before the walker went quiet again, Arturo regained enough physical control to sit up and hold his gun. His voice had fully returned by now, and he had been talking to the girls quietly while I patrolled the walls, helping them keep steady. Radio updates from the other groups continued, and eventually we got the news we were waiting for: Pine had linked up with the other groups, and now he was on his way with their four Hatchies to pick up Mei and Aliyah. We told him to drive carefully; not only was he off-roading, but it was late at night, and the walker could potentially attack his truck. I can't tell you how much of a morale boost this gave us. Arturo and I would still be stuck out here until Pine could come back for us teachers, but we were just grateful that Mei and Aliyah would be headed to safety soon. We just had to hold out until then.

Around 3 or 4 AM, Mei and Aliyah had started to doze off, and Arturo and I were tiring as well. We expected that the walker might be waiting for this exact situation, so it wasn't entirely surprising when I saw branches moving outside the south side, the rear, of the building. Arturo was back on his feet now, so I beckoned him over and whispered for the girls to stay put. We hugged the rear wall, rifles raised as we watched the leaves shift ever so slightly. Then the mountain lion burst out of the night, and Arturo and I opened fire with our rifles through the wooden wall. The walker approached in zigzagging bounds, making it impossible for us to keep consistently on target. In moments, she had jumped to the top of a boulder that was at least 20 feet away from us, then took a single long leap from the rock onto the side of the building, shaking the entire structure as she landed.

Arturo swore in Spanish, and we backed up, shooting straight into the upper portion of the wall where we could see the walker's body blocking out the moonlight. She snarled and lunged up onto the sloped roof, then slammed down what must have been her front paws, rattling the whole building to the point where it seemed like it might collapse entirely. Mei and Aliyah also opened up with their own rifles as one gigantic paw burst through the wooden planks. The paw quickly pulled back, and after a moment, a single hazel-colored human eye looked through the hole for the briefest of moments, then vanished before I even had the time to blink. With perfect clarity, a woman's voice hissed something in what I recognized as the Navajo language, before the skinwalker dropped from the building in a single movement and darted back into the trees.

"She'll be back," Arturo said after a moment.

"Doesn't she realize that she's not getting anywhere?" Mei asked.

"We told you how she killed those animals. Messy, almost like she didn't know what she was doing," Arturo said.

I remember how Mei suddenly frowned, an expression that I'd seen her make when she was deep in thought. "When she had influence over you, you went to aim the pistol at yourself. If you had pulled the trigger, the walker would lose the person she already had a hold on. Why not make you aim at any of us instead?"

"And Aliyah snapped you out of it so fast," I added.

"I just did what seemed right. I didn't think it'd actually work," Aliyah said.

"Normally it wouldn't have..." I said.

Then there was the shape. From what I had been told in past experiences, the mountain lion is a very powerful and sacred animal, and a walker requires a lot of skill to take that form. Combined with our distance from Dinétah and the four sacred mountains, it seemed quite possible that although this walker was certainly strong, she was having trouble controlling her abilities fully. I can't say how valid this theory actually was, and it wasn't a total game-changer, but it was still important, so we radioed everyone to let them know. I also believe that our earlier praying and ceremonies helped protect us from the walker's non-physical attacks, and just to be sure, I continued to say some of the protection prayers I knew; they weren't Navajo ones, but they could only help. The sky outside was starting to get light by this point, but only slightly. Walkers can become trapped in their animal forms during the daytime, so I was hoping that our assailant would give up after sunrise. Adrenaline was keeping all of us in the game, but we were exhausted, and that would become especially hazardous once it was just Arturo and I together.

The walker paid us another visit shortly after that, this time managing to use some shadows to get right up to our protective line of ash on the ground. She must have stepped on it, however, because we heard a soft whine followed by the sound of scraping pebbles. It was reassuring to know that our defense had worked, but that would probably be the last time. Maybe half an hour later, just as the sky was becoming a medium shade of blue, Arturo shouted a heads-up from the right side of the barn, and I rushed over just as the walker slammed into the wall, nearly caving it in. The planks splintered and began to give, and all of us opened fire straight through them as the woman's voice outside screamed in anger, pain, or maybe both. Moments later, the huge gray cougar's head and one front leg bashed through the wood, and although she snarled and swiped out, we were well out of range of her claws. Then I think somebody's rounds hit her in the eye, because a jet of blood went up into the air, followed by a plume of smoke. The walker's body seemed to flash or flicker, and it quivered in a way that seemed physically impossible, a bit like it was a video with missing frames. She screamed, thrashing wildly to pull loose from the wall, and after a few seconds, she managed to tear herself free. She fell backwards, then whirled and raced away faster than any time previously, leaving behind a thick gray cloud and a rancid stench around the shattered planks.

"I think I got her!" Mei called. "Well, I think."

Even if it was impossible to tell, we gave Mei the honor anyways and took a moment to praise her and give some well-earned fist bumps. I never like to rejoice in any type of suffering or pain completely, but you can always appreciate fighting back against evil.

We used the opportunity to give Aliyah some fresh bandages, and just after sunrise, we heard the glorious sound of an approaching engine. Still keeping vigilant, we waved Pine's truck over to the barn. He pulled up right in front of the entrance, where Arturo and I practically tossed Mei and Aliyah inside the vehicle.

"Good job, you guys. Don't let your guard down, just in case it tries to hit the truck," I told the two girls as we sent them off.

Mei suddenly reached out and put her arms around me in a tight hug, seemingly out of instinct just as much as intention. It caught me completely off guard, but it was really nice, and I returned the gesture before quickly urging her into the truck; as much as I appreciate a good hug, I wanted them to get to safety ASAP. Arturo, Pine, and I helped Aliyah into the truck next, and then Pine gunned the engines and carried all six Hatches off into the desert.

That was the end of that, and although I was still tense, the knot that had been sitting in my stomach for hours finally began to unravel. I was worried that the walker might try to go after the truck, but they had seven guns and a good engine, so any of us teachers were far more exposed than them. Once they were gone, Arturo and I got on the radio and decided to meet the other instructors at a halfway point. The last thing I wanted to do was hike across the desert for miles after that horrendous night, but this was our best option to reunite. On a much more welcome note, Louis had called his Guide, who had sent out an emergency distress call. Almost immediately, the request had been picked up by two other veteran Hunters who had dealt with walkers before. They wouldn't be able to get to us until the following day, but once they arrived, we would leave things to them.

Louis didn't ask for me to go with the two backup Hunters; knowing him, he felt awful about the whole situation and didn't want to put me in any more danger. Even so, I planned to accompany the pair, if they would have me. No matter how tired I was, I knew the area, I had dealt with this walker already, and three guns are better than two. At least, that was my intention at first. But things didn't exactly go to plan...which seems to happen pretty often...

Arturo and I balanced speed with exertion, moving as fast as possible without pressing ourselves too hard. We had a lot of ground to cover, and as the day went on, it became clear that we weren't going to reach the other four teachers until after sunset. Regardless, we were going to push on; being caught by ourselves in the open at night would be disastrous. One thing we had going for us was plenty of fresh white ash from our supersized fire at the ghost town, and since we had already been able to do some damage to the walker, maybe this would be just what we needed.

In the afternoon, Arturo and I were roasting in the hot sun, with only a few scattered trees for shade as we trekked westward. Our route took us across a long, flat stretch of land covered with scrubby sagebrush, which ran along the south side of some lightly forested hills. Ahead of us was a large dust cloud, kicked up by a herd of about 30 to 40 brown and black cattle that we had sighted earlier. They were going west too, which was a good sign: as long as they felt safe, we wouldn't have to be too worried. The only problem was that, at around 4 or 4:30 in the afternoon, they *stopped* feeling safe.

Up until that point the herd had been pretty quiet, but Arturo and I stopped dead when we suddenly heard a whole lot of mooing coming from the dust about 50 or 60 yards ahead of us. The dust cloud started to grow, and we saw individual cows emerging from it, raising and lowering their heads and calling out as they ran back the way they had come...right towards us. Something had spooked them, and Arturo and I both had a good guess what.

We looked at each other for all of 3 seconds, then, without a word, took off running to the north, heading for the hills to get out of the path of the incoming stampede. Moving on only two legs makes humans slower than many animals, especially when we're lugging guns, packs, and gear. And if you've ever seen a cow run, you'll know that they can move shockingly fast when they need to. As Arturo and I plowed our way through the sagebrush and other shin-high ground plants, we very quickly realized that we might not get to safety in time. The herd was spreading out over the flat terrain, so the stampede was not in a single-file line.

What happened next was something you might have seen in movies, and that's because sometimes it really does happen. When the closest cows were maybe 10 or 15 yards away, Arturo and I found just what we needed. Several big fallen logs had rolled down the hillside sometime in the past, and now they formed a small pile about 4 feet high amidst the brush; it wasn't tall, but it was enough of an obstacle that the cows would want to avoid it.

I had pulled slightly ahead of Arturo as we ran, and I hurled my pack to the side of the logs before diving into a crouch behind them, rifle still in hand. A couple of cows rushed past Arturo, missing him by a few feet, before he reached the logs, flinging himself forwards as simultaneously yanked him behind the pile. We crouched as low as we could, sheltering behind the logs and shielding our heads while cattle went thundering by on either side of us. Over the sounds of mooing, grunting, and drumming hooves, a cow bellowed in pain, and we both instinctively readied our guns. A large brown cow stumbled past the side of the log where most of the herd was running, and hanging from its flank was a huge russet and gray cougar pelt, with a mess of black hair visible underneath. The walker was in human shape, draped in the cougar skin and latched onto the cow's ribcage; sheets of blood, at least a gallon or two, were running down the animal's sides and hind legs, and much of the cougar pelt was stained bright red. I looked at Arturo, silently asking whether to open fire, but he shook his head and signaled to hold position; if we were lucky, the stampede would continue past us, and we could keep moving without the walker noticing us.

The cow that was being attacked was kicking and bucking to shake off the walker, simultaneously trying its best to keep up with the herd, but nonetheless falling behind. The monster may have partially taken on physical aspects of the mountain lion, because she tore gashes in the cow's skin as she clawed her way onto its back and bit into its spine. The poor animal stumbled and collapsed onto its rear end in an awkward sort of sitting position, and I saw a hand emerge from beneath the cougar pelt, holding what I knew to be a knife made of bone; my throat tightened as the walker spun the knife to hold it in a reverse grip, then began to repeatedly drive the blade into the cow's spine. It was very difficult to watch, and even more upsetting because I couldn't see any obvious rationale to it. Walkers feed on pain and terror, so maybe this one was trying to use these to fuel one of her curses or rituals. Maybe she was venting her anger at not having gotten to our group in the ghost town, or maybe she was just being sadistic. None of these possibilities were out of the question.

Thankfully, the horror was interrupted a moment later. A second cow was unable to swerve out of the way in time and wound up plowing into the walker and her prey, bringing all three of them down in a heap and a fresh cloud of red and brown dust. Meanwhile, although Arturo and I didn't have a great view from behind the logs, most of the remaining stampede seemed to have gone by; the sounds of mooing and hoofbeats were getting fainter, so I looked at Arturo and motioned for us to take this opportunity. He nodded, and we grabbed our stuff and dashed out from behind the logs. We quickly resumed our earlier path towards the hill; although the wooded terrain there would make travel a bit tougher, we only needed to stay up there long enough to keep hidden from the walker.

I risked a look behind us when we had gotten about halfway up the hill, and to my surprise, the two cows that had collided with the walker had survived and were running after the rest of the herd. Animals can be amazingly resilient, although I sadly doubted that either of the cows would last much longer, given the corruption they had been exposed to. Arturo and I had made it about 50 yards away from the dust cloud kicked up by their struggle, and as I took in the scene, a woman came hobbling out of the cloud, covering her mouth and coughing audibly. She was too far away to see clearly, but I recognized her black hair and the mountain lion skin that hung like a jacket around her shoulders and down her back. The walker also wore what looked like brown jeans, and I noticed that she was walking with a slight limp. It was tough to tell her age, but she didn't look very old, although many walkers age differently than ordinary humans.

Just then, almost as if the walker had sensed my eyes on her (which she very well might have), she whipped her head over to look at me. Even from that long distance I somehow felt us make eye contact, and a piercing pain shot through my skull, much like Tom had described back at the petroglyphs. Arturo was right next to me, and I looked at him to break the eye contact, then grabbed his shoulder to warn him.

"She's to our 6, turn around!"

I spun back around and lifted my rifle, looking through the scope to where I had just seen the woman, only to find that she had vanished. I started hastily scanning the area, until Arturo shouted something like "She's going for the logs!" In a matter of seconds, the walker had covered a distance of what must have been 15 yards or more, and now she was running, faster than even any of the cows, heading for the pile of logs where we had just been hiding. Arturo opened fire, and although it was tough to get a bead on the woman given her speed, I also let loose a few shots. One of us must have landed a hit, because the walker staggered and slipped as she disappeared behind the logs.

My head was spinning, and I was feeling slightly nauseous, but I pushed myself to reload and speak to Arturo. "Do we keep on her?"

"No, let's get out of here. I don't know if we'll be able to kill her," he answered.

We were both thinking on the same page. The walker was hurt, but since she'd already recovered to some degree from the wounds that we'd given her in the ghost town, our makeshift countermeasures might not be enough to finish her off if we tried to press the attack. I also mentioned that she seemed to be limping, which I think meant that the two cows had done a number on her as well. Thanks, cows.

Arturo and I pushed ahead, continuing to purposefully travel via open terrain to keep clear sightlines and avoid being jumped. Despite the fatigue, we were running high with adrenaline, and not just because of the danger. In the moment, neither of us had hesitated to open fire, but once things slowed down, we were both rattled by having to shoot at a human, or at least something that had once been fully human and still took a human form. I've dealt with countless creatures that have humanoid body structures, and as I discuss in another letter, I've even shot at a vampire who was physically indistinguishable from a human. We had certainly done the right thing, and it made my blood boil thinking about what the walker had done to the pronghorn, the bull, this cow, and especially Aliyah. But it was unsettling to have shot at her human form. I think Arturo was more shaken up than I was, because he's never been in a similar situation, but we were able to keep each other steady.

The following hours were miserable. Arturo and I were haggard beyond belief, and after the adrenaline evaporated, we moved at a crawl. But we never stopped, because we knew that if we did, we probably wouldn't be able to get going again. The constant radio communications and updates helped to keep us awake and in touch, and it was a big boost to have all the other teachers reassuring and encouraging us. Night fell, and we kept walking, until, after nearly two days of sheltering and shooting and hiking, we saw the lights of four headlamps coming down a hill in the distance.

Louis practically lifted me off the ground in a hug, and there were lots of pats on the backs and shoulders to go around for me and Arturo. I'm sure that we weren't very appreciative, because we just wanted to go to sleep. All of us had been awake protecting our Hatchies and hiking through the desert for at least 36 hours at that point, but because Arturo and I had been fighting and running, we got the privilege of sleeping first while the others took turns keeping watch.

Sometime overnight, Pine radioed us saying that he was on his way back to get us, and the following morning, the two backup Hunters that had responded to the distress call arrived to hunt down the walker. I mentioned wanting to go with them, but they (very politely) made it clear that I would be dead weight, given my condition. Eventually I conceded and wished them luck, but only after Arturo and I gave them a map and a full briefing on the geography and the events of the past two days. Not very long after they set off, Pine arrived at our camp; the poor guy had been awake for even longer than any of us, and it was a miracle he hadn't fallen asleep at the wheel (well...that we knew of). Louis immediately took over the job of driving as we all piled into the truck, and that was how we ended our nearly three months in the field.

The rest is pretty much what you would expect. We all met up with our Hatchies again and had a full swath of purification and curing ceremonies with Navajo medicine people, a.k.a. hataałii, or "singers". Aliyah's wounds had quickly become infected by the poison, but one singer specifically tended to her, and eventually she was feeling much better. Fortunately, the walker's powers hadn't sickened her too badly or even scarred her beyond what you would normally expect from her injuries. This process took some time, but after isolating ourselves and going through repeated cleansing and healing ceremonies, we were in the clear.

After that, we wrapped up the program with a celebratory Italian-style dinner and plenty of hugs and handshakes, and then it was time to go our separate ways. One by one, we bid the Hatches farewell at the airport or the train station over a couple days. Finally, when Mei and I were standing next to the train tracks waiting for her ride home, I handed her the gift that I had been waiting to give to her. Over many chunks of downtime in the field, I had secretly crafted a medicine bag and a charm.

Medicine bags are used by countless American Indigenous cultures, and although the exact traditions vary between tribes and nations, the standard one is a little leather or woven pouch that you can hang from your waist or around your neck. Anybody can carry a personal medicine bag to hold important items; these are usually objects with sacred or spiritual power, like corn pollen, soil or stones from holy sites, or body parts of certain animals, but many people also carry things that are simply significant to them personally. Not all medicine bag traditions are the same, and every person's is private and unique to them. For Mei, I cut one from deerskin and added a twine rope to hang or carry it. Inside I put a little note: "Great work, Mei. Thank you for learning, teaching, and standing by this old owl's side. – Sam", followed by the traditional Chinese characters for "Thank you", which Mei had taught me to write (I was worried I hadn't gotten them right, but she later confirmed that I had!). Along with the note I also included a soapstone charm that I had filed.

Soapstone is a soft rock, very workable and easy to cut or file into all sorts of forms and shapes. For Mei, I had carved out a representation of a mink. You might know what a mink is; they're mustelids, relatives of ferrets and weasels, with the same long body, short legs, and pointy snout. American minks are great climbers, observant, and stealthy, which allows them to go after a variety of prey. They're also intelligent and good at solving problems, which goes alongside their ability to be playful. All of this makes minks adaptable and versatile survivors, and hopefully with that information in mind, you can understand why I carved one for Mei.

"Can you write all that down?" Mei asked me after I'd told her all of that information.

"Your train is about to get here. But we both know how good your memory is. You'll remember long enough to write it yourself when you have time," I replied.

Mei's train got there a minute later, and after a final hug, I waved her goodbye from the platform as she boarded.

"Don't tell your parents that I almost got you killed!" I called, only half-joking.

"I can't make any promises!" she replied, and we both laughed.

I've seen Mei in person once more since then, when Serena, William, and I went to visit her in California, and otherwise I talk to her on the phone every now and then. She's done some field studies and a couple solo hunts, and overall seems to be doing pretty well for herself. I'm very proud of her!

And there you have it, the training trouble of 2020. I didn't expect this letter to go quite so long, but I hope you enjoyed it and found it informative, as usual. I wasn't sure which of my experiences to include as the bonus letter for this book, but hopefully this one was a good choice. Looking to the future, Elías and I are moving on to put my last 9 original letters into a second book, likewise including some extras, so you can look forward to that.

I want to thank you again for all your support, especially if you've read or listened this far to my ramblings. It was good to tell you guys another story after this time! This isn't the end, so I hope to have you along with Elías and I for the rest of this journey. And now I'll say, as I have many times before, that we'll talk more soon. This has been Sam White Owl, signing out.

ACKNOWLEDGMENTS

To start, we need to acknowledge everyone who's been involved in this project from Day 1, all the way back to the earliest YouTube videos! If it wasn't for Swamp Dweller, and every one of you who watched and commented and engaged, this never would have happened, so I appreciate you tremendously. And a big thank you to Swamp Dweller in particular, for giving the world the voice of the Letters from a Cryptid Hunter, and giving me a place to share these stories.

Thank you to Danielle, for giving a face to the beings who walk with us.

Thank you to everyone who helped teach me as a writer and actor! There are far too many to name: Paul Park, Anita Mumm, Nelly Rosario, Chris Murrah, everyone from BSA like Richard, Tony, Donald, Denise, Nancy, Mama Maria, and many, many more. I could fill a book with all of your names, so I'm sorry if I left you out!

Thank you to Ms. Mary, Dr. Tomney, Dr. Chico, Dr. Maxwell, Jennah, Helene, and all the other pros and wise people who formed "Team Elías" helped support me and my growth.

Thanks to Silverback, Wakinyan, Dan, Eli Nelson, Matthew, and countless other Indigenous folks across many different tribes and communication forums.

Thank you to Tojira Joseph Jones, Adallindis Kourtney Vom Hillhaus, and Gigi Jezebel Bunkley for being equally hilarious, loving, and supportive.

Thank you to my family! Mom, Dad, all my grandparents, and all of you who supported, guided, and loved me (and still do!).

Thank you to you, the reader/listener, for your support and your time. I hope you enjoyed, and maybe learned something new, and I would love to have you with me in Volume 2 and beyond!

Elías Ramos

Sam White Owl

ABOUT THE AUTHOR

 Trained in the acting department of Baltimore School for the Arts and majoring in English at Williams College, Elías "Owl" Ramos is dedicated to writing and sharing engaging stories. A lover of animals, nature, and the outdoors, he has visited and lived in thirty-two countries across five continents, speaks three languages, and studies topics ranging from mythology and language to zoology and ecology. His first publicly distributed stories are *Sam White Owl's Letters from a Cryptid Hunter*, which relate the experiences of a member of a global organization that deals with cryptids and monsters. The nineteen-episode series of letters has received wide acclaim and hundreds of thousands of views on YouTube.

If you enjoyed Sam White Owl's stories, please consider leaving a review on Amazon.com - it helps a lot!

For extra content and updates on more Sam White Owl and Elías projects, visit eliasramos.com for social media links and a special free gift for signing up for the email list!

ISBN 979-8-9930573-0-9

Print edition layout and design, e-book design and development, and publishing and marketing consultation services: Matthew Wayne Selznick (https://www.mattselznick.com).

Front cover design and interior art by Danielle M. Caulk (https://dmcaulkart.portfolio.site).

Hunter's Wings Publishing, USA

www.ingramcontent.com/pod-product-compliance
Lightning Source LLC
Chambersburg PA
CBHW051935240626
47153CB00005B/1502